"YE WERE WAITING FOR ME TO WARM YE ON THIS COLD NIGHT, WERE YE?"

"No, I do not wait for you," Lady Claricia replied. "Indeed you are a pompous peacock to imagine such a thing."

Alexander gave a hearty laugh. "Och, ye show yer thorns, little English rose." He strode across the room, took off his tunic, and tossed it aside. He captured her shoulders and dragged her to him. "Ye wouldna use yer thorns on me?" he drawled.

Claricia pushed at his chest, but he had positioned her against the cool stone wall. She could not escape.

Deliberately, he began to caress her, moving his hands and body in the way he knew would please a woman. Lightly, his lips traced a path from behind her ear along the delicate line of her jaw. In the moonlight, he saw the tiny pulse beating at the base of her throat. He heard the quickened breathing, saw the misty look in her wide eyes. He sensed the quivering in her limbs which she was trying to suppress, and he knew she was awakening to him . . .

"Storytelling is an art and Nancy Richards-Akers shows exceptional ability."

Affaire de Coeur

THE HEART
AND THE
ROSE

NANCY
RICHARDS-AKERS

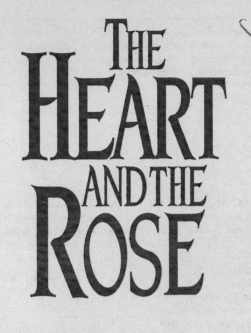

AVON BOOKS  NEW YORK

THE HEART AND THE ROSE is an original publication of Avon Books. This work has never before appeared in book form. This work is a novel. Any similarity to actual persons or events is purely coincidental.

AVON BOOKS
A division of
The Hearst Corporation
1350 Avenue of the Americas
New York, New York 10019

Copyright © 1995 by Nancy Richards-Akers
Inside cover author photo by Michael Pendrack
Published by arrangement with the author
Library of Congress Catalog Card Number: 95-94148
ISBN: 0-380-78001-1

First Avon Books Printing: September 1995

AVON TRADEMARK REG. U.S. PAT. OFF. AND IN OTHER COUNTRIES, MARCA REGISTRADA, HECHO EN U.S.A.

Printed in the U.S.A.

RA   10   9   8   7   6   5   4   3   2   1

Mo chridhe

Never believe it's anything less than a miracle to have a highly developed capacity for self-delusion.

Indeed, how could we survive without believing we were somebody else, if only for a little while?

PART 1

THE ROSE

Chapter 1

1314, The Lowlands, Scotland.

The New Year was six days old, and a cold gray dawn gripped the border fortress perched on a sharp rise overhanging the river Teviot. Patches of snow dotted the frozen ground, a thin sheet of ice covered the meandering waterway, and the woods below the castle presented an eerie scorched landscape. Blackened not, however, by the dead of winter but by the fires set that autumn by a passing band of rebels. Burn. Demolish. Destroy. Those were the renegade Scottish king's order. Leave nothing for the English. A gust of wind battered the skeletal remains of once-majestic trees, a charred limb crumbled to the ground, a great black rook took flight, and out of this wasteland darted the silhouetted figure of a man.

His movements were swift and silent as he made his way over the earthwork mote undetected by the lone warder on the castle rampart. The wall was lowest on this side, and the surface was uneven enough for a strong, agile man to get a foothold and climb. For an instant, he paused to secure the patchwork of hides that was

3

wrapped about his shoulders and torso. That done, he dashed across the final distance to the castle, and having reached his destination, he began to scale the north wall as if he'd done it a hundred times before.

The rocks were damp, and pockets of ice made them slippery. Although they were wrapped in rags, his bare hands were already numb. Soon his fingers had lost all feeling, and toward the top of the wall they began to bleed, but he made it to the top. Once there, he moved without a moment to lose, slipping into the inner bailey and disappearing into the lingering night shadow cast by the round tower wherein the household resided.

Soon it would be daylight, but the English garrison that occupied this conquered Scottish castle was sleeping off its Twelfth Night revelry. For a while yet, he was safe. Still, he didn't linger on his way to the tower entrance.

In the great hall, the fire in the massive open hearth had died to smoldering ash, offering scant warmth to either the hounds curled upon the littered rushes or to the soldiers who had succumbed to unconsciousness will he nill he. The long night of drinking and merriment had ended where'er it had been played out. Most of the snoring men were propped on benches; the two exceptions had collapsed atop one of the trestle tables, overturning trenchers and pitchers in their way, and the bittersweet aroma of spilled wine tainted the crisp air.

At the far end of the hall the man from the woods entered beneath the arched doorway and surveyed not the sleeping soldiers, but the remnants of the banquet. His stomach growled. One hand moved to his midsection, shifting his outer garment and revealing the woolen plaid of a Highlander. Again, his stomach rumbled. Even the unsavory odor of congealed grease did not stop the hunger that gnawed at him. It had been two days since he'd eaten more than a piece of moldy bread, let alone feasted until he could not take another bite. For a moment, the sight of a large bone that had been tossed to the dogs made his mouth water. His gaze moved to a nearby table, coming to rest on an untouched round of hard yellow cheese. There could be no harm in helping himself to a piece. Indeed, some might consider it his right.

He began to move forward when one of the soldiers atop the trestle shifted his position, flinging his arms in one direction his legs in another, and causing in the process a wooden-trencher to tumble off the table and land upon a wolfhound. The dog awoke and gave a startled yelp. The Highlander crouched in the doorway, his hand instinctively moving to grasp the dirk sheathed in a belt at his waist. His eyes darted about the hall. Still the English soldiers slumbered on undisturbed.

The Highlander exhaled a pent-up breath, straightened his tall frame to standing, and without a second glance at the cheese, he made his way toward the narrow winding stairs that led to the sleeping chamber. He knew the way well, for Hepburn Castle had belonged to his mother's family before the war with the English. More than a half century before, during the reigns of Henry in England and Alexander in Scotland, when there had been peace between the two nations, his great-grandfather had built the castle. It was where his mother had been born and wed, and it was where he had visited as a wee lad to bide the long winter months in this Lowland climate, less harsh than the western Highlands, which his father's clan had called home. It was here that he had celebrated the Christmas season and its culmination on the Twelfth Night with his grandparents and cousins, his parents, brother, and younger sister.

He was Alexander Kirkpatrick, grandson of the great laird, Malcolm, hero of the Battle of Largs, and like his grandfather, he was the Earl of Kilmory and Torridon. But times were different. Highlanders no longer looked to the north in fear of Vikings. Their enemy was to the south, and Alexander Kirkpatrick was an outlaw in his own land, hunted by the English for the handsome price that had been posted for his capture and death. But Alexander was no common felon. He was a patriot, whose only crime was the desire to see Scotland free of English domination and, in the process, to exact revenge for the crimes against his family.

Twelfth Night. The holiday of hope. "After darkness comes light," a line in the mummer's play promised. "After the dead of winter comes the sunny exuberant spring." Once in a time when the great hall in Hepburn Castle had been a different, brighter place, he had believed his grandfather when the old man had stood on the dais to raise his goblet and toast his guests: "After sorrow there is joy."

The Highlander's memories of those long-ago days were good ones. He saw his cousins laughing as his brother, Andrew, joined them in a *hulluchan*. His parents were smiling at each other, his grandfather was playing the bagpipes, and for a moment, he heard his sister calling to him.

"Dance with me, Alexander!" A comely lass with midnight-black hair picked up the skirt of her velvet kirtle and spun a playful circle before the dais, her tiny feet moving in perfect rhythm to the rapid music of drums and flutes. The traditional Twelfth Night eye mask that she wore disguised neither her fine features nor the bloom of color upon her cheeks. On the threshold of womanhood, she was as fresh and lovely as the Highland spring to come. "Dance with me, Alex."

But it was nothing more than the wind whistling through the rafters that arched above the sleeping soldiers. It could not have been Caitrine's voice, for she was gone, like the rest of them. His mother, his grandparents, and cousins had been murdered in their sleep the night the English took Hepburn Castle. It had been an act of retribution for the Scottish rebellion, led by William Wallace, who had first dared to challenge English authority. And it had not ended there. The rebellion had not died; it had become the War for Independence. After Wallace came Robert Bruce, and Alexander's father had been executed by the English in 1306, condemned for swearing fealty to the renegade Scottish king at Scone. His brother, Andrew, was dead, too, and his lovely fragile sister, Caitrine, had been kidnapped by the *sassenach* bastard, Sir Aymer de Clinton, who was to blame for the whole of his family's fate. Alexander was the only one left.

The last laird of the Kirkpatricks. He was the only one who could exact revenge for what had been done to his family, and so he proceeded up the stairs to the sleeping chamber.

On the landing he held his ear to the closed door. It was quiet within, and grim satisfaction settled upon his features. No doubt there would be those Highlanders who would disapprove of what he was about to do. They would rebuke him for putting his own interests above those of the king, and as his Irish-born kinsman, Rourke O'Connor, had pointed out there would be many who would say he was insane to have embarked upon this mission. Perhaps he had stepped beyond the bounds of sanity, Alexander conceded, as his thoughts drifted back to his parting conversation with Rourke.

"What madness is it that's wormed its way into yer brain, Alex?" the Irish warrior had asked with a disbelieving shake of his head. His features had been etched with grim concern. "I've fought by yer side through many a pitched battle, and until now I wouldna hesitate to trust ye with my verra life. But this, my auld friend, is naught but insanity." His offer to accompany Alexander to Hepburn Castle had been rejected. They had been in a secure haven, hidden from the English, safe for the winter, and Rourke's reluctance to bid farewell had been obvious. Their grandparents had been twins. Rourke was the grandson of Ingvar and Elspeth, while Alexander was the grandson of Ingvar's twin sister, Lady Isobel Kirkpatrick, and the bond between them was strong. They were more than friends, more than kinsmen, they were inseparable allies, who had sworn each to protect the other, but Rourke was not a Kirkpatrick, and he accepted the fact that, although he wished to stand beside his Scottish kinsman, this fight was not his. "I thought 'twas yer wish to destroy the bastard, not to deliver yerself into his hands."

"That's the beauty of this, Rourke." Alexander had met the skepticism in his gaze, and a slow cocky smile had crossed his lean features. " 'Tis beyond beautiful. Dinna ye ken that? 'Tis brilliant to slip into the beast's lair and strike when he least expects it. De Clinton knows I've vowed vengeance against him, and he's been watching his back in every glen and mountain pass since his men threw my brother's dead body off that wall. But the arrogant *sassenach* doesna think a Highlander has courage enough to invade his verra stronghold."

"Arrogant though de Clinton may be, he's no fool. I pray ye know what ye're doing." To speak of Aymer de Clinton was to speak of all that was treacherous and dishonorable. Rourke had asked, "Have ye not considered this could be a trap?"

"I've thought as much, but going into Hepburn Castle is a risk I must take."

There had been nothing more Rourke could say. "Take care of yerself, for I should miss yer skill with a lochaber axe and the deafening echo of yer wild war cry as we leap into the fray."

"Ye'll miss me smoothing a way for ye into the lassies' beds," had been Alexander's retort.

Rourke had tossed back his head in surrender to laughter. "It isna like that anymore."

"Aye. The lassies have grown used to yer over-sized hulk and untamed Irish ways."

"Nay, ye know 'tis not that." There had been a serene quality in Rourke's rebuttal.

"She's cast a spell on ye," Alexander had suggested, knowing that Rourke was thinking about the woman who followed the old pagan ways and had saved his life. When Alexander had been a lad, he'd lived at Eilean Fidra, the Kirkpatrick fortress on Loch Awe in the western Highlands. There, he'd heard the tales of the small community of old believers, but he'd never truly thought anyone lived there until the woman had pulled Rourke's battered body from the water and nursed him back to health. That had been almost four years before, and she was still on the island, despite the fact that Eilean Fidra had been sacked by de Clinton's order, after which the Scottish and English armies alternately had ravaged the countryside. Loch Awe was where Rourke went when he disappeared for days, if not weeks, on end.

"Perhaps she has bewitched me, for I'm as superstitious as the next fellow. I'll not be denying 'tis my Fate to return to her as surely as 'tis yers to seek vengeance against de Clinton, and I dinna suppose I could resist her any more than ye can resist going to Hepburn Castle," Rourke had concluded in a somber tone. "I shouldna be asking it of ye."

"*Slàn leat*," said Alexander. *Farewell*. The cousins had embraced.

"*Beannachd do t-anam is buaidh*," the Irishman had wished his friend in parting. *Blessing to thy soul and victory*.

Perhaps Rourke was right. Perhaps he *was* crazy, Alexander allowed. But then it would be equally as crazy to let this chance slip away. It would be, as Rourke had suggested, a defiance of Fate. He raised his hand to touch the amulet about his neck. It was the bottom half of a crucifix hanging from a leather cord. Crafted of silver with a large India pearl embedded below Christ's feet, the relic was tarnished and evidenced the passage of many decades. It had belonged to his grandmother Isobel, and the other half had belonged to Lady Isobel's twin brother, who had given it to his daughter upon her marriage to an Irish chieftain. That other half, the upper portion of the crucifix, now rested against Rourke's broad chest. His mother had passed it on to him with the wish that one day he might cross the Irish Sea to find his Scottish kin.

Alexander's fingers tightened about the pearl. By all that was holy, he had longed for vengeance. He had thirsted for it like a dying man. It had been his sustenance, his succor, and now it was within reach, on the other side of the door. Granted, today's deed would not be his final act against de Clinton. It would be only a beginning, and a blessed beginning at that, for at last, Alexander could cease worrying that he might not survive the next mountain skirmish before Sir Aymer de Clinton knew firsthand that the Kirkpatricks of Kilmory and Torridon did not tolerate English abuse. For that had been Alexander's greatest dread.

Death didn't frighten him. There was honor in shedding one's blood for justice, for one's clan, one's king and nation. But the prospect of departing this mortal domain before personally exacting vengeance upon de Clinton was something

Alexander much feared. Indeed, it was a shameful prospect, for there was no honor in failure. Aymer de Clinton had destroyed everything that was precious to Alexander, and in return, the last laird of the Kirkpatricks intended to take his enemy's treasure.

Alexander opened the chamber door and stepped inside, experiencing—much to his surprise—not the expected rush of triumph that revenge was near, or the usual ripple of tension when danger was at hand. Instead, it was shock that enveloped Alexander. Shock at how peaceful and clean, how warm and quiet it was inside that room that had once been his grandmother Hepburn's private retreat. The walls were whitewashed and coated with fresh lime, dried wild flowers mingled with fresh rushes strewn upon the floor, the newly stitched bed hangings were expensive, and the massive pieces of furniture were polished with pungent lemon oil. Everything was whole and orderly. There was nothing to hint of the chaos that ruled the countryside, and Alexander rubbed a hand across his eyes as if to rouse himself from a troublesome dream.

But this was no dream, and the tranquil scene before him struck a sorrowful chord in the depth of his soul. Peace and warmth, simple comforts and tranquility were as unknown to Alexander Kirkpatrick as a decent meal. It had been a long time since he'd slept in a bed, longer still since he'd passed a night in a chamber such as this, and with that thought images of the Kirkpatrick strongholds in the Highlands flooded his mind. There were no fresh rushes on the floors at Eilean Fidra, no whitewashed walls at Kilmory, where the furnishings had been destroyed, and family heirlooms had been looted before the English had put torch to the fortress that had stood guard over Glenacardoch Bay since Roman times.

The muscle along Alexander's jaw twitched, then stiffened at the awful memory of what the English had done to his clan. His hands clenched into fists, then relaxed. *Dhomhsa buinidh dioghaltas*, he repeated the vow in his head. *To me belongs vengeance.* His pledge to strike back was about to be fulfilled, and he entered the chamber, closing the door behind him.

With swift purpose, Alexander crossed to the bed and jerked open the hangings, only to experience his second shock in as many minutes. Lady Claricia de Clinton was there, as he'd expected. She was sleeping alone upon the crisp white linens, her face resting on her hands. Soft, white hands that caused his breath to catch, for she appeared as clean and fresh as the room, and she was lovely, too. Her skin was paler than mist, yet upon her cheeks was brushed a hint of color like that of rose petals. Her slightly parted lips were as plump as a ripe plum, and all about her face and shoulders swirled a mass of silken tresses so fine, so glossy that Alexander imagined her hair must have been spun from pure gold.

The scents of dried roses and lavender from sachets stitched to the bed hangings wafted about him as he leaned forward for a closer look. In sleep Lady Claricia was a vision of innocent loveliness that seemed in that instant to symbolize everything that had been destroyed in his world, everything that could never be Alexander's. Something perverse gripped him, and even though he knew it was wrong, the last laird of the Kirkpatricks reached out to touch his enemy.

Gently, so as not to awaken her, his finger trailed down her cheek to rest at the curve of her delicate jaw. The skin was as soft as it looked, and shock flared within Alexander as he looked upon the contrast of his dirty bleeding hand resting against that creamy soft skin. His heart lurched in his chest as her warmth was transmitted through his fingertips, and he couldn't suppress the sudden rush of shame that his own grandmother would not have recognized him. No laird did he resemble, but a hunted hungry beast, and it was because of the English, always the English, and because of de Clinton in particular, that the last laird of the Kirkpatricks had fallen so low.

The demon hate within Alexander rose, twisting his soul. Abruptly, he snatched his hand away from her face, reminding himself that not only was she English, but she was a whore. These comfortable trappings were those of a whore. Despite the title, Lady Claricia de Clinton was a whore. There was nothing innocent or pure about this woman, whose reputation was well known on both sides of the border. Her delicate beauty was naught but an illusion.

"*Drùthanag*. Harlot. Whore," Alexander whispered. His voice was laden with every ounce of the hatred that had sustained him on bitter winter nights and through every bloody battle against the English. It was a bitter palpable hatred, and each time another Kirkpatrick clansman had fallen beneath an English sword, his need for vengeance had hardened about his heart.

Lady Claricia awoke. Her eyes flew wide, her full lips parted, and Alexander stared. He could not shift his gaze from the vision of her tongue as it darted out to moisten those plum-ripe lips any more than he could prevent the pulse of desire that quickened in his loins. He couldn't help it. He was a man, after all, and it had been many weeks since he'd been with a woman, and she was a whore, one damned lovely whore. He watched her gaze travel down the length of his torso. Only a whore would search for the swelling between a man's legs. Her brazen appraisal confirmed everything he'd heard about Lady Claricia de Clinton. Maybe he should take her there, he thought, mount her and ride her with the same hard carelessness his sister had suffered at the hands of her people, the English. The prospect of hearing her scream beneath him was tempting.

Sweet Jesu, he was a beast to have such thoughts. Yet it was not shame that deterred him from possessing her. Rather, it was the fact that, while his loins might be sated, his lust for revenge would not be satisfied. Lady Claricia was used to such treatment, and it wouldn't be any sort of worthy vengeance to treat a harlot like a harlot. It would be too quick and certainly not public enough, for whatever Alexander did to de Clinton and his family, the world must hear of it. It must be known from Aberdeen to London that Alexander Kirkpatrick had bested Sir Aymer de Clinton.

Once more, Alexander ground out the harsh ugly words, "Harlot. Whore," but they didn't diminish the swelling in his loins. Driven by anger, he yanked her from the bed. A small gasp escaped those luscious lips, and she swayed as if she might collapse. Roughly, he gripped her arms and forced her to stand before him. Before his vengeance was complete, he would make certain she knew what it was like to lie beneath an enemy, but for now it was time to be on their way.

Claricia heard the door to the sleeping chamber open, and her entire body stiffened at the sound of footsteps. It was barely daybreak. She hadn't expected her uncle until later. He must have traveled through the night, and she forced back the onset of tears that threatened to spill down her cheeks.

She didn't want this idyllic solitude to end. Of course, she hadn't denied to herself that he would stay away from her for more than a week or two at best. He never had, not since that first night when he'd come to her. Claricia had known her uncle would come back. He always did. But this sennight of privacy while he had answered the Earl of Pembroke's summons had been bliss. It had been the longest time he had ever been away, and she had actually dared to imagine the impossible, that one day she might be free of him. Free of his carnal demands, his cruelty, and his violent jealousy. Heavenly Father, what did her uncle have to be jealous about, for what honorable man did he imagine would want her? She knew what they called her. She was Sir Aymer de Clinton's *whore*.

The Beast's Bawd.

It didn't matter that she was an unwilling partner. That did not alter reality. To all the world she was mistress of a man so cruel, his own soldiers called him *Beast* and *Barbarian*, and thus, Claricia had been ruined for any decent man. Her future was not much better than that of the harlots who plied their trade in Southwark alleys. She could hope for little more than survival.

Perhaps if she feigned sleep her uncle would leave, and come back later. Perhaps she might have another hour or two to herself. But it was not to be. She heard the bed hangings open, and, modulating her breath, Claricia peeked from beneath her eyelashes.

An unearthly chill gripped her. What she saw was far more horrifying than her uncle come to sate his carnal appetite. The man looming over her bed was not a dissipated English general with thinning gray hair, a sallow complexion, and lips drawn into a tight sneer, but a tall dark-haired young man. He was a *Highlander*, one of the savage enemy whom the English intended to tame, and for one wild moment, fear fled Claricia as she dared to believe it might be a messenger from Meg.

Although it had been almost five summers since she'd had any word from Meg, Claricia had not abandoned hope. It had been a miracle that they had managed to effect her escape from de Clinton's household, and an even greater miracle that in those first months after Meg had fled into the hills, she had managed to get a few messages back to Claricia. In turn, Claricia had sent coins and clothing into the forest. To have accomplished such miracles was reason enough to believe another miracle was possible.

Claricia almost greeted the man, but something

warned her to remain still. The garnet ring, she
reminded herself. Wait until he shows the garnet
ring. It had belonged to Claricia's mother, and
Claricia had given it to Meg as a means to secure
food and shelter. It was Meg who had decided to
use it to identify the messengers who traveled
between de Clinton's fortress and her hiding
place in the hills.

But this Highlander did not display the garnet
ring. He was no messenger from Meg. With that
sad realization Claricia's heart dropped, only to
leap in the next second with a fierce stab of terror,
and the breath caught in her throat as the Highlander's identity came to her.

It was *he*. Against the laws of God and nature,
it was the warrior she had murdered; the man whose
death had been a curse upon her. How could she
ever forget the hard angles of that masculine
face? She closed her eyes against the sight hovering over the bed, but the image of high cheekbones and haunting pale green eyes set beneath
heavy black brows was no less vivid. She peeked
again. His black hair was the same, plaited into
two braids that hung over his shoulders, yet he
was thinner than she recalled, and there was a
hollow quality to his cheeks that made his appearance all the more savage.

This was the man who was to blame for every
hideous thing that had befallen Claricia. If not for
him, her uncle would never have dared to touch
her. If not for the hell to which this Highlander
had sentenced her, Claricia might be wed to a
young lord in faraway Somerset or Kent, a chatelaine in a comfortable manor house with chubby
red-cheeked children at her feet. This man, this

uncivilized enemy of the English, had destroyed that possibility. This was the Highlander who had taken the future from Claricia.

But how could this be? a thin voice of sanity cried out. He was dead. It had been six long summers since she'd thrust the dagger into his heart. He was dead. She'd watched him gasp his final breath on the solar floor, his own blood pooling about him. He was dead. She'd seen her uncle's men toss his limp body off the ramparts.

The need to reason through this incredible turn of events brought Claricia fully awake as she tried to make sense of who was staring down at her. At first, she was certain it was his ghost come to torment her, as if she had not already suffered enough for taking a human life, no matter the justification. But when he breathed and puffs of air encircled his head, she could not deny he was made of flesh and blood and bone, and a renewed rush of terror seized her.

Why was he here? Was the castle under attack? She had heard the stories of rebel raids on the garrisons at Roxburgh and Linlithgow. Even the walls of the mighty fortress at Edinburgh had been scaled, and as of the New Year, only five strongholds remained within King Edward's control. It was only a matter of time before the rebels would seek to reclaim Hepburn Castle. Claricia had been concerned when her uncle had insisted that she accompany him to this border keep. But she had known better than to resist him. She knew she must never question his judgment or do anything to anger her uncle in any way. The quality of her daily existence, if not her ultimate survival, depended on the submissive facade she had taught herself to maintain in his presence. It would have served no purpose to argue the danger of taking up residence in hostile countryside. Aymer de Clinton considered himself invincible. There was no enemy bold enough to challenge him or threaten anything that was his, and Claricia was his as surely as his Spanish destrier or gold-handled sword. Indeed, she was his most treasured possession. He would never have parted with her.

Claricia listened for sounds of intruders, but she heard nothing to hint that the fortress was under attack. There appeared to be nothing out of the ordinary except for a dead man standing over her. The garrison, she knew, was sleeping off the night of high revelry. Before his departure, her uncle had exhorted his soldiers to enjoy themselves this Twelfth Night, and Claricia doubted any amount of screaming would have roused the guard to her aid. She was alone, and there was nothing she could do to protect herself.

Was it going to happen again? she wondered as the fear that had robbed the warmth from her feet set her stomach churning. Claricia held her breath. She needed to be brave, and the single thought that crossed her mind was that this time, she had no girlish dreams to be destroyed. This time, there was no innocence of body or soul that could be robbed from her. This time, she could prevent herself from feeling.

It won't matter if he lies between your legs again. This time, he won't be the first. He can't hurt you anymore. The damage has already been done.

Sensing his movement, Claricia stiffened, and, expecting to be roughly grabbed, expecting to feel

his weight collapse upon her, she did not understand the gentle tentative touch of his hand
against her cheek. It was almost a caress. Her
heart lurched. No man had ever touched her in
that way. Light as a feather, the tip of his finger
trailed down her cheek. It was the kind of touch
for which young girls yearned, the kind of touch
Claricia knew better than to fancy for her own.
Yet for the space of a heartbeat, the most peculiar
sense of well-being enveloped Claricia. It was as
if something almost bright was teasing her, and
the odd notion that there might be hope for her
beyond the existence she endured rose through
the terror.

Through slightly parted eyelids she saw his
calloused hand as it passed along her cheek. The
skin was blackened with dirt and crisscrossed
with rough red scars. His uneven nails were en-
crusted with grime. There was blood. She smelled
wet leather, wood smoke, and an unfamiliar salty
scent.

Tears pooled in Claricia's eyes. She could not
stop them.

It was such a rough hand. *A hand that had
known as much suffering as it had dealt.* The unlikely
thought filled her with sadness.

Why should she care? she wondered. He was
her enemy. It was not right that she should shed
tears for an enemy. Still her eyes burned.

Abruptly, his hand withdrew, and that bright
speck of warmth that too briefly had teased her
spirit withered. The tears dried as well, and harsh
reality returned.

"Harlot. Whore." The hiss in his voice was as
cruel as she had expected it to be. For the first

time, she opened her eyes wide, her lips parted to emit a tiny gasp of fright, and her tongue moistened her parched lips.

She stared up at him, and a familiar apprehension raced through her when she recognized the look in his eyes. It was lust. She'd seen it before. She knew all too well what was about to happen, and of its own accord, her gaze shifted down the length of his torso, searching for further evidence of the horrible truth she had seen in his eyes. But the loosely wrapped woolen plaid obscured her view.

"Harlot." He repeated the ugly word. "Whore." With a jerk, he pulled her from the bed and forced her to stand before him. He was breathing heavily, and the look in those green eyes had altered. An eerie fire continued to burn from their depths, but lust had been replaced by undeniable loathing, and Claricia observed this change in mesmerized fascination.

"Where's yer cloak?" he demanded. He spoke English with the heavy accent of one whose native tongue was Gaelic.

Claricia could not speak, indeed, she could scarcely connect two sane thoughts. She began to tremble, and, as she wrapped her arms in a protective gesture about herself, her gaze strayed from his face to a massive wooden chest at the foot of the bed.

The man followed the direction of her gaze, then took several steps, pulling her as he went around the bed, to kick over the chest. The lid opened, and a fur-lined cloak of maroon velvet tumbled out.

"Yers, *my lady?*" The mockery in his voice was

obvious. Clearly, he did not think she was a lady.
"Put it on."

Claricia didn't move. She tried to obey, but
could do nothing except stare at the cloak, which
reminded her at that moment of a great expanding pool of blood. His glance moved about the
chamber. There was a kirtle and tunic within his
reach. He tossed them in her direction.

"Go on. Put it on. And whatever else. Unless
ye want to freeze to death. 'Tis bitter outside."

Her eyes darted from the cloak to his face, then
returned to the costly garment as she considered
the meaning of his words. He was taking her
away. That much Claricia understood, and she
didn't know whether to laugh or to cry, whether
to invoke guardian angels or to give thanks to the
Lord. Was it possible that her prayers had been
answered and that she was finally to be free from
her uncle? Perhaps. But at what price? There
could be no freedom in merely trading one form
of captivity for another. Or could there?

Her thoughts sped onward. If the Highlander
did not kill her right away, she might escape. Perhaps this was, indeed, the blessing for which she
had yearned. Perhaps this was her chance to escape her uncle. She let her eyelids fall closed, certain that all of this was nothing more than
another bad dream, certain that when she looked
again it would be her uncle returned from his
audience with the Earl of Pembroke who was
standing before her, making demands and forcing himself upon her.

But the arms that pulled the kirtle over her
head, threw the cloak about her, and crushed her
against a broad, muscular chest were not those of

Aymer de Clinton. Again, Claricia's eyes flew open wide. She stared up into eyes as green as that awful color in the summer sky before a violent thunderstorm.

It was still him, the Highlander, hatred blazing in his gaze, his rage visible in the muscles twitching along his jaw. He stood so close, she heard the rasp of his agitated breathing. It was as tangible as the fury distorting his features. There was a far greater menace upon his face than she had ever seen before. His anger left her vulnerable, and more alone than Claricia could remember feeling in a long time. It revived the memories she had struggled to bury in a place where they could not hurt her, and although she fought against it, all the sights and sounds of the past began to crowd her mind.

Claricia began to pray, whispering a fervent *Ave Maria*. But invoking the Virgin Mother was not enough to prevent the nightmare from returning.

The Highlander was hurting her. Meg was hiding. There were flames everywhere. There was fighting, and a dead man lay at her feet. There was more pain. Searing agony ripped her apart. They were all calling her "whore," and her uncle was hurting her. Somewhere a baby was wailing for its mother. Somewhere a young woman cried herself to sleep amid broken dreams.

Reality melded with fantasy. A low wail of terror issued from Claricia's lips. The Highlander's grip about her shoulders tightened. The pain was returning. God's mercy, it was going to happen again, and Claricia began to numb herself. As the Highlander slung her over his shoulder, a merciful blackness swirled up to engulf Claricia.

Chapter 2

$\sim\!\!\infty\!\!\sim$

Somewhere in the snowy hills a wolf howled. The great black stallion upon which Claricia and the Highlander were riding neighed, partly in fright, partly in protest. It was long past time to rest. They had covered a remarkable distance since crossing the Teviot River, above Hepburn Castle. Any other traveler would have been more than satisfied, but the Highlander had his own idea of when and where to stop.

Claricia glanced toward the sky. They had been traveling in a northerly direction since midday. There was the North Star straight ahead, and a quarter moon was rising to their left. There were few precious hours of daylight at this time of the year, and the night wind was already blowing, yet the Highlander continued onward. As darkness descended over the land, Claricia could not help wondering if he was taking her to the farthest reach of the earth, where dragons lurked, waiting for lost souls who might tumble into the abyss.

The steep path was almost impassable. A wall of icy rocks, dotted by a few scraggly pine trees, rose sharply on one side, and as they went

higher, the wind became sharper. Claricia tilted
her face into the Highlander's chest for protection, and after a few minutes, she stole an upward glance at him. He was staring straight
ahead, his expression as gray and as hard as the
craggy gorge, and she knew better than to speak.
It would be pointless to tell him how cold and
tired she was. Her uncle had always expected
Claricia to abide whatever hardship she encountered, and her captor would expect no less.

Soon it began to snow, not large, soft flakes,
but small flakes as sharp as needles. Her eyes
were watering, her hands and nose and feet were
numb, and there was an awful burning sensation
in the pit of her stomach. Still Claricia forced herself to endure.

At the top of the pass, the Highlander reined
in their mount and glanced about the inhospita-
ble surroundings as if looking for something. He
slid from the saddle, then led the horse several
paces to the edge of the crest, where there was a
drop of several hundred feet to the valley below.
It was a perfect place for dragons. A perfect place
to dispose of an unwanted enemy. A perfect
place for retribution. She had tried to kill him
once. It made sense that he would return the act
in kind. A shiver seized her, and Claricia, determined not to reveal her fear, used every last
ounce of her energy to sit tall and stare him
straight in the eyes as if challenging him to do
his worst.

To her surprise, the Highlander did not have
murder on his mind. Instead, he pulled back several fallen pine boughs to reveal the entrance to
a cave. It was large enough for the horse to enter,

and once he had walked the beast inside, the Highlander replaced the thick evergreen shield. It was dark in the cave, but he appeared to know the way, and, having led the horse to the rear of the cavern, he untied the ropes that held Claricia's hands to the pommel and helped her dismount.

Claricia staggered on sore legs. Her arms flailed in the air, seeking support, and the Highlander came to her. His firm hands gripped her arms to prevent her from collapsing to the ground, and all the while, a grin animated his gaunt features. She bit back the natural impulse to thank him for his aid. The light was dim, but there was no mistaking her captor's expression, and it infuriated her. She was willing to accept death, but she was not willing to be the source of his amusement. Claricia set her chin at a haughty tilt.

Alexander was cold and tired and hungry, yet he could not stop himself from smiling. The situation couldn't have been worse. It was the dead of winter. They were nearing the foothills of the Highlands without food or proper shelter. He had no one to fight by his side, should he have encountered an English patrol. Death might have come for him at any time, nonetheless Alexander was inordinately pleased with himself, and he smiled. By now Aymer de Clinton had returned to Hepburn, and Alexander could only imagine the Englishman's fury upon discovering that the fortress had been breached and his niece had been stolen. It was a highly satisfying scene to consider. Revenge was sweet, and Alexander congratulated himself. It was a brilliant plan.

"Sit there, *whore*." Alexander motioned to a spot before a well-used charcoal hole in the middle of the cave.

Claricia tried not to wince at the callous edge in his voice. She fought back the tears that burned her nose and eyes. Her uncle called her that when she did not please him, but his opinion never made her cry. While visiting the court at Windsor, she had heard it whispered behind her back, but she had not cried then either. Yet somehow to hear *him* say the word made it more horrible, more shameful than those awful times when she pretended she had not heard her uncle or those ladies in London. Indeed, to hear him call her "whore" was far worse than seeing him smile at her expense. She struggled to conceal her humiliation and terror.

Where was he taking her? she wondered as she stumbled to sit before the charcoal hole. How long did he intend to let her live? Her posture remained erect, her chin was still pointed upward, her eyes were blazing with what she hoped resembled defiance, and she felt the heat of high color in her cheeks.

Alexander returned his captive's unwavering stare. By the Holy rood, she was an amazing sight. It was as if the arduous ride through the Buccleuch Pass had been nothing more stressful than an invigorating outing. He searched for signs of exhaustion but detected none. She was to be admired. There had been no tears since she had regained consciousness, no outburst when he'd set her across the horse and bound her hands to the pommel. There had been no begging for mercy. He could imagine how cold and tired she must have been, but there had not been a word of complaint from her the entire day. She was an uncommon creature, this English whore.

In the next instant, an unwelcome idea occurred to him. His smile vanished. Perhaps his prisoner was planning to escape. Could it be that the hope of freedom was her source of strength? The notion was unsettling. Revenge was only possible as long as he was in control. Alexander could ill afford to loose his greatest asset. Nor, in all honesty, did he wish to go chasing after her, should she have been foolish enough to try to run away. Although she might not have been tired, he was in need of a sound sleep.

Alexander picked up the length of rope that he had used to bind her wrists to the saddle. "I will not tie yer ankles if ye promise not to flee. This is where we stay the night, and it will be much more comfortable if I dinna have to bind ye."

Claricia nodded in agreement, managing against all odds to appear undaunted.

"Ye're a wise whore," Alexander taunted. He did not like her air of assurance. It was haughty. It was English to the core, and he loathed that. In an effort to weaken her, he added, "Ye'd perish in the elements before dawn's first light, if the Highlanders didna get to ye first." She cocked her head to one side. Clearly, she had not comprehended the meaning of his threat, and Alexander clarified. "There isna a Scotsman with an ounce of forgiveness for the English. Should ye stumble across anyone's path in yer flight, it wouldna matter that ye are a woman. Their hatred is so strong that even the wee bairns would delight in flaying ye alive and leaving yer remains in the forest for the night beasts.''

For an instant, alarm etched its mark upon her features. Quickly, Alexander turned away, for in that same instant, he knew both satisfaction and disgust at having induced that flicker of anguish in her eyes. But wasn't that what he'd wanted? She was naught but a pawn of war, and her sensibilities should not have concerned him. He rubbed his jaw. Why, then, this inner sensation of distaste? He did not understand it himself, and, annoyed, he set about making a fire.

Claricia watched the Highlander build a pyre out of the sticks and twigs that had been left behind by the last travelers to take refuge in this cave, but her thoughts were on what he'd said about being left in the forest. She had heard of the barbaric tortures Highlanders inflicted upon their captives. Indeed, she had already suffered the worst indignation to which a woman could be subjected, and she well knew it was not death, but surviving, that caused the most profound pain. Still his words upset her. Perhaps it was because he had not mentioned their past encounter, and she did not understand why.

It had been six years since she had last seen him, and much had happened in those years. The time had weighed heavily upon each of them. They were both changed in appearance. Yet she did not think that mere physical differences accounted for his failure to say anything about that day when the rebels had stormed her uncle's fortress. Perhaps he didn't remember that afternoon when he had come upon her in the burning solar. That was it, she told herself. Perhaps in deceiving death, his memory had been destroyed, and he didn't remember those minutes that had forever changed her life, those minutes that had seemed to stretch into hours, those brutally vivid minutes that Claricia could never forget. He remembered none of it, least of all her. Even if his mind had not been destroyed, it had happened in another time and place, and there was no reason to associate a frightened, knife-wielding girl with the woman he had kidnapped that morning. She had been someone else then, not the *Beast's Bawd*.

He struck the flints, and sparks jumped, igniting the dry twigs. Claricia dropped her gaze and extended her hands to the expanding circle of warmth. Outside, the wind howled, and Claricia knelt as close to the fire as she could. Flames lengthened along the pile of sticks, shadows danced on the cavern walls, and for a while she forgot about the nagging hunger within her. Her fear abated, the circulation was returning to her hands, for a while the past dimmed, and only the immediate comfort from the fire mattered.

Alexander squatted on the other side of the fire, legs apart and woolen plaid spread, letting the flames warm the chills in his thighs. He watched his prisoner rub her hands together and realized that he had yet to hear her utter a single word. He had read much in her eyes and upon her countenance. She had revealed anger and fear to him, but she had not spoken.

"Are ye always so quiet?" he wondered aloud. His low voice was laced with the lilting accent of the Highlands.

"Would you like me to speak, my lord?" Claricia asked, forcing herself to call him "my lord."

She did not know if he deserved the courtesy. That did not matter. She had learned much from her uncle and knew how important it was to treat men with modesty and deference. So she called him "my lord," implying she was accustomed to doing what it was a man wished her to do. She cocked her head to one side, stared across the fire and waited for his reply.

To Alexander's astonishment, her voice drifted through the shadowy cave like the caress of a spring breeze. It was English and educated, that much he had expected, but he had not thought to hear so gentle a sound. It was soft and pretty. Just like her, he was forced to admit. There was nothing harsh about the musical way she spoke, any more than there was anything coarse about the way she appeared.

He observed her as if she were a mystery to unravel. He'd been with a whore once in Ireland, an auburn-haired lassie named Finolla, who had rouged her cheeks and lips and had not said much either, except in the throes of passion. Would this delicate English whore be like Finolla? He closed his eyes and saw Finolla's great breasts, he heard Finolla moan and call his name, then he heard a musical voice. "My lord," the English whore had called him. He tried to focus on Finolla, but the vision of a lusty Irish lass faded away, to be replaced by that of a slender woman with flaxen curls swirling about naked shoulders. "My lord," he imagined she was whispering as she opened her arms to him.

Alexander opened his eyes and frowned. She was a bawd, a harlot skilled in the ways of tempting a man, and he shrugged, trying to ignore the quiver of desire in his loins as her lips parted to speak once more. But it was not possible. Whether whore or lady, she was a lovely morsel to behold, so fair in contrast to the dark beauties of the Highlands, and he knew there would be much pleasure in having her.

"Tell me, my lord, would you like me to speak?" Claricia asked again in a soft whisper. It required every ounce of fortitude to overcome her trepidation and utter that sentence. Sitting as he was on the other side of the fire, the flames projecting grotesque shadows on his face, he looked like a demon rising from the depths of hell. Everything about his appearance was dark and sharp and utterly without mercy. The sight of his gaunt face, with those ink-black brows and deep-set eyes, frightened her. Talking might help to remind Claricia that her captor was as human as she was. "What would you like me to talk about?"

"Talk if ye like," he muttered in a husky voice. Perhaps conversation would take his mind off *other things*. He scowled, shifting his weight to adjust the bulge between his legs. At least she was on the other side of the fire, and would stay there.

"Mayhap you would tell me, my lord, where are we going?" Claricia asked before she lost her nerve.

"Clar Innis." He did not look at her.

"Where is that?"

"Loch Lomond."

"I have heard of it." Meg had talked of Loch Lomond. She had been there as a child, and although much of Meg's memory had been lost, she had been able to describe the grassy green banks as they sloped down to blue water. It had been the faerie land of girlish fancies, and Meg had said that someday she would go there to live on an enchanted island, where there was nothing evil, only good. It pierced Claricia's heart to think that she was soon to see Loch Lomond, when Meg could never return. "Is it far?"

"Aye, at this time of the year 'tis verra far."

"And your laird is there?"

"I am the laird," he stated in a flat, emotionless tone.

"Ah," Claricia murmured, digesting this revelation and realizing that whatever reason he had for kidnapping her was his alone. "Your clan is there?"

"Clar Innis isna mine." The Highlander's tone came to life; it sharpened. He jabbed at the fire with a smoldering stick. "Besides, I have no clan."

"I don't understand," she said in that soft, lyrical voice, realizing that she did not even know the name of this man who had returned from the dead.

Anger surged within Alexander. It was not right that she should look so ingenuous. *I don't understand.* How could it be difficult to comprehend? His family was dead. Gone. Every last one of them. Didn't she know the horrors that the English had inflicted on every man, woman, and child who dared to call himself a Highlander? Didn't she know what her uncle had done to his family in particular? Alexander's lips curled in contempt.

"Silence, whore," he ordered. "Ye ask too many questions."

Claricia shrank back. Perhaps talking had not been such a good idea after all. He looked more sinister than ever, and she diverted her gaze to concentrate on the fire as it leaped higher. Lying down on her side, she brought her legs to her chest, and, resting her head on her hands, she stared into the blue flames and saw Meg standing in the bailey at Goswick Keep.

How long ago that had been when Claricia and her mother had resided in her uncle's coastal fortress south of Berwick. How long ago when the commotion in the courtyard had brought Claricia to the tower window to look down and see Sir Aymer de Clinton and his men-at-arms returning from their latest punitive assault on the Scottish rebels.

Robert Bruce had been crowned at Scone that winter, and the English thirst for retribution had been high in that summer of 1306. There had been numerous arrests, executions, and skirmishes, and after the June defeat of the rebels outside Perth, a savage vengeance had been exacted by King Edward. The normal code of warfare by which a knight could ransom his life had been discarded, and captives had been treated as common criminals to be hanged, beheaded, or drawn and quartered without trial.

Claricia had seen the rotting heads on spikes above the gates at Berwick Castle, and she had hidden her face in her mother's skirt at the ghastly sight, but it was the treatment of the Scots women that had truly horrified her. King Edward had ordered his heralds to proclaim that the wives and daughters of his enemies were to be treated as outlaws. Any Englishman could kidnap, rape, or murder them, immune from punishment, and it had seemed to Claricia that her uncle had relished this proclamation above all else.

"Look, Mother!" Claricia had pointed at the group of women being herded beneath the raised portcullis. They had been tethered together, the wretched creatures, exhausted from their forced march and terrified by what they had seen and were yet to endure. Their hands had been bound and their feet shackled to prevent them from running, yet they had managed to form a protective circle around a young girl. "Who do you think she is?"

"A prisoner." Lady Johanna had spoken with the constant indifference that had marked her demeanor since her husband's death.

"But she must be the daughter of an important laird or a knight. Do you not see how the others try to hide her? And her clothes. They are of a distinctly fine cut and fabric." Even from the second floor of the tower Claricia had been able to make out the quality of the girl's kirtle and overtunic.

"Come away, Claricia," Lady Johanna had urged. "You should not watch."

"Oh, Mother, can we not save her?"

The girl in the circle had appeared to be about her own age, and the sight of her had made Claricia recall how frightened and lonely she had been after her father had died. It had been two years before, during the first battle for Stirling, and how miraculous it had seemed to Claricia when her uncle had offered them sanctuary in his household. She had prayed to the Virgin Mother that she would not be separated from her mother, and when her prayers had been answered, Claricia had vowed to offer sanctuary to someone else one day. So that summer at Goswick Keep, being but a girl of twelve, Claricia had viewed that young prisoner in the bailey as her chance to honor her vow to the Virgin Mother. "Please, Mother, could you not send a message to uncle?"

There had been rare tears in Lady Johanna's eyes. "You are too kind for your own good, dearest daughter."

"It could not hurt to ask." Claricia's childish voice had been full of hope.

"And why, pray tell, would you explain we needed this girl?"

"For a maid, of course. I am old enough, you know."

Lady Johanna had pulled Claricia away from the window. The screaming had started.

"Oh, please, Mother, we must do something before it is too late," Claricia had pleaded.

"It would mean so much to you?"

"I would have a companion," had been Claricia's unguarded reply. From Claricia's earliest memories, Lady Johanna had been more friend than mother. Lady Johanna had taught her daughter to play the lute with the same splendid skill she possessed. She had taught her to read and scribe and to embroider delicate patterns upon the velvet kneeling pads for the chapel. The two golden beauties had been inseparable. Mother and daughter had attended daily matins together, they had managed the household, and had ridden and walked through the hills surrounding their home in England, keeping each other company in her father's absence and comforting one another after his death. Of late, however, that had changed. Ever since coming to live with her uncle, there had been a distance between Claricia and her mother that she did not understand, a distance that had left a lonely spot upon her heart and which she had yearned to fill. "I would like a friend my own age."

It had been that guileless admission that had prompted Lady Johanna to ask a favor of her brother-in-law, and thus it was that Claricia had rescued the Scottish girl who had no memory of who she was or from where she had come. The other servants had claimed the girl was bewitched. Perhaps she was a kelpie and would steal their souls, they had prattled. They would not let her share their quarters above the stables, shunning her presence out of ignorance and superstition, and so she stayed with Claricia and her mother in the tower. Lady Johanna had suggested they call her Meg, after Lady Johanna's long-dead sister, Margaret, and in quick time, the young mistress and her maid had become as close as any true sisters might have been. Two summers passed, and Meg never ceased to vow that one day she would repay Claricia.

"An eye for an eye. A life for a life. The debt I owe ye is eternal," Meg had sworn to Claricia. "And it wouldna be too great to pay with my own blood, should ye ask it of me, my dear friend."

And then it happened.

Claricia ran as fast as she could. The wind

tugged at her kirtle skirt, she felt the pebbles pierce her bare feet, but she could not get to Meg.

It was a dream, always the same dream, and Claricia was powerless to make it better.

Claricia was roused in the night by the jingle of bridles, and she opened her eyes to see the Highlander leaping up as fast as a bolt from a crossbow to kick out the fire. Outside on the ledge voices rose above the wind.

"*Na h-abair diog,*" Alexander warned her in Gaelic, then quickly he translated to English. "*Dinna say a word.* Dinna make a sound." He dropped to a crouching position, then pivoted toward the entrance. His dirk was drawn, and he was ready for a fight. "I will kill ye before I let them rescue ye."

Rescue. That was the one word that sank into Claricia's sleepy mind, not *kill*. *Rescue*. Her heart dropped. She shook her head. Let him think she was agreeing to be silent. In truth, she was shaking her head at the irony of her situation. As awful as her Fate at this Highlander's hands might be, the last thing she wanted was to be rescued and returned to her uncle. Indeed, it had not even occurred to her that anyone might be looking for her.

A sudden blast of frigid air burst into the cave. The entrance had been uncovered. Someone entered.

"*Ciod is gile na sneachd?*" It was not an English soldier come to rescue Claricia, but another Highlander. In Gaelic, he posed the childhood riddle, *What is whiter than snow?* It was the way to prove that he could be trusted, that he and his traveling companions were exactly who they appeared to be—fellow patriots, rebels, and enemies of the English.

"*Fìrinn*," Alexander replied in the language of his birth. *Truth*. He sheathed his dirk to greet his fellow countryman. "*Dia is Buaidh*," he identified himself with the Kirkpatrick motto. *God and Victory*. The two men embraced and proceeded to fall into low-voiced conversation.

Silently, a small band of refugees filed into the cave after their leader. Claricia remained by the fire and stared at the hungry faces, the sunken eyes, which seemed too exhausted to register their surroundings, and she wondered if Meg and the child were wandering the countryside in this manner. The child would be five years old. Meg, like Claricia, was almost nineteen. That seemed ancient, compared to when they had hidden behind the screens passage at Goswick Keep and giggled at her uncle's knights. It might as well have been a century since she had given Meg the garnet ring and sent her into the hills. Still Claricia did not doubt she would recognize her and the child. No matter how many lifetimes might pass, Claricia would always know the two souls on this earth who were the closest to a family she would ever enjoy. How could it be otherwise?

Somewhere in the crowd there was the thin mewling of an infant. The pitiful cries caused Claricia's chest to constrict, and a terrible emptiness washed over her as her regard came to rest upon a woman clutching a bundle beneath her tattered tunic. Claricia did not stop to consider what she did. She stood and walked around the fire to kneel before the woman. Without speaking, she draped her maroon velvet cloak over the woman's thin shoulders. She was little more than a skeleton, and, recalling the Twelfth Night feast she had enjoyed the night before, Claricia looked away in shame.

"Thank ye, my lady." The mother spoke Gaelic.

Claricia had learned a little of the heathen tongue from Meg but did not reply. She was afraid she might cry. Instead, she allowed her hand to brush against the babe's head, then she returned to her place on the other side of the fire.

"Why did ye do that?" the Highlander asked Claricia. He had watched as she gave her costly cloak to a stranger, and his mistrust was revealed in his voice as well as in the skeptical set of his expression.

"She needed it more than I." It was the only thing she could have done, but Claricia did not tell him that. No one would have understood.

"Ye won't be much good to me sickly." Alexander's eyes held hers, and try as he might, he could discern naught but honesty in what he saw. The man who had led the refugees into the cave said something, and gladly Alexander turned away from his perplexing English captive.

Claricia listened as the two men talked. While she could not speak Gaelic with any particular skill, she understood much of what they were saying.

"What do ye intend to do with yer prisoner?"

"What do ye think? She's a whore, and there's naught but one thing to do with a whore."

A tiny gasp escaped Claricia. There, it had been said. One hand flew to her chest, where her heart was beating like the wings of a tiny trapped bird. She wanted to pray for help, but Claricia knew she had only herself. It would always be that way.

The man gave a ribald laugh, then added with a sneer, "Ye'd go where the English bastard has been?"

"Why not? Isna she a bonny enough piece to plow?"

"Aye, she is." Again he chuckled. "And after ye've had yer fill? What then, on? Will ye be passing her on to another?"

But Claricia didn't hear the Highlander's answer. She was remembering the first time, and how foolish she had been to struggle. How foolish she had been to pray for help. Since then she had learned much. She was wiser, and when he came for her this time, she would not struggle. She would act the same as she did with her uncle. Quiet and compliant. She would agree with him. She would do what she must to please and appease him, and all the while she would not really be there. Claricia had become skilled at numbing herself. It worked much better than prayers. She had learned how to send her mind very far away and to forget about what was happening to her body. She did it with her uncle and would do the same with *him*.

> *Sleep, my little darling, sleep.*
> *My love is sweeter than honey,*
> *   better than jewels, softer*
> *   than wool.*
> *Dream, my only child, dream.*

She heard her mother's voice singing the old lullaby. Claricia had heard it a thousand times in English as a child. Meg had taught her the Gaelic translation, and her mind had played it over and over. It was the way to get away, the way to stop the pain.

> Dèan cadal, seircean, dèan cadal.
> A ghaoil is milse na a mhil,
>   fearr na seudan, maoithe na clòimh.
> Breisleach, m'aon leanaban, breisleach.

Claricia began to shiver. Without her cloak the chill rising from the damp earth floor permeated her, and in a vain effort to quell her trembling, Claricia wrapped her arms about herself. She pulled her knees close to her torso and tucked her head toward her chest. A few minutes passed before she became aware of someone standing over her. She peeked up. It was her captor, the Highlander, a scowl upon his dark countenance. He hunkered down beside her.

"Come, my lady. Lie beside me." This time, there was no mockery in his low whisper when he called her "my lady." He lifted his fur outer garment and beckoned her to come closer. "We can keep each other warm."

"Indeed not!" Claricia was horrified at his suggestion. She did not want to warm herself against his *body*, and she shrank back when he reached for her, fearing that he might do more than hold her near him for warmth. It was bad enough to consider lying beneath him at some later time, but she had not imagined it would happen in a public setting. Her uncle's men-at-arms often took their pleasures in the great hall for all to see, and the prospect of being treated in such a common fashion appalled her.

"Dinna fash yerself. There is nothing else I wish this night except sleep. 'Tis cold. A storm blows outside. Ye were generous enough to give yer cloak to someone in need. I merely wish to return that generosity. We can give each other warmth. I intend nothing more," he said, but he had not realized that lying next to her would affect him so strongly. As he pulled her into the cradle of his body, his senses reacted to her buttery skin where his hands slipped between her upper arms and torso. He inhaled the sweet scent of lavender in that golden hair and allowed his cheek to brush against a soft curl. He was aware of the rise and fall of her breasts and the curve of her slender legs against his thighs, and he could not prevent himself from holding her a bit tighter, a little closer, than was necessary.

"Is that not better?" he murmured against the nape of her neck.

"Yes," was Claricia's whispered admission. Oddly, there was nothing threatening about the way he held her, and it was a new experience. She had never slept in a man's arms. Her uncle had always taken his pleasure and left her alone when he was done. No one except her mother had ever held her through the night. He was warm, much warmer than she was, and little by little, that comforting warmth seeped into her bones. Tears prickled Claricia's eyes, and she shut her lids as tightly as she could to prevent those hot tears from spilling down her cheeks.

* * *

For the second time that night, Claricia was dreaming, and for the first time, in many, many nights, it was not a nightmare.

She was dreaming of a handsome young lord who had come to court her like a proper lady, to wed her and take her home to be his wife. She was dreaming of tenderness and of being able to trust someone. She was dreaming of strong masculine hands cupping her face, the tips of long fingers brushing against her mouth as a man bent his head to kiss her. Gently, he touched his tongue to her lips, and she felt herself melting at his caress, willingly opening her lips, eagerly arching her body closer to his. Her mind did not flee, nor was she numb. Claricia moaned at the pleasurable sensations flickering to life deep within the core of her being, her eyes opened in wonderment, and the lovely dream came to an awful end. It was no handsome young Englishman, but her captor, the dark Highlander, whose lips brushed against hers, and the expression upon his countenance held no trace of gentleness, nor admiration. There was naught but lust in those dragon-green eyes. The same selfish uncaring lust she had seen a hundred times upon her uncle's face.

"Liar!" Claricia tried to roll away, but he held her firmly. "Clearly, it was another kind of warmth you wanted. And 'tis a warmth I'm not willing to give."

"Nay, I didna lie," Alexander protested, although he did not understand why he felt compelled to explain himself. "It seems my mistake was in not consulting my body before I spoke, for it has betrayed me as surely as yers has played ye false, my lady."

She cringed at what he said and hastened to deny the truth. "Your lust trifles with your ability to reason. You are wrong, sir. My body desires no man, least of all a thieving Highland scoundrel such as yourself."

"Och, but ye're wrong, and I ken ye know it as surely as I do," he said. His lips teased her bare neck while one hand slowly trailed across her shoulder and down to her breast. He pushed aside the loose-fitting undertunic, but he did not look at her nakedness, as he wished. Instead, his heated gaze held hers as his palm rasped across her nipple. It puckered beneath his touch, she gasped as the whole of his hand closed over the soft mound, and a knowing grin edged up the corners of his mouth. The mockery returned to his voice. "Witness, my lady whore. Yer body tells the truth even if ye canna. But dinna fash yerself this night. There will be time enough later to prove my point. For now, ye need to sleep. Later we will let our bodies speak the truth."

Without further ado he withdrew his hand, and, lying on his side, he held her to him as he had done before. In a few minutes, he was slumbering.

Claricia, however, could not sleep as her mind replayed those moments when he had kissed her. It was only a matter of time, perhaps another few nights, before he would have his way with her, and because of this kiss, it did no good to tell herself it would not matter. She could only survive if she maintained the control to numb her senses. She could only be brave if she believed that she wouldn't feel anything. But something had happened this night, and for the first time in many years, Claricia was sorely afraid.

Chapter 3

The band of refugees was bound for the mountains northeast of Loch Lomond, where there was shelter from the English and food for the hungry at a secluded valley called Glen Doune. They were Colquhouns, distant kin to the Kirkpatricks, and Alexander, who had feasted and caroused with their laird in better times, chose to travel in their company. He kept counsel with their leader, the men riding side by side to cut a path through the deep snow, while Claricia shared a pony with two young girls. Each night, she slept in the company of the other women.

Mid-morning on the fourth day of the third week, they came to the Pass of Balmaha, and from there, they had their first glimpse of Loch Lomond. Even beneath winter's mantle, it was a breathtaking sight. The leagues-long frozen loch glimmered beneath the sun, and its many islands made Claricia think of how a giant's boots might mark the icy surface. To the north rose the peaks of Ben Lomond and Ben Vorlich. That was where Alexander was headed, he remarked. For another five days, they traveled with the Colquhouns, and upon reaching the fork in the trail that led into the Aberfoyle Forest, they parted company. The Colquhouns trekked east into the Aberfoyle, while Alexander, on his great stallion, continued to lead Claricia, now riding on the Colquhoun's pony, toward the mountains.

For several hours they wound their way along a path above the loch, following in the footprints of a herd of deer that used the same track as did human travelers. It was a magnificent day. Icicles hung from tree and bush alike, and new-fallen snow weighed down the evergreen boughs and lay thick upon the ground. The sun was high in a cloudless sky, the air was uncommonly calm, and here and there, a ptarmigan was flushed from its hiding place in the underbrush.

At length, Alexander stopped his horse, raised a hand to shade his eyes, and pointed to the distant outline of a fortress. "Our journey shall soon end."

"That is Clar Innis?" Claricia could not disguise her disappointment. Chilled to the marrow of her bones and more hungry than she had ever imagined it was possible to be, the notion of arriving at their destination had buoyed her on more than one occasion as they made their way through the snowy wilderness. But now her spirits plummeted. Clar Innis was nothing more than a burned-out hulk on a barren rise overlooking Loch Lomond. Three of its four towers were in ruins. It did not look fit for human habitation.

"Aye, 'tis Clar Innis," Alexander grunted in reply. He did not like her uppity English tone. "Where did ye think we were bound? Windsor?"

"There is no need to be snide." Claricia tried to sound indignant. In truth, his words wounded her, and Claricia could not stop herself from wishing that he might be kinder. In spite of herself, Claricia had been unable to forget those moments in the cave when the warmth from his body had enveloped hers. For a short time that night, he had been a far different man from the one she remembered in the burning solar, a different man even than the one who had kidnapped her, and the notion that he might have a gentle side disturbed Claricia in a way she did not want to understand. It made his scathing words bruise, when she should have been immune. Unable to face him without being confused, she kneed her pony forward and headed down the trail ahead of him.

Alexander stared at the proud way she sat in the saddle. The bright winter sun glistened off the mass of hair that swirled about her back like the finest silk from the Continent, and he could only think of how he was going to have her all to himself that very night. He had said they would let their bodies speak the truth to each other, and he had meant it. It was going to happen. He was going to kiss her again, hold her close, bury his face in that lavender-scented hair and feel her bare skin against his, and in response, she would moan and arch against him as she had done before. The prospect excited him, and he galloped after her. They could reach Clar Innis none too soon.

As they approached the fortress the shadows at the base of the ruined towers shifted. Men were standing guard about the old castle, and they moved forward with their battle axes and cudgels firmly in hand.

Alexander rose to a standing position, waved his sword overhead, and cried, *"Dia is Buaidh!"*

The Kirkpatrick battle cry rent the frigid air. It echoed across the frozen loch and into the surrounding hills. Several of the men returned the cry and hurried to meet the approaching riders. Rourke O'Connor was among them.

"Dhia beannaich sinn!" the Irishman exclaimed. *God bless us.* " 'Tis true, mon. Ye've succeeded! Ye took the wench from de Clinton and live to tell the tale! I never should have doubted ye, Alex."

Alexander dismounted and handed the reins to a lad, who led the horse away. Highlander and Irishman embraced each other with the familiarity of kinsmen and warriors, then broke into animated discourse while they walked the final distance across a makeshift drawbridge and beneath the castle gate. They both were of uncommon height, standing head and shoulders above the other men. Alexander, the Highlander, was said to have inherited the looks of his grandfather, Malcolm, and he was as dark and lean as Rourke, whose looks were distinctly Irish, was fair and broad of face and form. Both wore their hair in long braids; they were well muscled and toughened by battle, and the resolute confidence of leaders marked their features. The other warriors deferred to them, making way at their approach.

Claricia's pony followed in their wake, and she sat in silence as she passed between the curious Highlanders who lined the roadway to the crumbling entrance. The warriors at Clar Innis were a filthy lot, their clothes were nothing more than tattered rags, their hair was matted, their features were hidden behind thick beards and grime, many of them had bare feet despite the icy ground, and the look of hunger and hatred was keen upon every face. They crowded close to Claricia's mount, poking at her legs, pawing her kirtle, and talking about her as if she were not there. Although their Gaelic was heavier than what she was accustomed to hearing, she was able to comprehend the crude things that they were saying about the kidnapped English whore.

She bit her lower lip to still its trembling and dared not glance into their eyes, lest her composure be altogether shattered. Although it seemed to Claricia that she had ridden to the most remote corner of Scotland, it was evidently not far enough. *Drùthanag*, they called her. *Harlot*. Even this unwashed lot of ignorant Highlanders knew who she was, and they expressed some vivid notions of what it was they wished to do with the Beast's Bawd.

For the first time since her captor had kissed her in the cave, Claricia found herself fervently hoping that he had meant what he'd said about letting their bodies speak the truth. She did not truly want that, but she could not bear to think of being left to the mercy of several men, especially these coarse creatures who looked more animal than man. It was what her uncle had done to the Scottish women he had taken prisoner. It had happened to Meg, and Claricia did not think that was something she could endure. Better one man than many, she decided. It was hard to believe she had come so low that such would be her best choice, but it was, and so it happened that she prayed the dark Highlander intended to use and, perhaps, if she was fortunate, to keep her for himself.

Her eyes sought out her captor, and once again, the wish that he might be kind came to her unbidden. It was a silly, foolish hope, but one that lingered because of those few brief moments in the cave when he had kept her warm. There were many things that Claricia had grown accustomed to living without, but kindness was not one of them. She could not help herself.

Alexander sensed her gaze and glanced up from his conversation with Rourke. What a remarkably lovely sight she was, with that delicate English complexion, those plum-colored lips, that proud little chin, and that mass of golden hair tumbling over the patchwork of furs she clutched about herself. He overheard what the men were saying, and experienced a peculiar surge of possessiveness. She was *his* captive. The other men could ogle and leer all they wanted, but she was his, and Alexander grinned. Lady Claricia de Clinton was his flaxen-haired whore, and this night, she would be his in every sense of the word. Quickly, he called out orders, and the captive was escorted to the only standing tower while he went with Rourke and the others into what remained of the great hall.

There was scant furniture in the tower chamber except a lopsided chest propped against one wall and an old pallet covered with a pile of pelts in the middle of the floor. At least there were four walls and a roof overhead, and the old man who had escorted Claricia up the winding stairs returned with a torch and small brazier, so there was light and a little warmth. He did not speak to Claricia, and, having decided not to reveal that she knew a little Gaelic, she did not thank him for the food he set before her.

There was a trencher scooped out of hard dark bread, which was filled with some kind of soup. It smelled like leeks, and there were several pearls of barley floating about the steaming liquid. It did not look bad, especially since it was the first hot food she'd seen in more than three weeks, but Claricia could barely manage more than a few tiny sips.

As hungry as she was, her eyes kept straying to the door. She could not even force herself to finish the smallest bite of bread. Any minute he would come up the stairs and through that door, and the thought of what was going to happen after that made her stomach twist into anxious knots.

Time passed. The soup turned cold. She pushed it into a dark corner, for the sight of it made her queasy. Minutes turned into an hour, then a second hour and a third, and as Claricia's appetite had failed her, so did her ability to sleep. She could do naught but stare at that door, reminding herself as she waited that this would not be the first time. She could survive.

When at last the door opened Claricia hardly recognized the man who ducked beneath the lintel to enter. The Highlander had shaved off the heavy black beard that had hidden his features those past few weeks, and he had retied the long black braids into a vague semblance of order. He looked almost decent.

Alexander crossed the threshold. The light in the tower room was poor, and he paused, needing a few seconds for his eyes to adjust as he searched her out. There she was, standing a few paces away, but he did not notice the quiver in her chin, or the way her eyes widened and her shoulders stiffened. He saw only the cloud of flaxen curls that encircled her face like a halo, the tempting shape of her lips, and the delicate color of her skin, which glowed with the promise of silky softness. He detected the firm roundness of her breasts and the gentle curve of her hips beneath the tunic and kirtle. He did not notice how the wind had burned her nose, or how the days of travel had reddened her hands. To Alexander, she was the most desirable woman he had ever set eyes upon, and he knew the reason why it seemed this way. It was because she was his alone, and no one else's. With one foot he kicked the door closed, then barred it with a large wooden bolt.

"Ye dinna sleep yet, whore." He strode across the room, took off his tunic, and tossed it aside. There was a large sword in the wide leather belt about his waist, but he did not remove that, and, coming to stand before her, bare chested and wearing only his leggings, he grinned like a lad. "Ye were waiting for me to warm ye on this cold night, were ye?"

"My name is not whore. It is Lady Claricia." She backed away from him, but he followed her around the pallet, and with each step, he came closer to her. She sharpened her voice. "And no, I do not wait for you. Indeed, you are a pompous peacock to imagine such a thing."

Alexander gave a hearty laugh. "Och, ye show yer thorns, little English rose." That was what Rourke had called her, and Alexander found he liked that description. It suited her, fair and delicate, with a hint of color. She was like the flower of the hawthorn. A white rose, *ròs geall*, and he wanted to taste her sweetness. Alexander captured her shoulders and dragged her to him. "Ye wouldna use yer thorns on me?" he drawled.

She saw the light of lust in his eyes and recoiled. This was not the kind man who had held her in the cave. Those hands that seized her were the brutal hands that had haunted her dreams. This was the savage who had burst into the solar, who had thrown her to the floor, and soon he would abandon all control, as he had before. She felt those fingers grip her shoulders as she had felt them before, and when he crushed her against the same hard-muscled chest, a blurred vision of flames crowded her mind. She heard screaming, saw Meg run to hide, and she felt the pain. She had fought as if her life depended on it, but she had failed to ward him off, just as she had failed to exact justice for what he had done to her. Now he spoke of thorns, but she remembered the knife and how easily it had sunk into his flesh.

"Indeed, I shall use my thorns . . . and more. I shall use every weapon at my disposal," she hissed. "What better way to kill you for good this time?"

"What?" The single word exploded from him. His eyes tightened into slits.

Claricia pushed at his chest, but he had positioned her against the cool stone wall. She could not escape. The anger in his face intimidated her, yet Claricia's wits did not abandon her. Her gaze narrowed to match his. Her voice hardened, as did her resolve. "Given a second chance, I will not fail to snuff out your miserable life. This time, sir, I will not miss your heart. This time, you will not come back from the dead."

Alexander listened in disbelief. She could mean only one thing, and as he considered what she'd said his fingers dug into her shoulders. He wanted to hurt her, but she didn't flinch. If it was possible, that delicate chin tilted yet higher.

"Whatever you intend to inflict upon me this night there is nothing you can do that would be worse than what I've already suffered. Rape me if you will. It will not matter, for I've already had that from you, and this time, sir, when 'tis done, I will make certain you do not live to return and try a third time."

With those words Alexander knew the truth. "Bitch," he snarled, staring eye-to-eye at the person who had killed his brother. "*It wasna me* ye stabbed in the heart."

"How could that be?" Her eyes widened in astonishment. She looked at the black braids, the thick dark eyebrows, and the strong prominent nose. Her eyes moved over the sharp jaw and high sculpted cheekbones. She stared at the firm mouth, with the lower lip that was thicker than the upper. It was he. It had to be. There could be no other man with those deep-set dragon-green eyes. Claricia swallowed hard in a suddenly parched throat, and in a voice that was barely above a whisper, she asked, "Who are you?"

"I am Alexander, Earl of Kilmory and Torridon, and the last laird of the Kirkpatricks," Alexander declared with an eerie formal significance. He knew what he had to do, and braced himself to perform the deed. " 'Twas my twin brother, Andrew, ye murdered, and I do this for him. I do this for all my Kirkpatrick kin."

Grasping the hilt of his sword, he pulled it from the wide leather belt and raised it high above his head in readiness to smote her where she stood, pinned between him and the wall.

"*Dia is Buaidh*." The Kirkpatrick battle cry reverberated through the tower room. *God and Victory*.

"Murder me?" Claricia cried out. Quickly, she made the sign of the cross. "Go ahead." She saw his gaze flicker over her face, and she held her breath. He swallowed, then sucked in his cheeks. The muscle along his jaw twitched, but he did not lower the sword. She might still have a chance. Frantically, she whispered, "Do what you will, Alexander Kirkpatrick, but know that it is I who will win. The murdering English whore will be dead. You will set her free."

Alexander observed the cost of what she'd said. Although she had encouraged him to kill her, he saw the quiver of terror shoot through her body. He watched the color drain from her cheeks. She had revealed more of herself in those brief seconds than she had in all the days of traveling to reach Clar Innis. Somehow she managed to maintain unwavering eye contact with him. Her chin was held high with that haughty English pride, and in spite of himself, he was humbled by her courage.

There was upon her face an expression of de-

termination and defiance that reached deep inside him. He knew that she had not been trained
to face her enemy as a warrior, yet he could not
think of many Highlanders who were as dauntless as this English whore. If these sentiments
could be called empathy in Alexander, they were,
however, short-lived, as the unbidden memory of
the last time he had seen his sister rose before the
tapestry of his mind's eye.

I can be brave, his sister had promised when de
Clinton's horsemen had surrounded them in the
clearing. Alexander and Andrew had been overcome without a fight and trussed up like game
birds ready for the spit. They were to be taken to
Berwick to await execution, and although Caitrine had been little more than a child, her fate
would have been only slightly less harsh. Everyone had heard stories of the Scottish noble-
women who had been imprisoned in cages and
hung out of doors for swearing fealty to King
Robert. It had been a dreadful thing to consider,
yet there were things far more horrendous. Caitrine might not have been so fortunate as to be
suspended in a cage. She had become withdrawn
since their mother's death, so brittle since their
father's execution, so dependent on others those
last months.

*I can survive. Dinna fear, Alex, I will not dishonor
the Kirkpatrick name. No matter what torment the sassenach devil deals me I can be as brave as yer best
warrior.* Her valiant words had shocked him. She
had tried to be brave, but he had known how
truly delicate her mind had become, and that the
bravery could not last. Whatever speck of compassion Alexander might have felt for Lady Clar-

icia de Clinton evaporated as quickly as Caitrine's image had vanished that afternoon when
she'd been taken away. Having slung Alexander's sister across the rump of his Spanish war
horse, Aymer de Clinton had galloped into the
mist that was rising from the forest floor. It had
been raining, and the soggy ground had absorbed
the retreating thunder of hooves. How unreal it
had seemed. The summer day had been unseasonably hot and muggy, but there had been no
way to stop the cold hard hate that had encircled
Alexander's heart. Their younger sister had been
taken by Sir Aymer de Clinton, and Alexander
and Andrew had exchanged a speaking glance
that their captors did not see. They would escape
from Berwick to rescue Caitrine, or perish in the
attempt; that had been the silent vow between the
brothers.

To gaze upon this English whore and know
that she lived while his family did not, consumed
Alexander with a bitter rage over which he had
no control. His grudging admiration turned to lethal hatred.

"Ye're not afraid of me?" he taunted, leaning
closer, until he had trapped her against the wall
with his lower torso. The seconds ticked by, and
for reasons he would never understand, Alexander lowered the sword. It landed on the stone
floor with a loud clatter. The sword was no
longer a threat, but he did not move away. Instead of putting distance between them, Alexander began to move against her in a suggestive
fashion.

"No, I'm not afraid of you." A crimson blush
stained Claricia's cheeks, and her breath came in

quick shallow gasps as he rubbed himself against her.

Alexander knew she was lying. "Ye should be," he warned with a sneer, deliberately sliding up and down against her, pulling her kirtle higher with each movement. He brushed the tangled mass of long golden hair from her face, then he set his hand beneath her chin, tilting her face up to his, feeling his heart swell with a strange mingling of triumph and desire at the way in which her eyes fell before his. "It is time, whore. Time to let our bodies speak the truth between us."

He lowered his head and covered her mouth with his. It was not a tender kiss, but a hard and demanding one, filled with hunger and a thirst for vengeance. He was going to punish her. Roughly, he pulled her away from the wall and down to the pallet in the middle of the floor. "I've wanted ye ever since I saw ye sleeping in that clean bed," he murmured. "And I know ye want me, too, whore."

Claricia shook her head in denial. "You are a thief and a liar."

"Nay, lady, though I may be a thief, I am no liar." Alexander chuckled. "And ye canna hide from the truth." His lips moved against hers, pressing and sucking, and his tongue pried open her lips to swirl about her mouth. The length of his body lay atop her. Beneath his bare chest she was soft and warm, beneath his thighs her legs were shapely and delicate, and his body molded to hers while he kissed her. In a voice made rough with unquenched passion, he whispered in the space between their lips, "Do ye remember when we kissed in the cave? How ye moaned for me? How ye arched yer body and couldna get enough of me?"

Claricia did not answer, instead she held her breath and lay very still. She did not struggle when his hand pushed back the bodice of her tunic. She did not pull away when he caressed her breasts. Her mind began the lullaby.

> Sleep, my little darling, sleep
> Dean cadal, seircean, dean
>   cadal.

She did nothing but shut her eyes and think about Meg's faerie island when he slid the tunic over her hips. The kirtle was gone, too, but she did not feel the cold air on her bare skin.

> My love is sweeter than honey,
> better than jewels, softer than
>   wool.
> A ghaoil is milse na a mhil,
> fearr na seudan, maoithe na
>   cloimh.

She did not feel his lips brush across her nipple, or the hardness of his male flesh when it grew to thrice its size and pressed against her inner thigh. Her mind was drifting to a distant place, and Meg, who had taught her how to withstand the pain and how to turn hours into seconds, would be there.

> Dream, my only child, dream.
> Breisleach, m'aon leanaban, breisleach.

At length, Alexander raised his head from her breast. Something was not right. He pushed himself up on his elbows to stare at her. She was limp as a child's doll.

"God's blood," he swore in a harsh voice, suspecting what it was that she was doing. The whore was resisting him. "Open yer eyes and look at me!"

From faraway, Claricia heard him. He was furious, just as her uncle had been on more than one occasion, and she braced herself for her punishment, for the shouting and the blows, but it did not come. Instead, she was vaguely aware of his lips lingering behind her ear. She felt his warm breath on her skin, and there was an odd throbbing in her ears. Still she did not move. She did not obey and open her eyes to look at him when he feathered kisses up and down the length of her neck.

"No woman, especially not a whore, denies me." Alexander controlled his anger and made his voice low and provocative. "Ye will look at me before this night is done. Ye will feel me, whore. Ye will know me, and ye will surrender to me."

Deliberately, he began to caress her, moving his hands and body in the ways he knew would please a woman. Lightly, his lips traced a path from behind her ear, along the delicate line of her jaw. Erotically, he nipped and teased at the corners of her mouth. In the moonlight, he saw the tiny pulse beating at the base of her throat. He saw her eyes open, and it did not matter that she had not reacted to his words, for her body was reacting to his touch. He heard the quickened breathing, saw the misty look in her wide eyes. He sensed the quivering in her limbs that she was trying to suppress, and he knew that she was awakening to him.

"No!" Claricia cried out, drawing her hand across her mouth as if she could wipe away his kiss, as if she might stop the melting sensation that was spreading up and down her legs. This had never happened to her before, and she was horrified by the acute awareness she had of his hard stomach and corded chest muscles, of the warm dizzying sensation that was building inside her. This wasn't right. She must not feel anything. Claricia fought to move away from him, but he held her close. His hands were everywhere, and where his hands did not touch her, his chest or thighs or stomach did. It was horrible. Her flesh was tingling all over, as if she had taken ill with an ague.

Alexander slid his hands over the gentle curve of her buttocks and across her hips. Provocatively, he sought out the secret female spot at the apex of her legs. His fingers moved like feathers, teasing and circling until they reached their goal. For an instant, he did not know who was more surprised when his fingers slipped inside her. She was moist and hot, and his swollen manhood leaped at the sensual discovery of her readiness. It throbbed and pressed between their bellies, and he heard her cry out when his fingers began to stroke her.

In desperation, Claricia tried to free herself from him, but while the fingers of his one hand were deep inside her, his other hand held her firmly to him. *Concentrate*, she screamed at herself. *If you cannot free your body, free your mind.* But her body was betraying her, and she couldn't divorce her mind from what was happening.

"Sweet Jesu," Alexander moaned as he rose over her. He had never known a woman to be so ready for him. Try as she might to deny it, her body was reacting to his. A shudder of pleasure coiled through him. He widened the space between her legs. She was quivering, the musky scent of her was intoxicating, and, unable to hold back any longer, he descended quickly to sheath his manhood in her velvety warmth.

With a guttural cry he entered her, and Claricia, who had expected pain, was stunned by the white-hot thrill that coursed through her. She braced herself for the agony that accompanied a forced invasion, but there was none. Her body was warm and relaxed as she felt herself take him in and close about him. Her hips arched upward. Willingly, she let him wrap her legs about his waist, and as his thrusts became deeper and he slid to the hilt, her body seemed to open to him of its own accord. There was no pain. It was an overwhelming realization, and tears began streaming down her cheeks.

"God in heaven, ye're so lovely, so sweet," Alexander uttered from low in his throat, then a moan began deep inside him, building until it burst forth with raw unleashed power. His movements became faster. Despite the cold tower room, a thin sheen of sweat covered his upper body, and he knew it was almost time to withdraw. Although he might sheath himself inside the English whore, he could never allow his seed to flow into her. Just a few more exquisite warm moments, and then he would pull out of her. But the sensual pleasure was too much, and while an inner voice cried, "*Out now!*" it was already too late.

"Och, God!" Lost in the abandonment of an excruciating pleasure, Alexander shuddered as his seed exploded into her. He emitted another deep moan. His body was wracked by an uncontrollable contraction, a second, and a third. He thrust deeper, harder, bursting, filling, exploding, and then he collapsed on the pallet beside her.

Staring into the darkness, Claricia heard his agitated breathing, felt the sticky moisture between her legs, and she was devastated. She had allowed herself to feel his lips and hands, to experience the masculine hardness of his chest and the strength of his arms, the caress of his fingers between her legs, and the totality of his possession. He had been potent and tender and seductive, and she had felt it all. Even now she could not deny the warmth that was radiating from his body. She could ignore neither the raspy sound of his breathing nor the salty scent rising from his moist skin.

In the moonlight, Alexander saw tearstains upon her face, but he did not wonder at their source. He could only think of how he had failed. How he had allowed her to control him at that final moment. He saw her swollen lips, and he thought of how she had moaned beneath him, of how moist and hot she had been. A fierce desire pulsed through his loins. He wanted her again. His desire was even more intense than before,

and he could not help wondering if she had bewitched him.

He had never felt the renewed demands of desire so soon after release. He had never lusted for
another woman the way he did for her. He had
buried himself within her, he had ridden her hard
and deep, and that should have been the end of
it. That should have been enough, but Alexander
could not prevent himself from thinking that
maybe he would never have enough of her. The
prospect provoked him, but not nearly so much
as the fact that he had not been able to control
himself in the end. She was like the poison of too
much wine. Inebriated by her charms, he had dis-
honored his Highland blood by allowing his seed
to enter his enemy's womb. It disgusted him to
think that any woman might wield such power
over him, least of all the English whore who had
murdered his brother. It was abhorrent to consider that she might be with child, his child, a
Kirkpatrick bairn, and the hostility that was always lingering below the surface of his emotions
took control of his actions.

"I was wrong, whore. I dinna want any part of
ye." He spoke this lie as much to convince himself as to persuade her. He must not want her.
He must never allow her to control him again.
Although it was naught but lust between them,
it sickened him to think that this woman might
hold any power over him. She was his enemy, a
spoil of war, and nothing more than a means toward his end. His vengeance. He must not let her
affect him in any way. After a long hard stare, he
decided what to do. "In the morning, I'm giving
ye to my men."

Claricia's chest contracted, her breath caught in her throat, and she clapped her hands to her ears.

It gave Alexander a perverse sense of satisfaction to witness her reaction. He was in control again, and could not stop himself from adding, "My men have been a long time without the services of a woman, and are not particular when it comes to whores. Ye will please them."

A fist of fear clutched Claricia's heart. She remembered the screams in the bailey at Goswick Keep, and what little color had remained in her face was drained, until it became an unearthly white. One slender hand trembled at her throat; her gaze darted from his dark demonic face to the barred door, then back to his face, where she saw an unmistakable measure of satisfaction. He had seen her fear, and it pleased him. What a loathsome, unfeeling beast. He was as bad as his brother, as bad as her uncle. Perhaps worse.

She looked away and caught sight of a possible means of escape. There was a window only a few feet away. It had to be a long way down, but it did not matter whether she lived or died. Either way she would escape. It had been rumored that that was how Lady Johanna had died, and until now, Claricia had never understood what might have caused a mother to leave her only child. She had never believed it was possible that her mother could have flung herself from the tower window at Goswick Keep. They had been happy, the three of them, Claricia, Lady Johanna, and Meg, and it had not made sense to think her mother's death had been intentional.

Time seemed to slow. An afflicted cry echoed off the cold stone walls. Until this moment Claricia had believed that she could survive anything. But not what the Highlander had threatened. She knew the anguish and humiliation one man could inflict upon a woman, and to think of the same from ten or twelve or twenty was unbearable.

Claricia's grip on sanity began to slip. Pushing back the tangle of flaxen hair from her face, she rose from the pallet, dragging one of the fur covers behind her. She was only vaguely aware that the thin, high-pitched cry reverberating off the walls came from within her as she leaped onto the window ledge and flung wide the shutters to hurl herself forward, but she went nowhere.

An arm pulled her back.

Alexander was trembling. He had not imagined a whore would react like that. He had wanted to torment her. He had wanted to destroy the impression that what had happened between them was anything more than what might have happened between any man and any whore. He had not wanted her to know that he needed her again. He had merely intended to push her to the brink of her endurance. She had seemed so haughty. Impervious. But he'd been wrong. Once again, he was reminded of Caitrine, and when he jumped up to pull his English prisoner back from certain death it was an instinctive reaction. He could not let her perish.

"Why?" Claricia pleaded for an answer. Her teeth were chattering. Long strands of golden hair flew about her pale face and slender shoulders. There were tears welling in her eyes, upon her lashes, and they spilled over to mark new trails down her cheeks. "Why do you bother to stop me?"

"I dinna murder women," was Alexander's solemn reply. He hardly understood it himself. He wanted nothing more to do with her. She had killed Andrew. Why did he care whether she lived or died? "Not even murdering English whores. Yer blood will not stain my hands."

"Yet you are willing to strip me of my dignity." She spoke in a small sad voice.

Dignity? He'd never thought of a whore possessing a shred of self-esteem. But he refrained from saying so, for at that moment, everything about her was dignified. Though her feet were bare and she was naked except for the fur coverlet, there was an undeniable pride in the way she met his gaze. At length, Alexander said, "I willna send ye to my men."

He felt her relax, yet fearing that she might again bolt, Alexander's arms tightened across her chest. He had not come this far to let anything happen to her. He needed her for his plan. That was the only reason he had saved her, nothing else, and he renewed his vow for revenge against de Clinton before he turned his head from her tearstained face to look out the window.

A blanket of new-fallen snow shrouded the countryside. It was a beautiful white coverlet to hide the ugliness of war. As a lad Alexander had delighted in playing in the snow with Andrew and Caitrine. The first snowfall of the season had always been the best, and especially fine when it had been deep enough to flop oneself down and sink into several inches of soft white flakes. The three of them would lie side by side, arms extended, with fingers barely touching, and while Caitrine's merry laughter floated on the crisp winter air they would swing their arms and legs back and forth across the snow until they had each left the impression of a winged angel upon the white surface.

Alexander leaned against the stone wall and stared into the night mist that engulfed the surrounding hills, as anger and loneliness raged within his soul. They were as familiar emotions as the blind lust for vengeance with which he lived. Sometimes it seemed that he'd felt this way his entire life. But there was a new emotion stirring within him, something he did not understand, and he had never felt more hopeless than he did leaning against that wall and gazing into the night.

There was nothing for him. Not here or there or anywhere. What a pitiful relic of his former self he had become. There was nothing for him except vengeance. There were no angels. There was no heaven. There would never be light after the dark. There was only this hell. Something sharp and searing twisted in his heart as he stared down at the young Englishwoman in his arms, and he cursed the tragedies that had brought them to this awful reckoning.

Chapter 4

He was gone when Claricia awoke, but that did not blunt the intensity of her emotions when she thought about what he had done to her. She reached out for her garments, which had been cast on the floor beside the pallet, and as she put them on, a lingering male scent rose from her skin. Her stomach churned. He'd told her his name was Alexander, the last laird of the Kirkpatricks, and he had said he was not the one she'd killed. It had been his brother, a twin named Andrew, but what he had done to her the previous night had marked her more vividly than what his brother had done six years before.

By all that was holy, she hated Alexander Kirkpatrick more than she knew it was possible to hate. It was such a real thing, this anguish, this loathing, that her body seemed to ache from it, and Claricia prayed that if there truly were a God in Heaven, He would damn Alexander Kirkpatrick to the eternal fires of hell.

She despised him. He had robbed from her as surely as his brother had, and this time, the theft had been even more irreplaceable than her virginity. Until the night just past, Claricia had not believed there was anything more precious that could have been taken from her against her will, but she was mistaken. The night before, the man whose brother had set in motion the destruction of her future had purloined the final shard of dignity she'd managed to retain.

The coals in the brazier were cold. Outside the tower the wind howled and the shutters rattled; a draft swirled around the room. Claricia wrapped her arms about herself and gave a despairing shudder at the bleakness of her situation. The horror of what Alexander Kirkpatrick had done to her extended beyond dignity. He had pillaged the faint hopes that had lingered in a corner of her heart. There would never be a handsome young lord or a manor house in England to call her own; there would be no small children clutching her kirtle, and no devoted husband to treasure her. Gentleness and kindness were forever beyond her reach. She was, indeed, the whore his brother had made her.

"So, niece, you enjoyed it, did you?" Aymer de Clinton had accused Claricia when she had no longer been able to hide the truth. It had been four months since the rebels had attacked Goswick Keep and set fire to the tower. Four months during which time Claricia had slowly become aware of the different way in which her uncle was looking at her.

"Nay, sir," Claricia had cried out in vehement denial. What was wrong with her uncle, to imagine she might have found any pleasure in what had been done to her? In God's name, why did he want to punish her? She had not done anything wrong.

"Do not lie. You felt it. Indeed, you enjoyed it,"

her uncle had sneered as his gaze roamed over her body. "It appears 'twas not rape after all." The disapproval on his face had altered to a sort of hunger Claricia had never seen before. His lips had thinned into a knowing leer, and an awful light had appeared in the back of his eyes. Then her uncle had used the word for the first time, and she had finally understood why he had been staring at her in such a different fashion, "You're a *whore*, my young Claricia. A fair temptress with the heart and soul of a harlot."

Whore. Claricia heard her uncle say it over and over. She put her hands over her ears, but it did no good. The hideous memory was too compelling. Finally, a knock at the landing drew Claricia back to the present. The chamber door opened, and the man who had escorted Claricia to the tower the night before stood on the threshold. He did not enter, but motioned for her to come with him.

"What?" She did not rise from the pallet. "Why?"

"You must come with me, my lady," the old man replied in Gaelic.

"Why?" Claricia asked again, but she did not need to hear an answer. The old man was going to take her to the laird, but she did not want to leave the relative sanctuary of the tower chamber. She did not want to see Alexander Kirkpatrick in the light of day.

"Please, my lady, dinna disobey." The old man's voice was sympathetic. "We dinna want to offend the laird. I only follow orders."

Reluctantly, Claricia pulled one of the furs about her shoulders and rose to follow. Just as it would have been foolish, if not fatal, to try to escape during the long journey from Hepburn Castle, it was pointless to refuse Alexander Kirkpatrick's request now. She would gain nothing by offending the laird. It was a lesson her uncle had taught her well.

He was Lachlann of Kilmory, the old man introduced himself in Gaelic as they descended the winding stairs, babbling, as he went, of his small farm on the Kintyre. The land had always belonged to his family. It was rugged beautiful country, and no one, not Romans or Norsemen nor *sassenach* devils, could claim it. He was distant kin to the last laird of the Kirkpatricks, he told Claricia with a note of pride, and Alexander Kirkpatrick was his *toìseach*, his leader.

At the entry to the hall, old Lachlann stopped his chattering and drew Claricia aside.

"*An sibh, mo Eilidh? Mo nion?*" he asked in an almost conspiratorial whisper, and Claricia strained to hear him above the noise coming from the great hall. *Is it ye, my Eilidh? My daughter?* "Have the *sassenach* bastards let ye come home to yer da at last?"

For the first time, Claricia saw the light of lunacy in Lachlann's rheumy eyes. The poor old man had lost his child, and Claricia's heart skipped a beat. How many families had been torn asunder by this terrible conflict? How many souls had been pushed beyond the bounds of sanity? Claricia thought of her father, of Meg, and of Lady Johanna, and she almost answered, but stopped herself. It was better not to let anyone know she understood Gaelic, not even this half-witted old man. Instead, she gave him a small sad smile and patted him on his forearm. He seemed satisfied, and led her into the crowded hall.

A momentary hush fell over the room as Claricia walked behind Lachlann, her eyes downcast, her arms drawn close to her sides. She could not bear to think that she might have been given to these savages. Every one of them focused his attention on her, but no one uttered a word, and after Lachlann had directed Claricia to sit on the floor a few paces from a cavernous hearth, the warriors began to talk amongst themselves again. Claricia tried to relax. Although the stone floor was cold and there were no rushes, this was the warmest spot she had enjoyed in days. It was much better than the drafty tower chamber, and she inched as close as she could, not only for the warmth, but to position herself as far away from the warriors as was possible. Lachlann set oatmeal cakes and something to drink before her, but Claricia could not eat, and from beneath lowered lids, she peeked at her surroundings.

Clar Innis was a hovel. Claricia saw traces of former elegance. A few specks of red paint remained on the timbers overhead, and although thick soot stained the walls, there was the fading design of grapevines painted on the woodwork. Debris was everywhere. Broken timbers from the failing roof lay about in haphazard piles. There were the usual discarded bones upon the floor, as well as assorted excrement from the chickens, cattle, hounds, and rooks that inhabited the end of the hall opposite the hearth. Torches soaked in mutton grease provided light, and their stink, along with that from the unwashed bodies and animals, was horrible. In this rebel fortress, the great hall was used day and night for sleeping, meeting, training, and eating by man and beast alike. The furniture was scant. There were only two trestles and a few benches, not enough to accommodate the more than fifty warriors who were living at Clar Innis.

Claricia's regard strayed more than once to Alexander Kirkpatrick. In spite of herself she noted how his black braids fell over well-defined shoulders. She tried to look away, but stared at his long legs stretched before him. He was thin, but he was a big man, taller than her uncle, and much stronger, too. She had discovered that the previous night, and she watched in morbid fascination as the hands that had touched her with unspeakable intimacy splayed in the air, then motioned this way and that. He was deep in conversation with the stocky Irishman, and although Claricia could not see his dragon eyes, she could close hers and imagine what his face looked like. She could see the sharp masculine jaw and the high cheekbones, the faint beard stubble, and a tiny scar that resembled a star, high on his cheek, near the corner of his right eye. She could hear him, too.

Ye will look at me before this night is done. Ye will feel me, whore. Ye will know me, and ye will surrender to me.

Her hands clenched into fists, until her knuckles turned white. She would never let him touch her again. She would never surrender to him, and if he tried to make her, he would suffer the same fate as his brother. What had happened the night before would never happen again.

Alexander rose from the bench. He was coming

straight toward her, and Claricia tensed. She tilted her chin toward the rafters.

"Do ye cook?" Alexander asked without preface when he stood over her. He knew she had been watching him, and he didn't like that. It had not been a good idea to bring her into the hall. It was much too distracting. Even in the cold light of dawn when he had stood over the pallet before leaving the tower chamber, he had felt the renewed stirring of desire. Alexander could not concentrate when the memories of the previous night kept crowding his mind. He could not think as a warrior must think.

"If you would like me to cook, I can do so, my lord," she said in that soft sweet voice that did not reveal the kind of woman she was.

Alexander stared at her. He did not think she knew the first thing about cooking, but like any whore, she would try to please. She knew her place. That was good. And she would be out of sight. That was good, too. "Lachlann will show ye to the kitchens. As long as we've a female at Clar Innis, there's no need for any mon to be doing woman's work."

Claricia said nothing. She detested kitchens and cooking, but that did not matter. At least she would not be anywhere near him, and she breathed more easily when old Lachlann led her to the kitchen.

Rourke O'Connor, who had been watching his kinsman, was sitting on a nearby bench with his feet propped on the trestle table. He raised a carved drinking horn to his mouth and savored the bragot. While food might be scarce, it seemed they never ran out of bragot or ale. He studied

Alexander's expression after Lady Claricia had left the great hall, and at length, he set aside his drink.

"Now that ye've had yer way with her what do ye intend to do with Lady Claricia?"

"Why would ye say such a thing?" One of Alexander's thick, dark brows shot upward. He did not like to think that Rourke might know what had happened the night before.

"Well, as ye could barely keep yer eyes off her, and since I know ye're not a mon who denies his pleasures, it seemed fair enough to assume ye've had her and still burn for her."

"She's a whore, after all," Alexander muttered between bites of bread that had been soaked in stew. "And a fair one, at that."

"Aye, 'tis verra true. Fair as an English rose. White and sweet."

A vision of purity raced its way across Alexander's mind, then faded quickly. It was absurd. Lady Claricia was no rose. His response to Rourke was defensive. "Then dinna fault me for being as human as the next mon."

"But when does a mon have second thoughts for a whore? Unless, of course, ye've a mind to keep her." Rourke paused to measure Alexander's expression. To the best of his recollection his friend had never had second thoughts for any woman. Although they were blood cousins, sharing the same great-grandparents, the Highlander and Irishman had distinctly different perspectives toward women. Rourke appreciated every woman for the totality of her being, while Alexander never looked beyond the physical. Indeed, Rourke suspected that this was intentional, and once, when he had criticized Alexander for the way in which he discarded lovers as quickly as he'd seduced them, Alexander had made the bleak remark, "When a mon can offer nothing to a woman, 'tis unfair to prolong a relationship." Rourke considered that attitude to be unfortunate, but no less strange than Alexander's preoccupation with his prisoner. There had been numerous daughters of powerful lairds in Alexander's bed, many fair lassies to whom he might have given a second thought instead of this Englishwoman. "Neither is a good thing, Alex. Second thoughts or keeping her. Both should be avoided."

Alexander gulped the bragot, hoping the deep red juice would drown the truth in its heavy vapors. By the Holy rood, if Rourke knew the whole story of what had happened in the night, he would surely accuse him of having abandoned his senses. He thought of his brother's bloody crumpled body when it had been brought to him. Lady Claricia de Clinton was a murderess. She was the *Beast's Bawd*, and there should have been naught but loathing in his soul for her. He could have been done with it and killed her, but he hadn't. He could have let her toss herself from the tower window or he could have passed her on to his men, but he hadn't. He should have been in control, but he hadn't been. Second thoughts were the least of his worries. Rourke had posed the proper question, and Alexander must not hesitate to act. He must proceed with the business of playing out his vengeance.

"I shall ransom her," Alexander declared, finding a curious sort of comfort in the notion that something good might yet come out of this. "An English lady, though a whore, should fetch a good price, and we are in desperate need of food and other provisions. Lady Claricia will help supply us for the battle ahead." Alexander grinned. "That will be the final stroke of irony against de Clinton. He will finance his king's defeat, and my vengeance will be complete."

"A wise course to pursue." Rourke raised his drinking horn in salute. "And it will placate King Robert, who wasna pleased to learn what ye'd done. His Majesty didna like to think one of his strongest supporters would take such a risk and engage in a private war, perhaps at the expense of Scotland."

"His Majesty would have done no less in my place."

"Aye, 'tis true, there isna a Highlander who doesna seek justice, but His Majesty intends that his lairds will fight united."

Alexander tore off another piece of bread and took his time chewing on it. He was thinking. "Would ye be willing to escort Lady Claricia to Loch Awe? If de Clinton dares try to rescue her instead of paying the ransom, 'tis less likely he would succeed if she were at Eilean Fidra."

"I had intended to leave in the morning," Rourke replied. "I would be happy to take Lady Claricia."

"Och, Rourke, I should have known. Ye return to *her*." It was not a question, but a statement of fact. Alexander was referring to the young woman who lived on the Old Believer's Isle in Loch Awe, the young woman whose hold over Rourke had never been denied by the Irishman.

Indeed, Rourke, who believed in Fate as strongly as had his grandfather, who had been raised among the Norsemen, had never tried to pretend it was not so. She was his fate, and Alexander, who had never understood this easy acceptance of a female's power, found it particularly incomprehensible that morning.

"Aye, I am going to her, for I dinna like to think of her alone on that island at this time of the year."

Alexander surveyed his friend. "She has survived without ye before."

The Irishman tried to disguise how this remark made him feel. He did not like to think she did not need him. He owed her his life, and beyond that, there existed a link between their hearts, yet she remained a mystery to him. Worse than that, Rourke did not think that she would ever need him as he needed her—indeed, he was afraid it was so. This need was a different emotion than he'd dealt with in the past when it came to women. Although he found great pleasure in their lovemaking, the bond between them was of a spiritual nature. It nourished his soul and enriched his heart, and the incessant thought that she might not be on that island the next time he returned was a distressing one. The thought that she might leave without telling him where she was going was difficult to consider. Sometimes it seemed he had not truly lived until he had awakened on her island almost four years before.

Rourke had been bleeding for two days and nights. The battle in the Pass of Brandir, a narrow defile between Loch Etive and Loch Awe, had been fierce. The Highlanders had been assailed from both sides by English infantry, as well as by archers who had come over the top of Ben Cruachan to rain a storm of arrows upon them. Rourke's wounds had been numerous, and he had been left for dead when the Highlanders retreated in a headlong flight to the safety of the sea. There had been two deep gashes across his back and another across his shoulders. An arrow had impaled his thigh, and the wound had been festering badly, yet he had managed to limp and crawl to the shore of Loch Awe. Rourke was not himself a Kirkpatrick. It was his great-aunt, Lady Isobel, who had married Alexander's grandfather Malcolm, and therein lay Rourke's Highland ancestry. The bonds were fresh enough for him to have joined in the fight against the English, and while on this side of the Irish Sea, Rourke considered Eilean Fidra home.

It had seemed like a miracle when he hobbled out of the forest to gaze across the water at Eilean Fidra, its towers rising straight out of Loch Awe. The island fortress had not been totally demolished, and, having seen signs of life on the ramparts, he had raised a weary hand to his mouth to call out, but before he might utter a sound, he had collapsed into the shallow water. He had struggled but had been unable to rise, and Rourke's last conscious sensation had been of being swept away by the current as he sank deeper and deeper into the cool water.

Later, he was to discover that more than a fortnight had passed since he'd stumbled onto the shore. He had returned to consciousness, lying on his back and staring up at a low roof made of vines and branches. He had been sleeping on a bed of ferns. There were lady's-smock and fox-glove, mountain ash and hemlock, and for a moment, he had wondered if he'd been taken away by fairies. His body had been wet and clammy, and he had tried to rise, but the pain in his leg had been excruciating. Before closing his eyes, he'd seen the moss poultices on his chest and thigh. He'd smelled the mugwort and vervain. Rourke's Irish grandmother had been a healer, and he had realized someone was taking care of him. His feverish mind had conjured up visions of witches and trows. The little green shelter smelling of herbs and wet earth had seemed otherworldly, but it had been nothing like what the priests described as the afterlife, and Rourke had fallen back to sleep believing that he had survived.

> *In the blood of Adam death was taken.*
> *In the blood of Christ it was all to-*
>   *shaken,*
> *And by the same blood I do thee charge*
> *That thou do run no longer at large.*

But it had not been fairies or trows that had tended him. There had been no otherworldly magic at work. Just a girl, for he had heard her voice, chanting, "In the blood of Adam . . . In the blood of Christ," as she'd changed the poultices and spooned a bitter broth between his lips.

The next time Rourke opened his eyes was the first time he saw her, and he would forever hold the image of her rising from the loch like some magical water kelpie. He had been propped into a sitting position, and had been able to see her through the leafy wall of the hut. Her black hair had coiled about her arms and down her back, her skin had been the color of fine cream, and drops of water had glistened on her arms and legs like so many stars when she entered the bower.

She had been wearing nothing but a knee-length tunic, and when she had seen that he was awake, she had smiled with such radiance that Rourke had momentarily doubted that he lived, for surely this was Heaven. Or, if not Heaven, it must have been the faraway faerie isle of child-hood tales, for he could not imagine any human female being so enchanting.

"Ye're awake," the smiling, dark-haired vision had said in Gaelic, but her soft accent had sounded different to his ear. Light, musical. He could tell she had not always lived in the western Highlands.

"When I was a lad I wondered if mermaids could talk," Rourke had whispered.

"Mermaids?" She had stepped backward to stare at him, as if deciding whether or not he was dangerous. After a few moments, a slow smile of comprehension had crossed her features, and she had clapped her hands together in a sort of delight, surrendering to a ripple of laughter. "It would be wonderful, aye, to be a mermaid. And I suppose some folks might think I was one if they'd seen me pulling ye from the water."

"Ye can swim?"

"Aye."

"Ye went into the water after me?" Only a mer-maid would have done that, for 'twas ill luck to save a drowning body. Even a Christian knew there were spirits in the water. They had been there since the beginning of time, and if a mortal was saved from a watery grave, the spirits would claim the rescuer in his stead. "Aye," she had replied in a solemn tone. "What else was I to do? Stand by and watch ye die in the reeds while the eels nibbled yer toes?"

Rourke had shut his eyes, thinking that this was still some fantastic creation of a feverish brain, and he had not yet found his way back to reality. All his life he had dreamed of finding a woman so bold and beautiful, and there she was, kneeling before him in a soaked tunic, with wild black hair swirling about her shoulders. "Ye pulled me out of Loch Awe?"

"I dinna know what the people in yonder castle call it."

"Ye live alone? Ye dinna commune with yer neighbors?"

"Aye to both yer questions." She had cast the first of countless furtive glances over her shoulder. In the next moment, she had regained her composure and emitted another light trill of laughter as she went about the task of changing the poultice on his thigh. Lightly, she had chided, "Ye ask too many questions for an ailing mon. What am I to expect when ye regain yer strength?"

The days had passed, May blossoming into June, and the summer months had turned to autumn while she tended him with her radiant smile and musical laughter, and always looking over her shoulder. She had been kind and full of concern for him. She had wanted to know everything about him, his family, his home in Ireland,

and his past. She had always listened, but she had never answered a single simple question about herself except to tell him that she was called Viviane. It had suited her, mystical and mysterious and at peace with the watery realm of the loch. At first, Rourke had thought Viviane's reticence to talk about herself owed to shyness or modesty, and it was not until his time to leave had drawn nearer that he had discovered the truth.

Rourke knew he could not possibly repay Viviane for everything she had done for him, and when it was time to depart, he had known his absence would not be forever. He would return to Viviane time and again. In addition to his life, his lovely black-haired water maiden had given him joy and laughter and the first true sense of what it meant to see himself reflected in the glow of someone else's eyes.

He could never repay Viviane for all that she had bestowed upon him, all that she had willingly shared and given, and for the time being, the best form of repayment was to look after her. He must return to the island. It had been three months since Rourke had last been there, and although the supplies he'd left behind had been sufficient to last until the spring thaw, he always lived with the fear that an English patrol might have seen the smoke rising from her hut and crossed the ice to inspect the isle.

Alexander was saying something, and Rourke cleared his head to focus on his friend.

"So, Rourke, ye were staying at Clar Innis only long enough to make certain I didna get myself in dire trouble and need to be rescued from de Clinton?''

"Something like that." Rourke grinned. He was an imposing man, with a hulking form and heavy, masculine features set against a ruddy complexion, but when he smiled his eyes twinkled with such merry lights that even the most timid bairns could be charmed.

"*Gun robh math agad,*" said Alexander. *I thank you.* He was not offended that Rourke had been worried for him, for he would have done the same if their situations had been reversed. One of his fondest childhood memories was of walking in the hills above Loch Awe with his grandmother Lady Isobel, while she told him the story of her twin brother. It was a glorious tale of treachery and death, of loyalty and triumph. The babies had been separated at birth. Isobel had been the infant bride of Malcolm Kirkpatrick, while the boy had been sent into hiding in Ireland, and it was not until they were grown that either knew of the other's existence. It had been the summer of the last Viking invasion in the Highlands, when the lad, who had been named Ingvar by his adoptive Viking father, had returned to the land of his birth, and the molten silver crucifix had spoken the truth that neither child had known. Twice that summer, Ingvar had saved Isobel's life, adventures that Lady Isobel had related to young Alexander with much dramatic elaboration. The bond between Isobel and Ingvar had been strong, Lady Isobel had told her grandson, and so, too, would the bond be between Alexander and Rourke when the cousins met. Lady Isobel had been right. Indeed, there was more than blood between them. There was the bond of companions-in-arms, warriors whose lives depended on each other.

Rourke nodded at Alexander as if to acknowledge the trust between them; then he motioned toward a nearby table. "A messenger from King Robert arrived late in the night. The mon wishes to speak with ye."

A Scotsman as gaunt and weary as any of the other warriors came forward. "*Toìseach*." He addressed Alexander with the respect due a Highland laird. "I am Douglas of Carrick, come from His Majesty."

"His Majesty is well?"

"Aye, King Robert is well, but he is troubled by the news from across the border."

"Does the English king intend to make good his threat?" Alexander asked the question that had been on everyone's mind since the end of November, when King Edward had issued a proclamation declaring that he would lead an army by the twenty-fourth of next June against his enemies in Scotland.

This pronouncement had been the English monarch's response to an agreement between the Scottish king's brother, Edward Bruce, and Sir Phillip Mowbray, the English commander of Stirling Castle. During the previous year, rebel forces had expelled the English from Galloway and Nithsdale. The Scottish military enterprises had prospered with additional victories over Rutherglen and Dundee, and on the twenty-eighth of February, the first day of Lent, 1313, Edward Bruce had laid siege to Stirling. But the rebels had failed to rout the English from Stirling. By the twenty-fourth of June, the mighty fortress had not surrendered, the siege was called off, and Edward Bruce had consented to a treaty with Sir Mowbray stipulating that the castle would be surrendered to Scotland one year hence, if not relieved by English reinforcements before that date.

"Aye, *toìseach*, there is no doubt the *sassenach* king is preparing for an expedition to liberate Stirling before the deadline."

Alexander swore. Rourke echoed his sentiments, and as the news rippled through the great hall, the warriors moved closer to hear what was being said at the head table. Every Scotsman knew Edward Bruce had made the agreement without consulting his brother, and no one liked the invitation it had offered to the English. There had been slim hope that the politically weak *sassenach* monarch would not follow through on his threat.

Douglas of Carrick had more news to impart. "Our spies tell us the English will come by sea as far as Berwick and then make for Stirling Castle."

"Edward's barons will bring their knights and ride with him?" Alexander asked.

"Whether or not the barons agree may be of no import. 'Tis rumored King Edward will summons his Welsh allies, as well as the Irish chieftains in the Pale. We have also heard that emissaries have been dispatched on the Continent to Gascony, Poitou, Provence, and Brittany."

A dark expression hardened Rourke's features. The English had been ruthless in their subjugation of Ireland, and he did not wish to see them victorious in their attempts to dominate Scotland.

Alexander gave a grim nod. The *sassenach* king could assemble a force in the tens of thousands. The battle for Stirling Castle would be costly. It might very well be the decisive fight for Scottish independence. "Where is King Robert?"

"On the move." Douglas of Carrick pulled a missive from beneath his plaid and handed it to Alexander. "His Majesty requests that his loyal servant Alexander, Earl of Kilmory and Torridon and laird of the Kirkpatricks, call up all warriors and patriots from the western Highlands to rendezvous with the Scottish army no later than the first of April at the Torwood north of Falkirk. The Earl of Moray, James Lord Douglas, and Angus MacDonald from the Isles will be there, as will His Majesty's brothers, with their warriors."

Alexander unrolled the missive and scanned the written message. It was signed "Robert de Brus." This was a solemn moment. His king had called upon him, and Alexander stood to extend his hand to Douglas of Carrick. His reply was formal. "Tell my liege lord that we will be at the Torwood, ready and willing to shed our blood in the name of independence."

"*Dia is Buaidh,*" a warrior cried out. *God and Victory.*

Other men answered the wild shriek, and the Kirkpatrick motto reverberated through the hall, as did the battle cries of every sept and clan taking shelter at Clar Innis that winter.

Chapter 5

The stew that Claricia presented at the evening meal was an unappetizing concoction of mutton and leeks. There had been something on a shelf that smelled vaguely like ginger, but when she sprinkled it into the pot the result had not been for the better. The stew was a putrid gray color, and as she carried a serving kettle around the head table the pungent greasy aroma was making her nauseous.

Move around the table, feet. There were only two more warriors to serve. She was grateful that Lachlann was attending to the other table, and she sent up the silent plea: *Please, legs, keep me upright. Just let me finish this, so that I can go back to the kitchen.*

It had been peaceful in the dark room below the hall, warm and quiet, and although she did not usually like windowless, musty spaces, the kitchen was as far away from Alexander Kirkpatrick as she could get at Clar Innis, and she could not return there soon enough. While she might have been willing to do his bidding and work like a kitchen slave, she was not willing to let him have his way with her again, and Claricia intended to remain in the kitchen for the night.

The fair-haired warrior who was seated beside Alexander Kirkpatrick gave a pleasant smile when Claricia ladled stew into his trencher. He was Irish. Claricia could tell by the silver collar he wore about his neck and the brooch crafted of intricate swirls and knots that clasped his plaid at the shoulder. He pushed a thick fringe of blond hair away from his face and raised his head to Claricia, revealing eyes that were a startling, vibrant blue. He muttered a thank you in stilted English, calling her "my lady," and Claricia, who had always been told the Irish were even more loutish than the Scottish, was touched by this effort. She nodded in acknowledgment, and the stress lines imprinted upon her forehead momentarily relaxed, then she took two stiff steps to stand behind Alexander Kirkpatrick's place. It was upsetting to be near him. Clenching her teeth, she squeezed the kettle handle as if it were his neck while she reminded herself that soon she would be back in the kitchen.

Alexander, who had been trying to avoid glancing at Claricia as she walked around the table, peered into the kettle. "It appears ye didna try hard enough to perfect yer cooking skills." His tone was deliberately insulting. It was happening again, and he was angry. Disheveled and pale as she was, and smelling of mutton grease, he could not prevent himself from responding to her as a man responds to a woman. She was lovely, and he wondered whether having her beneath him just one more time would be enough. There was an intense pulse of lust down the length of his manhood, and when he swallowed, his throat was dry. If only she were not so desirable, this would not be so complicated. "Do ye expect me to eat that swill?"

"It willna kill ye," injected Rourke, who'd had his first taste. Lady Claricia was not looking well, and Rourke did not like to think Alexander was going to berate her in front of his men. Friend or foe, she was, after all, a woman, and Rourke had always been inclined to defend any female, no matter her nationality or circumstances. That this prisoner was the niece of Aymer de Clinton did not make her any less a lady, in his consideration. " 'Tis on a par with the usual fare our Lachlann is wont to prepare."

"Which isna saying verra much," growled Alexander. The damned girl was standing so close to him that he imagined the swell of her breast had brushed against his upper arm. Perhaps, she knew the effect she had on him and was doing it on purpose. Perhaps it was not her intent to escape or fight him, but to torment and bewitch him.

" 'Tis nourishment, and a hungry mon canna afford to be picky. The bread is fresh baked and still warm," Rourke added by way of further encouragement.

Alexander took one of the small loaves. He was hungry, and mayhap if he satisfied one desire, he thought, the others might be dulled in the process. Without looking at Claricia, he mumbled, "Go ahead."

Claricia glared at his head, where the ink-black hair was combed away from his forehead, and she had the most incredible desire to ladle the stew right on top of him. He was behaving like the swine he was, and it would have served him right to be covered with greasy mutton chunks. She almost laughed aloud at the vision, and at the satisfaction it would have provided her, but she didn't. She also controlled the impulse to douse him with stew and began instead to serve his meal.

As the large wooden spoon dipped into the thick liquid a plume of steam rose to circle her head. Her nostrils flared at the disagreeable odor. Her stomach churned, she gagged and averted her face from the steam. But it didn't help. The stench was horrible, and despite the unremitting winter chill, moisture beaded her upper lip. Her knees would not sustain her much longer.

The great hall started to spin. The voices and laughter of the men receded, and a ringing noise crescendoed within her ears. She could not hold the kettle. It was getting heavier and heavier. Her fingers lost all sensation, her grip relaxed, and the kettle fell from her grasp as her legs folded beneath her. She had fainted in a heap upon the floor.

"Christ crucified!" roared Alexander. He leaped to his feet, toppling the bench. Hot liquid had spattered his leggings. "What's wrong with the wench?"

"Hunger, I'll be supposing, *toiseach,*" said Lachlann. He frowned. The lass was a mess, and the wolfhounds were stepping on each other to lap at the spilled stew. "She didna eat the *aran corna* last night, nor did she touch the oatcakes this morning."

Rourke rose to aid her. Lachlann was already kneeling beside her and clucking like an old biddy hen.

"Dinna touch her," snapped Alexander, shocking himself into momentary inaction by the possessive tone in his voice. His surprise was mirrored in Rourke's expression. His Irish kinsman raised his hands in a motion of deference and backed off. But old Lachlann continued to cluck, and, swearing beneath his breath, Alexander kicked at the dogs. The animals yelped and scampered away. Without considering why, Alexander took Lachlann's place hovering over her.

First things first. Lifting her up off the floor, he gripped the collar of her sodden kirtle and with a quick motion split it open to pull off the soiled garment. The undertunic was relatively clean, and he left that in place. Deftly, he wrapped his own woolen plaid about her, then used the ruined kirtle to wipe her arms.

Claricia's eyelids fluttered open. The first thing she saw was that his face was only inches from hers. His dragon eyes were ablaze with intense anger, and she cringed at this turbulence. Then she felt his touch upon her, she saw her ruined kirtle in his hand, and, fearing the worst, she tried to get away from him. "It w-was an accident," she whispered as she attempted to fold her arms across her chest to protect herself from him. "Please d-don't. I didn't mean to."

"I didna think ye did." Alexander's voice remained sharp. He scowled at her. "And stop staring at me as if ye were gazing upon the devil himself."

Claricia glanced away. Feebly, she rubbed at the muck on her legs.

"Fetch something clean for her to wear and something bland to drink," Alexander instructed

Lachlann. Then he scooped her into his arms and rose to carry her to the tower room.

"Ye must take better care of yerself, my lady." Alexander was coaxing Claricia to taste the clear broth that Lachlann had prepared. Sitting with his back propped against the lopsided wooden chest, he held her upon his lap as if she were a small child. She was clean and wearing a dry, albeit ill-fitting, kirtle, but she had neither spoken nor taken a sip since they'd left the hall. Ten minutes before he had not wanted her near him, now he was holding her. Alexander wondered what had possessed him to take charge of her in this way. Recalling how she had given her cloak to the woman in the cave, he told himself that was the only reason he was showing her this attention. She had been kind to a stranger, no less an enemy, and he was repaying that kindness. Besides, Alexander suspected that if he didn't take care of her, he would have to explain himself to her self-appointed guardians, Rourke and Lachlann. "I ken ye're a survivor, my lady. Ye've come too far to give up now. Ye must at least stay well enough to see a Highland spring."

Claricia thought that was a strange thing to say, and she responded in a dull little voice, "I had not imagined being your prisoner for so many months."

"Och, perhaps not," Alexander replied in a sympathetic voice. "But 'tis a rare sight when the heather on the hillsides turns from brown to green. Magical it is when the birds return to sing in the trees, and bright blossoms dot the slopes and valleys where all was gray and dead not weeks before. Everywhere a body looks there is color, and all around ye the sounds of life echo through the hills. Wee lambies bleating and calvies calling, fledglings in their nests chirping for their mamas, and the constant drone of bees flitting from flower to flower. Along the riverbanks and shores the does lead their spindly-legged fawns to drink. 'Tis a wonder to behold. Why, even the glittering salmon jump from the water in delight. Doesna that sound like a worthy scene to set yer eyes upon?"

Claricia did not answer. His words were at odds with almost everything he had said or done up until that moment. Evocative and poetic, they had soothed her. Even his voice was different, and for a moment, she had forgotten reality. She had been imagining that the hand holding the spoon to her lips and that the gentle voice speaking to her were those of a handsome young lord and that she was at her own manor house somewhere in faraway gentle England. She imagined reaching up to caress his cheek. Then she saw the young lord's deep-set green eyes, wary and intent like a forest beast's. She glanced about her. Her throat tightened. Of a sudden, she wanted to cry, for England was, indeed, faraway, and although she knew now what the future held, she knew it was bleaker than it had ever been.

Alexander did not like it when she was quiet. The remote look upon her features was unsettling. It seemed Lady Claricia had the ability to travel great distances without ever moving. In an effort to bring her back, he asked, "If not spring,

isna there something in yer life for which ye wish
to live?"

"That's a foolish question to ask a whore,"
Claricia answered. The passing daydream was
ruined. *Of course there's something. Even whores
have wishes, but I would never tell you mine.*

Alexander stared at her profile. Her complexion was uncommonly ashen. There was a fragile
quality about the high cheekbones, aristocratic
chin, and perfect nose that only made her pret-
tier. Her thick lashes offset her wide eyes, and for
the first time, he noticed their color. They were a
lush, regal purple, a hue as deep and vivid as that
of the wild iris growing at the water's edge. How
strange that he had not seen their beauty before.
Like everything else about her they were delicate
and refined, and he knew the toughness in her
voice had been forced.

She was lying to him again. But why? What
was she hiding? Perhaps nothing more than tarnished dreams. To Alexander's astonishment, it
was not difficult to imagine that once upon a time
Lady Claricia de Clinton had cherished the same
girlish dreams as any other young lady. Of
course, such thoughts made no sense. She was a
whore and murderess, and he didn't understand
how his mind could have conjured up such contrary notions. Lost dreams should not have mattered. He was the last laird of the Kirkpatricks,
and must avenge his family. Still he could not
lighten the heaviness that lay upon his heart.

Alexander raised the spoon for another try.
This time, she opened her lips, and after several
sips, a touch of color returned to her cheeks. He
continued to feed her, mesmerized by the sight

of her lips each time they closed over the spoon. He watched her tongue slip out to lick away a drop of broth. Her moist lips glistened in the rushlight, and Alexander shifted her weight on his lap. Finally, the bowl was empty, and he set it aside, but the arm that held her upon his lap did not release her. Instead, he continued to stare at her lips.

Sweet Jesu, he wanted to kiss her. It had been foolhardy to pretend he could hold her like that without wanting to touch her in other ways that were far more intimate. He wanted to feel her bare skin against his. He wanted to run his hands across her breasts, her soft stomach, and up the inside of her legs. He wanted to . . .

He sensed her power. It was a palpable thing, reaching out to touch him, tempting him and working its sensual magic again. Already he was forgetting that she was the one who had killed Andrew. His body was betraying him, and he feared—nay, he knew, to his immense shame— that if he took her it would end in the same disgraceful way it had ended the night before.

A shudder of repugnance ripped through him. He was a trained warrior, and one whore should not have been able to exert such influence over him. It was disgraceful; a dishonor to his name, his clan. Such weakness went against everything he had been taught as a Highlander and a warrior, and he was glad Rourke did not know the truth, did not know how easily he had abandoned his honor, for he could not have borne to see the pity in his kinsman's eyes.

"Yer lips are a bonny wonder," he said on a soft breath before he could stop himself. It was the sight of those lips, so close, so tempting. They made him speak those words, and out of nowhere the idea came to him. He would kiss her just once more, in order to prove that he could stay in control. He would do that, she would leave in the morning to be ransomed back to de Clinton, and this gnawing guilt would be gone with her.

Claricia gasped. Seated upon his lap, she was vividly aware of his muscled thighs beneath her bottom. She felt his fingers where they held her shoulder, and she closed her eyes to think of Meg's faerie isle, but the image was too far away. She opened her eyes to stare down at her lap.

"Do ye know what I'm thinking?" he drawled in a low husky voice.

"I'm not a fool," came Claricia's stiff reply. She didn't want him to kiss her again, didn't want to be close to him or to feel any part of him touching her.

Alexander chuckled, and with the hand that had held the spoon, he tipped her chin upward. Her skin was warm, and her chin trembled. His gaze lingered upon her lips, and, using a fingertip, he traced the outline of her mouth.

Claricia jerked backward. She tried to angle her mouth away from him, and, taking a deep breath, she dared to deny a man. "Just because *I know* what you're thinking does not mean *that I shall let you* kiss me." Her uncle would have struck her for saying such a thing; she expected no less from this Highlander.

"Was I so terrible last night?" Alexander's voice was a seductive drawl. He did not let her move away from him. Slowly, his fingertip continued its path around her lips.

"Aye, you were vile. A whoremonger and rapist." But Claricia's accusation was barely above a whisper. He was not livid with fury, as her uncle had been. His touch was like a caress. There was nothing cruel or punishing in the way he was treating her, and her heart twisted in confusion.

"Och, lassie, but ye're wrong about last night. 'Twas not rape." Alexander's finger lifted away from her lower lip. The back of his hand trailed along her jaw, then down the column of her neck, to stop at the little pulse quivering at the base of her throat. "Ye were ready for me. 'Twas not rape."

"But was I willing?" Claricia retorted. She was trembling but did not understand why, and she wished that she had not posed that question, for she knew the answer and did not like it. The truth was that some part of her had been willing. By the Holy rood, her body had been more willing to accept a man than it had ever been, and she feared her uncle had been right. Truly, she had been born to be a whore. Her trembling worsened. There could be no other explanation for the way she had reacted, the way she had failed to dull her senses and keep herself from feeling everything that he had done to her, the way her body had accommodated—indeed, welcomed—his.

Alexander's hand moved from the pulse at the base of her throat to push a thick length of pale golden hair off her shoulder. His voice became huskier. "Ye shouldna resist," he said as he coiled a long strand through his fingers, moving his hand in such a fashion that it wrapped round and round them. " 'Tis a waste of time when we both ken the truth." With each wrap about his hand the length of hair became shorter. Gently, slowly, he was pulling her lips closer to his, and the languid seductive movement of his hand matched the tone in his voice. "Must I show ye once agin the way it is between us?"

Their lips were only inches apart when Claricia's heart skipped a beat. If only she could remember how to get to Meg's faerie isle. If only Lachlann would return to the tower chamber and interrupt them. If only she were not sitting upon his lap. If only . . .

"Tell me true how ye felt last night, else my manly vanity shall be mortally wounded," Alexander whispered against her lips. "I couldna be any worse than that bandy-legged *sassenach* bastard ye welcome between yer thighs. Did our rutting not give ye pleasure?"

Claricia diverted her gaze to stare at her folded hands. In a small voice, she said, "I am not used to such foul language."

Alexander stared at her. A visible blush stained her pale cheeks, and, looking down as she was into her lap, she presented a picture of innocence. No maiden true could have been more demure, and oddly, he regretted his words. It was strange, but he could not help feeling the same stab of youthful remorse he had experienced when his mother had reproached him for blaspheming in the presence of his sister. He tried to shrug off his discomfort.

"Och, well, 'tis a good thing, then, that ye'll be gone from here in the morning, my lady."

"Gone?" Claricia raised her head and met his eyes.

"Aye, I've dispatched a ransom letter to de Clinton, and ye'll be going somewhere else to await his reply."

"You're going to return me?" Claricia asked, unable to comprehend what this kidnapping and mad trek halfway across the length of Scotland had all been about in the first place. Why had he done it? She shuddered, unwilling to believe that she was soon to be her uncle's prisoner once again.

Alexander heard something odd in her voice. She was looking at him very strangely. Faith, she did not appear happy at the prospect of freedom, and Alexander thought that he must have been mistaken about the distress in her expression. "Dinna tell me ye like it here?" he asked, not entirely serious, but unable to stifle the query.

"Nay," Claricia shot back. She glared at him. "I do not like it here. 'Tis filthy as a stye, lacking in any of the amenities to which I am accustomed, and mine host is most displeasing."

There was nothing confusing about that answer, and Alexander grinned. She had tilted her chin upward in that defiant fashion that he found appealing. "Then it should be most pleasing to consider that after tomorrow ye'll never see my vile face or suffer my foul tongue agin. After tomorrow ye'll be gone forever from yer displeasing host." His voice fell to a smooth whisper, he angled his lips toward hers, and his breath caressed the corners of her mouth. "One more kiss canna be such a terrible price to pay."

"You'll get no ransom from me." Claricia put

her hands against his chest to push away from him. Inadvertently, her lips brushed his, and she tried to escape, but his fingers were still entwined in her hair. He held her close. There was nothing she could do to get off his lap.

"Just a kiss," he drawled, letting his lips graze her chin, her jaw, her cheek, below her ear. "Nothing more. Just one kiss." His tongue began to trace her lips, as his finger had done.

Claricia inhaled sharply as he drew a moist path about her mouth, and when his tongue had been around once, his lips replaced it. His mouth was barely touching hers, feathering light kisses at the edges and along the bottom lip. He nipped and tasted, licked and swirled, and Claricia did not move. She kept her body still, her lips pursed into a repellent, tight line, but still he kissed, meticulously, softly.

"Come, my lady, ye dinna play fair," Alexander murmured in the second before his mouth claimed hers. He knew what she was trying to do, and he could not let her do it. She must respond to him. She must surrender to him, and he would make it happen. His caress was as passionate as it was tender, beckoning and beguiling, one kiss fusing into another, and then it happened. He heard her little moan, he felt her lips relax. The tension fled her shoulders, and in that unguarded second, his tongue slipped between her lips. Her teeth were no barrier. Easily, he entered her mouth.

Claricia drew a breath, more of a little gasp, as a quiver of heat skirled through her. His probing tongue was hot, and to her dismay, she was not repulsed by its exploration of her mouth. Her body was weakening, softening, melting, and Claricia tried to numb herself against the sensations he was arousing within her. *Sleep, my little darling, sleep.* It had always worked with her uncle. Where was her resolve? *Dream, my only child, dream.* Claricia had to force herself to think of the lullaby. Her mind should have been able to ignore what was being done to her. Why couldn't she hear her mother's voice? Why wasn't it working now?

She was vividly aware of everything that was happening. His beard stubble chafed against her skin, his corded torso muscles were hard against her breasts, and his manhood pulsed beneath her buttocks. He smelled salty and tasted like bragot. This Highlander, her enemy, her captor, was awakening a desire within Claricia she had not known existed, and in a moment of horrific revelation, she knew why her resolve had abandoned her. The truth was that she couldn't shut down her senses, no matter how much she thought she wanted to stop feeling him and everything he was doing to her. She moaned again, perhaps at the shocking, dismal discovery, perhaps at the delicious sensations coiling through her.

Alexander loved it when she moaned, such a yielding, sweet sound. She was warm, and a musky scent rose from her skin as he bent her within his embrace, molding her breasts to his chest and pressing himself closer and closer. His swollen manhood was pressing upward between her buttocks, straining against the fabric that separated them, and gently, he moved her back and forth on his lap to simulate their joining, but it was a mockery.

A harsh groan rose from deep in his throat. There was an intensifying desperation within him for more than a single kiss, for more than this futile adolescent rubbing of himself against her while clothed. That was not enough. A kiss would never be enough. He had to be inside her, fully and completely. He had to have her beneath him, his naked flesh against hers. It was an awful sensation, this wild need, as if a horde of devils had taken control of him. Something beyond his power was taunting him, tormenting him, and like a madman possessed, he roughly pushed her off his lap and onto her back.

With lightning speed, Alexander thrust her tunic over her hips. She was wearing no underclothes, and was sprawled backward in a fashion that fully exposed her sex to him. Vainly, she tried to close her legs, but he was kneeling between them. She tried to wrench herself free and roll away, but his hands held fast to her wrists, pinning them to the pallet above her head.

"No," Claricia pleaded. Even in the dim rushlight, she saw the lust burning in his eyes. It was emblazoned upon his angular features, and she wanted to escape, wanted to close her eyes and go away, but the fire in his gaze immobilized her.

Alexander leaned down between her legs, closer, closer, until his body held hers, and one hand slipped between them to delve into that secret feminine place. He moaned. She was wet and hot, and ready for him.

Claricia bucked upward. Sweet God in heaven, her entire body jolted with shock at the ease with which his fingers slipped inside her. The moisture that had been between her legs the night before was there again. Tears welled within her eyes, but he was not hurting her. There was no pain. She cried from shame and confusion.

Nothing like this had ever happened to Claricia in the past, and to confront the reality of her character was appalling. She wanted more from him. It did not matter who he was. She wanted him to do these things to her, and admitting to that terrible truth, Claricia sensed more than ever how important it was to resist. She must not surrender to him, for deep inside she knew another terrible truth. Deep inside she knew that somehow this man could scar her more profoundly than anything or anyone before, and she must not let that happen.

Mustering every ounce of her strength, Claricia yanked one hand free and slapped him as hard as she could across the right cheek. "Liar, that is more than a kiss. Do not touch me, else I shall kill you, as I did your whoremongering brother."

Alexander's hand flew to his stinging cheek, and he narrowed his eyes menacingly. "*Eist!*" His exclamation was sharpened by anger and disgust, but it was her words that echoed through the tower chamber, ridiculing him for the fool he was. She was right. This was much more than a kiss, and once again, he had failed. Once again, his willpower had not been able to withstand whatever sorcery it was she wielded over him.

He withdrew his hand to pull down her tunic. Wordlessly, he covered her with furs, then lay on the pallet beside her. But he did not release her.

His hold remained tight and stiff. It was almost as if he were afraid that if he moved even a fraction of an inch it would start again. Even the muscles along his jaw that stung from her blow remained tense. He was angry at himself and at her. Violence churned within him.

How easy it would be to squeeze the life from her, an inner voice chanted the foul thought. To be done with her now and forever. But he did not murder women, not even this one, and Alexander struggled to suppress his rage, not moving, barely breathing, and reminding himself that soon it would be morning and she would be on her way to Eilean Fidra. Then he would be free.

It would have stunned Alexander to know how similar Claricia's thoughts were at that precise moment. She, too, tried not to move or breathe too deeply, in an effort to dull her awareness of the long, lean male body beside her. She, too, reminded herself that soon it would be morning and she would be leaving, never to see this insensitive, lying, thieving Highlander again. But her last thought before she fell asleep was an inexplicable one.

Mine host's language was not always foul. He was not always insensitive.

That night Claricia dreamed of heather turning to green and of the coming Highland spring that she would never see.

" 'Tis a good day for traveling," Lachlann muttered as much to himself as to Claricia when he fetched her from the tower chamber. A midwinter thaw had come on a gentle wind at sunrise, and the clear morning was unseasonably warm.

It was a good thing the weather had turned, he said to no one in particular, especially since the lass had nothing more than a threadbare plaid about her shoulders.

In the bailey, the old man helped Claricia mount a sturdy Highland pony. Nearby, Rourke was preparing to travel. He was tightening the girth on his saddle, and from a low shed on the other side of the yard, Alexander appeared, first to wave toward Rourke, then to walk toward Claricia. Her hands tightened about the reins at his approach, her back stiffened, and despite the urge to look away from him in shame, she managed to hold her head high.

In a few long strides, Alexander stood beside Claricia. "I see ye're ready to depart," he said bluntly, and before he might change his mind, he thrust a large bundle at her.

"What's this?" Claricia inquired in a trembling voice. A rush of hot pink colored her cheeks. She did not like to see him, to be near him, and think of how he had made her body betray her, of how he knew the truth about her. He had been absent from the tower when Lachlann had roused her at dawn, and when she had been allowed to sit before the fire and break her fast in the great hall, he had been absent then as well. She had not expected to encounter him before she left. She certainly had not expected him to give her anything.

"Why dinna ye look and see?"

Claricia obeyed, and unfolded a wondrously heavy cloak. It was amazingly unsullied, and made of a rich, fur-lined fabric, with elaborate clasps at the collar. Quickly, she secured it on her shoulders. There was even a hood, but there was no need to pull it up that day. The luxurious material pooled about her neck and down her back. It was wonderful, warm, and elegant, and she glanced down at Alexander Kirkpatrick, bewilderment etched upon her face.

"I didna want ye to catch a chill." Alexander saw her curiosity, and gave the answer for which he thought she asked.

"Of course, I would be no good to you then," Claricia reminded him. Despite his kindness—indeed, perhaps because of it—she could not keep the mockery from creeping into her voice. Why was it so hard to accept this gesture at face value? "My uncle would not pay a single farthing in ransom for a sickly whore."

That was not why Alexander had given her the cloak, and he scowled. He had merely been thinking of how she had not been repaid for her generosity to the Colquhoun woman. He had not been thinking of de Clinton or the ransom, and he was startled to discover that he had, for the briefest moment, forgotten she was a whore. He was even more startled at how hard it was to say good-bye to her.

"I merely wanted ye to return with all that ye had when ye started on this journey," he said.

Claricia's heart twisted. Why did he have to play at being kind? He knew not of what he spoke. Although she had willingly parted with the cloak, there was much more that had been taken from her, much more that could never be given back. Gone was her finely developed ability to distance her mind from her body. He had rendered her vulnerable in the worst possible way, and she did not know how she would survive when she was returned to her uncle. Alexander Kirkpatrick would never have understood such a thing, and although she wanted to hate him with every ounce of her being, some part of her did not. She had hated him upon waking the morn before, but somehow that feeling had faded. He had been cruel and brutal, yet there had been other moments she could not explain. Moments that gave way to the illogical impulse to reach out to him.

"Rourke O'Connor will take ye to Loch Awe, my lady." As he was speaking, Claricia looked at him, thinking how he had once called her "my lady" with contempt. There was none of that now. "When yer uncle delivers the ransom, ye'll be returned to the Lowlands. I willna see ye agin. *Soirbheas leat*," Alexander ended in a quiet voice. *Good luck to you.*

Claricia gave a bland nod, while her heart was contorting with exquisite agony. "Thank you," she whispered as the unbidden image of a young English lord with hair as golden as her own crossed her mind's eye.

"For what?"

It would have been simplest to say, "For the cloak," but it would have been a lie. Instead, and without understanding why, Claricia spoke the truth: "I'm not certain."

Then, before she might stop herself, Claricia reached up and gave way to the illogical. She allowed her fingertips to trail across Alexander Kirkpatrick's cheek. He had stolen from her, but he had given her something as well: a tiny moment of kindness. Briefly, her fingers lingered. Briefly, she thought of the young English lord

who did not exist except in her dreams. She
thought of how this man had coaxed her to take
the broth, of how he had held her to prevent her
from leaping from the window ledge; she saw a
vision of his Highland spring, and they were
strolling on a path down the greening hillside.
None of this made sense. She frowned at the absurdity of what she was doing and snatched her
hand away.

An aching sweetness ran through Alexander
when her fingers lifted from his skin. How wonderful it had been. How quick was the touch of
her fingers, and how freely given was that caress.
He thought not of sorcery or of willpower diminished by overwhelming lust. This was a golden
moment, unbearable in its genuine tenderness,
for he knew that such a moment would never
come again between bitter enemies, and he tried
to memorize it on the spot. He tried to seize upon
an image of Lady Claricia that would allow him
to remember her as nothing more than a woman.
But he failed.

He looked away from her. This was all wrong.
"Take care of her," he ordered Rourke in a voice
that sounded far too rough.

His Irish kinsman nodded, and wheeled his
horse toward the gate.

Claricia gave a mirthless laugh.

"I've said something to amuse ye?" Alexander
asked, realizing that he had never before heard
her laugh.

Her laughter stopped. "Not really."

"What, then?"

She hesitated and shook her head as if to deny
that there was anything to tell. Her pony whin-

nied, and the jingle of bridles was carried away on the winter breeze as her mount tried to follow Rourke's. In a moment, she would be gone from Clar Innis and Alexander Kirkpatrick forever. They would never cross paths again. It would not make any difference if she spoke the truth.

"There has been no one to care for me in a very long time, my lord," Claricia said in her musical voice. She tried very hard not to sound as miserable as she felt, and she prayed that somehow, having spoken the truth, the burden that it had placed upon her heart would leave her as quickly as had the words. "I was merely pondering how strange that it should be my enemy who cares, even if it is for the wrong reasons."

It was not what Alexander had expected to hear, and he found himself at a loss for a reply. In silence, he walked to the portcullis, where he watched Rourke and Lady Claricia make a path through the melting snow. Aye, he was her enemy, and enemies they would always be. Nothing would change that. It would take a miracle, and as the English whore, with her uncommonly brave demeanor and flaxen curls trailing down her straight back, disappeared into the gray winter hills, Alexander reminded himself that miracles were no more real than angels.

Chapter 6

❝Is something amiss, my lady?" Rourke reined his horse to a halt and twisted sideways in his saddle to better look at Lady Claricia. As it had each day since their departure from Clar Innis, a bright sun shone overhead, and he raised a hand to shield his eyes. "Ye've been glancing over yer shoulder all morning."

"I heard a noise," Claricia lied. In truth, she was scanning the landscape for Alexander Kirkpatrick. Of course, he wasn't there. She knew that. Still it was impossible to shake the awful feeling that he was hovering over her. It had been that way since their departure from Clar Innis. They had traveled the length of Glen Lochy, and as their horses plodded over trails made muddy by melting snow and ice, it seemed to Claricia that they could not go fast enough or get far enough away.

Rourke looked from the lady's anxious countenance to gaze across the countryside. "We've been on Kirkpatrick land since dawn, and although ye canna see them, the laird's clansmen patrol these hills and ravines. We are safe from outlaws and beasts alike. Dinna fash yerself, my lady."

The Irishman's kindly meant words did not re-assure Claricia. Instead, they were proof that she could not escape Alexander Kirkpatrick. From the recesses of her mind, his low, lilting accent rose to conscious memory, and it was not the fierce voice that had called her whore that she heard. Rather, her mind replayed the kindly tone when he had coaxed her to sip the broth, and the achingly gentle tenor when he had described the Highland spring, the quiet voice when he had wished her good luck.

Oh, how easy it had been to hate his brother, and easier yet to loathe her uncle. Indeed, such emotions were right. They made sense, just as it made sense that she should loathe Alexander Kirkpatrick with equal intensity. But she didn't, not exactly. Indeed, there were moments when Claricia felt an empathy with him. By the blessed Christ, how she wanted to hate him. How she wanted to forget him. But neither was possible, and resentment prompted Claricia to make the snide rebuttal: "Your laird's protection is of little comfort to me."

Rourke frowned at her bitterness, but he knew better than to say anything more. In his experience, it was pointless to dispute an indignant woman. Silently, he prodded his horse onward. Lady Claricia's pony kept pace as they made their way alongside a widening river. The ice had melted through in patches, and the water ran black and swift, gurgling as it made its way toward Loch Awe. For a while, Lady Claricia's gaze did not waver from the rocky path, but once they'd rounded the next bend, she stole another glance over her shoulder, and Rourke began to

understand. It was not unseen beasties of which
Lady Claricia was afraid, but a man, flesh and
bone, by the name of Alexander Kirkpatrick.

At length, he spoke. "Although ye will never
know it for yerself, my lady, Alexander Kirkpatrick is a good laird. Loyal and honest and a
brave warrior. I dinna know a mon who isna
proud to call him friend. Dinna judge him too
harshly."

"You ask too much, Rourke O'Connor. Alexander Kirkpatrick kidnapped and forced himself
upon me. There is nothing good or honest about
that."

Rourke acknowledged this with a sober nod.
Although that did not make it right, what Lady
Claricia had suffered was not unique to Scotland
in these times. "Alex has sought vengeance
against yer family for many years. It is the
Highland way, especially for a laird."

"I trust he is now satisfied," Claricia said in a
brittle voice.

"I canna answer that." Rourke reached out to
grab her pony's bridle. "Let us rest here." They
had reached the crest of a gentle hill. He dismounted and assisted Lady Claricia from the saddle, and as he lowered her to the ground, his gaze
held hers. "Is he satisfied? ye ask. I know only
that there is a vindictiveness festering in Alex
that which may never heal. He has lived too long
believing that retribution will make things right,
and in all that time, he has not reckoned with the
fact that there is nothing that will bring them
back."

"*Them?*" Claricia could not stop herself from
asking. Although one part of her wanted to forget

Alexander Kirkpatrick, to stop thinking about him, there was another part of her that wanted to know more. She smoothed out the folds of her cloak in an effort to divert her thoughts. But distraction was not possible. "Who are *they*?"

"Who *were* they?" Rourke put grave emphasis on the past tense. "They were his parents. His entire family."

"What happened?" This curiosity, she knew, was a dreadful weakness, and although she did not like it, neither could Claricia suppress it.

"They're all dead. Alex's father was beheaded for swearing fealty to King Robert at Scone. His mother and grandparents were killed in their sleep when yer king declared Kirkpatrick lands forfeit and the *sassenach* army stormed Hepburn Castle."

"Hepburn was his family's?"

"Aye, his mother's clan."

"I did not know." She found a large boulder upon which to sit and brushed the twigs and pine needles off it, trying to pretend it did not matter that she had been living in a home that had once been his.

There was much Lady Claricia did not know and thus did not understand, but Rourke did not say this aloud. Instead, he went on. "After Hepburn, Kilmory and Eilean Fidra were sacked. Alex took shelter in the hills, living in caves and on the run. It was then that his sister was taken prisoner by de Clinton."

"My uncle," Claricia whispered beneath her breath, wrapping her arms about her waist to control the sudden shudder that slid up her back. It was horrible to imagine what must have happened to the girl, tragic to consider how her family must have grieved for her innocence, and in that moment, Claricia began to understand the demons that tormented Alexander Kirkpatrick.

"Aye, Caitrine was taken by de Clinton. Alex was imprisoned at Berwick. He was flogged and tortured and left to rot, but managed to survive, and before the year was up he escaped. Soon after that his brother was killed."

"His brother?" One slim hand touched Claricia's throat. Whether she wanted to know it or not, she was going to learn more about the man who had been the first to use her, and the seconds before Rourke continued seemed to stretch into hours.

"Aye, his twin brother, Andrew. They were close. Verra close. And so similar in appearance the lassies couldna tell them apart. But they were not so similar in temperament. Andrew was the rash one. Mayhap there was a touch of madness in the lad. Some even whispered 'twas the tainted blood of his great-great-grandsire, the auld outlaw Murdoch MacWilliam, that drove Andrew to go off half-cocked to rescue Caitrine. He took a small band of clansmen, and against the odds they stormed an English fortress. But Andrew didna find her, and he was slain during the raid, his poor body discarded by the English like a diseased sheep. I dinna ken what troubles Alex the more: to think of Caitrine's fate at the whim of de Clinton or to recall the sight of Andrew's bloody corpse. Alex has sworn vengeance against de Clinton and death to Andrew's murderer."

But he did not kill me. Like a bolt of lightning, the reality burst upon Claricia's mind, and, peculiar although it might have been, the thought was accompanied by a twinge of wonder. That Alexander Kirkpatrick had not killed her when he'd had the chance was more than a mystery. It was a miracle. Claricia did not doubt that it must have troubled him to let her leave Clar Innis alive. But that was not her worry, she told herself. That he had failed to avenge his brother had been his choice. He'd had the opportunity, he'd held the sword above her head, but he'd let her live. He had shown mercy. And when she'd tried to throw herself from the tower window he had stopped her. His action had been hard to understand then. Now it was incomprehensible.

"What will happen if he does not find his brother's killer?" she asked Rourke, feigning an offhand manner as she accepted the flagon he offered and took a sip.

"Och, he will find the bastard. I've no doubt of that, and when he does, then Alex will at least have reclaimed his honor."

"Are you saying his honor will not be restored until he kills Andrew's murderer?"

"Aye."

Claricia stared at the Irishman, but it was not him she saw. Instead, she saw Alexander Kirkpatrick's dragon-green eyes as she contemplated the enormity of what he'd done. Her enemy had sacrificed his honor for her life. But why? It did not make sense. She was an Englishwoman, and a whore in his eyes. Certainly, Alexander Kirkpatrick did not value her life above his honor. Nonetheless, she lived, and his vow had gone unfulfilled. Tears stung her eyes and nose, and she swiped them away with the back of her hand.

"It means much to Alex to know that he will die with honor." Having seen Lady Claricia's distress, Rourke tried to allay it. "Honor is all-meaningful to a Highlander."

"But what of life and living?" The heartfelt question burst forth from Claricia in a voice weighted by unmistakable sorrow. "What of forgiveness? Two wrongs can't make a right. I do not accept that."

"Are ye suggesting that lassies should be in charge?" Rourke posed the query in an attempt to lighten the conversation. He had intended to defend Alex, not to submerge Lady Claricia in melancholy. He had wanted to take her mind off whatever was making her look over her shoulder with such nervousness. Instead, he was making matters worse.

Claricia refocused on the Irishman. There was an undeniable twinkle in his eyes. "I think you tease me, Rourke O'Connor."

"If it would make ye smile, my lady, I do. Ye should do it more often. Smile."

"Only with good reason. Smiles are too precious to waste."

"Och, my lady, surely ye're not as auld as ye sound."

"Perhaps not in years, but there are times when I feel as if I've lived a lifetime, and then some." The momentary levity was gone as quickly as it had come, and as if to punctuate the bleakness of what she'd said, a rook cawed from his perch in the upper branches of a pine tree, the somber lonely sound echoing across the gray landscape.

"So there has been little joy in yer life," Rourke said, unable to prevent a trace of cynicism from creeping into his voice. He leaned against a sun-warmed rock to study Lady Claricia. Her cheeks and forehead were reddened by the wind and cold, and her chapped hands were wrapped in rags. The past weeks in the Highlands had made their mark upon the lady. It was easy to see she was not accustomed to hardship. " 'Tis a strange thing to credit, living as ye were, in comfort, with yer every want satisfied. Ye had good, plentiful food despite famine, rich clothes from abroad despite war, and the warmth of a secure fortress despite the scores of homeless folk roaming the countryside. Living like a princess, I'm told ye were, at Hepburn, with all the costly trappings a lassie could desire. What would ye ken of adversity?"

Less than a month before Claricia would have taken offense at such a remark, but not now. Indeed, much to her surprise, she liked Rourke O'Connor. He was an honest man and deserved an honest reply, and she did not hesitate to speak from the heart.

"Luxuries I may have enjoyed, and I may have been relatively safe from the suffering the war has brought, yet surely you must know that such things can never replace one's family or the emptiness that being alone entails. Alexander Kirkpatrick is not the only one to have lost everyone who mattered to him."

"But ye were with yer family at Hepburn."

"There is no comfort in kinship with a man who would take his niece to whore!" Claricia shot back before she might stop herself.

So the lady did not share her bed with de Clinton willingly. Rourke's regard narrowed. There was

much more to Lady Claricia than was quickly revealed. From the first, he had owned a natural
protectiveness toward her because of her gentle
sex, now he sensed the depth of her carefully hidden vulnerability, and realized it went beyond
the revelation that she loathed de Clinton. Indeed, Rourke entertained the suspicion that she
harbored an awful secret. He saw something else,
too. He saw a vision of Lady Claricia and Alexander Kirkpatrick not as enemies, but as two
souls who might have found solace with each
other if they had met in another time and place.
Although neither would ever realize it, they were
much alike, Lady Claricia de Clinton and Alexander Kirkpatrick, and Rourke wondered aloud,
"But ye've never considered revenge, like Alex?"

The color drained from Claricia's cheeks, and
despite the fur-lined cloak and brilliant sun, a
chill settled over her. If the Irishman only knew
the torment she had already suffered for taking
one life, he would not have asked such a thing.
If only he knew how hard it had been for her to
listen when Meg had assured her that she should
not feel the slightest remorse for killing the savage who had raped her. Her action had been jus-
tified. But nothing Meg said had been able to
erase the fact that she'd taken another human life.
Her greatest crime was not being *The Beast's
Bawd*. It was murder. Taking another human life
was a mortal sin—rape and whoring were not—
and, far from plotting vengeance, Claricia had
sought penance for the sin she had committed.

When at last, atonement had come for her, she
had known what it was she must do. Claricia
closed her eyes. She heard Meg's frantic plea for

help above the crackle of gathering flames, a baby was crying in the far hills, and her uncle was calling her "*whore*." Claricia did not like to dwell on the past. It was almost as desolate as the future. Opening her eyes, she injected a false measure of brightness into her voice.

"So, Rourke O'Connor, we've been talking of me. Now you must tell me of yourself. How is it that an Irish warrior comes to be allied with rebels in the fight against King Edward?"

"I am only half Irish," Rourke explained. "My father was the son of a lord of Connacht. My mother was of Scottish ancestry. Her mother was from the Lowlands, and her father, though raised by Vikings, was a Highlander by birth." His hand rose to touch the upper half of the broken crucifix that hung from a leather cord about his neck. "My five sisters were all married to English overlords in Ireland, part of a grand scheme to further dominate the Irish by bringing their warriors under the Crown's control." He spoke with obvious contempt. "I was my father's only son to survive more than ten winters, and I would have no part of it when my da pledged me to a kinswoman of Robert de Burgh."

Rourke's features altered when he muttered the name of the staunch ally of the English king. Robert de Burgh, the Earl of Ulster, was as loathed in Ireland as de Clinton was in Scotland. It was his Anglo-Norman ancestors who had colonized Ireland in the previous century, seizing the lands of the native Celtic chieftains and subduing the populace to their bidding, and Rourke had not intended to serve such a master by marrying into his family. "Instead, I crossed the sea to seek out my grandfather's kin. My grandfather talked often of his sister, and I wanted to find her family and join their fight against the English. If the English could not be driven out of my father's country, at least I might prevent them from taking control in Scotland.

"At first, I couldna find Alexander. It was the year Robert de Brus was crowned at Scone, and Alexander's da had been executed. Alexander was on the run with his brother and sister. So I fought with the king's brothers, and when the queen and her ladies were taken prisoner, I was among the warriors who tried to rescue the little princess Marjorie. It was not until after their sister was captured that I met Alexander and Andrew."

For a moment, Claricia was quiet. It was not of Rourke O'Connor or Alexander Kirkpatrick and his brother that she thought, but of the Scottish princess, Marjorie. She knew the story well. It had been in the days when King Edward had proclaimed that the wives and daughters of his enemies should be treated as outlaws. The punishments for those who were not slain had been abhorrent. King Robert's sister, Mary, and Isabel, the nineteen-year-old Countess of Buchan, who had been the only noblewoman at Scone, had been imprisoned in cages of wood and iron and suspended from the castle walls at Roxburgh and Berwick. At the Tower of London, a similar cage had been built for Princess Marjorie, and although rescue attempts had failed, the *sassenach* king had relented in his punishment of the eight-year-old princess and her mother, Queen Elizabeth. But it was not mercy that had motivated Edward. The queen was the daughter of the Earl of Ulster, and Richard de Burgh was an ally too valuable for Edward to risk offending. If it had not been for military and political considerations, the child and her mother would have been caged like animals and exposed to the elements, as had the other captured ladies. Claricia's mind skipped to thoughts of Meg and the women in the courtyard at Goswick Keep, and she bowed her head. "Sometimes I am ashamed to call myself English."

Rourke understood. "We canna help the circumstances of our birth. We can only be responsible for the conduct of our daily lives." He studied Lady Claricia's downcast expression. Her sincerity was touching, and he was moved to say, "Alex told me of your generosity to the woman in the cave. Charity is a virtue that transcends birth."

The corners of Claricia's mouth began to edge upward. How odd it was that hearing this should have occasioned a rare smile. It should not have mattered that Alexander Kirkpatrick had talked of her in a favorable light, and as if to ruin the agreeable feeling, as if to punish herself, Claricia sharpened her voice. "But I am a whore. God-fearing men and women should not see virtue in a whore."

"Then they do not look with adequate care."

Claricia studied Rourke O'Connor. It would have been easy for a woman to surrender her heart to this warrior, and for a moment, she wished that she might hear the bells and thunder of which the ballads sang when a man and a woman gazed into each other's eyes and knew they were destined for each other. How wonderful it would be to find someone like Rourke O'Connor, she thought, someone with whom to share the good and bad, someone who could discover who she really was and treasure that woman, even if she was a whore. But there was no such sensation of destined hearts when she looked at this man. Indeed, the longer she stared at him the harder it was to prevent herself from seeing Alexander Kirkpatrick.

"Tell me, is there some lady who is special to you?" she asked in an effort to expunge the gaunt, dark features imprinted upon her mind's eye.

"Aye," was his soft reply. "There is a lass."

"Your lady wife?"

"Nay, we are not married, although for her, our arrangement may be the closest she will ever come to marriage."

"I do not understand. What nature of woman does not yearn for the vows of matrimony?" The unguarded question popped forth from Claricia.

Rourke had no answer, nor did he focus upon the significance of Lady Claricia's question. Instead, beginning to be a bit uncomfortable with the conversation, he took a long drink from the flagon.

"Is she in Ireland?"

"Nay, at Loch Awe."

"That is good," said Claricia, and, sensing his uneasiness, she made a conscious effort to smile at him. "I should like to meet the woman who has captured your worthy heart."

"Nay, it isna possible."

Claricia's smile evaporated. There was sadness in her eyes at having been rebuffed by Rourke.

"I'm sorry. How foolish of me to forget I am not a guest, but a prisoner."

"It is not that, my lady. She is a recluse, and doesna live at Eilean Fidra, but on an island some distance from the castle."

Claricia allowed several moments of silence to elapse before asking, "Tell me her name."

"Viviane."

"Ah, the Lady of the Lake. She has always lived there?"

"I dinna think so."

"Then she is a lady of mystery."

Rourke's uneasiness made it impossible to look Lady Claricia in the eye. He did not like to admit that he knew nothing of Viviane's past. As far as he knew, she had not existed before pulling him from the shallows and nursing him to health. She could have been anyone or anything. He shoved the flagon into a sack and tightened the plaid about his shoulders as he rose from the rock upon which he'd been resting. "Come, my lady, we must be on our way. There are still a few hours of daylight remaining. We should not tarry."

A sharp high-pitched ping reverberated through the hills and glens.

"What is that?" Claricia asked. They had reached Loch Awe and were standing on a hillock several hundred yards above the shoreline. To the northwest rose the snow-capped guardian peaks of Ben an Oir and Ben Cruachan, below, in the middle of the loch, was the island fortress, Eilean Fidra, and from somewhere above the mountaintops came the noise, which made Claricia think of a mythic giant working at a forge, tapering a sword on a great anvil.

"It is the unseasonably warm weather. The ice is cracking."

"How will we get to the castle?" The silver, frozen surface was crisscrossed with black lines stretching from the shore to the island fortress, which seemed to rise directly out of the loch. It was a small castle built in several stages, each of its four towers being of a different height. Even the color of the great gray stones varied from a very dark hue at the base of the walls, which disappeared beneath the frozen water, to the pale color of the restored ramparts, which were touched with flecks of something that sparkled. Eilean Fidra was neither grand nor imposing. It reminded Claricia of the manor house in England where she'd long ago lived with her mother and father. It made her think of home.

"There is a tunnel," Rourke explained as he dismounted. He assisted Claricia from her pony and tethered the animals. "Someone will return for the horses. Come this way." They walked to a clump of rocks and edged between the two largest boulders, to find themselves at the entrance to a cave. There were steps hacked from the rock, and as they went down it became darker and warmer. "Stay close," Rourke advised when they reached the bottom and began to make their way along a narrow passage.

It was ink-black in the tunnel. The walls were dank, the ground uneven, and the air was absolutely utterly silent except for the sound of their breathing.

"Give me yer hand, my lady." Rourke helped Claricia climb over a pile of objects.

"Why, this is a bench," Claricia said. Her hand skimmed along a smooth surface.

"Aye, and whatever else was left of the furnishings from Eilean Fidra."

"But it will be ruined down here."

"To Alex's mind, 'tis better to be ruined by his own orders than touched by *sassenach* hands."

Slowly, Claricia inched along in the space between the jumble of furniture and the moist wall, her fingers tracing a pattern of flying fish and unicorns in carved wood, her hand grazing over a heavy metal latch. It was a chest to keep precious belongings secure from one's enemy, but never to be seen by those who cared. Of a sudden, Claricia thought of her mother's garnet ring. It had been a betrothal token from her father to Lady Johanna, and while it had not been nearly as costly as the gold-and-pearl fillet with which her father had gifted her mother on their wedding day, Claricia had always thought the garnet ring was the prettiest piece of jewelry she had ever seen. She had always wanted one for her own. She had always wanted to be like her mother and have a husband as handsome as her father.

"Will you, Father? Truly? Will you give me a ring like Mother's when I'm grown up?"

" 'Tis true, sweetling, for your tenth birth-time celebration." The tall Englishman had knelt upon one knee to look his little daughter straight in the eye. One large hand had smoothed back the pale golden curls that tumbled across her brow, and he had smiled with deep affection at the tiny replica of his lovely wife. "And I'll slip it on your finger just like I did upon your mother's."

But her father had not lived to see his daughter celebrate her tenth summer. Claricia had never had her own ring. Instead, her mother had given her the garnet ring that had been her betrothal gift.

"You must never forget I love you," Lady Johanna had said when she'd put the ring into Claricia's palm and closed her fingers over it. "You must never forget me or your father, and whatever happens you must remember us and know that there is such a thing as true love."

An hour later Lady Johanna was dead, her neck broken by the dreadful fall from the tower window at Goswick Keep.

There was nothing in the whitewashed chamber at Hepburn or at Goswick that held any sentimental value for Claricia. Nothing so precious that she would drag it beneath the ground to hide. If Claricia could have saved anything, it would have been her mother and Meg. But one was in the unhallowed ground beyond the churchyard at Goswick Keep, her broken bones turning to dust, and the other was lost forever.

Ahead of Claricia, Rourke pushed open a door. A beam of yellow light shone at the end of the tunnel. They entered a storeroom, where a torch was affixed to the wall. Rourke took the light to lead Claricia through a kitchen, then up to the ground level. As at Clar Innis, signs of destruction were everywhere at Eilean Fidra. There had been a fire. Black streaks stained the walls, and most of the support timbers were charred. But there was not the filth of Clar Innis. A handful of

Kirkpatrick clanspeople, having taken shelter on the island, had kept it habitable and orderly, maintaining the fortress for the laird and living communally in the great hall, which had been restored as best as possible.

A group of men greeted Rourke when he and Claricia entered the hall. There was a large open fire, about which several hounds were sleeping, a young woman with deep red hair was nursing a babe, two little girls were playing with rag dolls, and a pair of stooped gray women were spinning wool about their distaffs. Claricia went to the fire, and the women of Eilean Fidra eyed her with curiosity while Rourke talked with the men. After a while, he escorted Claricia from the hall and up the winding stairs in one of the towers. No one had spoken a word to her. She thought of Alexander Kirkpatrick's warning and wondered if these folk wished her harm.

Upon reaching the uppermost chamber, Claricia was distracted by the good condition of the abundant furnishings. "How comfortable this is," she remarked with surprise. That the owner had wealth was apparent from the intricate design of the brazier, which was filled with glowing peat, and the mauve velvet bed hangings, which, although threadbare, had been embroidered in a grand pattern of blooming thistles. There were shutters on the narrow windows. Rushes covered the floor, and, while neither plentiful nor fresh, they had been mixed with dried heather. It could actually be called a pleasant room.

"This is where the laird said ye should stay."

"It is his chamber?" she inquired, noting the personal effects, a pair of boots standing beside a chest and a folded plaid draped over a massive chair near the brazier. There was a goblet on a trestle, along with a comb of carved bone, several belt buckles, and a large wooden laver.

"Aye. And always at the ready for his return."

Involuntarily, Claricia closed her eyes. One day Alexander Kirkpatrick would return to Loch Awe, but Claricia would not see him again. For a moment, she had forgotten the reality of her situation. She crossed to the trestle and found herself touching one of the heavy buckles. "How long before I am sent back to my uncle?"

"Not long. A month, perhaps a few weeks more than that."

"Before spring, then?"

"Aye."

"So quick." There was a wistful catch in her voice.

Rourke failed to notice how her eyes lacked luster at the prospect of being ransomed, and he made a chivalric bow. "One of the women will bring ye something to eat."

"You're leaving?"

"For a day or two."

She nodded in understanding and bid him farewell when he closed the door behind him.

Later Claricia opened one of the shutters to look out over the countryside. There was a curl of smoke rising in the distance, and she imagined it was coming from Viviane's island. Rourke would be on his way to see her, Claricia thought, recalling in that moment how her mother had welcomed home her father. She remembered the tears of happiness, the laughter and tender embraces. Claricia had not forgotten her mother. She would never forget her father. But she did not believe there was such a thing as true love, and she knew there would be no tender embraces when she was returned to her uncle. There would be no joy for her.

Viviane came out of the shadows to stand in the firelight. She was the vision of a pagan high priestess walking through the blue smoke that filled the hut. Her black hair, cascading below her waist, glistened like iridescent raven's wings, about her face the wild curls formed a halo in startling contrast to a flawless creamy complexion, and there was upon her countenance an expression that was both untamed and wise. It was not hard to imagine her standing upon a high crag, calling out to the old gods, the wind sweeping her hair about her like a tattered cloak, her arms outstretched to touch the invisible powers that ruled the universe.

"Did ye miss me, lass?" Rourke dared to ask. She was an achingly beautiful sight, and he had yearned for her more than he could have imagined possible. Until he'd met Viviane, Rourke had not believed there was any human bond deeper than that between warriors on the field of battle, but the longer he knew this woman, the clearer it became that the bonds between a man and a woman could transcend all else.

"Aye, *a mhorair*," Viviane dared to reply, calling him *my lord*. She had not wanted this to happen. She had struggled not to care one way or the other about this man, but the longer he was gone, the more she thought of him, the more she wondered where he was and what he was doing, the more she yearned for his return. "Ye are well?"

"No new wounds," he said with a roguish grin. "Although I have suffered some pain being away from yer more intimate attentions."

Viviane laughed. "Did ye travel far?"

He recounted how he had spent the past months. "I couldna come back until I was certain the *toiseach* had been successful."

"The laird has embarked upon his vengeance?" Viviane asked. She had heard Rourke talk about Alexander Kirkpatrick's pledge to avenge the crimes against his family, and while she did not approve of such actions, she understood them. There was far too much violence in the world. It was self-perpetuating, and the only certain way to escape it was to stay away from the world.

"Aye, the retribution begins. I've brought a prisoner to Eilean Fidra. 'Tis the niece of Aymer de Clinton."

Abruptly, Viviane turned away from Rourke, her hand rising swiftly to her mouth to still the small gasp that she could not stop. It was almost as if she had been frightened by unseen spirits or compelled by some invisible hand as she hurried across the hut to an alcove, where a child was curled into a tight ball beneath a mound of fox pelts. She looked down at the sleeping boy with midnight hair as glossy and thick as hers.

The lad rolled onto his back and opened his eyes. "Mam," he said with a wide yawn, his green eyes lighting with recognition, then bewilderment.

"Dinna fash yerself, Simon, love." Viviane leaned down to kiss him on the forehead and tuck the pelts snugly about his small body.

"I heard voices," he said in a little-boy voice that tried to hide his worry.

"Rourke has returned."

"Rourke," the lad whispered a drowsy greeting and squinted to look past his mother.

"Go back to sleep, Simon," Rourke said, standing now behind Viviane. "I shall see ye in the morn."

"Promise?"

"I promise."

Together, Viviane and Rourke walked away from the child in the alcove, and when they reached the far corner of the hut, Viviane glanced over her shoulder. The lad had fallen back to sleep.

"Tell me, what does the laird intend to do with his prisoner?" she asked, her eyes still focused on the sleeping child. Involuntarily, she reached beneath her tunic to clasp a ring hanging from a leather cord about her neck.

"Ransom her."

Viviane looked back at Rourke. Her gaze narrowed. She thought of when she had been taken by force to live among strangers who did not speak Gaelic or understand why she could not remember the past. It was not often that she allowed herself to dwell on those years. The less memory the better. She did not want to remember; what she knew of the past hurt. The pain was too fierce, and it stoked an anger she did not like. Disapproval rang in her voice. "And yer laird has treated this niece of his enemy well?"

"As well as can be expected."

Viviane did not like to consider what a man meant when he said, *As well as can be expected.*

Taking a deep breath, she asked, "Did he—" But she could not finish the sentence.

Rourke understood, and answered, "The laird is a mon, after all, and his prisoner is a woman, a verra bonny woman."

Disgust settled upon Viviane's features while she studied the planes of Rourke's face. She knew he was a warrior, but she had never seen this side of him. He was a man as bold and hard as any other, but she had not seen that either. This cavalier remark was the closest glimpse of that other part of him she had ever seen, and it sickened her to know that anyone, in particular the man she'd allowed into her life, could rationalize domination over a woman with such ease. It was so contrary to the person she had thought he was, and Viviane did not like to think she might lose him, not physically, but spiritually. She did not like to consider that she might have made of Rourke the kind of man she wanted him to be while failing to see the man he truly was.

Every time Rourke returned to Loch Awe he seemed to have become a bit harder, and Viviane feared that one day she would not know him when he returned. That one day the outside world, not another woman, would claim him, and she would be alone again. This fear was at the core of why she did not trust him. She did not possess sufficient faith to believe that their relationship would last. Indeed, the depth of his friendship with the laird ignited a spark of jealousy. "I dinna think I like this *toìseach* of yers, no matter what ye think of him."

Rourke could not help grinning. It appeared he had come face to face with another one of those

times when it was pointless to dispute a provoked woman. He extended his hand to her.
"*Pax?*"

A few moments ticked by. A log fell in the fire.
Cinders popped. The child mumbled in his sleep.
Rourke took a step closer to Viviane. Their fingers
touched.

"*Pax,*" she whispered in reply. Her fingers entwined with his, then she raised his hand and
held it to her chest. Her heart was beating rapidly
as she tilted her face upward to his. "*Na h-abair
smid. Dinna say a word.* Kiss me."

He drew her into the circle of his arms and
gladly kissed her soft lips, slowly, thoroughly,
with unbearable tenderness. When at last he
paused to catch his breath, his eyes were luminous with desire, but he knew he revealed more
in those sparkling blue depths than mere lust,
and the words he had been afraid to speak came
with unexpected ease. "I love ye, lass, do ye
know that? *Le m'uile mo chridhe.*" *With all my heart.*

"Why now?" She was peeling off his plaid and
undertunic, baring his chest to her touch and running her fingers through the thick blond hair. She
splayed her palm across the well-developed muscles, then raised her eyes to his. "Why tell me
now?" she asked in the second before his lips
claimed hers again.

"I dinna want to lose ye," Rourke said between
hot hungry kisses.

"I'm not going anywhere," Viviane murmured
as she kissed him back with all her heart, her
fingers eagerly helping him to loosen her tunic.
"*Bi clis,*" she said in a raspy voice. *Be quick.* The
tunic slipped off her shoulders, over her hips, and

down her long legs, to pool about her ankles. "I'm not going anywhere. At least not now."

"I know that." Rourke held her at arm's length to appreciate the full beauty of her naked body. She was slender as a maid, with a flat stomach and narrow hips, and although her breasts were not large, the nipples were a deep shade of rose that begged to be suckled. She stood there without shame or reservation, knowing the pleasure he derived from gazing upon her. He watched as she widened her stance and smiled at him while her hands slowly moved over her hips and down across that flat stomach, lower, until her fingers disappeared into the triangle of soft dark curls. Rourke moaned from deep in his throat, and his manhood became rigid with desire at the sight before him.

Viviane would do anything for him, enjoying his pleasure as surely as her own. His heart ached at the wonder of it all. She gave herself to him so freely, so completely, and Rourke tried to tell himself it didn't matter that she had not said she loved him. But that was self-deception of the worst kind. Rourke O'Connor had given the one thing to Viviane that he had never shared with another woman, and it mattered that she had not answered in kind. It mattered profoundly. The pain of it was sharp and deep. It cut to the marrow of his bone, and Rourke could not banish the bittersweet quality from their lovemaking that night.

Chapter 7

It was dark when Viviane rolled away from the cradle of Rourke's warm body. She had been awake for several minutes, listening to his steady breathing and comforted by the familiar scents and sensations of absolute physical contentment. It was wonderful to have him back. "I love ye," he had told her. *Le m'uile mo chridhe. With all my heart.* It might have been perfect, she might have been able to return his affection if he had said those words the last time he'd been there, when there would have been nothing more important than Rourke and his love. But that was not the case this day, and there was much she must do, with little time to spare. It was only a matter of a few days, perhaps a sennight.

Quietly, Viviane slipped from beneath the wolf pelts to dress in several layers of crude woolen tunics, then she stepped into loose-fitting high boots, which she secured with long laces about her calves. A morning chill permeated the hut, and, crossing to the wooden laver beside the door, she wrapped a plaid about her shoulders. A thin sheet of ice had formed in the roughhewn bowl. She broke the ice before dousing her face, then moistened her hair and wound it into a thick coil, which she secured with a piece of polished bone at the nape of her neck. Rourke and Simon were still sleeping. Neither moved nor uttered a sound as she added peat to the brazier before going outside and closing the door behind her.

Despite the frosty clouds that escaped her lips, she could tell it was going to be another unseasonably warm day. The Highland winds were calm that morning, as they had been for several days. Such a perfect silence cloaked the pine forest surrounding the hut that she could hear the beating wings of awakening wildfowl. Holding her skirts above her ankles, she headed down a path, taking note as she went of the muddy animal tracks in the melting snow. After a few minutes, the path came out of the woods, and the wall of evergreens fell away to a narrow expanse of beach. Viviane paused to stretch her arms overhead and look toward the thin line of golden light widening over the horizon. The gloomy gray of night was giving way to the clarity of a silver dawn.

The laird's castle was not visible from that spot, so Viviane continued along the path to the northernmost tip of the small island, where a series of large, flat rocks created a natural bridge that extended several yards into the loch. There, standing on the last rock, it was possible to glimpse the outline of Eilean Fidra. It always appeared the same, no matter the time of year. From there it was merely a hulking, dark outline, its irregular towers rising from the water to the sky.

It had always been the same scene, except for the night when the English had set torch to it. Viviane would never forget how those great orange flames had leaped toward the moon, their fierce light illuminating the woods as if the devil's spawn were stirring the embers of hell and the earth had split open to let demons rule the world. She had been too far away to hear the battle, but her memory had brought to life the screams of terror and the hideous war cries that must surely have echoed along the shore that night. She had not dared to stand upon this flat rock, instead, she had crouched on the beach, closing her eyes to the horrible orange light and holding the wailing toddler in her trembling arms.

Somehow she had convinced herself that they'd escaped the past. In the months since Viviane had found her way to the island in Loch Awe, there had been naught but peace in her solitary world. It was what she'd sought, yet the night of the battle a potent fear had seized her, shattering her sense of security and nearly rendering her incapable of caring for herself or the child. It was several mornings later, when she discovered the Irishman, who called himself Rourke, floating among the reeds that she had regained her inner strength. Over the next weeks, while taking care of him, and later, as their relationship had deepened, her fear had abated. Rourke was a warrior; he would protect them. But the fear within her had not truly been dispelled. It had merely been pushed into the recesses of her mind, and the night before, it was Rourke who had unwittingly brought the past to her very door.

Viviane had believed that this island was far enough removed from civilization for the truth ever to matter. It had been easy, perhaps too easy, to become someone else and to preserve the secret she had vowed to protect. It had been the right course, all the easier since she'd had no past of her own to deny, and when the plan had been devised it had never occurred to Viviane that a time might come when the lies could actually end and the truth be told. Indeed, the lie had become the very foundation of her existence.

"Mam!" a child's voice drifted from the pine woods. "Are ye there, Mam?" It was Simon, rushing headlong across the beach, leaping from rock to rock, his dark hair bouncing about his shoulders as he hurried toward her. "Rourke still sleeps, but I thought ye might be setting traps, and I came to help," he said with the breathless excitement of childhood.

"I wouldna set the traps without ye." Viviane smiled.

The lad flung his small arms about his mother and hugged her tightly.

Viviane returned Simon's embrace, leaning down to kiss him on the top of his head. His hair was still as soft and silky as it had been when he was an infant, and her heart swelled with such maternal affection it seemed it might burst. She had nothing except this child, no past except what she'd built with him. How could she tell him the truth? How could she do something that might destroy everything? And then there was Rourke. How would Rourke react when he knew the truth? Viviane looked away from Simon, frightened by the sudden impulse to burst into tears, and she bit her lower lip, for her eyes had come to rest upon Eilean Fidra, and she could not stop herself from wondering in which tower the laird's prisoner had slept.

A shiver ran up her spine. Simon was babbling about how much Rourke liked roasted woodcock, and wouldn't it be a fine thing to snare one that morning? But Viviane was thinking about the secret she'd been guarding. Until the previous night, secrecy had been the proper thing. She had done nothing wrong. She had been a good and loyal friend, but now everything was changed, and that it was cowardly and dishonest to continue to hide the truth she did not deny. But she knew herself well enough to realize that she could never force the truth from between her own lips. How could a child understand that he was not whom he'd believed himself to be since his earliest memory? And that the great wide world beyond this lovely island was filled with evil?

Someone else would have to tell Simon, and in order for that to happen, Viviane knew there was only one thing she could do. Wrapping an arm about the lad's shoulder, she led him across the stone bridge toward the beach.

"Och, Mam, did ye see the sack on the floor? Do ye think Rourke brought any treats with him this time? A honeycomb, mayhap? Or a piece of ginger?"

"I dinna know, Simon, love," she said. It was unlikely that Rourke would have brought a honeycomb in the middle of winter, or any other treat, especially when all of Scotland except for this remote loch was embroiled in violence, but her smile did not waver. "Shall we see if he's awake and ask him?"

The prospect of a sweet quickened Simon's

pace, and he skipped ahead of his mother.

Viviane sighed. It was awful that the right thing could seem so forbidding, and as she neared the shore she cast a final glance over her shoulder. The distant towers had disappeared from sight, but not so thoughts of the laird's prisoner and the vengeance the laird intended to exact at her expense. She must act before it was too late, and a merciful God willing, Simon would not turn away from her when he knew the truth.

For the first time since being kidnapped, Claricia did not awaken until late into the day, when the faint sounds of someone moving about the laird's chamber filtered through the heavy curtains that were drawn about the big bed. She'd enjoyed a restful night, and slowly she opened her eyes, realizing that for the first time in many weeks nothing ached. The throbbing in her lower back and legs had ceased, her chapped hands did not hurt, and the windburn upon her cheeks and forehead had finally subsided. Claricia could almost imagine it was the morning after Twelfth Night, and she was still the same young woman who had opened her eyes early that day in her whitewashed chamber at Hepburn. There was comfort in holding fast to the notion that she was awakening from a horrible dream and that nothing had changed, that she was still the same Lady Claricia de Clinton who could dull her senses to prevent herself from feeling what her uncle might do to her. That notion was, of course, a fraud. She was not invulnerable, if she ever had been, and now whatever the future held for her was a terrifying thing to consider.

Someone was singing on the other side of the bed hangings. It was a Highland lullaby, one that Meg had taught to Claricia, and thinking of Meg, she imagined the sound of an infant cooing. Rising to her knees, she parted the curtains. The red-haired woman who had been sitting by the fire and nursing a bairn in the great hall the night before was arranging something on the table alongside the belt buckles; she was singing in a pretty, lilting voice as she worked. A few paces away from her, in a shallow oblong basket woven of rushes, there was a baby, propped up and watching the woman, waving its little fat arms and making funny noises with its puckered mouth.

"Och, ye're awake, mistress. Good morning to ye," the young woman said with a broad smile when she saw Claricia peering out from behind the curtains. Her English was stilted and quaint, her voice as lilting in speech as it had been in song. "I didna mean to disturb ye with my singing."

"You did not disturb me. 'Tis long past time to rise, and your voice is most pleasant to hear first thing upon awakening," Claricia replied, feeling further cheered by the comfortable surroundings and this genial young woman. Her worries that the folk of Eilean Fidra meant her ill appeared unfounded. How different this place was from Clar Innis, and how simple it was to imagine that nothing bad had happened since Twelfth Night. "Do not stop singing on my account."

But the young woman did not resume the lullaby. "Look over here, mistress. I've set out some things ye might be needing." She indicated a comb and hair ornaments on the table and pointed to a low chest, where several garments were stacked in neat piles. "Would ye like to see for yerself? Perhaps there's something ye could wear while my mam is mending yer kirtle."

"She did not have to do that." Claricia emerged from the bed to inspect the clothes on the chest.

" 'Tis no bother, mistress. I am Frances, daughter of the Kirkpatrick *sennachie*. My father is Ewen, the seneschal of Eilean Fidra, and my mam is Sorcha," she said, introducing herself, stating with pride the high hereditary rank of her father in the household as official genealogist and historian of the clan. "The laird sent instructions saying to treat ye proper, and though my auld granny says we should be defying him—for there isna a *sassenach* alive who isna a devil, she claims—I dinna think ye look evil, no matter what they call ye. And my mam agrees. It couldna hurt to take care of ye after such a long journey, she said. Even a Highland lass wouldna find traveling in these snowy months an easy task. Ye must be verra brave, mistress, despite yer fair hair and skinny bones."

Claricia could not help smiling. "Am I such a sickly sight?"

"Och, mistress, nay. Ye're a bonny lady, I'm thinking." The baby in the basket made a fretful noise, and Frances picked him up, kissed his brow, then balanced him on her hip.

"Tell me, Frances, whose clothes are these?" Claricia inquired as she unfolded the items. There was a kirtle of soft wool that had been dyed a deep purple, leggings to match, and several overtunics in shades of blue and gold. There was even a simple girdle crafted of silver to secure the kirtle about the waist. The garments were too fine to belong to Frances.

"They were made for the laird's wife."

Claricia's heart lurched. "Alexander Kirkpatrick is married?"

"Nay, mistress."

"He is betrothed, then?" She did not understand. She had not thought of Alexander Kirkpatrick as anything more than a Highlander bent on vengeance, a warrior who had made the leap to manhood through such a brutal series of tragedies that he could be naught but a man whose heart had been hardened forever. She had not spared a moment's consideration for him as someone's husband or sweetheart.

"Nay, mistress, he isna now, but once upon a time he was promised to a lass." Frances paused as if deciding whether or not to continue. Like her father in his role as *sennachie*, she knew much of the history of the Kirkpatricks, some of it idle gossip, some of it truth. The expression upon Lady Claricia's face encouraged her to impart what she knew. "Her name was Moira; a lady, she was—like yerself—being the daughter of Malcolm MacCruarie, a powerful chieftain and Earl of Tay. Betrothed by their fathers, they were, Alexander and Moira, and when she was seventeen Lady Moira was brought here to Eilean Fidra. Those clothes were part of her trousseau—stitched with loving hands by the laird's verra own dearest mother, may God bless her soul." Frances paused to bow her head and make the sign of the cross in the name of the Father, the Son, and the Holy Ghost.

"They were all alive then—the auld laird and his lady-wife from Hepburn, and their other children, Andrew and sweet little Caitrine, who had been my playmate. We all helped with the preparations for the wedding feast, baking and hunting, stitching, decorating the great hall with boughs of greenery, putting on a coat of fresh whitewash and hanging the clan pennants from the rafters overhead. But nothing was grand enough, Lady Moira complained, and so she ran away the verra morning she was to have been wed. I shouldna be telling ye this, but she was a dreadful spoiled creature. Caitrine and I heard it all—hovering just outside the entrance to the great hall—and we even heard it said that it was Andrew she loved, instead of Alexander, to whom she was betrothed, and who, being aulder by a few minutes, would be laird one day."

Claricia gazed at the purple kirtle, running her hand back and forth across the soft wool. Although the fabric lacked ornamentation, the garment was surprisingly beautiful, and she tried to picture the kind of woman who would not have appreciated this. "Did Alexander Kirkpatrick love Lady Moira?" Claricia asked, being in the next instant troubled by this conversation. It was altogether inappropriate to ask such questions, and she did not like the sentimental, almost melancholy, feeling that had come over her at the thought of an Alexander Kirkpatrick disappointed in love.

"Love her? Nay, mistress, I dinna think so. Of course, he was verra angry, and I remember it

well when Lady Moira's da threatened to fetch
her back and have her beaten before the whole
clan—a frightful thought it was to consider—but
Alexander told the MacCruarie chieftain nay. He
said he couldna blame Lady Moira, and he asked
his father to release them from the betrothal.
While he didna believe in love, he said that at
least there should be civility in a marriage, and
he wouldna have an unwilling wife, especially
not one who'd been beaten into submission."

Claricia continued to stroke the kirtle. She did
not dare look up, else the flush of color upon her
cheeks might reveal how it pleased her to know
Alexander Kirkpatrick had not loved Lady Moira.
Sweet Saint Aidan, what pestilence could have
infected her brain that she could care one way or
the other about Alexander Kirkpatrick, or what
he thought of love and marriage? Swiftly, she
changed the subject.

"Am I to be confined to this chamber?" Claricia
inquired as she began to dress.

"Nay, mistress, ye may come and go as ye like.
There is a merry fire in the hall, and my mam
and sisters are curious to ask ye questions about
the south. Although I must warn ye my granny
is an opinionated old biddy. Ye mustna let her
sharp tongue hurt ye."

"Your granny is the one who believes I'm the
devil?" Claricia smoothed the kirtle over her
hips. It fit nicely. The snug bodice flattered her
firm, rounded breasts, while the loose sleeves and
flowing skirt gave it practical comfort.

"Aye, her name is Maeri, and she puts great
store in fear of all things unholy. No doubt she

is wearing an amulet to protect her soul, should ye cast yer evil eye upon her."

"I shall endeavor to charm her, then." Claricia secured the girdle about her waist, then quickly plaited her hair into a single braid.

"Before we go down to the hall there is one more thing I want to give ye, mistress." Of a sudden, there was a sober tone in Frances's voice. She shifted the child to her other hip and held out a small drinking gourd.

Claricia accepted the gourd, cocking her head to one side in query before she held it close to peer at its contents. Immediately, a peculiar odor assailed her. She brought it nearer and sniffed. The smell was rich and dangerous, and with a sinking heart, she recognized the bittersweet scent of crushed hempseed. Some women had no qualms about adding a few drops of hempseed oil to a cup of warm cider or broth. It was a way to expel a babe from its mother's womb before birth. But doing such a thing was not something Claricia's conscience would accept. A child, no matter what the circumstances of conception might be, was an innocent. Life was too fragile not to nurture every bit of it.

Her free hand rose to touch her flat belly. It was an involuntary reaction as she found herself wondering what it would be like to feel life stirring within her. It would be *his* child, a little bastard, half-English and half-heathen, yet the notion did not repulse her. Her hand fell away from her stomach, and she glanced at Frances, who was staring at her with open sympathy.

"It is not necessary," Claricia said, handing back the gourd, and intense sorrow settling over her, for it would never be necessary. The physicians had told her the damage was permanent, and her uncle had told her to stop sniveling and be grateful that she would never have to worry about bearing an unwanted bastard ever again. Her uncle had not understood. The child had not been unwanted. Granted, he had been conceived from the seed of her rapist, but that had not mattered to Claricia when she had held his tiny body. It had not mattered earlier when she had felt the stirrings in her womb. He had been her child, her flesh and blood, and even now she could not bear to be apart from him. *Dream, my only child, dream.* The lullaby drifted through her memory as she recalled how her breasts had ached after he was gone. *Dean cadal, seircean, dean cadal.* How the milk had stained her tunic like tears and how she'd had to listen to her uncle spew a litany of curses about the little Highland bastard and how fortunate they were that the brat had died. But he hadn't, not truly, and that alone sustained Claricia, for in saving her son's life she had triumphed over her uncle. Frances's bairn cried out, and the sound of the hungry child brought Claricia back to the present.

"Did *he* tell you to give this to me?" Claricia's voice was sharpened with bitter disdain at the thought that Alexander Kirkpatrick would destroy his own child rather than allow it to be born of an English whore.

"The laird? Nay, mistress, it was my mam and sisters. We didna mean to offend ye, but were thinking ye might be needing it." Frances hesitated before adding, "We werena certain what ye'd been through these past weeks."

It was a pitiful gesture of compassion between women who were strangers, indeed, who were enemies—a bond that only women could share. "Thank you," Claricia said, visibly moved by Frances's kindness as well as by the fact that it had not been Alexander Kirkpatrick's idea.

Frances walked to one of the narrow embrasures, opened the shutter, and emptied the contents of the gourd into the loch. "There is already too much suffering," she remarked. "And women always take the worst of it."

Claricia nodded. They understood each other. Despite the differences in rank and birth and in national identity that would have divided two men, those things did not matter between Claricia and Frances. "Praise be to God, hempseed is not necessary," Claricia repeated in a whisper that sounded like a prayer. Although she had once before been able to protect a child from her uncle, it would have been impossible to accomplish such a deception a second time. She crossed herself. It would have been an unthinkable fate to consider returning to Aymer de Clinton carrying another bastard. Thankfully, that was not the case, and this time, she had that much for which to be grateful.

But as Claricia followed Frances from the chamber, she had never felt more sorry for herself than she did at that moment. There was nothing for her. No purpose, no dream. She fought back the tears welling in her eyes at the sheer waste of it, and for the first time, she found herself questioning God's will. Why had He bothered to let her live? What was the point? No one needed her.

No one would have missed her except her uncle, and there was no solace in that.

From Clar Innis, Alexander traveled in a northeasterly direction, following the glens and frozen riverbeds that were fed by Loch Tay. He was bound for Finlarig Castle, ancient fortress of the MacCruaries, which had been built on a low rise overlooking a marshy flatland where the burn flowing from the loch split into several smaller streams. It was an unremarkable keep, hidden by intersecting hills and thick foliage, and there, Alexander would await de Clinton's response to his ransom demands.

The plan was a simple one. Alexander himself would not deal directly with de Clinton. Rather, another Highlander serving as a decoy had arrived at a priory to the south. He was waiting in a village called Dunblane, a few miles from British-held Stirling Castle. There, in the sanctuary of the Lord's house, protected by the Holy Mother Church, the Highlander, who resembled Alexander Kirkpatrick, would face Aymer de Clinton. In his laird's behalf, the decoy would negotiate the terms of where de Clinton would deliver the ransom supplies as well as the precise location where he wished his niece to be deposited in exchange for those supplies. Once the terms had been agreed upon, the decoy would begin the first leg of a relay to convey the details of the agreement to the laird at Finlarig.

For Alexander, the wait at Finlarig was interminable. Since he was a man of action, it was difficult for him to sustain his patience in any solitary setting, and Finlarig was desolate. It had been deserted by its laird and his clan for more than five years. Ever since the English had cut a swath of destruction across the breadth of the Highlands, the fortress had served no greater purpose than temporary shelter to passing travelers or homeless lepers. Looted of its contents, Finlarig was nothing more than a cold gray shell nestled in the thick pine forest, a perfect place to hide and wait, but frustrating for a man who did not wish to sit idly while others did his bidding.

How long would it take to learn what had transpired at Dunblane? Was a messenger already on the way? Or had some misfortune befallen one of the runners? Perhaps the plan was not so clever after all. There was always the chance that de Clinton would act with treachery to retrieve his niece without paying the ransom, and Alexander was forced to accept the fact that there was always the possibility his vengeance would not succeed. Perhaps he had been followed from the moment he had taken Lady Claricia from Hepburn. Perhaps de Clinton was toying with him, letting him believe his whereabouts were unknown, only to strike at any moment to take him prisoner. If that were the case, Alexander would never let de Clinton take him alive. Failure was his greatest fear, and in the solitude of Finlarig, that fear gnawed at him.

On the sixth day at Finlarig, the monotony of waiting came to an end. Alexander was making his hourly inspection of the countryside from the allure that spanned the front battlement when he sighted a rider at the crest of a nearby hill. Quickly, he dropped to a crouch, so as not to be seen. He had not expected a messenger to arrive by horse, or from that direction, and warily he watched the approaching traveler, straining to make out the cut and identifying markings of his clothes. Closer the rider came down the hill, over the raised hump of earth that formed a natural bridge across the mote, and then beneath the portcullis into the bailey. Alexander moved to the other side of the allure to look down.

The rider, cloaked in a ragged woolen tartan and wearing the loose-fitting buskins favored by Highlanders, slowly circled the bailey, as if searching for something. Pausing, he leaned down from the saddle and peered into a row of dilapidated fore-buildings, which were positioned against Finlarig's single donjon tower, then he urged his mount back beneath the portcullis. Alexander crossed the allure again and watched as the rider rose up in the saddle to wave an arm overhead. The back-and-forth movement caused the cloak to fall down, revealing a heavy, waist-length auburn braid. The rider was a woman, and she signaled toward the hill, whereupon a line of refugees appeared over the crest to begin the trek down to the castle. They were a bedraggled lot, and whoever they were, they could have posed no threat to Alexander, who descended to the bailey to greet them.

There were eleven women in all, not a man or child among them, and they were a miserable sight, poorly clothed against the elements, their gaunt faces presenting stark evidence of constant hunger, and their skin blackened with dirt from months, if not years, of hard living. Alexander was shocked. He had seen much suffering and hardship, but this band of women struck a nerve deep within him. A queasy sensation twisted at his belly as he found himself searching for his sister among them.

Although Alexander neither spoke nor moved from where he stood at the bottom of the stairs, several of the women had spotted him, and they manifested fear. Alarm widened their eyes as they huddled closer to one another. The woman on the horse wheeled the animal around to see what had alarmed them.

"I thought the castle was abandoned," she said without introduction. There was authority in her tone. She stared at Alexander with a measuring look. Her horse ambled toward him.

"*Dhia dhuit*," Alexander said. *God today.* The huddled women appeared to relax at the familiar Gaelic greeting while the woman on the horse continued to study him. He moved away from the stairs. "Usually it is abandoned. I've only taken shelter here for a few nights, and there is more than enough room for ye and yer companions. Sadly, there is no peat for a fire, and I'm verra sorry to tell ye there isna much to eat, but the roof doesna leak and the walls are secure against the night wind."

"We come with our own provisions." The leader spoke in a flat tone. Her frozen expression was entirely lacking in emotion. Having positioned herself between Alexander and the other women, she dismounted, an uncommonly tall woman, who stood almost eye to eye with Alexander.

"Do I know ye?" Alexander asked in a slow, cautious tone. He did not like the way this wraithlike creature was staring at him. It was almost as if there were no one beneath the flesh and bone. Her legs might move to walk, her lips might move to talk, but it was easy to imagine that inside her chest there was nothing more than a dead woman's heart.

"Aye, ye do know me." She handed the reins to one of her band, who led the horse toward the shelter of a ramshackle lean-to against the donjon tower. "That is, if ye're Alexander Kirkpatrick of Kilmory and Eilean Fidra."

"Aye, 'tis me," Alexander affirmed in a voice muted by confusion. He took another step nearer to discern who she was, and the closer he got, the older she appeared. The hair at her temples was not auburn, but gray and dry. Her cheeks were sunken, there were deep lines flaring out from her eyes, and the lopsided shape of her mouth made it obvious that she did not have all her teeth. Alexander did not recognize this woman. Not even his grandmother Hepburn in her seventh decade had been as worn and haggard as she.

"I dinna blame ye, Alexander Kirkpatrick, for not recognizing this pitiful creature." She spread her arms wide, like the wings of a raven. "Are ye thinking I should be better off dead than dragging this bundle of bones about the snowy hills?" She laughed. It was a dry noise, without a trace of mirth. "Och, I wouldna recognize my own reflection, if I had the time to be as vain as I was in days gone by. Do ye remember it then, Alexander, when we were lairds and mistresses of our own land? When we could hunt in our forests, and banquet and make merry in our warm, dry halls, surrounded by kith and kin?"

A sharp bitter mockery weighted her voice, and her identity came to him then, for he had heard that scornful tone before. She was Moira MacCruarie, the spoiled lass who had defied her father instead of becoming his wife.

Chapter 8

⁓⁓⁓

"Moira?" Alexander whispered her name in disbelief. *"An tu?" Is it you?* Although he had not spared much more than a moment's consideration for Moira Mac-Cruarie in many years, if called upon to remember her, he would have envisioned a young woman with the bright light of ambition in her eyes. She had wanted so much, and although she had been conceited and shallow, Alexander had admired her energy and determination. Now it was a profound shock to gaze upon this aged woman. Alexander had to remind himself that Lady Moira was actually younger than his twenty-six years. Then he did the right thing and extended a hand to her in a gesture of greeting.

She gave a grim shrug and accepted his hand, but there was little strength in her cold, bony fingers. "Who else would make the trek to Finlarig in the middle of winter?"

"But why?" Alexander repressed a shiver. Their momentary grasp was broken when they stepped away from each other, and he stared beyond her to the huddle of women who were waiting to be told what to do next. That they had traveled at all seemed a miracle. "Were there no

160

other safe havens where ye might have taken shelter?"

"Nay." Lady Moira's expression cracked. A flicker of pain rippled across her dirt-blackened brow, and a glimmer of sorrow—or was it shame?—was reflected in her eyes. She looked away from Alexander to her traveling companions. "There was no place for us."

There was no anger in her voice, only bitter resignation, and Alexander considered the meaning of this. Highland hospitality was a proud tradition. Even in miserable times such as these, strangers were always welcomed, and one could expect at least an offer of shelter, if not of sustenance. "Tell me who turned ye away, Moira. They've no right to call themselves Highlanders. 'Tis unthinkable that any laird would have turned away a band of women in need, unless—" His voice broke off abruptly.

Moira looked up to meet Alexander's gaze. Her expression was once again impassive. Neither was there any trace of emotion in her voice when she spoke aloud what he was no doubt thinking but could not say.

"Unless," she whispered, "unless we were traitors. Aye, 'tis true, Alexander. We're traitor whores. And dinna look so shocked, so disparaging. Tell me, what was I to do after they'd killed my husband, burned my home, and stolen all but the clothes upon my back? What was I to do when more *sassenach* bastards than ye could count on the fingers of both hands and feet had their filthy, lustful way with me? I could have rotted to death in that stinking prison hole beneath Edinburgh with the other rebels' wives or

I could have agreed to be a willing whore. I had a choice, and I chose to live." She glanced back at the other women. "They, too, had a choice and chose to live. Is that so wrong?"

For a moment, Alexander could not reply. There was a bitter taste in his mouth, and a sort of horror etched itself in lines about his eyes as he wiped at his lips with the back of his arm. He was thinking of his sister and wondering if, sweet Lord forbid, this had been her fate. He saw her black hair and heather-green eyes and swallowed hard, his mind dashing onward to another haunting face. By all that was holy, his next thought was of Lady Claricia, and Alexander found himself wondering if somehow she had been forced to make a similar choice.

"I canna fault ye for surviving, Moira," he answered in a voice that was weighted with rough emotion. "It canna have been an easy choice to live with."

Moira responded with another grim shrug. "There's no need to be kind. I dinna deserve it, least of all from ye, Alexander Kirkpatrick."

Alexander ignored this reference to the past. Instead, he indicated that Lady Moira and the other women should accompany him into the donjon tower. The massive oak door that led to the great hall at Finlarig had long ago fallen off its hinges, and Alexander held it open with the weight of his body as the women filed past. Once inside, they settled against the walls, legs drawn to their chests, heads resting on their knees. Ragged sighs of relief drifted through the empty room. A few of the women closed their eyes and surrendered to exhaustion. Moira sat on the edge of the raised dais and stretched her legs out in front of her. Alexander stood a few paces away and watched as her gaze moved about the room.

Thin beams of sunlight streamed through the high, narrow windows. The sunlight crisscrossed on the bare floor, making a pattern not unlike leafless dead trees in the winter forest, and in those narrow branches of light, dust motes swirled like flakes of ice. It was an altogether desolate scene, and although the roof above the great hall still held, Finlarig reeked of abandonment.

"I didna expect to find so many ghosts," Moira remarked in a voice barely above a whisper, and Alexander had to sit down on his haunches to catch her words. "Is it true about my family? They're all dead?"

He nodded.

"What of the clan, my father's warriors, and the MacCruarie cousins at the other end of the loch? Where are the crofters and their families?"

"Those warriors who have survived now ride with the king or one of his brothers. As for the others, they've all gone into the Grampian Mountains, living in caves or seeking shelter where best it can be found."

"And yer family, Alexander?"

Another grave nod.

"Andrew?" There was a revealing little catch in Moira's voice when she said his name.

"Dead, like all the others."

Lady Moira made the sign of the cross, and her lips moved in a silent prayer. There were tears in her eyes. With two quick blinks, they were gone. She sighed. "Dead? Och, well, then it is a good thing, for I am as vain as always, and would not want him to see what I've become."

Alexander's jaw tensed. He understood only too well what she was feeling. That acrid taste returned to his mouth, and he had to swallow before asking, "Ye havena by any chance seen or heard any word of my sister?"

"Caitrine was taken captive?"

"Aye, by de Clinton in '06. We were ambushed in the Lowlands."

"That is a long time to survive."

"But ye did." He motioned over his shoulder. "They did."

"Is this what ye would want for Caitrine?" she challenged. "The life of a *diobrachan, an outcast in exile* in yer own land is an awful thing to endure."

Without waiting for Alexander's reply, Lady Moira proceeded to tell him of her imprisonment after her husband's execution, and then how she had spent the ensuing years in the company of Gillemin de Fiennes, a knight from Burgundy, an ally of Edward's, and warden of English-occupied Roxburgh Castle. As a noblewoman, Moira had been luckier than the others, and de Fiennes had kept her for his own pleasure; the other women had been at the disposal of several hundred foot-archers and spearmen, and no worse collection of loutish, flea-infested peasant scum could there have been. Freedom had come the preceding March, she told Alexander, when the Scottish had assailed Roxburgh on Shrove Tuesday and liberated the fortress. De Fiennes had surrendered to James Douglas on the condition that he be allowed to return to England,

and upon his departure, Lady Moira and the other women had been left behind.

"Can ye imagine how it felt when I realized that I'd survived? What an incredible miracle that the pain of all those times I'd wanted to give up and die suddenly faded away, with the realization that the degradation and suffering hadna been for naught? It was over. My spirit soared, and we cried with joy and danced in the bailey, embracing James Douglas and his men when the *sassenach* bastards surrendered." Lady Moira emitted a hollow laugh. It was an awful sound, laden with self-mockery. Her lips trembled in a visible show of vulnerability. "But the Douglas didna share in our rejoicing. His warriors wouldna dance with us. *Drùthanagan. Brathadairean.* They called us *whore* and *traitors,* and they wouldna let us travel with them after they had demolished Roxburgh. We were on our own, and when word spread that a band of traitor whores was traveling north, the door to every hut, the gate to every fortress, and the hidden entrance to every cave was barred to us. We've been on the move since then, bound for Finlarig, and though it isna such a great distance our journey has been a harsh one. Five of our company sickened along the way, and we were forced to make several lengthy stops to nurse them, and twice to bury our dead."

In all their wanderings, Lady Moira told Alexander, she had not seen Caitrine in any of the *sassenach* army camps while she was with de Fiennes, or among the refugees they had encountered since the liberation of Roxburgh. "Ye've been holding out hope all this time?"

"Aye," Alexander confessed. Rourke had never understood how a warrior could cling to such an impossible hope.

Moira actually smiled, and surprised him by saying, "Such honesty is a rare thing, Alexander Kirkpatrick. If I allowed myself the luxury of regret, I should be verra sorry I didna take the time to know ye all those years ago."

Three of the women stepped forward to speak with Moira. That they considered her their leader, if not their saviour, was obvious in the way they called her "my lady," with all the respect due the daughter of a Highland laird. One woman said that she wished to search for kindling, and two others volunteered to set snares in the nearby woods. Several hours later, Alexander was marveling at the sight of flames crackling in the fire pit, over which a quartet of deftly plucked woodcocks began to cook on a makeshift spit.

Later, after they had licked the last of the dinner from their fingers, Moira, who had been studying Alexander, remarked: "Now I understand why ye kidnapped de Clinton's niece. It didna make sense until ye told me about Caitrine."

His head snapped up. "What do ye know of that?" Alexander demanded quickly, sharply. The momentary calm that had settled over him from a full stomach and warm fire evaporated.

"Stories of yer foray into Hepburn are taking on the proportion of legend. Rumors are everywhere, and there has been much talk about yer ransom demands in the past few weeks." She saw the suspicion in his eyes. The question, *How could you have heard anything, if you were traveling in exile?* was written upon his face. It was to be expected, and Moira clarified bluntly. "There is many a mon who will rut with a traitor, and we did what we had to for a crust of bread or a few moments out of the winter wind. Twice we spent a few hours in the company of some Highlanders. They wanted sex; we needed food. The first time was outside a place called Dunblane, and then again, but two days past, at a rebel camp in Glen Ogle. Both times we overheard talk of how ye'd outwitted de Clinton and stolen the Beast's Bawd.

" 'Tis a cause for much pride and celebration in the Highlands. A laird has bested an Englishman, and even the king was pleased when he learned the terms of yer ransom demands. Ye're a hero, Alexander Kirkpatrick. *Curaidh*. Indeed, 'tis said ye employed the powers of the auld ways, that ye bewitched the *sassenach*, else how could a single warrior have overcome an entire fortress? Yer strength is great, and 'tis whispered ye ken the magic of the *drùidheachd*."

"Do ye believe such things?" Alexander raised a midnight-black brow.

"What I believe doesna matter. Men will believe what satisfies them, and in these times, it is good to believe in a little bit of magic. 'Tis good to believe in heroes."

Alexander frowned. "I want nothing more than to avenge my family," he said, thinking, in the next instant, that a hero did not kidnap a helpless woman. An honorable man did not make war upon women, even whores, and Alexander was sickened by the depth of his hatred. Thank God, the deed was nearly completed. Soon his vengeance would be fulfilled, and the whole sorry business would be behind him. He was no hero, but a cruel, angry man, and he looked away from Lady Moira.

The hall was dark. There were no torches, and the fire in the pit had burned to embers. About them were the muffled sounds of the women readying to sleep where they had dined. He bid Moira good night, then lay on his side, facing the smoldering embers, and closed his eyes.

But he could not sleep. Instead, he saw Lady Claricia's abundant golden tresses cascading down her back when she tossed her head and tilted her chin to stand proudly before him. His mind painted a picture of how that abundant hair had clouded out about her slender shoulders when she lay beneath him, and how he had noticed the scent of lavender that first time he had seen her asleep on those pristine linens. With his eyes closed, his memory rushed onward to the time when he had lain beside her on that shabby mattress. It was easy to re-create her little moans of pleasure when their flesh had touched and their bodies had melded into one. By all that was holy, she was lovely, and he could not help but wonder who she really was. Had she been forced to make inconceivable choices? Had life truly been as easy for her as he'd assumed? Or had she struggled to survive?

Something ripped at his innards as a fleeting image of their parting crossed his mind's eye. He did not like to think of how he had called her "whore," of how he had mocked her when she spoke of dignity. He was no hero, and, God save him, there was an awful feeling inside him, as if he needed her forgiveness. It was a feeling he did not like. Lady Claricia de Clinton was the niece of his most bitter enemy, she was the one responsible for his brother's death, and he was a warrior. Warriors did not need forgiveness from an enemy. He did not owe her anything; nor did he need absolution. Still the feelings lingered, and as he drifted to sleep, Alexander's final thought was that it was a good thing she was going back to her uncle. It was a good thing he would never see her again.

During the night a great blizzard blew in from the North Sea, making it impossible for anyone to reach Finlarig. Once again, Alexander could do naught but wait.

In the glow of firelight, Rourke and Simon sat cross-legged, staring with serious intent at carved Viking warriors arrayed upon a hide that had been divided into a geometric pattern of squares. They were playing King's Table, *Hnefatafl*, as Rourke's grandfather, Ingvar, had called the old Norse game, which was similar to draughts. Rourke had learned the game from Ingvar, and, in turn, he had found much pleasure in teaching Simon, who had demonstrated a sharp mind for one so young. The lad let out a quick whoop of victory. His white king was safe, and he had captured one of Rourke's knights.

"Have ye won?" Viviane looked up and asked. She was seated on the other side of the small fire, working on a pile of old pelts. Some of them needed to be mended. All of them needed to be softened. A combination of age and exposure to snow and rain had caused the furs to stiffen, but with repeated rubbing, it was possible to restore them to their original condition. It was a time-consuming task, and Viviane used a miniature broom to brush vigorously at them. Her hand stilled while she awaited his reply.

"Almost," Simon said with a rush of enthusiasm.

"Aye, the lad is a skilled tactician," Rourke said to Viviane; then he turned to Simon. "I shouldna like to be yer enemy. Ye dinna allow a mon to make a single mistake."

Simon glowed with pride. " 'Tis how ye taught me."

" 'Tis how it should be." Rourke leaned across the playing cloth and tousled Simon's dark hair.

Viviane smiled. While Rourke had filled the lonely spot in her life, he had been a blessing for Simon. The devoted friendship of the Irishman had made every difference in the world to the boy. Although she had reached the island on her own, she did not think that she and the baby could have survived so many years, had it not been for Rourke. But what he meant to them went further than mere survival. Rourke had made their circle complete, and there were countless things that only he could have done for Simon. Paternal things, and she was afraid that when the truth was revealed, Rourke, too, would be hurt. She did not want to hurt Rourke any more than she wanted to hurt Simon, and Viviane wished that the storm might never end. She knew that nothing stayed the same, and once the storm had passed, there was no guarantee that they would ever be together as they were at that moment. She closed her eyes to capture the warmth and companionship and hold them as close to her heart as she could.

On the sixth day the snow stopped, and the last of the heavy gray clouds drifted away. The winds died down. In the woods surrounding the hut, birds began to chatter and caw as they emerged from snow-shrouded trees to search for seeds. It was going to be a splendid, sunny day, perfect for a brisk walk. Viviane, Rourke, and Simon bundled up in layers of furs and woolen cloaks to venture forth from the hut. Somewhere in the distant hills above the shore a wolf howled. Another answered, a third joined in, then a fourth, and their baying echoed back and forth across the frozen loch. Hungry beasts were on the prowl.

But the anxiety that Rourke saw on Viviane's face as they began to wade through the snow had a deeper meaning. He could not quite put a finger on it, and he did not like it. Something wasn't right. He had noticed it earlier when the falling snow had started to taper off. He had seen it in the way she stared at Simon with an expression so wistful and sad it made him think her heart was going to break. Perhaps they had been cooped up inside too long. Perhaps all she needed was a bit of fresh air. If there was one thing Rourke intended that afternoon it was to make Viviane smile and see her laugh. He would be returning to Eilean Fidra in the morning, and he did not want to leave her in such a melancholy state.

At the edge of the clearing Simon scurried ahead of them toward the beach.

"Hurry, Mam! Rourke!" His magnified voice carried easily over the cloaked landscape. "Ye canna even see the bridge of rocks. It has all vanished beneath the snow."

Rourke and Viviane followed in the trough Simon had made in the snow, walking as one and making the path wider as they went. He had slipped one arm beneath her furs to hold her tight, his hand wrapping about her waist and coming to rest against her stomach. She entwined her fingers in his. Rourke squeezed her hand and leaned close to drop a quick kiss on her temple, where strands of wild black hair had escaped from beneath the hood about her head.

"Have I told ye today how much I love ye, lass?" He wanted to see her smile.

Viviane's heart sank like a black rock. "Aye. More often than I deserve," she said before she could stop herself. She had nothing to give Rourke in return for his devotion, his love. But that was not the worst of it. She was about to destroy everything.

Rourke frowned. His first attempt to elevate her mood had failed. He began to sing, "*Tha teanga fhada, chaol, chruaidh; Aig mo luaidh an rìbhinn òg.*" It was a bawdy ditty sung by warriors flush with victory and deep in drink. *A long, slender hard tongue, Has my beloved, the young maid.*

"Hush," Vivian scolded. "Simon will hear."

"*Is ioma neach le am miann a pòg.*" Rourke did not stop singing, but the words were muffled as he nibbled at her ear. *Many a one desires her kiss.*

"Stop that!"

"Not until ye tell me that ye love me."

They had passed through the woods and were on the small rise above the beach, but the snow covered the land so completely, it was impossible to tell where the island ended and the loch began. The island, the loch, and the far shore all melded together into one continual sweep of white.

"Say ye love me," Rourke prompted. "Else I will sing again."

She wanted to tease him. *And why would ye think such a thing? Me? Love ye?* But, of course, she did love him. There was every reason in the world why she should. And when she gazed across that snow-covered loch and saw the gray castle, its irregular towers reaching toward the cloudless blue sky, she knew she could not lie to Rourke.

"I do, Rourke."

"What?" Firmly, gently, he held her chin in his big, strong hand to tilt her face up to his. "Say it," he coaxed.

"I do love ye," she whispered, as if it were a magic spell, and she knew not whether the incantation would invoke good or evil. She brushed her cheek against his battle-scarred hand.

"Och, lass, ye could make a grown mon weep," Rourke murmured on a quick, hot breath as his mouth swooped down to claim hers. She'd said it. She loved him, and he knew she meant it, for when their lips met the passion was there, as it always was between them, but there was a tenderness, too, aching and sweet, that skirled from his loins to his heart.

"Mam, *seall!* Look at the castle," Simon called out. "See how close it is. 'Tis magic. The storm has brought it nearer to us."

Rourke raised his head, the kiss was broken, and together, they looked at the castle. Indeed, surrounded as it was by an ocean of white, it appeared to be closer.

"Take me to Eilean Fidra when ye return," Viviane whispered before she lost her resolve to do the right thing, before she turned and hurried back to the hut, never to gaze across the loch again, never to think of the woman who had been held there for a few short weeks one winter.

Rourke wondered if he had misheard Viviane. She had spoken quickly, breathlessly, as if someone were chasing her. A chill of apprehension touched his spine. "Ye want to move into the castle?" It was not uncommon for those living in the countryside to seek shelter in a castle, especially during a hard winter. Although Viviane would have been more secure if she had lived in such a community, Rourke could not help feeling threatened by the notion of sharing her with anyone else. His jaw tightened as he waited to hear her answer.

"Nay, I only wish to visit."

"What about the lad?" Rourke wondered if she could hear the relief in his voice as he exhaled a breath he had not even realized he'd been holding fast. "Do ye want him to visit as well?"

"Aye, Simon needs to go, too."

After a few moments, he spoke. "Why after all this time?" He did not like the way she had said "needs."

" 'Tis for Simon that I ask this of ye, but dinna ask me to explain."

A few more moments of silence ticked by. At length, Rourke dared to ask, "Will I lose ye?"

Viviane heard the ragged note in his voice. Her heart caught, her gaze was drawn to his crystal-blue eyes, where she saw his affection and generosity, his love and tenderness, tainted by apprehension. To see that this warrior could be so human and vulnerable made him all the more loveable. But to know that she had caused that vulnerability to be revealed was a painful burden. "I was right, ye know; I dinna deserve yer love." She touched his cheek with the back of her hand. "I willna be going anywhere. Indeed, Rourke, after we visit the castle I will be needing ye more than ever before. 'Tis ye who must promise not to leave me."

Rourke reached up to slip his fingers through hers, where they lay against his face, and he brought her palm to his lips for a lingering kiss. "Ye know I would do anything for ye, lass."

"Anything?" she teased lightly, while her thoughts tumbled into darkness. She was thinking something unutterably horrible, something unimaginable. *Would ye kill yer laird if I asked it of ye?* It was an awful thing to consider. Vengeance was abhorrent, especially if it entailed violence. It had never solved anything. It only created more misery and hardship, more violence. Indeed, part of the reason Viviane had chosen to live in isolation was to avoid being part of the vicious cycle of violence. How could she, of all people, think such a thing, even if only for the briefest second? she wondered.

But the awful truth was that this wasn't the first time she'd thought of seeing the laird called Alexander Kirkpatrick dead for vengeance's sake, murdered by her hand or Rourke's. The thought had occurred to her quite a few times since Rourke had told her of the English prisoner in the castle, since he had implied that the lady had been forced to endure the laird's carnal advances. And as the prospect of visiting the castle and seeing that prisoner were about to become reality, the possibility of vengeance became more insistent.

"Aye, if it were within my power." Rourke did not suspect Viviane's darker thoughts, and, seeing that he had at last succeeded in making her smile, he kissed her hard to seal his promise. "I would do anything ye ask of me, lass."

Chapter 9

~~~ ⊙⊙ ~~~

Maxwel of Ballimeanoch, a clansman of Alexander Kirkpatrick's, sat on a bench inside the entrance to the great hall at Eilean Fidra. His back and head rested against the dank stone wall, his focus was straight ahead, and the deep lines etched across his brow and flaring out from his thin mouth were dour. But there was nothing in his expression to indicate he noticed the women gathered about the fire pit in the center of the hall, or that he was even awake, for that matter. The women called him *Foghuinteuch Sùilean*, *Valiant Eyes*, for Maxwel of Ballimeanoch was blind, a result of wounds inflicted upon him during the same battle in the Pass of Brandir that had brought Rourke to Viviane's island. It was said that even after the blood streamed forth from his eyes, he had continued to fight, slaying every *sassenach* in his path. Ballads had been written in his honor, and the laird, even the king, had praised his bravery and loyalty, but Maxwel of Ballimeanoch did not revel in any of the glory.

He was a bitter man, unforgiving—indeed, disbelieving—of a God who would let him live, only to stay behind with the women and children while the English king was still undefeated. In his

177

own mind, he was nothing more than a breathing gargoyle, a freak, who could not even do the simplest task, as a warder on the castle rampart. Only because leaving would have broken his mother's heart did he remain at Eilean Fidra, instead of finding the deepest cave into which he might crawl and never come out. He kept his distance from the everyday goings-on, having as little to do with human intercourse as was possible, sitting, as he did this day, as far away from the women as he could.

Their quiet murmurings reached out to him. He recognized each voice. Two of them were ancient. The two Maeris were in their eighth decades, and their voices were weak and thin, sometimes punctuated by the raspy cough of an old one. The Maeris spoke very little, but when they did, what they said was sharp and opinionated. The old women had lived too long, and Maxwel of Ballimeanoch often agreed with their snipings. There were other times, though, when he could not stomach their barbs, and then he focused upon Giorsal, who did not speak so much as sing, in a voice as light and sweet as a meadowlark's. There was Frances, usually pleading with one child or another to behave, and her sisters with their children, and her mother, Sorcha, whose authority over the others rang clear in her voice. Of late, there was a new voice, that of a *sassenach*, and try though he might to loathe the woman, he could not, for he heard naught but kindness and bravery when she spoke, a bravery that masked a dreadful loneliness.

Blind though he might have been, Maxwel of Ballimeanoch's abilities to hear and discern were uncanny, and little transpired within the island fortress of which he was unaware. Of a sudden, he cocked his head to the side. There were footsteps outside. Someone—nay, two persons, perhaps three—was coming down the corridor. He sat straighter, reached for his dirk, fingered the hilt, and listened closely, then relaxed when he recognized the flat footfall of the giant Irishman who was a distant cousin to the laird.

"Rourke O'Connor, welcome." Maxwel spoke in a low voice, not loud enough for the women in the hall to hear.

The three newcomers came to an abrupt halt on the threshold.

"Maxwel," Rourke acknowledged as he stamped the last of the snow from the bottom of his boots.

"Do ye bring yer friend from the Auld Believer's Isle?"

"Aye." Rourke was not surprised that Maxwel would know who was by his side. "'Tis Viviane."

"Welcome." Maxwel reached out a hand as if in greeting, and Viviane, realizing that the warrior could not see, stepped forward to make contact with his outstretched fingers. "Are ye as bonny and wild as Rourke brags?"

Her breath caught. She raised her eyes to look at Rourke. He was grinning, amused and proud.

"I make ye blush?" Maxwel whispered.

She snatched her hand away. "How did ye know?"

"Yer hand warmed in mine."

"Och," scolded Viviane. "And next ye'll be telling me ye've the sight of the fairies."

Rourke chuckled. This was not a bad start to Viviane's first encounter beyond her sheltered island.

"There is someone else with ye?" Maxwel tilted his head as if he could see beyond Viviane. He had heard a soft shuffling. There was someone—a smaller woman, mayhap a child—hiding behind her skirts.

"Rourke!" Sorcha called out from her place by the fire pit. As wife of the *sennachie,* she was mistress of Eilean Fidra until such a time as the laird took a wife, and, seeing that Rourke O'Connor had returned with visitors, she began to cross the hall to greet them. They had long wished that Rourke would bring his friend from the island, and now that she was there, Sorcha intended to make a fuss. "Welcome to Eilean Fidra. We are only a small fortress, but what we have to share is—" The words caught in Sorcha's throat, and both hands flew to her mouth as if to extract them by force.

Maxwel leaned forward on the bench. Something was amiss.

"Sorcha?" Rourke began to move toward the woman, as if to aid her.

The other women at the fire pit looked up from their mending or set aside their distaffs, and in the next instant, the hall echoed with their gasps and cries.

"Caitrine!" Sorcha recovered from her initial shock and rushed forward with open arms. The other women were on their feet and staring at Viviane, and the name Caitrine rippled from their lips to circle the rafters. "Praise God in Heaven. Ye've come home to us, Caitrine, and what a blessed miracle ye have brought us, Rourke. Where did ye find her?"

Viviane's reaction was swift and immediate. She snaked an arm through Rourke's and clung to him, not moving an inch toward the tall woman who held her arms open to her. "I swear I've never seen these people before. Not a one of them," Viviane told Rourke on an agitated underbreath, searching the huddle of unfamiliar faces for the one person she hoped to recognize. Frantically, Viviane reached behind her with her other arm, and, finding Simon, she clutched the child close to her.

Where was the prisoner? Viviane scanned the faces once again, and when she did not see Lady Claricia, when the women in the hall pressed nearer and extended their arms as if to embrace her, she moved closer to Rourke, wondering whether her decision to come to the castle had been a terrible mistake. It required immense fortitude not to turn and flee.

Rourke heard the panic in Viviane's denial. He felt her resistance when the women tried to welcome her with embraces. Such a reaction was not entirely unexpected. It had been a long time since she'd been around other people, but there was something more to this. He was reminded of the expression on her face when the wolves had howled in the hills, and, remembering what she'd said on the snow-covered beach, *After we visit the castle I will be needing ye more than ever before,* he wrapped his arms across her chest, pulling her to him in a protective, possessive hold. "This is Viviane," he said in a firm voice intended to stave

off the women of Eilean Fidra. "I dinna bring Caitrine."

"Viviane? Nay, 'tis our little Caitrine come
back to us from the dead," challenged one
woman, who peered over Sorcha's shoulder. It
was not safe to get too close, the woman thought.
While this person looked like Caitrine, it could
easily have been an evil spirit, mayhap the devil
himself, in possession of her body and soul. The
woman made the sign of the cross and began to
pray aloud, "*Ave Maria.*"

Another woman fell to her knees. "*Ar n-Athair
a ta air Nnèamh.*" *Our Father which art in Heaven.*

"My name is Viviane," she insisted above the
rising invocations.

"Ye're Rourke's lady from the loch?" inquired
Sorcha, who appeared to be the only one able to
maintain a shred of sanity. "Not Caitrine?"

"*Ach saor sinn o olc.*" *But deliver us from evil.*

"Aye. I am Viviane. One and the same, from
the Auld Believer's Isle. Not yer Caitrine."

The woman on her knees set to a horrible keen-
ing, and Maxwell, who seldom exchanged two
words with the females of the household, had
had enough. He rose to his full height, an imposing Highlander made even more forbidding by
the odd, sightless focus in his eyes, and when he
spoke, others still took heed.

"Hush, ye silly biddie," Maxwell chastised the
woman on her knees. "Get up. 'Tis no ghost, nor
ghoulie come to haunt us, but Rourke's Viviane.
Behave yerselves. Bridle yer tongues, and stop
acting like superstitious heathens. Ye should be
welcoming yer guests like proper Highlanders."

To his amazement, the women fell silent, and,

satisfied, Maxwel of Ballimeanoch resumed his seat on the bench.

"Ye should have warned us, Rourke," said Sorcha.

"That she was so beautiful?"

"Aye, and that she is the image of the laird's sister."

"I didna know such a thing."

"Aye, I forget. Caitrine was gone before ye came to us."

Viviane was appalled at the notion of a blood tie to the laird. "My name is Viviane," she repeated. Then, remembering her own despair at once having been lost from all that was familiar to her, she added in a more sympathetic tone, "I am sorry to disappoint ye."

"Och, sorry? Dinna fash yerself, lass. I see now we were mistaken. Though the hair is the same, Caitrine wasna so tall. Will ye pardon us? Rushing at ye like a bunch of rooks on the attack. I am Sorcha, wife of Ewen, the laird's *sennachie*. Welcome to Eilean Fidra."

"No pardon is necessary. It was an honest mistake."

"Won't ye come closer to warm yerselves by the fire?" Sorcha motioned to the other women that they should return to their places.

"Thank ye." Viviane moved forward with Simon at her side. The covey of women dispersed, and it was then that Viviane and the one woman who had remained seated by the fire saw each other for the first time.

It was Claricia in a fine-woven purple kirtle, her golden hair braided and woven about her head like a splendid crown. She let out a startled cry, one hand covering her lips to prevent any more sound from escaping. But Claricia did not think she could have heard herself if she had screamed, so deafening was the frantic pounding of her heart at the sight before her. *It was Meg and he.* Found, at last, here, of all places, when she had almost given up any hope of finding them. It was the bairn she had called Simon. He was alive and safe and healthy, and it was the hardest thing she had ever done to stand there, instead of rushing forward to take him in her arms and rain a thousand little kisses across his brow and nose and cheeks, to blurt out who she was and how a day had never passed that she had not prayed for him.

On the other side of the fire, Viviane stopped abruptly, and her hold on Simon tightened, causing the lad to look sideways at his mother in confusion. Viviane stared straight ahead with the same kind of fear and astonishment that only moments before had marked the features of the other women. She was staring at the woman in purple, who was coming toward her.

"Rourke, I am glad to see you," Claricia said in English when she was near enough to be heard without raising her voice. Although she addressed Rourke, she was staring at the woman and child. "Is this your friend?" she asked, wondering if anyone else noticed how odd her voice sounded. It was hollow and brittle. Her skin felt clammy. Was she as pale as she felt?

Rourke nodded and introduced the two women, first in English, for Claricia's benefit. He repeated the introduction in Gaelic for Viviane.

"My lady." Viviane spoke in Gaelic, then began to curtsy, not so much as an act of deference but as a means to hide the confusion that most certainly must have been reflected in her eyes.

She had not thought through this reunion. She had been so determined to do the right thing before she lost her courage that she had not considered what would happen once she had brought Simon there. Most important, she had not imagined that in coming to the castle there would be so many onlookers and strangers. Nor had she imagined that her entrance into Eilean Fidra would cause the stir it had when she'd been mistaken for someone else. Staring at the ground, Viviane suppressed the urge to rush at Lady Claricia and hug her. She wanted to ask her a hundred questions, to tell her a million things, but she didn't move a muscle. She must do nothing to give them away, especially if there had been no signal, nor hint of recognition, from Claricia.

"No." Claricia motioned her to stop. *Do not curtsy to me*, the expression in her eyes implored as they stood face-to-face. She had not spoken aloud, yet her friend understood.

Rourke watched with fascination the wild Scottish maid wrapped in coarse wool and wolf pelts standing opposite the slender *sassenach* with golden hair, dressed in a fine kirtle befitting a laird's wife. There were tears in both of their eyes, and as different as they appeared upon first glance, it was startling to realize that their gazes were marked by identical wariness. The two women shared a past. Rourke's instincts had never been as strong as they were at that moment. The proof was revealed in the way Viviane was avoiding his regard and in the way Lady Claricia could not take her eyes off Simon.

"And who is this?" Claricia's voice was quivering as she looked at the lad with what she hoped was a suitably bland yet polite expression. Here it was! The impossible dream had come true, but she could not reveal her joy. She swayed slightly, her body moving of its own accord, as if to rush forward and enfold the lad in an affectionate embrace. She steadied herself.

"This is Simon," replied Rourke.

"Simon." Claricia whispered his name as if trying it out. "Simon," she repeated, her eyes never moving from his small, dark face. Sweet Jesu, he was a Kirkpatrick, with midnight-black hair and deep-set green eyes. Her heart leaped to her throat. Even his features were sharp and lean. He was a handsome lad, and when she gazed upon him she did not think of his sire, nor of the painful manner of his conception. She thought instead of his birth, of the gentle newborn cooing at her breast. She thought of the tiny, perfect hands and the mother's love that had come so naturally, so unconditionally into her heart when she had held him in her arms.

Simon, having heard his name upon the lips of the beautiful, golden-haired lady, stepped closer to her. Since they had entered the hall he had been overwhelmed by the strangeness of it all. Everything was big. The ceiling was as high as the sky, the great rocks in the walls were the size of the ones in the loch that he could not budge, and the fire in the pit looked like a bonfire that should have been out-of-doors instead of inside. Were not these people afraid of the hazard? But the most amazing sight of all was the woman in purple, and he could not stop staring at her golden crown of hair and pale skin. It was so unlike his own coloring or his mother's; even Rourke's yellow hair did not shine as hers did. She was soft and delicate as an early summer iris growing at the loch's edge, swaying in the breeze, and he had never imagined that anyone could be so lovely. He took another step toward her and bowed as his mother had long ago taught him when they'd played at games of knights and lairds and faraway places. A shy smile played across his face. He whispered in awe, *"Aingeal."*

Tears sprang to Claricia's eyes. She had heard his little-boy voice, and she had understood. *Angel.* The child had called her an angel, and she blinked several times to prevent the tears from pouring down her cheeks. This was almost more than she could bear.

"If you will excuse me I must go to the solar," Claricia said hastily. "Frances has been feeding her baby there, where it is warmer and not so noisy, and I promised to sit with the child, so that she could come into the hall and help her mother."

Rourke translated this for Viviane and Simon.

"A bairn," exclaimed Simon, casting an eager glance at Rourke and the two women. He hurried on in Gaelic. "I've never seen a bairn. Och, Mam, may I go with her? If only for a moment?"

"The lad has never seen a bairn and would like to accompany ye," said Rourke. Once again, he translated to English, but this time, he kept a close eye on Lady Claricia, and he could not help concluding that there had been no need to translate. He had noticed the lady's expression while Simon was speaking, especially when he had called her *aingeal*. He was certain that if she did not speak Gaelic, at least she understood the spoken word.

The lad's request was unexpected. Claricia glanced toward Meg. A thousand emotions were skittering across her friend's countenance. Clearly, Meg was as confused as she was by all of this.

"Yes." Claricia addressed Rourke. "He may come with me. I would like that, if it is all right with Viv-Viviane," she said, stumbling over the name.

Viviane nodded, not stopping to think that Rourke had noticed how she'd understood what Claricia had said in English. She could only think that this was the beginning of the end, and she shut her eyes tightly against the vision of Simon following Claricia away from her.

Rourke saw Viviane's distress. He leaned down and whispered in her ear, "Dinna fash yerself. The lad will be fine with Lady Claricia. She isna a devil."

"I didna imagine she was," came Viviane's reply.

"Go after them, if it bothers ye." He gave her a tiny nudge. "The solar is off that passage." He encouraged her, knowing full well that this might be his best chance to uncover the mystery between these two dissimilar women. Rourke intended to lurk outside the door to hear what he might of their private conversation.

* * *

The solar was a snug chamber. Once it had been an elegant, well-appointed retreat for the laird's wife and the other women of Eilean Fidra, a place to sew and gossip, to play the lute and teach one's children their daily catechism. But those elegant furnishings and wall hangings—the Flanders tapestries, the mirror from Venice, and the chairs whose legs had been carved to resemble flying fish—were rotting in the tunnel beneath the loch. The room was still snug, the winter drafts being kept out by an assortment of furs hanging on the walls, and it was warm, being the only chamber at Eilean Fidra with a hearth in the exterior wall.

The women, one dark as night and the other as fair as snow, having embraced and cried and rejoiced in their reunion, now sat side by side on a pallet while they watched Simon playing with the baby on a pile of furs. Claricia had shown the boy how to roll a smooth wooden ball to the baby, who squealed and laughed and clapped his chubby hands in delight. Simon laughed, too. It was a wonderful sight to experience this momentary glimpse of how her life might have been at that manor house in faraway England, in a withdrawing chamber filled with merry children.

"A day has not passed that I havena thought of ye, my dear friend," said the woman known as Viviane and Meg.

"And you have always been in my thoughts and prayers," Claricia replied. "Just to know that you have survived is more than I dared to expect. Of course, I dreamed. Ah, *bhruadair mi. I dreamed* and wished and yearned, and I always told myself that it was possible to endure anything, because one day I would find you."

"It canna have been easy. Five years is a long time to endure with only a wish and a dream."

"Not nearly so hard as what you've been through. I never imagined that you would have come so far from Goswick Keep. I could not have done on my own all that you have accomplished, and with an infant. You have triumphed over many struggles."

"There are different kinds of struggles, my friend. While ye marvel at my feats, ye shouldna forget that I would never have been able to survive de Clinton as ye did." She looked from Claricia to Simon, and after a long silence, she asked, "Did ye recognize him?"

"*An diobair mathair a ciochran?*" was Claricia's whispered response. *Can a mother forget her suckling?* "What have you told him?"

"Nothing. I wasna sure what to say. I always thought when the time was right I would know. Now the time has come, but I still dinna know."

Claricia patted her hand in understanding. She was not certain either. "First, you must tell me everything. I want to know every little detail. His first step. His first word. Is he brave? A good hunter? And does he mind you?"

They were a mother's questions. Outside in the dim corridor, Rourke wondered if he had misheard, or mayhap Lady Claricia, who was speaking Gaelic, did not know what she had said. Surely Viviane's son could not be hers. The lad looked exactly like Viviane. The black hair. The green eyes. Rourke leaned his head against the cool stone wall in disbelief. How could it be?

Lady Claricia was Aymer de Clinton's whore, and the Englishman's possessiveness was well known. Could it be that five or six years before there had been someone else? A girlish indiscretion with a young knight, or perhaps a Scotsman, given the lad's dark looks? Was this the secret Viviane had been protecting? The bastard child of de Clinton's whore. But why? What bond was there between the English rose and the Highland lass, that such trust and sacrifice might exist between them? Rourke could not begin to make sense of it.

"Would that I might see your island before I am sent back to my uncle," said Claricia when her questions about the boy had been answered. She smiled. "I should have known an island would be where you ended up. I should have guessed."

"So ye didna forget my stories of fairie isles."

"I never forgot," she said in a quiet voice, remembering all the times she, too, had fled to the safety of an island.

"I went to Loch Lomond. Do ye recall my telling ye about Loch Lomond?" Claricia nodded, and Meg went on, "But there were too many people. Too many soldiers. And then I heard of this place from an auld woman. The Auld Believer's Isle, she called it, and only those who dared to confront the water spirits could make the crossing. It was a perfect spot, with a small shelter and fruit trees, some tools for fishing and trapping. There was no one until Rourke."

"What have you told him?"

"He doesna know anything. Indeed, he doesna know me by any name except Viviane."

"Wherever did you get that?"

"Do ye not recall Queen Guinevere's tutor? The Lady of the Lake?"

Claricia stared past Meg and blinked as if seeing nothing at all. Lady Johanna had related the legend of the Grail Maidens to the girls on many a winter night at Goswick Keep. It seemed such a long time ago, and Claricia knew a moment of terrible shame that Meg had remembered but she had forgotten. The notion squeezed at her heart, making it even emptier. She was nothing. She had nothing. She forced a semblance of a smile. "It was good of you to come to the castle to let me see him."

"Good of me? What nonsense do ye speak? There is nothing of goodness in what I do. 'Tis the right thing. Ye're his mother, for God's sake. Ye have the right to see him." Meg paused for what seemed like the longest moment in her life. Here it was, the thing she had dreaded. The right thing, which would change her life and take away her precious child. She braced herself and rushed into speech. "And he has the right to be told about you and how—"

"No!" Claricia stopped Meg before she might say another word. She looked at the lad, who had none of her English characteristics. It was a strange sight to behold, for he seemed to look like Meg. They both had distinctly Celtic looks, with dark hair, high cheekbones, and eyes the color of heather. They looked like mother and child. She had heard that people who spent time together could come to resemble each other. That was surely what had happened. "No. He does not need to be told anything. You are the woman who has raised him and loved him and nurtured him. You are the one who protected him. The one who saved his life. You are his mother, and there is nothing more than that which he should ever know."

"*Gun robh math agad.*" Meg said, exhaling a pent-up breath. *I thank you.*"

"Don't thank me," Claricia snapped, sounding angry, and a flush of shame brought high color to her cheeks. "I'm sorry. You must forgive me."

"I understand."

"Do you, Meg? Do you really? Can you imagine how I have lived for this day, thinking that I would get him back, that I would have some claim to him? But I don't. I see that now. I never asked how you felt about being sent away with him. You accepted the responsibility in exchange for an earlier favor, but—"

"And I would not have it any other way. Every moment, every hardship, has been a joy. It was almost perfect, until—"

"Until Rourke told you I was here, and you thought you had to give him back."

Meg answered with a grave nod. "*Bha mi sgathach.*" *I was afraid.*

"And your heart was likely as twisted and aching with fear as mine, thinking that the world would never be the same."

"We are too much alike," said Meg, with affection.

"In many ways," Claricia agreed. "Which is one more reason why Simon should—nay, why he *must*—stay with you and never know the truth. There would be no point in telling him. It would endanger him. I cannot take him back .

with me when I am returned to my uncle. His past has been with you, and you have given him a good life. His future will be a good one, but only if he stays with you."

Meg could not stop herself from dissolving into tears. She knew what it had cost Claricia to say those words, and it grieved her deeply to realize how much she had, when Claricia had nothing.

"What is wrong, Mam?" Simon rose from the fur and walked across the chamber to comfort his mother. "Dinna be sad."

"I am not sad." She wiped her eyes and gave a little sniffle before going on. "The angel has given me a wonderful gift. These are tears of happiness."

Simon left his mother's side to stand beside Claricia. "If it is a good gift, then ye should be happy, too. Why do ye not smile?"

"Ah, but I do. My heart is smiling." Claricia ended with a true smile upon her lips. It was easy to be happy, gazing upon this child. He was handsome and kind, a wonderful son, and her eyes drank in the sight of him, memorizing every feature, every detail, and then she saw the garnet ring on a leather cord about his neck.

Simon noticed the direction of Claricia's gaze and held out the ring for her to see. "It belonged to my grandmother. Her name was Johanna."

Claricia's composure wavered. "Ah, then you must treasure it."

"Aye, and I'm only allowed to wear it on special occasions like today, when my mam said we would come to the castle. I am glad we came. I have always wondered what it was like on the other side of the water. And it is nice to meet you.

Maybe you will visit our island in the spring."

Claricia swallowed hard. "I should like that."

The baby called out for attention, and Simon went back to the fur rug.

"When do you leave?" asked Meg.

"*Gu goirid. Soon.* The ransom is being negotiated, and I expect someone will come for me in another sennight, maybe two, but not longer than that. I will be gone long before spring comes."

Rourke had heard all he needed to know, and he moved away from the door. Although there was much he did not understand, their secret would be safe with him. He walked away and did not hear the rest of their conversation.

"Will you marry Rourke?"

"He would like that, I think."

"You're right. Will you?"

Meg sighed. "Aye."

"Then, you will stay here at Eilean Fidra?" Claricia found it was a comfort to know where they would be. There was a certain reassurance in being able to hold a picture in her memory of where they would be living.

It was then that the awful irony of the child's relationship to Alexander Kirkpatrick unfolded itself to her. She did not have to think for more than a second to know that as long as she was the only one who knew the truth, she would not reveal it to anyone else. There was no reason to do so. She did not care about birthright and clan lineage; neither did Meg. Simon did not need to be the laird's nephew. He did not need to be a Kirkpatrick. In truth, Claricia could not stand to think of Alexander Kirkpatrick trying to lay claim to Simon in any way. She feared that if he knew his dead brother had fathered a child, he would try to get that child even if he was the bastard of an English whore, and she could not bear to think of Simon's being taken from Meg. Claricia did not want the lad to grow up in a world ruled by hatred and vengeance. Meg's island was a thousand times better than this castle, and Meg had proven herself able to protect Simon. She loved and cherished him. That was enough. There was no need to reveal the truth.

"Nay, we willna stay here. Perhaps we will return in the summer, but for the time being, we will stay on the island. It is what we know."

This brief reunion was coming to an end, and Claricia struggled to make the most out of the final minutes she would spend with Meg and Simon. Before, when they had bid farewell, there had been the faint hope that it would not be forever. This time, there would be no such hope. This time, when they said good-bye, they would do so in the knowledge that they would never see each other again, at least, not in this worldly plain.

Claricia took Meg's hands in hers, a gesture of sisterly affection. "There are no words to tell you how much I love you—you know that, don't you? No words to fully explain what it means to me to see the result of what you've done, to know that you've survived."

"Och, it is a blessing, indeed, to known that *our plan* succeeded," Meg said. "But ye mustna fash yerself with thanks and trying to find proper words. What I did was nothing between friends, and although it began as a means to repay a debt, it has become my life and love and joy. It is I who am beholden to you for entrusting me with such a precious gift."

"You will take care of him?" There was a clear note of maternal anxiety in this question.

"As I always have, and should anything happen to me Rourke will be there for him."

"That is good. I can think of no better man than Rourke O'Connor to guide your son—"

"Our son."

"—into manhood."

Suddenly, the baby cried. Claricia and Meg looked toward the fur rug, where Simon was trying to appease the child.

"How can I make him stop?" asked Simon.

"Watch," said Claricia. She rose to pick up the babe, then she sat down beside Simon, and, cradling the child, she began to sing in Gaelic, *"Dean cadal, seircean, dean cadal."* She cooed at the babe, *Sleep, my little darling, sleep,* and beside her a thin, childish voice joined in.

"A ghaoil is milse na a mhil, fearr na seudan, maoithe na cloimh," sang Simon in his young bright voice. He cuddled close to the pretty golden-haired woman, who not only looked like an angel, but sang like one, too, and he smiled down at the infant as she was doing, an angelic smile, at once as radiant as it was serene. *My love is sweeter than honey, better than jewels, softer than wool.*

Tears welled up in Claricia's eyes. They were bitter and scalding. Her eyes burned. Her nose prickled. *"Breisleach, m'aon leanaban, breisleach,"* she sang, finishing the lullaby, her voice entwined with Simon's. *Dream, my only child, dream.*

That was the moment she would treasure until the day she died.

PART 2

THE HEART

Chapter 10

Claricia awoke with a start. But it was not a nightmare that roused her. She did not have dreams anymore, neither good nor bad ones. It was the thud of metal landing upon wood, a sword, perhaps, and a second sense warned her to resist sitting bolt upright or calling out. She lay still, listening.

Someone was on the other side of the bed curtains, but the movements were not familiar. Claricia was accustomed to the early-morning sounds of Frances bustling about the laird's chamber, lighting a new layer of peat in the brazier, and freshening her kirtle from the day before. But this was not Frances. It was a man. Claricia could tell by the heavy tread on the floor and by the height at which the torchlight was being carried above his silhouetted form. Although Rourke had reported no sign of English patrols in the area, Eilean Fidra was vulnerable to outlaws, *sassenach* deserters, or Scotsmen with no allegiance to anyone save themselves. Such men were ruthless, and might invade a fortress to steal food from women and children, to pillage and rape with no remorse. Slowly, Claricia reached beneath her pillow, and, finding the ceremonial dirk that used to sit upon the laird's chest, her fingers tightened about the handle.

The hour must have been close to dawn. The hot stones that Frances had stuffed beneath the mound of furs to warm Claricia's feet during the night had turned cold. The enclosed interior of the sleeping compartment was chilled. Her breath came forth in small white clouds, and with her free hand, Claricia held the fur coverlet over her nose as she turned on her side to watch the intruder's lanky silhouette secure the torchlight in a wall mount. That done, he moved straight toward the curtained bed, his shadow becoming elongated in a ghoulish pattern against the threadbare hangings.

Claricia held her breath, but she did not close her eyes, as a roughened hand slipped between the bed curtains. Long, masculine fingers parted the fabric just wide enough for a bearded face to peer inside the dark compartment. The outline of shoulders and an upper torso became visible, and as the light from the torch made recognition possible, Claricia's grip on the dirk relaxed.

It was Alexander Kirkpatrick, his lean face hidden beneath a thick beard. But not so hidden that Claricia could not detect the frown that was set deeply upon his countenance. Something was not right, and Claricia found little comfort in discovering that the intruder was no outlaw. A strange tremor pulsed through her as she gazed up at Alexander Kirkpatrick's angular features. He was the epitome of a dangerous man. Powerful and virile and filled with rage.

"What is wrong?" She spoke without preface, choosing to remain buried beneath the furs, her fingers toying with the handle of the dirk. She sensed his troubled gaze resting upon her face, but his expression did not alter. He was as fierce and savage as she recalled, all dark and chiseled, his eyes piercing her, holding her as a wolf holds his prey before attack. She knew the angry strength of which he was capable, and Claricia forced herself to say, "I did not expect to see you again."

Alexander could not speak. He had spent the past ten days trekking through the snow and preparing for this interview, readying himself to explain to Lady Claricia why he had made the journey to Eilean Fidra instead of a messenger.

Good evening, Lady Claricia. Have ye been treated well? he had planned to begin.

But now that he saw her he could not spit out the words. The little speech that he had prepared was lodged in his throat like a dry lump of porridge.

Ye did not suffer during the blizzard, I trust? Nay? That is good.

Instead, he stared down at her face, pale in the light that came through the crack in the curtain above his head, and he was struck by the unexpected sensation of how glad he was to see her.

It had been more than a full month since he'd bid farewell to Lady Claricia at Clar Innis, believing that he would never see her again. The parting, in his mind, had been a final one, and in those first days at Finlarig, he had not thought much about her. But as time had passed, particularly during the blizzard that had followed Lady Moira's arrival, he had found himself thinking of her. Little by little the memories and images of

Lady Claricia, the sights and sounds of her, even the smell of her, had returned to him, until it seemed hardly an hour passed that he did not pause to think of her.

"Are you come to take me to my uncle?" Claricia asked in a cool clear tone. She had managed to prevent her voice from trembling, but she had not managed to hide the horror that had widened her eyes with desperation.

Alexander could not bear to see the evidence of what her eyes revealed. Wanting to believe she was as evil as Aymer de Clinton, he had turned away from every hint to the contrary. He had let his hunger for vengeance cloud his common sense. Until now. *Are you come to take me to my uncle?* An awful sickness churned in his belly at the thought of that beast touching her. It had suited his purpose to believe she was a whore, and in the end, his treatment of this lady had made him no better than the *sassenach* bastard. He had done much that was dishonorable, and, feeling the weight of his shame, Alexander shifted his gaze away from the lady's eyes.

Claricia knew his silence could mean only one thing. It was time to leave. Time to say farewell to Frances and Sorcha, to kiss the bairn in the solar one more time, and to savor one final glimpse down the length of the loch at the distant curl of smoke rising from the Old Believer's Isle. Somewhere in the gray hills rising above Loch Awe her uncle's men-at-arms were waiting, and at dawn's first light, Alexander Kirkpatrick would take her to them. She knew that, but she needed to hear him say the words, and so she persisted. "Why are you here?"

Alexander raised his eyes to meet hers, green melding with blue, as a measure of her despair flowed into him. He shuddered, ragged and tired, never having felt so close to defeat. "This is my fortress. My chamber. My bed," he said in a dull voice as he sat down on the edge of the mattress. There was no greater meaning behind the words than what he had said aloud. He was bone-weary, and disgusted with the events that had brought him there. He was supposed to be on his way to join King Robert, not trekking through the snow to deliver an unpleasant message to a whore who was no whore, to a hostage who was no hostage.

Alexander rubbed the back of his hand across his eyes. Why was he there? The answer was not easy. Could it not have waited until morning? At that moment, he wanted nothing more than to lie down, close his eyes, and sleep for eight or nine hours. "I willna touch ye this night, my lady. I have traveled long and hard, and want nothing more than to rest in a true bed, in my own bed, for the first time in months."

"And I don't believe you." His words did not allay Claricia's anxiety. In a defiant little voice, she challenged, "You want nothing more than to rest? I seem to recall that you said something to that effect once before, but you were not true to your word then." Oh, how clear was her memory of that kiss in the cave, how vivid were a hundred other images of this man, and she was glad for the darkness within the curtained bed, glad that Alexander Kirkpatrick could not see the warmth rising in her cheeks. It was wrong to re-act like this, wrong to hold even a single favorable memory of this man. He was her enemy, her captor. He was a liar and a thief. "I do not trust you," she stated.

Alexander was too tired to smile. Of course, she was right. There was no reason for her to trust him, and when he saw that delicate chin tilting upward and her lips pursed in a stalwart defiant pout, warmth embraced him. As if by magic the winter chill faded, his blood quickened, and every nerve in his body awakened with awareness of the woman only inches away from him. But there was something more than the rising heat of physical desire that enveloped him. There was a certain contentment with a familiar sight that was pleasing to behold. He liked the look of Lady Claricia, and wished the light were not so dim. He could only imagine the flashing color in her eyes, the plum-ripe hue of her lips, and the hint of a blush across her brow and cheeks.

"Please go back to sleep. Ye're safe with me this night." He lifted the furs to crawl beneath them. The bed moved beneath his weight, and, lying on his side to face her, he supported his head on the palm of his hand. "Dinna fash yerself, my lady. I wouldna hurt ye," he vowed, but he knew right away the foolishness of making such a promise.

Staring down at Lady Claricia, Alexander could not avoid the truth. In the long miles through the glens from Loch Tay, he had been forced to reckon with many an unpleasant fact. Foremost among them was that he was guilty of hurting Lady Claricia no less than her uncle or, he was loath to admit, his brother, Andrew, had hurt her. And the worst of it was that he was going to do so again.

How easy it would have been if the message delivered from Dunblane had been a different one. How simple if that parting at Clar Innis had, indeed, been final. How uncomplicated if he looked at her and still saw naught but the niece of his most hated enemy. But that was not the case.

He had been the one to launch this plan to satisfy his thirst for vengeance, and he would be the one to see it through to its conclusion. There was much about his conduct the past weeks that was dishonorable, and with that in mind, Alexander was not going to allow himself to take the easy way out. By Christ's nails, what an unholy web he had woven.

"I am sorry, my lady," he whispered across the small distance that separated them.

Claricia's breath caught with bittersweet pleasure. No man had ever said that to her, and she trembled with the wonder of it. But could she forgive this man? she asked herself, studying him in the faint light that seeped through the threadbare hangings. What she saw upon Alexander Kirkpatrick's face and in his eyes touched her profoundly. There was no trace of rage, no hint of disdain, nothing to make her believe he did not mean what he said. This was neither the Highlander who had pulled her from the bed at Hepburn, nor the man who'd had his way with her on the straw mattress at Clar Innis. "You are forgiven," she whispered. The hatred had to stop somewhere.

"Nay, my lady, dinna pardon me, for ye know not yet every wrong I've done ye."

A chill ran up Claricia's spine. She could not imagine what he meant. What could be worse than what he'd already done? Sweet Jesu, had he found out about Simon? "Tell me," she demanded. "You must tell me what you mean."

His eyelids fell closed. He could not bear the fear and pain he saw in her eyes. Slowly, Alexander began. " 'Tis yer uncle—"

"He has paid the ransom, and I will be returned to him," Claricia said briskly, speaking on his behalf and wondering why Alexander Kirkpatrick should ask her pardon for this. It was where she belonged, as far as he was concerned; indeed, it was where he believed she wished to be.

"Nay, my lady."

She detected the effort he required to speak. That was curious, as was his answer. "What do you mean?"

"De Clinton has refused to pay the ransom," came Alexander's flat reply, followed by an awkward pause.

"I see," Claricia said in a quiet, stricken voice. While she did not wish to be returned to her uncle, his rejection was a blow nonetheless. How bitter it was to realize that her one living blood relation would not help her. It was hard to believe, even of a man who delighted in cruelty. She was, after all, his brother's only child. "My uncle refuses to pay for my release?"

"Aye," Alexander confirmed as he watched the pain he'd anticipated worm its way onto Lady Claricia's pretty face. She didn't deserve this utter abandonment, and he vowed that she would never know the content of de Clinton's message. *A soiled, ungrateful bitch,* Aymer de Clinton had called his niece in the missive. *. . . an unsatisfying shard of ice that is likely better off with a savage Highlander who might succeed where I have failed.* And that had not been the worst. De Clinton had concluded with wishes of good luck to Alexander Kirkpatrick, in the hopes that the laird would be able to teach the frigid wench how a woman ought to treat a man. *Mayhap I was too generous, and she will respond to your heathen ways.* The bile rose in his throat.

"What am I to do?" Claricia voiced the question aloud before she could stop herself. What did this man care? "Nay, sir, do not answer that. I want nothing from you save my freedom to leave this place at first light."

"I canna allow that."

"What say you? Why not? You have no need of me any longer."

Alexander shook his head. *Och, my lovely lady, but ye're wrong.* His whole body was aching for her. She was no shard of ice, as de Clinton asserted, but a woman trying to protect herself the only way she could. There was a sensual creature dwelling within Lady Claricia's heart and soul; he knew that as surely as he knew he could not let her go without showing her that there could be beauty in the joining of a man and a woman. Nay, Alexander corrected himself in the same heartbeat. He would show her that beauty but he could not let her go, and not because it would be wrong to turn her out, but because he had suddenly realized he wanted her for his own, not merely for one night of passion, but for always.

"Speak, sir," Claricia implored. She did not like
the expression upon his face. He had the look of
a hungry animal. She was afraid of what he
might do next. "Say something. Why won't you
let me go?"

"I have wronged ye. Indeed, I am not the only
one in my family who has wronged ye. I am as
guilty as my brother, perhaps more, for I sought
to avenge yer uncle's cruelty with another act of
cruelty. That was wrong. I said once before I
dinna murder women, but what I forgot in my
blind obsession to get at yer uncle was that it was
wrong to wage war on women. If I set ye free, ye
have no future, not with yer people or with mine.
And so I intend to marry ye."

"Marry me?" Claricia spat out in shock, too
stunned by his pronouncement to move away.
"Do not flatter yourself or make this attempt to
be noble. It doesn't become you." But the truth
was that it did become him. There was an uncertain softness about his eyes. Sweet Heaven, was
he worried that she was going to reject him?
Well, what else did he expect?

"If ye'd had the choice, I know I'm not the kind
of mon ye would have wanted to wed. Having
had a sister, I ken that lassies have pretty dreams,
and since ye're English, I'm sure yers were of a
comfortable, rambling house with tidy gardens,
not some bleak gray fortress at the end of nowhere. I'm told England is verra green, and lush
with posies. Mayhap ye dreamed of a handsome
English lordling, fair of face and hair like yerself.
A devoted lord who wouldna leave yer side to
fight or shed blood. And I'm sure yer dream was

filled with plump English bairns with rosy cheeks, tugging at yer skirts and playing tag in that tidy garden while yer fair-haired lordling husband held yer hand and vowed his undying love." There was not a trace of mockery in his words, only sorrow, as if he actually felt the emptiness of her lost dreams. In a low, sad voice, Alexander ended with, "None of that can ever be, but I can promise ye the protection of the Kirkpatrick name and clan. Ye will be honored as my wife and chatelaine, and my loyalty will be no less than that of the clanspeople of Eilean Fidra."

A lump lodged itself in Claricia's throat; her lower lip began to quiver, and she held it between her teeth to keep it still. How could *Alexander Kirkpatrick* have seen inside her heart and known about the children and the manor house in faraway England? Tears pooled in her eyes. Even in the dim light of the curtained bed they shimmered like tiny dewdrops on the ends of her long lashes.

"Please, my lady, dinna cry," he said on a soft whisper. "I didna mean to distress ye."

There was infinite gentleness in his voice. It rang with the very kindness for which Claricia had so desperately yearned. A single tear escaped one eye, then a second, and a third. Rourke O'Connor had been right. Somewhere inside Alexander Kirkpatrick there was a good man. It was this awful war that had made these men into such twisted creatures. Everyone deserved better. She sniffled back the tears. "But am I the sort of woman you would have chosen for yourself?" she asked, wondering what manner of man would marry a whore and a murderess.

"That isna important," Alexander said in a gruff voice meant to hide the truth. There had never been any other woman to inflame his senses as Lady Claricia did, no other woman with whom he could imagine spending more than a few nights without being bored, no other woman who had infected his blood like a fever. It was a shameful thing, this weakness, this obsession, and Alexander did not want her to know there was another, much more personal reason, why he must wed her. Marrying Lady Claricia would take away the guilt, for a man could not shame himself by surrendering to his own wife, even if she was a *sassenach*.

"*Am pos thu mi, ròs geall?*" Alexander leaned closer. Beneath the furs, he found one of her hands and held it between his as he looked into her eyes and whispered, "I'm asking ye right and proper, my lady. *Am pos thu mi, ròs geall? Will ye marry me, white rose?*"

Within Claricia, heart and sense collided. The touch of Alexander's long, slender fingers wrapped about her hand sent shock waves through her body, while his words rocked her heart. Alexander had called her "my lady" with naught but sincerity. He had called her "white rose" in a voice vibrating with tenderness, and Claricia's heart skipped a beat. The beginning of a smile tugged at the corners of her mouth. Being his wife would not be half as bad as being her uncle's whore. Although there would not be love, there would be kindness, something that was perhaps rarer than love. She could not turn away from that. And the best, of course, was that if she married Alexander Kirkpatrick, she would not be leaving Loch Awe. She would be able to stay at Eilean Fidra, where she could see Meg and Simon. Marrying Alexander Kirkpatrick was not a hard price to pay. Only a fool would have tried to refuse him.

"Och, my lady, is that the whisper of a smile I see upon yer bonny face?" One strong, masculine hand reached out and lingered at the corner of her mouth. She nodded, he grinned, and in that moment, something started to blossom between them, something fragile and inexplicable. He felt it as surely as she must have done, for he witnessed the mystified widening of her eyes; he felt her hand relax in his as a little bit of warmth was transmitted from her to him and back again. "While I would like to take credit for that hint of happiness, I willna be so arrogant. Though I do promise to try to make it happen more often."

Claricia's pulse was racing. Her skin tingled where Alexander had touched her face, and her tongue flicked out to moisten her lips, inadvertently brushing his fingertip. She heard his sharp intake of breath, saw the fire that lit his dragon-green eyes. Her mouth parted slightly. Was he going to kiss her? Oddly, the idea did not repulse her, and she waited. The pad of his thumb rubbed against her cheek as if to restore the tiny smile, then his hand fell away. He did not kiss her, and in the dim light, she saw a curious look of something like regret sweep over his face.

"Go back to sleep," he murmured. His fingers were in her hair, brushing it gently off her brow as he settled her back against the pillows. "Go back to sleep. There will be much to discuss on

the morrow, my lady, for my lady ye shall truly
be before the week is out."

Several hours later the familiar sounds of
Frances attending to her morning chores filled the
chamber. Claricia stretched her arms and legs.
There was someone in the bed beside her. It was
Alexander Kirkpatrick, and as the memories of
what had happened in the night returned to her,
Claricia experienced a most unusual sense of ex-
citement to begin the day.

She scooted from beneath the covers to sit at
the bed's edge, her feet dangling toward the floor.
In the past weeks at Eilean Fidra, she had become
a member of the household, and while Frances
might have lit the brazier and set out her kirtle,
Claricia could not lie in bed as if hers were a life
of leisure. Every able-bodied soul was needed to
help maintain a fortress, especially in the dead of
winter. That morning, she was going to help with
the baking. In the past, she had never liked cooking, but that was not the case anymore. There was
something comforting about attending to domes-
tic tasks in the company of other women. She
must hurry. In addition to her chores, Claricia
wanted to find Rourke and ask him to take her
to the island. She had to tell Meg about her
change in plans.

Before pulling the bed curtains closed, Claricia
glanced over her shoulder to look at Alexander
deep in sleep. This man was soon to be her husband, and the idea left her more than a little
breathless. In repose, the anger and bitterness
that usually marked his features were not there.
Still, he was nothing like her fair lordling, and

she tried to picture this rugged Highlander in the rose garden of some faraway English manor house. Alexander Kirkpatrick's image was oversized and awkward in such a setting, and she frowned. Then the image was gone. Instead, she saw a clear vision of him standing on a gargantuan gray rock, the ragged mountains rising behind him, wind tugging at his black braids. He was pointing toward some distant sight, as if he ruled the whole of the wild, untamed world. Claricia didn't know why, but seeing this pleased her enormously. Indeed, she suddenly didn't care about that garden, with its perfectly pruned rose bushes.

What Alexander Kirkpatrick was doing for her extended far beyond mere kindness, and while it would never erase the past, Claricia was determined to ensure that he would never regret his decision to make her his wife. *His wife.* To consider what the words meant made her at once hopeful and thankful, nervous and uncertain. She would do her best to please him in every sense. It was the least she could do. Indeed, it would be her duty.

Claricia stood and closed the bed curtains. She held a finger to her lips. "We must be quiet, Frances. The laird needs his sleep."

"Aye, mistress," Frances replied in a low voice. After Claricia had visited the garderobe, Frances helped her slip the purple kirtle over her undertunic and brought a pair of snug boots, and a length of leather to tie back her hair. Then the two women exited the chamber. "We have visitors," Frances informed Claricia as they made their way down the narrow winding stairs to the hall.

"Warriors?"

"Nay. It is some women from Finlarig, where the laird bided his time during the snow. *Sassenach* soldiers were sighted on Loch Tay, and the laird offered the sanctuary of Eilean Fidra to the women." Frances paused to turn toward Claricia. "Lady Moira is among them. She is their leader, in fact."

"The girl who was once the laird's betrothed?"

"Aye, and she got her dream, it seems. Married a rich Edinburgh merchant, she did. But all that gold and a fine town house were no protection when the English army took the city and hung her rebel husband. She was taken prisoner and forced to whoring. *Diobrachan*, an outcast in exile, is what some might call her for having carnal knowledge of the enemy. But my mam says to pay no heed to what others say, and to be charitable," Frances hastened to add, failing to notice that Claricia appeared to be absorbed in her own distant thoughts. "And when I look upon Lady Moira, Mam says, I ought to be telling myself that 'There but for the Grace of the Almighty Father—' "

Goswick Keep. An image flashed across Claricia's memory. She saw the huddle of bedraggled, desperate women in the courtyard below the tower window. All the gold in the world could not have stopped those soldiers or her uncle, and for the first time, she wondered if there was anything that might have stopped Andrew Kirkpatrick. She did not imagine there was. Men were the same, it seemed, no matter to which monarch they owed allegiance.

"There but for the Grace of the Almighty Father . . ."

Some of what Frances was saying seeped into Claricia's consciousness, and her mind returned to the present from its troublesome reverie in the past.

Two more steps brought Frances and Claricia around the final bend in the stairs, where the noise from the hall carried into the stairwell, to be magnified by the cold stone walls. Eilean Fidra was a bustle of activity that morning. There were more mouths to feed. So, too, were there more hands to help. Sorcha and Moira were busy when Claricia entered. They had been to one of the storerooms hidden deep beneath the castle for another sack of barley flour and a few precious yards of wool. Four of the women would serve as warders, and for them, there would be new shawls. The others had eagerly accepted responsibilities in the kitchens or stables. The outcast women were eager to work in exchange for the chance to be part of a community.

Sorcha glanced upward and saw Claricia. "Here is our other visitor," she said by way of beginning an introduction between the Englishwoman and Lady Moira. Sorcha smiled warmly. "Lady Claricia comes to break her fast. Good morning to ye."

"You are entirely too civil, Sorcha," said Claricia, making reference to how everyone at Eilean Fidra so delicately skirted the truth. They all knew she had never been a visitor. She was a prisoner, kidnapped to avenge the wrongs against their clan, and although the look upon Lady Moira's face made it clear that the Scottish noblewoman also knew the truth, there was nothing in her voice to hint of that truth when she spoke. Despite her wretched appearance and the folly of her youth, Lady Moira was a lady. After the introductions, Claricia said, "It appears my visit shall be extended. My uncle has refused to pay the ransom."

Sorcha's expression softened with concern. She had suspected as much when the laird had returned in the night with a troubled expression upon his face. "And does that please ye, my lady?"

"Yes, it does," was Claricia's reflective reply as she studied Sorcha's and Moira's faces in an attempt to discover how much Alexander Kirkpatrick had told them. It did not appear that either of them knew their laird intended to make his English prisoner his wife. Nor did it appear that they were surprised by her answer.

"We would have missed ye." Sorcha spoke with affection. Like everyone at Eilean Fidra, Sorcha had become fond of Lady Claricia. No one had been able to reconcile the rumors of the Beast's Bawd with the gracious young woman who had been delivered into their keeping by Rourke O'Connor. Even the two old Maeris had come to accept her, and Sorcha had been praying for the strength to bid Lady Claricia farewell when the time arrived to send her back to Aymer de Clinton. Sorcha made the sign of the cross. Her prayers had been answered, although not in the way she had hoped. "The good Lord has been merciful, I think."

"You are a true Christian, Sorcha."

"Nay, only honest. I follow the lead of Alexander Kirkpatrick and the auld laird, and all the lairds before them. The Kirkpatricks have always been tolerant, generous, just, and forgiving." Pride laced her voice.

"Eilean Fidra is a special place, I discover." Moira spoke up, her words seeming to imply how lamentable it was that she'd been too vain not to have made the discovery all those years before.

"That it is," agreed Claricia.

The double doors to the main entrance opened, and a gust of wind carrying a whorl of snow heralded the arrival of Maxwel of Ballimeanoch and Rourke O'Connor. The two men, bundled in furs, shuffled into the hall, clapping their arms against their chests for warmth. Rourke strode toward the fire pit, leaving a path of melting snow on the stone floor, but Maxwel did not approach. Instead, he went to the bench and sat, as he always did, at a distance from the others.

"Who is that?" Moira asked Claricia.

"Rourke O'Connor."

"Nay, the other one who doesna venture near us."

"He does not venture near anyone. He is Maxwel of Ballimeanoch."

"Och, ye dinna mean it." Moira emitted a disbelieving clucking noise. "It canna be Maxwel of Ballimeanoch, not with such gray hair and the stooped walk of a verra auld mon. I recall a handsome young clansman, flirting with all those lassies and trying to get beneath every kirtle he might."

"Do I hear ye, Moira MacCruarie?"

Moira paled and averted her face from the corner bench upon which Maxwell brooded.

"Speak up, lass."

"I dinna want him to see me," Moira whispered frantically, positioning herself behind Claricia so that she could not be seen.

"While I dinna usually come into the hall to break my fast, I made an exception when I heard the bonniest lassie in the Highlands had deigned to come to modest Eilean Fidra. Come, Lady Moira, speak up. Dinna disappoint an auld friend."

Claricia was moved by the panic and embarrassment that Lady Moira revealed. Only moments before, she had seemed strong and resilient, and Claricia had been admiring and envious. She noticed that Sorcha was looking at Moira with undisguised impatience, but Claricia understood. Softly, she said, "Do not worry, Lady Moira. Maxwell will see only what he wants."

"I dinna recall such a kindly mon."

"He is blind, Lady Moira."

The expression on Moira's face altered as if she had been struck in the chest. "I forget I am not the only one to have suffered."

Claricia had never heard a truer word, yet she could do nothing but nod as a feeling of great humility washed over her while all thoughts of past suffering gave way to the consideration of how her life was about to change: just when it seemed everything of value had been taken from her and she had no future, she was going to have a husband, a family, and a home. It did not matter that she would spend the rest of her life in this wild corner of the Highlands or that there would be no love in her marriage. That was not important in comparison to all that she would be gaining. For the first time since her mother's death, the future did not seem a bleak, unendurable thing. Gently, she nudged Lady Moira toward the bench in the far corner. "Go on, talk with him. Mayhap you could encourage him to come within the arc of the fire's warmth. I have tried but failed."

Something in Moira relented, and a measure of her earlier fortitude returned. She grinned. "I have always liked a challenge." And with that, Lady Moira turned and walked toward Maxwel of Ballimeanoch.

Claricia looked around. Rourke was standing by her, looking at her with a quizzical expression. *He knows*, she realized. Alexander Kirkpatrick had told his Irish kinsman the whole of what had occurred and what was still to happen. "Good morning, Rourke O'Connor."

"Lady Claricia, *dhia dhuit*," he replied with a polite nod. Since Viviane's visit to the fortress, Rourke had interjected increasingly more Gaelic into his discourse with Lady Claricia. At first, it had been a sort of test to discover the extent of her knowledge of the language. It was, as he suspected, extensive. Now the use of Gaelic was more of a habit.

"I've a favor to ask of you."

He tilted his head in query.

"Would you be able to show me the way to Viviane's island today?"

It was as if Rourke had known Lady Claricia would ask this of him, and without question, he complied willingly. "Aye, I should be pleased to take ye across the ice. 'Tis a fine day. The sun shines brightly in a clear blue sky. If ye have no pressing tasks, we can leave within the hour and be back before nightfall."

"I can be ready."

And they were off before Alexander awakened.

Chapter 11

"**Y**e're going to marry him!" Meg fairly screeched at Claricia. She stood with her arms akimbo, that wild black hair falling to her waist, as she glared at the delicate golden-haired Englishwoman sitting on a crude stool in her one-room hut.

"You need not sound so disgusted." Claricia retorted. This rapid exchange was in Gaelic. Rourke and Simon were not present, having gone to check the snares that had been set the afternoon before in the woods beyond the clearing.

"But he raped ye."

Claricia neither denied nor affirmed this. "It does not matter. It can't matter."

"*Eist!* I think ye're besotted with him. Or possessed by the fairies. There are evil ones, y'know. Wee little devils that tempt good souls to do bad things."

"Nay, Meg. I'm neither besotted nor possessed. 'Tis practical I'm being. Think on it; what other future is there for me, now that my uncle has refused to pay the ransom? Can you imagine there is anywhere in England for the Beast's Bawd? Anyone who would welcome me into their household?"

223

"Bi'd thosd!" Meg hissed beneath her breath in the way an angry parent would chastise a child. *Hold yer tongue!* She could not bear to hear Claricia speak disparagingly of herself. "So Alexander Kirkpatrick announces he'll marry ye, and ye tell yerself ye should be grateful for such a blessing."

"It is no little thing from which to turn away," Claricia said with cool certainty, but Meg was not convinced.

"Consider what ye're doing, and how willingly ye trade one devil for another! *Bheil thu ad chiall?*" Meg demanded. "*Are ye in yer wits?*"

"Alexander Kirkpatrick is not as awful as my uncle." Claricia spoke in an oddly composed tone. How strange it was to hear Meg voice aloud the very thoughts that she had managed to dismiss from her mind. "There is not a shred of goodness in my uncle, but with Alexander Kirkpatrick, it is different. I trust his promise that there will be no pain or humiliation for his wife."

"Trust him?" Meg threw up her hands toward the low ceiling in a display of sheer consternation, then wagged a finger at Claricia. "Ye're defending the mon, and ye'll regret it. Mark my words. Ye'll regret it."

"Perhaps," Claricia admitted, knowing better than to believe in nursery-tale endings. Although there might have been a kindly, honorable man beneath the angry warrior, there was no way to predict which man would be her husband. "But I cannot afford to worry about possible regrets. Only the here and now matters. What matters is that marriage to Alexander Kirkpatrick means that you and I do not have to bid each other farewell. Instead, we shall be able to renew our friendship, and I shall be able to see Simon as he grows from a small lad to a young man. You can move to the castle and—"

"Nay!"

"Whyever not?"

"Ye may be able to forgive Alexander Kirkpatrick, but not I. He has behaved no better than the *sassenach* scum in yer uncle's courtyard, and he shouldna be allowed to call himself a Highlander or a laird. A mon such as Alexander Kirkpatrick doesna deserve to breathe the same air ye do."

Claricia was taken aback by this vehement assertion. "I did not know you were so stubborn."

Meg shrugged as she tossed back her head, a thick curl tumbling over her shoulder. Her green eyes narrowed. Her voice was sharp. "And dinna expect me to attend yer wedding and give ye my blessings."

"I had hoped—"

"Och, dinna cling to hope. Have ye not learned by now?" Meg stared at Claricia, her mind churning with the same thought that always came to her when she considered Claricia. Her English friend had been, and still was, too charitable and tenderhearted for her own sake. It amazed Meg to see how Claricia could remain innocent and hopeful in light of all that had happened. "I am sorry to sound so disparaging."

"You should be," Claricia said with a gentle smile. "Oh, Meg, can't you see just the tiniest bit of goodness in all of this?"

"Aye, 'tis a good thing ye're not going back to yer uncle. That much I will admit."

Claricia grinned. "And was that so hard? The words did not poison you, did they?"

Meg returned the smile, and a light ripple of laughter passed between them as they embraced. "I will be glad for ye, if that is what ye wish. But I willna attend yer wedding. And while I will gladly continue to be your friend, dinna expect me to pretend I like yer husband. Dinna ye remember our pledge?"

Many fervent adolescent pledges had been made between the girls, and Claricia could not imagine to which one Meg referred. They had never talked of husbands or weddings. They had never thought that far ahead. Indeed, they'd never imagined such futures for themselves.

Meg saw Claricia's uncertainty, and a sense of loss enveloped her like a heavy cloak. "We promised to protect each other, and I vowed to repay ye for rescuing me from yer uncle's men. I said I would do anything, even shed another's blood, if need be, to see ye safe."

"That debt has been repaid, Meg, a thousand times over. I want nothing from you but your friendship. Besides, when we made those promises we had no one but each other. Now you have Rourke, and I will have Alexander Kirkpatrick."

The mention of Rourke brought a glow to Meg's cheeks that faded in the next instant. She opened her mouth to challenge Alexander Kirkpatrick's motives, when the sound of Simon's voice in the clearing outside the hut stopped her.

"Mam! Mam, wait 'til ye see. 'Tis the biggest, plumpest pheasant ever caught in the Highlands."

The door burst open, and Simon rushed inside,

holding forth a dead bird for Meg's inspection. Rourke entered behind the lad and stood off to one side as Simon launched into a recitation of how he'd set the snare. The Irishman watched the two women, and, sensing the bond between them, he was glad for both of them. Glad that his Viviane would again have the companionship of another female, and glad for Lady Claricia that she would not be going back to Aymer de Clinton, although marrying his kinsman was unlikely to produce any sort of happy ending. He knew that Alexander Kirkpatrick wasn't entering into this union with any intention of being a husband for very long.

It had been sometime after the household had retired the previous evening when Alexander had slipped into Eilean Fidra. He had roused no one except Rourke, who had assisted the women from Finlarig up the slippery path to the front gate, and after settling the travelers on pallets in the hall, the Highlander and Irishman had removed themselves to the privacy of the solar. It was there that Alexander had told Rourke of de Clinton's refusal to pay the ransom.

"And what of Lady Claricia?" Rourke had asked. "What do ye intend to do with her?"

"I will marry the wench," Alexander had stated without any trace of emotion as he sat down in a chair and leaned over to unlace his boots. He had not removed them from his feet, but had stretched his legs out before him and wriggled his toes to restore their circulation. He had not even looked up at Rourke when he added, "And at the first sign of a thaw, I will leave for Stirling."

"To make Lady Claricia a widow." There had been an accusatory edge in Rourke's manner. He admired his kinsman for deciding to marry the lady. It could not have been an easy choice, given the circumstances. On the other hand, he did not think well of Alexander for the cold manner in which he could so easily dismiss his life, so easily turn away from a chance at happiness. It was possible, Rourke believed, for a man to find peace and contentment even with the niece of his most bitter enemy. The powers of the heart were beyond man's control. It was Fate, his grandfather Ingvar had asserted, that dictated the destiny of one's heart, and Rourke did not like to consider what might happen if Alexander were to deny his Fate.

Alexander had raised his head. "It will not matter one way or the other. If death awaits me, Lady Claricia will at least have survived with a place to call home."

But Rourke had sensed something more behind Alexander's reasoning. He had sensed that Alexander had felt Fate tugging, not upon his mortality, but perhaps upon his sensibilities. "Ye have a tender heart for the lass."

"I am human, after all," Alexander had rejoined, again avoiding Rourke's gaze by directing his attention to his toes. " 'Tis nothing more than that."

"It would not be hard to fall in love with a woman such as Lady Claricia, who has remained beautiful and kind in spite of all that has happened to her." This time, there had been sympathy and understanding in Rourke's voice.

"What would ye ken of such things?" Alexander had demanded, sitting bolt upright on the chair. "Ye speak as if ye know Lady Claricia."

"We talked during our journey from Clar Innis."

"Talked?" Alexander had tilted his head to the side, one thick black brow had shot upward, and his gaze had narrowed with suspicion upon Rourke. "And what else?"

"Is that jealousy?" Rourke had asked.

At that, Alexander had lunged forward in a half-seated position from the chair. His arm had swung upward as if in readiness to strike his Irish cousin.

"Whoa." Rourke had taken a sideways step out of his way. "If ye wish to defend the lady's honor, I'm not the one with whom ye have a score to settle."

Alexander had collapsed back in the chair, where he had remained motionless for a few heartbeats. A muscle along his jaw had twitched as he reached for a wooden goblet on a nearby table. He had taken a long, deep drink, then wiped his mouth with his sleeve. "I am tired. Tired from the journey, weary of this war, and of the bloodshed and brutality. Ye're right, Rourke. An incurable disease festers in me, and as always, de Clinton is the source. I am nearly spent, and want it to end, but I fear only death will assuage the sickness churning within me. Nothing else will suffice. I will wed Lady Claricia and depart as soon as possible to join King Robert's army gathering in the Torwood, and when the English army arrives, I will seek out Aymer de Clinton to drive a sword through his heart. Only then will I be able to die with honor."

Only then will ye be able to live, was what Rourke had thought the night before, but he had not spoken those words aloud to Alexander, for he did not think his kinsman had yet found any reason for which to live, save vengeance, and therein lay the greatest tragedy in all of this. He was turning away from Fate. He was turning away from the future.

Standing in the cooking corner of Viviane's hut, Rourke studied Lady Claricia and wondered if Alexander had concluded his proposal by informing his betrothed that he would be going into battle shortly after the wedding. Did she even care? Probably not, considering how he had treated her, and doubtless that was a good thing, since Alexander Kirkpatrick was bound to break Lady Claricia's heart whether he lived or died.

"Rourke, I am glad you return," said Claricia when Simon had finished his hunting tale and handed the bird to Meg to be plucked and readied for roasting. "Your aid is needed. Can you not convince Viviane to come to the wedding ceremony?" During their walk to the island, Claricia had confided in Rourke, who had informed her that he already knew of Alexander Kirkpatrick's marital intentions. But he had not said anything more, and, as on more than one previous occasion, Claricia had sensed that Rourke O'Connor knew much more than he showed he did. He knew that she and Meg were not strangers to each other. He knew that her relationship with Alexander Kirkpatrick had gone beyond that of captor and prisoner. He was a wise man. She could tell by the reflective way he observed people and events, his was a mind both keenly logical and intuitive. But was he discreet? Soon Claricia would try to discern the extent of what Rourke knew, and if he had told anyone of it.

"Convince me? Dinna even venture to try such a thing, Rourke O'Connor. And, mind ye, none of yer sweet kisses will tempt me either." Meg's eyes flashed with determination, and Rourke knew better than to go against her. Abruptly, she changed the subject. "There were visitors who arrived with the laird, ye say?" She looked to Claricia for response.

"One of them is Moira MacCruarie, the daughter of an old ally of the Kirkpatrick's. She has been leading a group of *diobrachain* through the Highlands." Claricia did not mention that this was the same Moira MacCruarie who had once been betrothed to Alexander Kirkpatrick. It made no difference any longer. "They were captives of the English, but were released some months ago. Lady Moira led them to her father's castle, but it was not safe there."

Meg closed her eyes as the memory of being a captive revisited her. She recalled the constant pain from the harsh treatment, the countless miles traveled on foot while shackled, and how even the smallest glance from any one of the soldiers had caused her blood to chill. They had touched her and fondled her, pinched and delved and squeezed, only to laugh at her humiliation. So, too, did she recall how the older women had tried to protect her, to disguise her as a lad or hide her beneath a plaid, and when that had failed, how one of the women had let herself be taken in her place. The name Moira MacCruarie struck a chord in Meg's memory. Perhaps she knew this woman. Perhaps they had been imprisoned or had traveled together. Mayhap Moira MacCruarie would know who she was. But Meg did not toy long with the notion of seeking out this Lady Moira to ask her about her past, for Meg did not want to know the truth any longer.

Her life with Simon and Rourke was a full one. It was more than many women had ever dared to dream of having, and one day in the spring, there on her island, in the pretty green clearing, she would exchange vows with Rourke. That was what Meg wanted. Perhaps it was wrong of her, but she did not want to revive ghosts or go backward and make sense of her past. What if she had discovered something about herself or her real family that could destroy her present? Meg did not want to take that risk. The past was not important to her. Only the future mattered.

Their small hut was warm and dry. It had been built by caring hands. Rourke had constructed the exterior with a system of double walls, which he and Simon had filled with earth. Together, the three of them had whitewashed the interior, made the simple furnishings, and gathered the wild flowers, which Meg had dried and hung from the beamed ceiling. It was her home. Indeed, it was their home. She was not surrounded by a large extended family of parents and cousins, grandparents, aunts and uncles, but Meg was secure with those she did have. She could trust Rourke, and now she had Claricia. She did not need anything more, anyone else. The very notion of stirring up the past was a threatening proposition to Meg, and thus, she did not mention the familiarity of Moira's name to Claricia.

Meg did not want anyone mucking up her past, and she knew all too well that Claricia would try to make it right. Claricia would not understand why Meg would choose to turn away from uncovering the truth.

It was time for Claricia's brief visit to end. Soon the sun would slip below the horizon and winter darkness would cloak the loch. Rourke would walk Claricia halfway across the ice before returning to spend the night with Meg on the island. In three days, he would go to Eilean Fidra for the wedding ceremony, and Claricia promised Meg that she would return to the island as soon as possible.

Rourke led their way along the narrow passage that had been cut through the deep snow. The path was rough, uneven, and extremely slippery, the afternoon's bright sun having melted the top layer of snow, which had turned to ice when the sun began to set. Carefully, Claricia tried to place her boots into existing imprints, and for about ten minutes, she and Rourke were concentrating so hard on keeping their footing that they did not speak. After a while, they became accustomed to the slow and cautious manner in which they had to walk, and Claricia dared to glance at Rourke from beneath the hood of her cloak.

"You have figured it out," Claricia said in a way that sounded more like a question than a statement. She had to find out how much he knew and what he might have said to anyone else, in particular to Alexander Kirkpatrick. "You know that Meg and I were friends in another time and place."

"What did ye call her?"

Claricia nearly lost her footing on the icy surface. Rourke grabbed her elbow to steady her as she looked up at him and whispered, "Meg." There was no point in pretending she hadn't let the name slip. "But it is not her name. My mother and I gave it to her, for she had forgotten hers."

"She remembered naught of her past and family when ye knew her? Not even her own name?"

"Yes," came her reluctant reply.

Rourke looked at Lady Claricia and saw that this discourse was deeply troubling to her. Obviously, there were secrets she did not wish to reveal, but Rourke could not ignore this chance to learn more about the woman he loved. He considered what Claricia had said. She had mentioned her mother, which meant that all of this must have been a very long time ago. Carefully, he fished about for more information. "You and your mother found her, then?"

"No." There could be no harm in revealing this part of the truth, and Claricia told Rourke about that day in the yard at Goswick Keep. She mentioned the years they had lived together more as sisters than as mistress and maid, growing ever more dependent upon each other after Lady Johanna's death.

Rourke listened and gave a grim nod, understanding at last the dimension of the bond between the two young women. His Viviane probably would not have been alive if it had not been for Lady Claricia. Swiftly, his mind considered the implications and possibilities, and like piecing together an old Roman mosaic, he knew without being told that Meg, or Viviane, or whoever she was, had been more than willing to raise another woman's child to repay such a priceless debt. But Lady Claricia had not mentioned the lad, and Rourke did not venture to pursue that subject. Instead, he tried to find out more about from where his Viviane might have come, and therefore, to which clan she might belong. "Goswick Keep is below Berwick. She was a Lowland lass, then?"

"Do not try to figure out the puzzle," Claricia warned softly. She wanted to reassure Rourke. Uncertainty and worry were visible upon his features, as was his devotion to Meg. This was not a man who was prying with the intent of bearing tales. "The answer is often worse than the mystery. You should know only that no matter who she once was, Meg is yours now. Nothing will change that."

"I wish I had yer optimism."

Claricia nodded, but she could not speak. She knew only too well how fragile was the future, and she turned away from Rourke to look straight ahead. They had come halfway across the loch. She could cover the final distance to Eilean Fidra on her own. "Thank you for showing me the way to the island."

"It was nothing. I will see ye in another few days, and I shall be pleased to dance at yer wedding," he said with a smile. "In the meantime, ye mustna fash yerself, for I willna breathe a word to anyone about"—he paused, then said— "Meg."

Claricia was satisfied with Rourke's promise to keep their secret. They went their separate ways. Claricia hurried through the gloaming afternoon

to the fortress that was to be her home, and
Rourke returned to Viviane and Simon.

Alexander stood beneath the raised portcullis
while Claricia ascended the steep path from the
frozen loch to the castle gate. It had been several
hours since he'd awakened, to learn she had gone
with Rourke to the Old Believer's Isle, and in that
time, he'd caught himself straying outside to look
across the expanse of white. He was waiting for
her, he admitted to himself with no little sense of
shock. Even more surprising was the realization
that he did not like the fact that she'd left Eilean
Fidra, if only for the space of an afternoon. He
had never considered himself a possessive man
when it came to females, and this reaction toward
Lady Claricia was unexpected. It was not as if
there were any sentiment of the heart attached to
his decision to marry her.

She neared the top of the icy path, where the
footing became treacherous, and he stepped forward to extend a hand and help her up the last
few steps to level ground.

"Hello!" Claricia said as if she'd known he
would be waiting for her. Her demeanor was cor-
dial, but she did not smile. It made Alexander
recall how she had almost smiled the night before, and all he could think was that he wanted
to see a smile as broad as the sea and as bright
as the sun upon her face.

"What were ye doing?" Alexander asked, letting her hand drop as they walked side by side
down the length of the covered entry that led into
the outer bailey.

"I was walking," she answered simply. The

wind tugged at her cloak, the hood fell back, and she brushed several golden strands of hair from her face.

Alexander frowned. He did not like this half-truth. He knew she had been to the Old Believer's Isle. "Is that all?"

"Did you think I had left?" She asked the question before she might stop herself.

"Of course not," came his quick, defensive response. But he had thought that, if only for a moment. So, too, had he worried about the quickly descending night. Hungry beasts prowled the hills, and a woman on her own would have very little chance of warding off an attack.

Claricia paused to try to measure the meaning of his behavior. It appeared that the sudden change in their relationship was as strange for Alexander Kirkpatrick as it was for her. "Where would I have gone?" she asked. "Indeed, sir, why would I leave?"

Her candor caught Alexander off guard. "I didna treat ye well," he replied, matching her honesty.

"Better than my uncle ever did," she said in a soft sad voice. "Besides, you have offered me a future. My uncle never did that."

Alexander's gut lurched. *You have offered me a future.* Rourke had been right to berate him for the carelessness with which he had been willing to dismiss a future with her. The circumstances of their union would not matter once they had exchanged their vows. In becoming his wife, she would no longer be Claricia de Clinton. Her name would be Kirkpatrick, and beyond marrying her to give her a home, beyond marrying her to justify his lust for her, he found that he wanted to make her days as his wife good ones. It was an ambition both sobering and humbling.

It had been a long time since he'd thought of his parents in a way that didn't entail their brutal deaths, yet in that moment, standing with Lady Claricia in the darkening outer bailey, a vision of his mother and father came to Alexander, a vision that recalled the affection and tenderness that they'd had for each other. As a lad, he'd watched them sitting at the head table, often holding hands, his mother always willing to dance a *reel o tullochgorm* with his father, who began and ended any dance with his wife by placing a lingering kiss upon her lips.

In his youth, Alexander had thought that sort of marriage might one day be his, but his illusions had long since been dashed. Starting with Lady Moira's rejection and ending with de Clinton's crimes against his clan, he'd lost all belief in love, all hope for anything other than vengeance and dying an honorable death. Now he saw his parents: he heard his mother's pretty laughter in response to something his father had said. His father had flirted with her even when their eldest bairns had grown to men and gray hairs had appeared amongst the ink-black braids encircling her brow. He had loved her to the end.

"Come with me, my lady," Alexander said to Claricia. Recalling this vision of his parents had reminded him there was something he must do. He took Claricia's hand and pulled her toward the tower entrance.

"What?" she stammered, bewildered by his sudden urgency.

"Just wait," was his mysterious reply. Alexander did not elaborate as they ascended the stairs to his chamber, and upon entering, he directed Claricia to sit upon the heavy carved chair positioned near the brazier.

Claricia watched as he crossed the room to crouch down by the far wall, his long legs folding beneath him with a grace that seemed impossible for any man. Slowly, he ran his palm back and forth along the floor, and not finding what he wanted, he moved several paces to one side, where he ran his hand over the stones once again. This time, he located what he was searching for, and, using his dirk, he loosened one of the stones, then lifted it from its place in the floor. With his other hand, he reached inside the hole.

There was something in his hand when he stood, and Claricia sat at the edge of the chair, eager to see what would happen next. As he walked toward her, he opened his palm to reveal a small leather pouch.

"There is a story behind this," Alexander said. He untied the cord at the top of the pouch to get at whatever was inside. "Hold out yer hand."

Claricia obeyed, and wondered as she did why her hand was trembling, why the oddest flush of warmth was spreading from the tips of her toes to the top of her head. For a second, she closed her eyes, partly in anticipation, partly to absorb the warmth radiating through her.

Something cool touched her palm. Instinctively, her fingers closed about the object. It was a smooth, odd-shaped stone. She unclenched her fingers, opened her eyelids, and stared in wonderment at a dappled green stone that had been carved into the shape of a heart. It was attached to an old velvet cord, and Claricia could not help herself when she held the stone heart against her cheek. "How lovely it is."

"It was my mother's," he explained. "She was a Hepburn. Catherine was her name, and my father gave it to her upon their betrothal. Before that, it belonged to my grandmother, Lady Isobel. It was a gift from her husband, Malcolm Kirkpatrick."

"You imply it was not a betrothal token."

"Aye, for Isobel and Malcolm were wed when my grandmother was an infant in swaddling, and there were no betrothal gifts exchanged."

Claricia's eyes sought Alexander's in an unspoken question.

" 'Twas in the middle of the previous century, and Malcolm was but a lad of eleven years when the outlaw laird Murdoch MacWilliam waged a brutal war against his Highland neighbors. Isobel was MacWilliam's newborn granddaughter, and she was wed to the lad to keep her safe from MacWilliam, who was determined to see her dead. She spent most of her childhood alone here at Eilean Fidra; then she lived in the royal household as the king's ward. Theirs wasna a true marriage in any sense, and when my grandfather gave my grandmother this heart pendant, he gave it to a lass he had rescued from thieves, a lass he was falling in love with but didna know was his verra own wife."

"My grandmother wore it always, and only took it off when their son—my father—was betrothed to his Catherine. Then Lady Isobel gave it to my father for his wife, telling him to pass it on to his firstborn son with the message that the heart's destiny can never be predicted. My grandmother believed it was a sin to turn away from happiness, and this heart is a reminder of that. She would want ye to wear it. 'Tis yer right. 'Tis yer betrothal gift."

No words of love and devotion could have touched Claricia more deeply. Her hand that was not holding the little green heart rose to rest lightly against her chest, as if to subdue her accelerated heartbeat. She had not expected a betrothal gift. Not at all. Her lips moved upward into a smile that animated her entire countenance, brightening her eyes and coloring her cheeks a delicate shade of pink. She could not suppress her delight. Indeed, she could not suppress the physical reaction of her heart to this kindness. Alexander Kirkpatrick did not have to treat her like a normal bride. But he was doing so. Her heart contracted, then expanded with warmth, and as she gazed upon the somewhat apprehensive expression shadowing his gauntly handsome face, she was not certain why it seemed as if her heart might break. Still she smiled, for she sensed that was what he wanted.

"Ye see, it works already. A smile lights yer face. I'm glad to see it and verra pleased I can claim a bit of responsibility for putting it there," Alexander murmured warmly. He had wondered on the way up the tower stairs if giving the heart pendant to Lady Claricia was the proper decision, considering the circumstances of their betrothal. Now he knew he could not have done anything less. "Ye must come stand before me and turn around so that I can slip it over yer head."

Perhaps too eagerly, Claricia complied, and when she had her back to Alexander, he slipped it over her head, then lifted her hair so that the pendant might rest properly. His fingers brushed against the nape of her neck. Claricia shivered and held her breath, waiting, wondering what would happen next.

Alexander let her silky hair fall back in place. "There ye go. Let's take a look at ye, now," he murmured, and, setting his hands on Claricia's shoulders, he gently turned her around. She did not meet his gaze for long, but shyly glanced from the heart to his face and then quickly back to the pendant. There was a pretty rose blush upon her cheeks, and, glimpsing the disbelief mingling with pleasure upon her features, he realized how badly he had misjudged her. Coming upon her in that whitewashed chamber at Hepburn, he'd thought she had everything, that she was spoiled and pampered, but in truth she had very little. Indeed, it struck him that even Moira had more, for she, at least, had the companionship of other women. His heart twisted anew as he gave her a smile, setting his forefinger beneath her chin to raise her face so their eyes would meet. "It suits ye."

"Thank you," she said with all the modesty of a maiden pure. Her fingers caressed the heart, her eyes darted downward again, for his green dragon gaze had been too penetrating. It seemed as if he saw things about her that she did not even know. He was staring at her. She felt his gaze, his finger against her chin was warm, and the back of her neck was tingling where he had brushed against the bare skin. Of a sudden, she was acutely aware of him, of his warmth and strong masculine odor, and of herself, her rapid heartbeat and the strange heat radiating from her middle. She lifted her gaze, her eyes filled with uncertainty.

The thick black beard that had covered his face the night before was gone. Claricia admired the sharp lines of his nose, high cheekbones, and brow, liking very much the lean, masculine look of him. It made no sense. She had never before found men attractive. They had always been vile and ugly, hurtful beings, in her eyes. Why, then, did she think such a thing when she gazed upon Alexander Kirkpatrick? What was this tingling, this awareness? Again, she lowered her gaze in confusion.

Jesu, Alexander thought, drawing in a sharp quick breath. He saw the flush upon her cheeks and brow, and he knew it could mean only one thing. She was drawn to him in the way that a woman is attracted to a man. Perhaps she did not know or understand it, but her body had a will of its own. She was reacting to his touch, his nearness, and in that instant, his entire body ached for hers as a hot, swift erection engorged his manhood. Desire set a ragged edge to his voice. "Now that I've presented ye with the official Kirkpatrick betrothal token, would ye be willing to seal our agreement with a kiss?"

Claricia's heart leaped into her throat. She looked up, her lips parted, and she could not tear her eyes from his while the pad of his thumb rubbed gently against her lower lip. She could barely breathe. There was a fire crackling the air as they stared at each other. It was frightening and exhilarating to consider his touching her all over, and the rose hue on her cheeks deepened as her breath quickened and tiny puffs of warm air encircled her head. *Yes*, she urged herself, *yes, you must let him kiss you.* After all, it was her duty to please him. It was the least she could do, and she whispered, "Yes."

Alexander slid one arm about her waist. He pulled her hard to him, so close that he felt the pounding of her heart against his chest. It was a delicious sensation, hinting at the wealth of pleasures to be found in intimacy between a man and woman. For an instant, he gazed at her face, only inches from his, captivated by the luminous light in her violet eyes. She was unbelievably lovely and delicate, and Alexander ached with the knowledge that she was going to be his. Not merely for a brief moment in time, but for eternity.

It was not a sweet kiss. One hand held the back of her head firmly, keeping her steady so that his lips might caress hers in a way that was hard and deep and demanding. His tongue entered her mouth, caressing, probing. She was open to him, and returned his kisses with equal ardor, pliant within his embrace. Her body was molded against his where surely she must have felt the evidence of his desire. Alexander was hardly able to breathe. Kissing her was like drowning, and he had to force himself to lift his mouth from hers.

"I want ye." His voice came out on an aching sigh. He swallowed quickly, convulsively, and speaking with urgency against her lips he repeated, "I want ye. Do ye know that? Can ye *feel* that?"

"Yes," she whispered in the tiny space that separated their lips. The length of his male hardness was pressing against her inner thigh. She knew what he meant and knew that she must not refuse him. She was soon to be his wife, and conjugal obedience was a wife's duty. She must please him in every sense of the word.

Chapter 12

Alexander feathered a line of kisses along Claricia's jaw. He nestled them beneath her ear, inhaling the sweetness of her, reveling in the softness of her skin. "I want to be inside ye, where it's hot and wet and tight," he whispered in a voice roughened by passion.

His husky words excited Claricia, as did his firm lips nipping against the sensitive flesh behind her ear, as did his splayed hands sliding up the length of her back and down her thighs. He cupped her buttocks, squeezing them as he pulled her to stand between his legs. Claricia did not resist. Instead, she swayed forward, overwhelmed by a sudden light-headedness when the urgency of his swollen desire pressed against her. Then he was lifting her in his arms, kissing her deeply as he carried her toward the bed.

"I dinna want to hurt ye." His lips seared her neck, behind her ear again, across her chest from shoulder to shoulder. "There is pleasure in this, my lady, and I want to show it to ye. I want to give it to ye." Alexander set her down on the bed, and, standing between her legs, he slipped a hand beneath her partially rucked-up kirtle. Slowly, his fingertips traced their way up the soft flesh of her inner thigh. She quivered beneath his touch. "Does this pain ye?" he asked. He stopped moving his hand but did not raise his fingers from her bare skin.

"Nay," she said on a whisper between a series of shallow, irregular breaths.

He drew a hard, uneven breath of his own. "And this?" His hand began to move again. Upward. Higher. His fingers were moving toward the secret female place between her legs.

"Nay," she said softly, huskily, and her eyes closed as she drank in the sensation of his hands moving over her skin. It was tempting, tantalizing, arousing. She gasped at the responses he was arousing within her, at the languid heat spreading outward from her belly and down her legs, at the increasing moisture between her legs.

This was the way it had been at Clar Innis, and she did not understand it now any more than she had then. Even her breasts were straining against her bodice with some strange anticipation. These reactions had nothing to do with obligation. All thought of duty fled, and Claricia trembled with the discovery that she liked what Alexander Kirkpatrick was doing to her. But there was more to this than what she experienced at Clar Innis. Then, she had felt things she had never known before. Her flesh had tingled: her heart had pounded. She had felt what he was doing to her, but this time there was more than that. This time there was a yearning within her body, which she had never thought to have for any man.

"Does this pain ye?" Easily, one of Alexander's fingers slipped inside her. He stroked her.

"Nay." It was barely a word as he raised her

kirtle above her waist, and Claricia opened her eyes to see Alexander Kirkpatrick gazing at her most private parts. He was watching his finger work its way in and out of her.

"Lovely," he murmured. His gaze did not stray from the sight between her legs. "Ye were made for loving, my pretty rose. *Mo ròs geall.*" *My white rose.* "Delicate and lovely and overflowing with honey. Tell me, *mo ròs geall*, how does this feel?" He slipped a second finger inside her along with the first, then there was a third finger stroking and delving alongside the other two. "Does it pain ye or pleasure ye?"

"Pleasure," she murmured, feeling with that simple admission as if she had revealed the whole of her soul to him. There she was, sprawled backward on the bed, her legs spread wide, her female parts exposed before him, and yet that was not nearly so earth-shattering as the admission that she was feeling pleasure. This was all too new, and uncertainty flickered across her features. When she had thought of submitting to Alexander Kirkpatrick, she had only considered this act in a physical sense. She had never known that there might be an emotional aspect to what went on between a man and a woman. She was confused, for the enjoyment she experienced went beyond the immediate sensations he aroused in her. This was nothing like the feelings he had stimulated within her at Clar Innis. The pleasure when he touched her so intimately extended deep into her soul, and she did not know what to make of that or what it could mean. She had never felt any connection to her uncle. He had come to her bed a hundred times, but he had never affected her as this man did.

Alexander gazed upon her. There was a hungry, roguish look in the depths of his dragon-green eyes, but his smile was tender, promising, as he moved onto the bed and kneeled between Claricia's legs. With a few quick motions, he released his erection from his leggings.

Claricia gasped. Alexander Kirkpatrick was nothing like her uncle, who had often forced her to do things to stiffen his pale member when it would not awaken. Alexander Kirkpatrick, in contrast, was thick and long, and so firm it seemed as if he might explode. Indeed, the end of his manhood looked as large around as her fist, and if she had not known otherwise, Claricia would have been unable to imagine that any woman could take such a thing inside her.

"Ye havena truly looked upon a naked mon before? Ye have always shielded yer eyes?" Alexander wondered aloud. Having grown accustomed to the dim light of the chamber, he had seen her obvious surprise when she gazed upon him. He had heard her little gasp.

"Until now," she answered softly, shyly.

"Does the sight pleasure ye?"

She swallowed, embarrassed and intrigued at once by the notion. "I—I've never thought of it."

At once, his grin turned from tender to roguish as he leaned forward between her legs. "Och, then tell me this, my lady. Does the feel of it pleasure ye?" Alexander held his erection in his hand to rub the tip of his swollen desire at her moist opening.

Claricia's response was immediate. A luxuriant

sigh of enjoyment floated forth from her parted lips as she arched her back and widened her legs in a centuries-old instinctive reaction. Alexander's erection slipped inside her, then he withdrew. She made a little noise that sounded like frustration, and in the next instant, he slipped inside a second time, a little deeper than before, then he pulled out again.

Alexander could barely control himself. He wanted to plunge in deep and hard. He wanted to experience that sensation of being sheathed within her, of that wet velvety heat enveloping him, holding him tight. He wanted it so badly he would almost have traded his life for it at that moment. Claricia's possession over him was nearly total, his need for her was powerful, and he was afraid. But not afraid this time of losing control and releasing his seed within his enemy. He was afraid that if he let loose he might hurt her—or worse, he might frighten her away from him forever. Slowly, he entered her again. Slowly, he began the pleasing sensual rhythm. He heard her sigh, felt her opening wider to him, accommodating him, and he paused an instant to pace himself.

"What is it?" Claricia had sensed his tiny hesitation. She gazed up at him with passion-misted eyes.

"I dinna want ye to leave me," Alexander said with stunning honesty.

She knew exactly what he meant. It had nothing to do with going away from Eilean Fidra, but everything to do with her mind leaving her body to travel to Meg's faerie isle. He might not have known where she went, but he knew she'd tried to go there, and her heart contracted as she put her arms about his shoulders, letting him know it was all right. It was true. There was a kind soul within this Highlander who would be her husband, and Claricia was determined to find that man and hold fast to him in the days ahead. He was not hurting her, and she was not going anywhere that night. She moaned softly, her fingers threading through the thickness of his black hair.

That was all the encouragement Alexander needed. He began to move within her again, knowing that it would not be long before he surrendered himself entirely to her. Wildly, swiftly, the passion mounted within him. It was like being swallowed into a vortex at the edge of the earth. With each thrust, his body was reaching toward the highest height, and then, with a ferocious burst of energy, he lurched forward, harder, deeper into that blissful vortex, his very life force flowing out of him like a raging river that overflows its banks in spring.

It was over. Claricia did not stir beneath him, and Alexander cradled her in his arms, pulling a patchwork of furs over them as the glow of passion faded and the chill in the chamber settled about them.

"I am sorry, my lady," Alexander whispered against her soft hair.

"Sorry?" Claricia said in confusion. "You were not pleased?"

"Nay, *mo ròs geall*, my pleasure was great. 'Tis yer pleasure for which I am sorry. I was greedy, and failed in my promise to show ye the full extent of pleasures a mon and a woman can share."

"I don't understand." It had been wonderful. What could he mean?

"Och, 'tis as I feared," Alexander said with a touch of sadness for this evidence of all the times she'd been taken against her will, taken by men who cared naught but for themselves. At the same time, it was also a good thing to know she had never experienced the ultimate pleasure with another. It was a splendid thing to anticipate that he would be the one to give her that satisfaction. Alexander knew why she had fought so hard to numb herself. It was the only way to prove she was not truly the whore her uncle had tried to make her. Mayhap that was the greatest tragedy of all.

"There is more, *mo ròs geall*. More pleasure to be had between a mon and a woman, and it will be my delight to give it to ye."

"Why do you do this for me?"

"Because ye're to be my wife, and ye've pleased me more than I could ever have imagined. And someday, mayhap, ye might say the same about me."

"I don't deserve it."

"Hush, dinna say such a thing. Say nothing more." He dropped a light kiss upon her brow and brushed a strand of hair away from her eyes, wondering how it could be that this was the one woman for whom he would move heaven and earth if it were possible. Above all else, Alexander hoped that once she had been able to experience the fullness of physical pleasure with her husband, the ugly past would fade away. "If nothing else is to come of our marriage, if ye're never to have yer dreams of a fair *sassenach* lordling, at least ye'll learn there is something rare and special to coupling that can raise us above the beasts of the forest. That is my wish."

Claricia did not know what to make of this little speech, and so she did as he'd suggested. She said nothing, and lay with her head upon his arm, listening to his breathing, staring up at the mauve velvet canopy above her head. The faint light in the chamber had given way to the darkness of the long winter night. It was surely time for the evening meal. At length, she said, "Should we go down to the hall?"

"Are ye hungry?"

"Not particularly."

"Why go, then?"

She blushed. "There will be talk."

Alexander laughed. He could not see the flush upon her cheeks, but he felt her face grow hot where it rested against his upper arm. "Aye, there's bound to be clackiting tongues in a hall with too many women. But it will be nothing more than jealousy."

"You've told them of your intention"—she paused before finishing—"to wed me?"

"Aye." He turned all the way on his side to study her in the darkness but could not make out her expression with any certainty. "Do ye care what they think?"

"Yes, for I have grown fond of them. Of Rourke and Sorcha and Frances, of Maxwel of Ballimeanoch, even the two old Maeris. And I had thought they might have come to like me, as well. I would not want them to have any reason to resent me now."

"No one could ever resent ye, my lady. And

should that contrary creature exist, I wouldna tolerate such behavior. What I said last night will always be true. Ye will be honored as my wife and chatelaine, and my loyalty will be no less than that of the clanspeople of Eilean Fidra. Ye must believe me, my lady. If nothing else, I am a mon of my word, and I would guarantee that promise with my last breath.''

Down the length of the loch on the Old Believer's Isle, it was not different than any other night for Rourke and Viviane, who could barely contain their passion until Simon had fallen asleep. Viviane was especially impatient, tossing sultry looks over her shoulder while she prepared a leek-and-potato stew, allowing her hand to linger against Rourke's arm when she served the meal, and intentionally brushing her breasts against his back when she leaned over to clear the table. It was a familiar prelude in anticipation of the hours that would be theirs alone once Simon had settled into his bed in the alcove.

At last, the lad was asleep and the wooden trenchers had been cleaned. Rourke added a peat brick to the brazier while Viviane pulled the curtain across the sleeping alcove. Then she turned around to face him, and as she knew it gave him pleasure, she unlaced her tunic and tugged open the fabric to reveal her breasts while he watched.

"Are ye ready, *a mhorair*?" *My lord*, she called him, and her smile was playful, tempting, flirtatious, as she shrugged off the tunic. The garment tumbled about her ankles, and she stood there naked, raking her hands through her thick midnight-black hair, holding it high off her back, her round firm breasts rising with the motion. Viviane walked toward Rourke, her nipples puckered and hips swaying, her creamy white skin an enticing contrast to the mass of wild black curls trailing down her back as well as those that were nestled between her long slender legs.

She stood before him, so close that her bare breasts grazed his tunic, her thighs brushed against his, and Rourke, letting out a lusty groan, bent his head to her. But he did not kiss her lips. Instead, his mouth fastened over her nipple, and while Rourke suckled her breast, Viviane undid his leggings to free his hard male flesh. It was her turn, and her caressing hands encircled him. Rourke let out another groan, long and low and deep, in response to her fondling. His lips took a tiny bite of her nipple, and his tongue flicked out to trail a moist path to her other breast.

Viviane laughed, arching her back and thrusting her breasts upward to his ministrations. It was a low sensual sound, and her voice was huskier than usual. "Och, *a mhorair*, we are always too eager."

"Aye." His hot breath fell against her nipple. " 'Tis always like the first time I held ye in my arms."

Together, they slid down beside the brazier, joining as one before her back had even touched the waiting pallet. Viviane's legs wrapped about his waist, one hand playing across his muscled back, the other against his chest and belly where the blond hair became thicker beneath her fingertips. They were moving as one, hot and quick, and Rourke's hands scooped beneath her bottom to tilt her, opening her to him as wide as he might.

"I love ye," he said, raising up on his arms to look her in the eyes. *"Le m'uile mo chridhe." With all my heart.*

"And I love ye, Rourke." Her lips made contact with his, and she kissed him.

"Truly?"

"Le m'uile mo chridhe," she whispered. "I think I must have loved ye from the first, but I canna say why I didna tell ye long ago. Can ye forgive me?"

"There is naught to forgive." His eyes closed as he modified his pace to move in and out of her with excruciating, taunting slowness, making each entry seem as if it were the first. His voice was very hoarse. "What went before doesna matter. It only matters that I have yer love now."

"My love and my body and my soul." She moved her legs from his back and draped them over his shoulders, and with the next entry of his manhood, he slid to the hilt, encased so deeply in her lush feminine ripeness it felt as if he had touched the very core of her being. "I am yers for always," she murmured, intoxicated by the pleasure he was giving her. This ecstasy that they created together was so pure, so intense. It had always been that way, and it always would be: Viviane was certain of that.

They were perfectly matched. The potency of their passions surged in tandem, neither outpacing the other as they hungered and strained, then glided and soared toward that peak of final euphoria.

When it was over, Rourke gathered Viviane

into his arms. Her breathing was low and quiet, and he gently placed a tender kiss upon her brow, then upon each of her closed eyelids and the tip of her nose. He thought she had fallen asleep and was surprised when she spoke.

"Will ye kill him for me?" Viviane asked.

"What?" Rourke experienced an eerie chill. "Who?"

"The laird. Will ye kill him before he can wed Lady Claricia?"

"Nay!" He sat bolt upright. Viviane tumbled from his arms, landing before him on her knees in a semicrouched position, her wild hair tumbling about her face, trailing down her arms to touch the pallet, and Rourke stared at her as if she were possessed.

"But ye promised."

"I did no such thing."

"Aye, ye did. Dinna ye not recall what ye said? Ye would do anything for me, ye told me . . . if it was within yer power. *Anything* I asked of ye."

"But I never imagined ye would ask such a thing as this, and I am sorry to tell ye that what ye ask isna possible. Murder? My own cousin? 'Tis true, I would do anything for ye, lass, but not that."

"How can ye forget that he raped her? Kidnapped her. Used her against her will. Lady Claricia is no whore, but a noblewoman, and those are crimes for which he should be called to pay . . . with his verra life, if need be."

Rourke stared at Viviane, struck by the realization that he had misjudged the power of the bond between her and Lady Claricia. Indeed, he wondered if Viviane would ever believe her half of the debt had been satisfied. At length, he reached out to her. "Come, lie with me again, and let me tell ye what I think."

She jerked away from his outstretched hand. There was danger in being too close, for he could all too easily make her forget, all too easily distract her with a single caress. "I will listen to what ye have to say, Rourke O'Connor, but I will stay right here." She sat back, pulled up her legs, wrapped her arms about them, and, resting her chin on her knees, waited to hear what he had to say.

"As ye wish." Rourke offered her a fur before he continued. "I have known since we went to the castle with the lad that ye and Lady Claricia somehow knew each other."

"But ye said nothing," she said softly, casting that familiar glance of cautiousness toward the sleeping alcove.

"I didna wish to worry ye, nor have I any wish to probe about for the whole truth. I know much of the story—"

"How much?"

"Enough."

"How much?"

He sighed. "I know ye were a prisoner and that Lady Claricia saved ye. I know she calls ye Meg."

"She told ye this?" Viviane asked with an obvious note of betrayal.

"Aye, but that was all."

"Still, ye were able to figure out something more?"

"Aye, that the lad is hers, and I surmise ye took him and raised him in repayment for what she'd done for ye. Please, Viviane, Meg, dinna look like that," he implored. Her eyes were wide with fright and something else, like emptiness, or perhaps fear of abandonment. It hurt him to see her scared, thinking that he would harm her in any way. "This is not as terrible as it seems. There's no threat in my knowing. I always knew ye had a secret, and it didn't matter. Now I ken part of that secret, and it still doesna matter. Nothing will change, not if I can help it. I dinna want to hurt anyone, least of all ye or the lad."

He paused for a moment to measure her reaction. She had averted her eyes from his, and he knew he must speak from his soul. "I love ye with all my heart, and I want a future with the both of ye. I'm only telling ye I know because I think ye've paid yer debt to Lady Claricia. What ye did was brave and selfless, and I canna think of any other woman so loyal and honorable. But it's over. The debt's paid. Ye're safe. The lad is safe. Lady Claricia is safe. It's all over. The past is behind ye, and we've all of us naught but the future to consider," he said in conclusion, sending up a silent prayer that Viviane would accept this, that she would not challenge him, because he did not want to be forced to tell her what else he'd figured out. As far as Rourke was concerned he'd revealed enough.

But she argued. "I canna accept that."

"Ye must. It is the only way."

She looked up, the light in her eyes crackling with indignant challenge. "And who are ye, Rourke O'Connor, to be acting like the Lord Almighty, speaking of 'the only way'? Are ye all-knowing, all-seeing?" she taunted him, unable to prevent herself from feeling threatened, unable to

stave off an encroaching sense of loss. "What special powers do ye possess to make ye certain the
debt is paid? Certain that the only right course is
to look to the future?"

Rourke did not want to tell her that there were
facts she did not even know. Things that he had
begun to suspect about the child's father that
would have complicated matters. Indeed, there
were things about Viviane herself that were so
unbelievable, he could not bring himself to mention them to anyone. But should any of his suspicions have proved to be true, Viviane's
animosity toward Alexander Kirkpatrick would
have been painful to reconcile. "Can we not set
the past aside?"

" 'Tis not possible for me."

He tried another angle. "What if this marriage
was what Lady Claricia wanted? Would ye go
against yer friend? Would ye take that from her?"

"*Eist*." She spat out the sound of disgust.
"Lady Claricia is so grateful not to be going back
to that bastard de Clinton, she canna think
straight."

"But what if—what if there was a chance for
happiness between them? What if Lady Claricia
might touch my cousin in a way that would make
him a better mon? A worthy mon?"

"What if?" Viviane did not need more than a
few seconds to consider her reply. "Then it
would make killing him harder," she said without much emotion.

"Don't do it," Rourke warned, alarmed by her
implication that she would be willing to do the
deed herself. His expression was adamant, his
gaze narrowing as he frowned at her.

"I have lost ye," Viviane said on a sigh of anguish, reacting to the distance she heard in his voice and saw upon his face. "Over this I have lost ye."

"Not yet." His tone softened, and when he reached for her, she did not pull away.

"But I will. I will lose ye, if I do what I believe is right." There was no fight in this statement, merely a sad sense of resignation. Tired and confused, she allowed him to cradle her against his body.

Rourke did not know what to say. His hand was trembling as he brushed a long strand of hair off her face. "Go to sleep," he whispered. "In the morning this will all seem verra different."

Chapter 13

In the morning, Alexander gathered up his personal items that had been arrayed atop the chest in the tower chamber. He removed the belt buckles and ceremonial dirk, the comb of carved bone and the silver dragon clasp for his Kirkpatrick plaid, plus the few things he had brought with him to Eilean Fidra. He handed them to Frances.

"What are you doing?" Claricia asked after the *sennachie's* daughter had carried them away. It was late in the morning. Sunshine was streaming through the cracks in the shutters, crossing the chamber with streaks of bright light, and before they descended to the hall, Claricia and Alexander broke their fast with bread and cheese and warm cider.

Alexander set aside his wooden cup. "I am moving out of this chamber until we are properly wed. A groom should not share quarters with his bride before the ceremony. For the next two nights, it is yers alone."

Claricia had not expected such gallantry. It was disconcerting, and she required a deep breath before she could say, "That is not necessary." She was acutely aware of the way his gaze moved over her face. His deep-set eyes were intense and penetrating. It was unnerving, and her reaction was to sit a bit taller, with her hands folded upon her lap. "I am no maid, nor are we strangers to each other, my lord. There is no reason to inconvenience yourself because of convention. Lest you forget, there is nothing conventional about our coming nuptials."

"That is true enough," Alexander agreed in a quiet voice. His eyes narrowed, his green gaze held hers, and, while his voice was confident, a momentary shadow of uncertainty wavered upon his face. For the space of a heartbeat, his features seemed more gaunt, his skin paler. "All of what ye say is true enough, but ye will humor me in this and not question my motives. It is what I want."

"If you like," Claricia consented, wondering why her heart was fluttering. It should not have mattered. But it did. Indeed, it changed the way she perceived this man. It would have seemed improbable that something so simple as removing himself from the tower chamber would make any difference. Nonetheless, in that instant, it seemed she was marrying not a stranger, but someone she knew well, someone who truly cared for her, and Claricia could not control the girlish fluttering of her heart. "This is your home. You are the laird, and I would never naysay you, my lord."

Alexander listened carefully to catch the slightest hint of that submissive-whore tone in Claricia's voice that he had heard in the cave, when her words and the way in which she had spoken had implied she was accustomed to doing what it was a man wished of her. This morning, he heard nothing of that. It simply was not there, and Alexander experienced an unexpected rush of relief. Emboldened, he dared to speak again. "There is one other thing I would like."

"Yes?" Claricia's eyes widened, and a fresh pink blush stained her cheeks in anticipation.

"Ye call me my lord, but I would like for ye to call me by my given name."

She nodded her assent. Her mouth curved upward into the beginning of a shy smile. Another barrier between them was coming down. Involuntarily, her hand rose to touch the polished green heart, where it rested against the woolen kirtle. If only Meg could see how it was between them. Surely then her animosity toward Alexander Kirkpatrick would abate.

"Can ye say it for me now?" He caught the upward movement of her hand as she touched the little green heart. Warmth flowed through him to circle round his heart. "Can ye say it? Alexander."

The pretty pink upon her cheeks deepened, and she lowered her lashes, then peeked up at him. "Alexander," Claricia said softly, timidly. It was not as hard as she had thought it would be to speak his name aloud, not so hard to put behind her the memory of the stranger who had taken her from her bed, and to see instead the man who had given her his grandmother's heart pendant. "And what will you call me, my lord?" Quickly, she corrected herself. "Alexander?"

He grinned. "If ye dinna mind, I willna call ye by yer given name. Claricia, 'tis comely enough, but I would prefer to call ye *ròs geall*, for that is what suits ye best. White rose, delicate and sweet."

"I do not mind in the least," she said. Her heart went from a flutter to a leap; then it was soaring somewhere outside of her body. The flush upon her cheeks spread up and down her arms and legs, and she could not stop herself from adding, "In truth, I like it very much."

Well satisfied with her answer, Alexander sat back in the great carved chair to look at her. The flush on her face was appealing, and he liked the way she fondled the pendant. What a marvel it was to consider the chain of circumstances that had brought them together. Perhaps Rourke was correct, and he had been too quick and too cynical in the way he had denied the power of Fate. Everything about this seemed right to Alexander, especially the way her slender hand cupped the little green heart as if to reassure herself it was really there. He could not resist murmuring softly, "Aye, 'tis yers, *mo ròs geall.*"

Claricia followed his gaze to where it rested upon the pendant. His words reminded her of the first woman who had worn it, and she could not help wondering aloud. "Tell me about your grandmother. About Lady Isobel."

"Och, ye would have loved her, as did everyone who knew her," Alexander began eagerly. There were few things from the past that he cherished so much as his memories of his Kirkpatrick grandmother. "She was a lady as admirable in heart and soul as in face and form. Always putting others ahead of her, always lending a hand, and a true Highland beauty, she was, with wild black hair and eyes the color of heather when 'tis full and lush and green. Even in her last years, she never seemed auld to me, always smiling and forever singing in a voice that my grandfather Malcolm said was the sweetest in the Highlands. Och, she was truly lovely, and my grandfather called her Heather."

Claricia was touched by this effusive discourse. If only someone might one day say the same about her. Her smile wobbled, and she blurted out the first thing that popped into her mind, "Then you, too, marry a flower, as did your grandfather. Mayhap it is the destiny of Kirkpatrick lairds," she teased, mortified in the next instant that she had presumed too much. But he showed no offense.

"Aye, *mo ròs geall*." Of a sudden, Alexander's voice became enigmatic. "When ye speak of Destiny, there may be more truth in that than either of us can comprehend at this time."

She did not know what to make of that statement. Uncertain, she set aside her piece of unfinished cheese and stood, smoothing down the skirt of the purple kirtle. "If you will excuse me, my lord, Alexander, I must go below."

He did not speak, finding such immense pleasure in hearing his name fall from her lips that he merely nodded and waved her away in an indication that he would join her later.

There was nothing, with the exception of the birth of an heir, that could generate as much excitement in a Highland fortress as a laird's wedding. Even an impromptu wedding in the middle of winter, in the midst of a war, could mobilize an entire household, and by the time Claricia entered the great hall, preparations were already underway for the coming festivities. Of course, there was much sweeping and dusting, and the last of the fresh rushes, spread to dry the past summer on the banks of Loch Awe, were scattered across the floor. The benches and trestles were being rearranged so that the laird and his bride might sit at the head of the hall and so that there would be adequate space for dancing and entertainment. The fire pit was being cleaned and laid with fresh logs, over which two large spits were being erected. On the morrow, the logs would be lit, and two of the pigs that were presently rooting in the frozen garden behind the stable would be slaughtered for roasting.

Sorcha, who was overseeing the work at the fire pit, saw Claricia enter. She wiped her sooty hands on her overtunic and, smiling, crossed the hall to embrace her with motherly affection. "I couldna be more pleased, mistress. The laird has made a wise decision."

"I am glad to hear you say so."

"Ye didna imagine I would feel otherwise?" The *sennachie's* wife was taken aback by Claricia's implication. "Ye didna imagine that I—or any one of us, for that matter—would harbor resentment?"

"To do so would not have been without cause," was Claricia's calm reply. "And I would not have thought ill of you."

"Och, mistress, ye mustna trouble my ears with such nonsense. The Good Lord acts in strange ways, and I think 'twas His hand—and not that of Highland honor and revenge for the clan—that was at work when the laird sent ye here. Ye're a blessing and a treasure."

"As you are, Sorcha. As is everyone at Eilean Fidra." Claricia glanced about the bustling hall. "When I cherished girlish dreams of what kind of home I would have as a bride, this was not what came to mind. I never dreamed of being so far away from where I grew up, and certainly not in a foreign setting. But now, grown and having experienced something of life, I can see that I will be content here. It is true that one can travel very far from those things both familiar and cherished and still find a place to call home."

"Enough of this sentimental talk. Enough of it." Sorcha made a gruff clucking sound and rubbed at her eyes with the back of her hand. "Are ye trying to make me cry? This is supposed to be a time for celebration and joy. Ye're a bride, and ye mustna be so serious. Yer wedding is a mere two days hence, and there's still much to be done."

"May I help?"

"Aye, there is something for ye." She took a torch from its wall mount, lit the taper in the embers of the fire pit, and motioned to Claricia. "Come with me."

Sorcha led her to the kitchen level, beneath the great hall. There in a small room a number of heavy chests, which had been removed from the tunnel, were set out; their heavy lids were propped open, so that the contents might be aired and inspected. Sorcha secured the torch, then knelt down before the nearest chest to rummage through its contents, and, not finding what she wanted, she delved through a second and a third chest.

"At last," she exclaimed, pulling forth some sort of garment. "This is what I want to show ye." She unfolded a length of saffron-tinted wool. A bridal kirtle was revealed, with gold and deep-rose-colored embroidery in a knot-work pattern about the squared collar and wrists. Sewn at the hem in bright golden threads, there was a continual design of interlaced birds accented with the same dark rose color about the neckline and wrists. "Do ye think it will fit ye?" Sorcha handed the kirtle to Claricia.

Carefully, Claricia held the garment against her torso, extending one of the narrow sleeves down the length of her arm. The wool was as soft as the finest down, and although it smelled of age and moisture, the quality of the garment itself had not suffered, hidden, as it had been, in the tunnel beneath the loch. Claricia had never expected anything so special. It was an unexpectedly emotional moment, and she required an instant before she could answer Sorcha. "It could not be more perfect had it been made for me."

"And these?" Sorcha produced a pair of pointed slippers crafted of vermilion leather. Claricia tried them on, and, finding they were a perfect fit, she lifted her skirt to display them. Sorcha gave a nod of approval. "The laird will be pleased."

"This was his idea?"

"Aye. I didna even know these things were still here. I had imagined they were destroyed when the *sassenach* looted Eilean Fidra. But they were saved along with everything else precious to the clan. 'Twas the laird's doing, putting these things into the tunnel, as if he knew there would come a day when he would need such a link with the past.''

Gazing down at the wedding outfit, Claricia spoke from her heart. ''I could almost feel like a real bride.''

''Och, ye poor dearie, but ye are a true bride,'' Sorcha retorted. ''Ye didna imagine the laird would be marrying ye if he didna truly want ye for his wife?''

''I don't know what to think,'' Claricia said, then wondered aloud, ''Were these meant for—''

''Moira?'' Sorcha understood her hesitation. ''Nay. They were his mother's. Lady Catherine, the young bride from Hepburn. I remember as if it were yesterday. The kirtle came with her from Hepburn, but the shoes were a gift from her mother-in-law, the Lady Isobel. They came from a Cordovan merchant at the Glasgow market.''

Claricia closed her eyes for a moment, not to envision the long-ago bride from Hepburn in the saffron-tinted woolen gown, but to think of Meg on the Old Believer's Isle. If her friend could know of this—how the laird wished her to wear his mother's wedding finery—and of the heart pendant, then she might be able to put the past behind her. Claricia had promised to find the man who Rourke had asserted existed beneath Alexander's harsh exterior, and to her surprise, that had not been a hard promise to keep. Indeed, it had been easy, which gave Claricia reason to hope that perhaps one day Meg would understand that if one ever hoped to heal, if one ever hoped to have a future, one would have to let go of the past.

Two days later, Claricia stood before the double doors of the chapel that occupied a building adjacent to the main donjon tower. In addition to wearing Lady Catherine's wedding kirtle, the polished heart pendant, and the pointed leather slippers, Claricia wore the traditional bridal wreath of flowers, patterned in a crown of heather entwined with other dried wild flowers.

It was shortly before sunset, and in the waning light of the late afternoon, Alexander stood beside her, garbed in a woolen *breacan* woven in the Kirkpatrick plaid of green and purple with a touch of gold. The *breacan* was wrapped about his torso, and the end was draped over his shoulder, where it was secured with a large silver clasp. Beneath this, he wore a knee-length white shirt, which was cinched at the waist by a wide leather belt with a buckle crafted in the same dragon pattern as the silver clasp at his shoulder. His thick black hair was not plaited into braids that afternoon, but combed loose and secured with a single strip of leather at the nape of his neck.

On the step above the bride and groom stood Brother Luthais, his ankle-length black robe flapping in the breeze, his pate shaved bald, and his only adornment being a wooden cross he wore about his neck. Brother Luthais was a Colquhoun kinsman of Alexander's and a Franciscan friar, who in these times of unrest had gladly given up his mendicant ways to reside over the small chapel at Eilean Fidra. On the cold ground below these three was assembled the household, Moira and her women, plus a significant gathering of Kirkpatrick clansmen and allied warriors, who upon short notice had ventured forth from their safe havens to stand witness for Alexander Kirkpatrick.

"I take ye, Claricia, to my wedded wife, to have and to hold." The groom, prompted by Brother Luthais, was the first to make his vows. "From this day forward, for better, for worse, for richer, for poorer, in sickness and in health."

When it was her turn, the bride spoke the identical vows. Claricia concluded with the same words that Alexander had spoken only moments before. " . . . Till death us depart, if holy church it will ordain, and thereto, I plight you my troth."

Brother Luthais, who had not officiated at many weddings, let alone a laird's, smiled and raised his hands. "Let this woman be amiable as Rachel, wise as Rebecca, faithful as Sarah. Let her be sober through truth, venerable through modesty, and wise through the teaching of Heaven."

The ceremony was completed. Brother Luthais made the sign of the cross, blessing the newlyweds and the fruit of their union.

"*Beiribh beannachd*," invoked the good friar. His words echoed off the gray stone walls and into the crisp winter night. *Be ye blessed*. Overhead, in the dark sky, silver stars were already twinkling brightly. It was a good sign.

The clan piper struck up a march. The youngest male in attendance, one of Sorcha's nephews, carried the Kirkpatrick pennant beside the piper, and the guests paraded behind the laird and his bride into the great hall. In addition to the roasted pigs, the trestles were spread with platters of eel, a variety of game birds, venison, and salmon, which had been smoked and stored in barrels for the winter, plus baked apples, pickled eggs, and assorted breads and pastries. Considering the exigencies of war, it was an amazing feast, which included an abundance of ale, cider from apples, perry from pears, and a potent sweetened wine called malmsey.

After a while, Alexander stood to offer a toast. The noise in the hall diminished only slightly. He addressed his guests in a rousing, strong voice. "First, I must extend my thanks to my clansmen and neighbors, who came to stand witness in my behalf under such extraordinary circumstances. I wish that it might have been a different time than this, and that yer families could have been with us. I dinna enter into this marriage lightly, and yer presence here today tells me ye understand and respect my decision. Thank ye for yer support. Yer blessing is indeed welcomed, for I know a dark future looms before our clan and before our nation. *Cinnidh Scuit saor am fine.*" Alexander lifted his goblet, and the silence was broken. The crowd cheered. *The race of the free Scots shall flourish.* He raised his goblet a second time and finished with, "*Dlighe flaitheas do ghabhail.*" *They shall prevail by the right of Heaven.*

"God bless our chief and the clan!"

"Blessing to King Robert!" one of the guests shouted.

"God bless Scotland." The cry was repeated up and down the benches, and everyone drank deeply.

Alexander remained standing and lifted high his goblet again, turning from the crowd to face

Claricia. "To my wife and yer lady, the mistress of Eilean Fidra." Having saluted Claricia with the goblet, he drank first from the vessel, then handed it to her.

By accident, his fingers brushed hers, and in the brief moment before she raised the goblet to her mouth, Alexander allowed his touch to linger against the inside of her wrist. Sensing a trembling within her, his hands reached upward to steady the goblet at her lips, and when she had tilted the vessel back to finish the draught, the guests and warriors, the clansmen and the *diobrachain* cheered their approval. Alexander let his hands fall away, and when she peeked at him over the rim of the goblet, he gave his bride a roguish wink, then extended his hand once again and, using a single fingertip, wiped away a drop of wine from her lower lip.

Next Sorcha stepped up to the head table. She motioned for the bride to stand.

Claricia hesitated. There was a rising flush upon her face, where confusion mingled with a wide-eyed expression brought on by light-headedness.

The sweet wine was potent. But even more potent was the way Alexander had been looking at her, and the way he had caught that little drop of wine. Claricia's senses were spinning. If the malmsey was not intoxicating enough, her husband was having a disconcerting effect upon her; Alexander's suggestive demeanor was making her decidedly giddy. It was almost as if he were putting her under his spell, relaxing her, warming her, and Sorcha's approach was like an unpleasant gust of wind. Claricia knew it was

Highland tradition for the *sennachie* to recite family pedigrees at weddings, baptisms, and funerals, and she did not want this moment to be tainted by an unpleasant reminder of who she was. Surely Sorcha did not intend to represent her husband and perform his ceremonial duties.

"Go ahead. Stand. 'Tis all right," Alexander reassured Claricia in a low voice that only she heard.

She complied, and although she tried to remain composed, her lips quivered. She could not deny the sensation of dread that her lineage might be discussed at this time.

But that was not Sorcha's intent. Instead, she raised a shortbread cake, which was broken over the bride's head.

Claricia heard Alexander laughing, not in mockery, but with merriment. It was a wonderful thing to hear. Alexander had said he was marrying her to right the wrongs he and his brother had committed against her, yet this unexpected display of genuine pleasure revealed the possibility of something more. For the first time, Claricia dared to feel like a true bride. Indeed, she even dared to think that Sorcha might have been correct, and that Alexander Kirkpatrick had made her his wife because he wanted her. It was an exhilarating notion to consider. Again, her senses were sent reeling. Magic was at work that night, and she joined Alexander in laughter.

At length, their laughter died down. The harp and bagpipes began to play. Everyone joined in a song:

> *Welcome to yer ain fireside;*
> *Health and wealth attend the bride!*

The bride's welcome with the breaking of a shortbread was a custom as old as the mountains rising above Loch Awe, a ritual with origins that were both Celtic and Roman. After the singing had ended, the welcome was completed when Claricia received a pair of fire tongs and a long broom, then she and Alexander ate together a piece of the shortbread, the remainder of which was distributed among the guests. Another cheer echoed through the great hall. It was time for the dancing to begin.

In another Highland tradition, the first dance was not between the bride and the groom. Instead, the bride and the groom's head witness— in this case, Rourke—were coupled. It was the bride's role to call the tune, and prompted by a discreet whisper from Rourke, Claricia asked for a *hullachan*. It was the only Scottish dance she knew; Meg had taught it to her.

Taking their places in the center of the hall, Claricia and the Irishman led off the reel. Soon they were joined by other couples. Many of the women from Finlarig had been paired off with one or another of the visiting warriors. Even Maxwel of Ballimeanoch was off his bench and on his feet, one hand raised above his head, the other wrapped about Lady Moira's waist, as they moved through the paces of the brisk dance.

The crowd sent up another cheer, and several ribald remarks were tossed amongst the clansmen when their chieftain strode into their midst to take Rourke O'Connor's place with his bride. This time, the dance was a *reel o tullochgorm*, in which the partners faced each other with one arm raised overhead, as in the *hullachan*, while the other hand rested on the hip.

" 'Tis not as hard as it appears. Simply follow what I do," Alexander told Claricia above the stirring cadence of the pipes. He began hopping on one foot while flinging the other, and she copied him, laughter lighting her eyes and escaping her lips. She was an enticing sight, flushed and breathless, and Alexander could hardly concentrate on the reel. In another moment, he was bound to trip upon his own toes, and when they passed each other shoulder to shoulder, he could not resist leaning toward her to whisper against the soft flesh behind her ear, " 'Tis almost time for us to bid our guests good night."

Back to back, they continued to circle around each other. Claricia was glad that Alexander could not see how her eyes had widened and her mouth had fallen open at his words. The skin on her neck tingled where his warm breath had touched her, and of a sudden, images of his body, bare flesh and long legs, a well-muscled chest, crowded her mind. She could almost smell the salty scent of him, almost feel the throbbing power of him, and she swallowed, her throat dry at the thought of what lay ahead of her that night.

They were facing each other again, this time hopping on the opposite foot, the positions of their arms reversed, but she could not concentrate. Instead, her eyes locked with his, violet fusing with green, and as her mouth parted, so did his. As the tip of her tongue came out to moisten her lips, so did his. As Claricia's hand moved from its position at her waist to touch the green heart resting against the bodice of his mother's wedding kirtle, Alexander watched and smiled. It was getting very warm, and she wished that she had not finished that ceremonial cup of malmsey.

The final notes of the song drifted upward to the rafters, and as the music of the bagpipes died away, the dancers went back to their benches. Alexander hooked his arm through Claricia's to escort her to the head table, and in a movement that caught her off-guard, he pulled her into a passageway. It was the one that led up the stairs to the tower chamber. There, the gaiety from the hall was slightly muffled, and for a moment, their breathing was strangely loud. They stood face-to-face, exhilarated by the dance and the wine.

"Is everything all right, Alexander?" Claricia asked, remembering to call him by his name.

"Aye, everything is fine, *mo ròs geall.*"

And before Claricia could utter a word of protest or query, Alexander swept her into his arms, and, holding her firmly against his chest, he carried her up the stairs.

Chapter 14

❝**W**hat splendid enchantment is this?❞ Claricia exclaimed when Alexander carried her across the threshold of the tower chamber. "I've never seen anything like it before," she marveled, taking in the wondrous sight before her.

The chamber was ablaze from the light of a myriad of tapers and torches. They were everywhere, and in every size and shape. Where only two wall sconces had been that afternoon, there were now four, each holding a blazing rushlight. Throughout the chamber an assortment of votive candles rested on the furnishings, while countless others had been set at random about the floor. Where there had been a single brazier, there were now three, placed in a semicircular fashion to offer the most warmth. The familiar setting had been transformed from cold gray to twinkling silver. So shimmering did it appear that the golden thistles on the mauve bed-curtains sparkled like jewels, disguising the timeworn condition of the embroidered velvet.

"It is lovely," she whispered. Alexander still held her in his arms, and she glanced upward to bestow a shy smile of appreciation upon him, thinking that if nothing came of this marriage at least she would have this brief memory of her wedding night.

Although Alexander did not smile in return, his expression was as tender as was his tone of voice. " 'Tis a fact that I'm not the husband of yer dreams, but this is yer wedding night nonetheless, and I wanted it to be a good memory." He set her on the rush-covered floor. A bashful, almost boyish cast settled upon his features, and he raked his fingers through his hair before adding, "I wanted ye to have something special this night."

Claricia's heart twisted. How was it that he could look inside and read her innermost secrets? Softly, she said, "That is the nicest thing anyone has said to me. Indeed, has ever done for me."

He shrugged, not liking to think of all the things she'd been denied, of all the things that had been taken from her. There was an odd sort of gruff edge to his voice. "Once, long ago, I was to wed a Highland lass. It was an arranged marriage, of course, but she wouldna have me—no matter what her father said—for Eilean Fidra wasna grand enough for her tastes. 'Twas hard to believe, for this used to be one of the finest castles in the whole of the western Highlands. Ye should have seen it, richly appointed, secure against mon and nature, with well-stocked storerooms and larders. There were many lassies who would gladly have been my bride then." He laughed. It was a brusque hard sound. Again, he raked his fingers through his hair, this time using both hands.

"Och, now it is little more than a mockery of

its former self. As am I. Now I have nothing to
offer a bride. There are no riches to be had. There
is naught but a roof, and mayhap a few favorable
memories. That is all I do this night but offer
what little I can give to ye as yer husband on yer
wedding night."

A veil of tears misted Claricia's eyes as she
gazed up at him, thinking of everything he had
done for her, of what he'd said and how obvious
was his humility. Her voice was unusually
throaty, and barely more than a whisper. "You
are a very different man than I ever imagined."

"That is a compliment, I trust."

"Very much so."

"Then ye arena frightened of me?" *Ye dinna see
my brother every time ye look upon me?* The question
had to come to mind again and again, but he did
not have the strength to voice it aloud. He did
not think he could have borne to hear her speak
of him and Andrew in the same vein, especially
not on this night. Alexander held his breath, waiting for her to answer the easier question.

"A woman would be foolish to be frightened
of her husband, and I would be foolish to be
frightened of a man who can work such delightful sorcery." She swept an arm in a circular motion to take in the chamber bathed in golden
light.

Alexander smiled. He exhaled the pent-up
breath. "I find I'm thirsty. Would ye join me and
have some wine?" He ambled to a nearby table,
lifted a large methir, which had been carved from
a single piece of wood and embellished with silver handles in the shape of ram's heads, and

poured generous servings of malmsey into a pair of matched drinking horns.

"Thank you." Claricia held the horn to her lips and took three quick sips. The sweet, powerful beverage swirled through her veins, causing that same dizzying warmth she'd experienced in the great hall to return. She set it aside. "I have had enough already."

Alexander nodded. He, on the other hand, had not had enough, and after a deep, fortifying drink, he was able to ask, "Tell me, did ye miss me the past two nights?"

"I did," came Claricia's hushed reply. In the next instant, she lowered her lashes demurely, shocked not only by what she had said, but because of the truth of her words.

"That is what I hoped ye'd say. And I promise that tonight I willna be selfish with ye." Alexander lowered his voice. He set aside his empty drinking horn and reached out a hand to her, noticing as though from a very great distance that it was shaking. "Come here. Come to me. *Trothad an so*," he murmured in Gaelic. *Come hither.*

Claricia took a small step forward. Her hand went out to him. His fingers entwined with hers, and gently he turned her hand over to kiss the palm. His lips moved along the sensitive underside of her wrist, which smelled of the exotic potions women used to soften their skin. He pushed up the kirtle sleeve and trailed kisses all the way to her elbow, inhaling lemon balm and honey, rose water and a distinctly musky female scent.

It was heady to feel her smooth skin beneath his lips, intoxicating to breathe in the mingling of sweet and musky aromas. His eyes closed, then slowly opened, and, seeing the funny little look, at once solemn and expectant, upon her features, Alexander could not resist cradling her pretty face in his hands. Where the pads of this thumbs rubbed against her cheeks, she was as soft and luminescent as a rose. His eyes narrowed as he looked at her, tracing the contours of her face, her delicate jaw, and her plum-ripe mouth. Her moist lips glistened in the candlelight as if touched by dew at sunrise. There was a little pulse at the base of her throat beating like the wings of a moth.

From the first, Alexander had desired this woman. Even when he could think of her as naught but a whore and his enemy, he had desired her above all others, and now he felt that desire slice through him with an intensity so beautiful it was almost painful. She was his for all time, and every ugly appellation and image was gone forever. She was his wife to cherish and adore, and he could scarcely believe that he could have her without any remorse or guilt.

"Och, *mo ròs geall*, I'm going to kiss ye," Alexander drawled as he caressed her lower lip with the tip of his thumb. "I'm going to taste ye and show ye the full pleasure a woman can enjoy with a mon. I'm going to adore ye with my mouth and with my hands." Lightly, quickly, his lips made contact with hers: then they lifted away. Next he kissed the end of her nose. "I'm going to adore every inch of yer loveliness, from the top of yer head all the way down to yer toes."

Claricia merely stood there. *Adore her with his mouth and hands.* She had never imagined such a thing.

"Has no one ever told ye how beautiful ye

are?" he asked, but he already knew the sad tragic truth. He whispered in a velvety voice, "Never told ye how kissable and desirable ye are? How worthy of admiration ye are?"

She responded with a tiny shake of her head.

"*Eist*, how the angels must weep at such transgressions. It appears there are a host of crimes that must be rectified this night," he said before settling his mouth upon hers. He shifted his fingers from cradling her face to threading through her hair. The bridal crown of dried flowers had tumbled to the floor, and while a braid still circled her head like a halo, a lustrous shank of her golden hair cascaded over her shoulders and down her back.

Claricia let her eyes fall closed. It was a delicious kiss, slow and provocative, and after a while, she opened her lips to his coaxing. His tongue slid inside her mouth, hot against hers, and she tasted the saltiness of him as well as the lingering sweetness of the wine they'd been drinking. His hands moved downward, splayed wide, and pressed against her; his fingers hooked beneath the edge of her kirtle bodice to slide the garment off her shoulders. She did not resist. Off came the kirtle, then the linen undertunic, and when she stood unclothed before him, he gently pinned her arms at her side when she would have crossed them over her bared breasts.

Although the chamber was warm, her nipples puckered as his gaze moved over her body, leisurely, thoroughly. He missed nothing. From her breasts, his adoring glance traveled downward over her stomach, then lower, to linger at the soft triangle between her legs. She marveled at the languid sensation seeping into her limbs when she saw him swallow hard in reaction to her nakedness. It was a feeling to which she would have liked to surrender, a feeling that made her glance toward his hands and wish that they might go where his eyes had been only a moment before.

"Aye, let me look at ye. There is no shame in such beauty. Such perfection. Can ye not imagine that looking is only the first step in adoring? This is only the beginning of a long night for us." Alexander lifted a strand of golden hair from her shoulder, wrapped it between his fingers, and held it to his cheek to enjoy its soft satiny feel, to inhale its clean scent. Then he let it tumble back over her shoulder, watching in fascination as the end of that strand of golden hair curled round the luscious mound of one breast. His throat went suddenly dry. Every nerve ending in his body burned hot, then turned cold, and between his legs his manhood stiffened, swelling far beyond its natural size, pulsing against his confining leggings. He could barely control himself to speak. "Now ye must undress me," he said in a voice so hoarse he almost did not recognize it as his own.

"I—I know not what to do," Claricia said, realizing in that moment that she wanted to please him but experiencing at the same time an awful fear that she might fail.

"Give me yer hands. I will show ye," he said.

His steady fingers guided hers, showing her how to unclasp the silver pin at his shoulder and how to loosen the *breacan* about his torso. The plaid dropped to the floor alongside the saffron-tinted kirtle. Alexander lifted the white linen shirt

over his head, and when he stood before her in
nothing more than his leggings, he took her hand
in his once again and placed it against his bare
chest.

Claricia's fingers flexed in reaction to the firm,
hard surface. Her eyes widened, and she uttered
a tiny "Ooooh," part in surprise, part in pleasure
at the unfamiliar yet agreeable feeling of his
corded chest muscles. "You are so different from
me," she said, letting her fingertips trail over his
chest, then downward over his stomach, and
even lower, along a line of swirling black hair
that disappeared into his leggings.

"Och, that is good, my sweet white rose." Alexander spoke in a raspy voice. He was en-
thralled by her timid, gentle touch. "Ye should
get to know yer husband, for that is who I am
now, and I shouldna be a stranger to ye in any
way. Aye, a mon's chest and stomach are hard
and muscled, while a woman's are soft as a
feather pillow." His hands moved over her
breasts, lifting and cupping the supple flesh, and
her nipples stiffened beneath his palm. "And this
isna the only place where a man's and woman's
differences compliment each other."

She knew exactly what he meant, and could
not prevent her glance from lowering to look between his legs. Although he still wore his leggings, she could see the outline of his rigid
erection. A sort of apprehension mingling with
excitement rippled through her.

Alexander saw her reaction. "Do ye understand what is happening? Do ye understand
why? It is ye, my sweet white rose, who does that
to me, and ye shouldna be frightened by yer

powers. Most women would be pleased. While ye are soft and pliant, I am hard and full of energy." He took her hand and guided it between his legs. Slowly, he moved it higher along his inner thigh. In another second, he would have the touch he craved, and, guiding her, he cupped her fingers along the ridge of his swollen desire. *Heaven on earth*. That was what this sensation of bliss was, and for a moment, he could hardly speak. At last, his voice came, roughened by passion. "That is the way it should be. Responsive to yer touch."

Claricia trembled all over. The turgid feel of him beneath her fingers excited her, as did the ardent words that he spoke to her. So, too, did a skirl of excitement unfold through her at the promise of where this would lead. They kissed again. His lips were hotter than before, more insistent, and when her hand lifted from between his legs to wind about his neck, she bent within his embrace, pliant and willing, as if a peculiar languor had assailed her limbs.

At length, Alexander broke away from kissing her. He felt almost as if he were drowning, and he needed a deep breath of air to clear his head, to steady himself. Holding her tightly about the waist, he studied her face in the rushlight, searching for signs of her readiness for him to move onward from kissing to something more. The flickering golden light enhanced her features with a special, expectant glow. Her lilac eyes were luminous, there was a flush across her cheeks and brow, her lips were parted, and her chest rose and fell in shallow agitated breaths.

They could be no clearer indication that it was

time to advance beyond mere kissing. In an instant, his lips had brushed across her mouth, then down the column of her slender throat. He heard her moan as his tongue and lips moved over her shoulders and lower, to her breasts. "I adore ye," he whispered, his lips moving over her nipple to suckle and taste it. His own moans mingled with hers.

Claricia had never imagined it might be possible to feel like this. Every touch, every sensation, was charged with a vividness of which she had never conceived. His hands held her firmly, wrapped about her waist, while his mouth moved from one breast to the other. His lips trailed down to her belly as he came to kneel before her, his hands sliding from her waist, over her hips. One hand moved behind to cup her backside, while the other dipped lower to that place between her legs. Gently, quickly, his fingers were inside her, spreading the petals of her sex as if he were searching for something. He massaged and fondled, rubbing the increasing moisture that was within her about the outer lips of her most feminine private places, and then his motions became smaller, more controlled. A moan fell from her lips. He had found a tiny sensitive nub. It was there that he concentrated his caresses.

"My lord, Alexander!" she cried out. "Sweet Heaven," she moaned. Her legs were weakening, her head fell back, golden tresses tumbling about her hips, and she wrapped her hands about his neck, her fingers threading through his hair. She could hardly bear it. Her legs widened of their own will, and she pulled on his neck, bringing him so close to her that his mouth brushed against her naked belly.

"Be careful," he cautioned. His groin cramped with excruciating desire. Perspiration drenched his brow. He wanted her. His skin was on fire, his erection was throbbing, and he was ready for her. But he forced himself to say, "Ye excite me, but 'tis yer pleasure—not mine—I wish to guarantee this night. We mustna go too fast, else I'll get greedy."

"I don't understand," she panted.

"Ye will soon enough, my sweet." His lips dropped a kiss upon her stomach. His tongue swirled out, and he kissed her flesh again. "Ye will soon enough. I willna fail this night."

His fingers were doing things Claricia had not dreamed were possible. It was unimaginably intimate, and he was achingly, tenderly attentive. Everything he was doing was to give her pleasure. Then he leaned forward, his mouth went over that nub, and his tongue slid inside her, stroking and delving where his fingers had been. She heard a whimpering sound. It was coming from her, and when his tongue flicked about the opening, sliding up and down, in and out, she cried out, her fingers digging into his shoulders.

Suddenly, Alexander rose from his knees, and her puzzled gaze followed him until he stood at his full height above her. " 'Tis almost time, *mo ròs geall*. Almost time," he murmured in answer to her unspoken question, and although his lips no longer caressed her, one hand slipped between her legs while he swept her into his arms to carry her toward the bed. He placed her upon the fur coverlet. Quickly, he unlaced his leggings, pulled them off, and climbed onto the bed, his legs sliding between hers as he lay atop her. Again, he sought and found that tiny nub.

She was aching all over from the pleasure he was giving her. As if his hands were not enough, now their skin touched without a shred of fabric between them. His hard thighs pressed against hers. His flesh was warm, and unfamiliar, maddening sensations were beginning to build up in her. Claricia shuddered, widened her legs, rubbed against him, and arched upward. Every inch of her, inside and out, was straining for something, but she did not know what it was. She hiked her lips closer to his touch. She arched and pressed and strained with increasing desperation.

"Aye, it's coming upon ye. Creeping up on ye to hold ye, ride ye, and take ye like the wind to a place ye've never been. Ye're almost there, and I'm coming with ye," he whispered as the caressing tip of his hard male flesh rubbed against the opening to her sex.

Once, twice, he rubbed the length of himself against those moist outer lips. He felt her shudder, heard her cry out his name again. She was frantic, and his blood raced even faster. Quickly, he entered her, sheathing himself to the hilt with one heavy stroke, and feeling in that exact moment the first contractions of her velvety flesh about him. She was shaking, convulsing. Her hands were clutching at his shoulders. It was as if she were trying to climb higher, and with a low moan, he followed her to that height, his body clenching in a series of explosive convulsions, surrendering to her as she was surrendering to him.

A large golden light burst within Claricia. She cried out as her world exploded, then she emitted several long soft sighs as the heat of that explosion flowed through her limbs, and she began floating back to the bed. Her body relaxed beneath his. Her arms were wrapped across his shoulders, her legs were still entwined with his, and for several minutes, they remained joined as one. As if from very far away, she heard the sound of their shallow breathing. Slowly, she became aware of the cool night air against her exposed skin. But she did not move, liking far too much this sensation of oneness, of closeness, of ultimate pleasure and trust.

"How did you know?" she asked in a voice ringing with the profound wonder of it all.

"It is not uncommon for some women to have that experience with any mon. Some never have it. And then there are other women, like yerself, who only find it with a certain mon. And for ye, I wanted to be that mon." Propping himself up on his elbows to look into her eyes, he said with touching humility, "I hoped it could be with me. There was desire between us from the first. That was promising. And I could not turn away from the fact that our bodies knew what our minds did not admit."

"What was that?" she wanted to know.

"That we were destined for each other," Alexander said with calm certainty. "Happiness or contentment in a marriage doesna depend upon whether one is *sassenach* or Highland born. In most marriages, contentment—not to mention affection—is a rare commodity. Even more precious is compatibility, particularly in the carnal sense. And though ye may not understand it yet, that rarity blesses our union. Such compatibility canna be nurtured. It is destined."

Claricia touched the polished green heart and smiled up at him. How fanciful it was to consider that they had been *destined* for each other, and with a startling jolt of clarity, Claricia realized that she had not abandoned her dreams.

She had a new dream: that this marriage with Alexander Kirkpatrick would be a marriage in truth. If their bodies were compatible, why not their hearts? Their spirits? Her hopes soared at the prospect, then plummeted at the absurdity of such an ambition. It was preposterous to fancy that the love and tenderness that had been the mainstay of her girlish dreams might be hers with this man. She should have been satisfied with his kindness and consideration.

"Dinna look so sad, *mo ròs geall*." Alexander was stricken by the bleak expression that washed across her pretty face. He leaned down to brush his lips across her forehead. "That isna all. There is more, I promise."

"More?" she gasped, relieved that he had not suspected the truth behind her frown. Sweet Heaven forbid that he might suspect she was falling in love with him. For that was the truth. She was falling in love with Alexander Kirkpatrick, if she had not already done so. But how could he even respect—let alone love—a woman who would act with such wanton abandon? She might be a wife, but she had acted like the whore her uncle had branded her. "Are you saying it is all right to feel that way? It is not a shameful thing for a wife to act like that?"

"Och, my sweet rose, there is nothing shameful between a mon and his wife. Nothing shameful in accepting the pleasure I wish to give ye," he said, understanding what it was she could not say aloud. Silently, he cursed de Clinton for every evil he had inflicted upon this lovely woman, but he revealed none of this anger to her. "Pleasure between a husband and wife is a miracle. And there are a thousand different ways to reach that astonishing sensual height. Rest awhile," he said. Alexander pulled the furs about them, and, moving to lie beside her, he rested his head next to hers. "Sleep, now. Then I will show ye other ways to soar with the wind. Other ways to adore ye."

Reassured by his tender words, Claricia dozed. The rushlights burned low, flickered, and went out. One by one all but a few of the candles reached the end of their wicks and sputtered into darkness. Several hours passed. Pale embers glowed in the braziers, and the crisp air bore the sweet smell of beeswax when Claricia opened her eyes.

The first thing of which she was aware was Alexander holding her in the cradle of his body. She was content to lie there in the dark listening to his even breathing, inhaling the familiar masculine scent of him, and enjoying the pressure of his thighs against hers, his chest against her back. She closed her eyes to recall the pleasure he had given her the night before. He had said there was no shame in experiencing pleasure or in the way she had reacted. He had said it was a miracle, but that was not the greatest miracle. In Claricia's mind, the greatest miracle was his gentle strength and restraint, and his eagerness to please her. She had never known that a man might treat a woman as he had treated her.

Enveloped by warmth and security, Claricia arched her back like a cat in such a way that the roundness of her bottom pressed against his limp member. Immediately, it grew longer and harder, pulsing with hot, insistent energy in the space between her legs. She had not meant to touch him in that way, but having done so, she was neither shocked nor frightened. It only made her memories of the previous night's pleasure more vivid. She imagined Alexander assuring her that it was all right for a wife to give in to the impulse to arch her back a little more. Perhaps even move her bottom a little bit against him. It certainly felt good to her, and by his reaction, she knew it must be pleasurable for Alexander as well.

She made several little rocking movements. Each time, she arched her back just a little more, allowing his erection to rub deeper and higher between her legs. The growing moisture from her sex anointed him, and a bittersweet yearning began to build within her. She was swollen with desire. Even her breasts began to ache.

"Och, my sweet little wife, what a joy it is to feel ye unfolding to me like a wild flower," Alexander murmured in a sleepy voice against her neck. His hands about her waist moved higher to caress her breasts. He had thought he was dreaming. What perfect magic was this, to have his wife awaken him in such a delightful fashion? He kissed her shoulder, the column of her neck, and beneath her ear. "And a good morning to ye, too, *mo ròs geall*."

"You're awake," she exclaimed, very glad that she was not facing him. She felt a red-hot flush flood her cheeks. It might have been all right for a wife to do this, but it was still wanton, and Claricia was not yet entirely used to such flagrant intimacy. She did not think she could have met his gaze if they had been face-to-face.

"So ye're ready to soar with me, are ye?" he drawled. One hand slid down from her breast to stroke between her legs. "Ready to ride like the wind?"

"I am," came her hushed and breathless reply.

Alexander made a growling sort of sound from deep in his throat. The willingness of his wife was thrilling. This was more than he had thought possible. Carefully, he moved her from her side and put her on her knees. He brushed her long hair off her back and showed her how to support her weight on her hands. Then, with a firm hold on her hips, he entered her from behind, sliding into her moist heat. She sighed when he buried himself in her. He watched the slender curve of her back arch and flex, and he heard a series of tiny moans when he began to move within her.

Claricia was too excited to wonder about the bewildering position in which he'd placed her. He must have known what he was doing, for from that angle, he had filled her more completely and far more deeply than she had imagined was possible. The sensations he was arousing within her were sharply erotic, and with each thrust, she was being carried skyward on a bed of clouds, going higher, as he had promised he would take her.

"It's happening," Claricia cried out in amazement at how quickly he was making *it* happen all over again. She writhed against him, then began to push backward to meet each of his thrusts. The heart pendant was swinging wildly between her breasts, her hair had fallen across her eyes, and she could not see, but these matters weren't important, as she gave in to a long, low sigh of pleasure.

He felt her begin to tighten about him. His hands moved from her hips to her buttocks. Hard, he squeezed her and pulled her against him as he exploded into her. An exultant cry was wrenched from him. "Och, Heaven on earth. Sweetling." His hot seed emptied into her, his thrusts slowed, then ended, and still he held her buttocks firmly to his groin, still he remained inside her as he prayed that his seed would take root. One of his hands moved around to her stomach. He splayed his palm across her belly. "Perhaps our child grows there already," he said in a soft almost reverent hush.

An awful frigid disappointment washed over Claricia. Her skin turned clammy, and she held her breath, fighting off tears and wishing that he had not said such a thing.

"It will be wonderful to hold the bairn born of our union." Alexander had not thought until that moment of his heir. Now it was a prospect that made his heart swell with a joyousness that laced his voice. "It will be nothing short of a miracle when the next laird of the Kirkpatricks is born, and no matter what the origin of our marriage, ye must know that I will be proud and pleased that ye are his mother. Believe me: I could never wish for any other woman but ye."

Tears dropped from Claricia's eyes, moistening the veil of hair across her face. The night before, she had thought she was falling in love with her husband: now she knew that she had done so. Being Alexander Kirkpatrick's wife and lover had nothing to do with duty. It was her heart, not her mind, that revealed itself to her, and she knew that she did not deserve him, for she would never be an adequate wife, no matter how hard she tried. There was something she must tell him, and it was one of the hardest things she had ever done. "I cannot be the mother of your child."

Her solemn words were a harsh assault on his state of mind. The intimate moment was shattered. "How do ye know that?" he demanded, withdrawing from her. She rolled onto her back to stare up at him, and the utter anguish in her eyes tore at his gut. He saw that she had been crying great, silent tears, and despite his own pain, he reached out to brush the tears from her cheek. "How do ye know that?" he repeated in a gentler tone. "Why do ye say such a thing?"

Claricia bit her lower lip, desperately trying to think of how to answer. She could tell him neither about Simon, nor how his brother's child had been torn from her body feet first, and how she had bled for days even after Meg had taken the infant into the hills. She could only tell him part of the truth. Very softly, she said, "In all the years with my uncle there was nothing. He said I was barren."

And ye believed the treacherous auld bastard? Alexander wanted to cry out, but he did not. "Did ye never think it was de Clinton's fault?"

"No," she whispered, wondering if it could

possibly be true. Had her uncle lied to cover his own inadequacy? Had his physicians told her only what he'd instructed them to say? Childbirth was often a harsh ordeal. Perhaps her experience had not been an uncommon one after all. There had been no one to talk with after Meg had left except her uncle and his loyal servants. No one to answer her questions. There had been no one Claricia could trust, no one in whom she could confide.

Alexander saw her uncertainty, and in an effort to lessen her unhappiness, he tried to reassure her. "That isna why I married ye, *mo ròs geall*. It doesna matter," Alexander said, but knew that he lied. In the space of a few hours, his expectations for their marriage had changed. To have a child of her womb would have been a treasure that had nothing to do with giving the clan its next laird, but everything to do with miracles.

"I am sorry to fail you," she said in a quiet voice. "When you said that you would marry me, I made a pledge to myself to fulfill my every duty to you as your wife, and although I fail you in this regard, I think that I can promise to please you in every other way. Have I not pleased you thus far?" she dared to inquire as a scarlet flush colored her cheeks.

"Duty? I dinna want duty. Is that what that was between us last night and this morning?" Alexander raised his voice. It was as if a devil had taken possession of him. Something evil was making him say these angry, horrid things to her. He sneered, "Duty? Did ye think the little moans and sighs would please me? Were you playing the whore with your own husband?" He spoke the poisonous words without thinking, but as soon as he heard them he regretted that such lowly thoughts had crossed his mind. "Och, God," he swore in agony, and pulled her into his arms. "What have I done?"

"No!" Claricia cried in anguish. She did not pull away from his comforting embrace but shook her head from side to side, muttering, "No." Alexander could not have hurt her more if he had lanced her with a sword. She wanted to tell him the whole truth, but she couldn't, and instead, she sobbed against his shoulder. "I am sorry you would think such a thing. You are a kind and honorable man, a worthy laird and Highlander, but this marriage will not work. I am not the right woman to be the wife of a Highland laird, and especially not to be your wife."

"Dinna speak such nonsense." There was an unexpected aching in his chest, the likes of which he had never experienced before, and he found himself having to fight tears. He did not understand the power this woman had over him. At first, it had been his physical nature, his lusty male desires, that he could not control. Now she had possessed his emotions, his thoughts, his very ability to think clearly and logically. It was almost as if she were holding onto a corner of his heart. "My tongue should be cut out for speaking to ye like that. It was the disappointment of what ye said about birthing, coming on top of all we've had together this past night. A child seemed like a natural outcome to such perfection; it didna make sense to hear anything to the contrary. I didna expect to discover such a sad thing at this time, not after so much joy and pleasure." He stroked her hair. He continued to hold her, and kissed her brow. "There is nothing wrong with ye. Ye're perfect."

"But can't you see?" Claricia said between little sobs. "From the moment I came into your life things have not been right. Verily, it is on my account that your vengeance has failed. I have sullied your honor."

"*Eist!*" His jaw stiffened. "There will be no talk of failure. No talk of tarnished honor. I have not failed," he stated in a voice made deadly by its sudden unnervingly calm tone. "The laird of the Kirkpatricks never fails."

Claricia looked at him with widening eyes, a chill seeping from the tips of her toes to the top of her head. His features had hardened into something dark and menacing. His gaze had narrowed, an eerie dark green light reflecting from the depths of his eyes. "What do you mean?"

"I will kill him yet. I will have my vengeance. *Ni mi dioghaltas air.*" *I will take vengeance on him.*

She lay on the bed for no more than a few heartbeats, yet it seemed like an eternity. She needed no clarification. She knew exactly what he meant, and who it was he intended to kill. Her voice was roughened by renewed tears. "When do you leave?"

"Before a fortnight elapses. I will join King Robert's army near Stirling for the coming fight with the English. He will be among the *sassenach* generals, and there, I will seek him on the field of battle. Vengeance will be mine." Alexander watched her expression change before his eyes. Of a sudden, she was uncommonly pale, and there was a brittleness to her appearance that made him wonder if she cared about him. If she knew of the size of the gathering armies, would she worry for his life, his safety? It was rumored that across the border, King Edward was appointing the largest military force ever to be arrayed by England. Aloud, he asked, "Would ye miss me?"

"Yes."

Her honesty touched Alexander deeply, as did the trust that was revealed upon her face when she made that sad little admission. The hold she had upon his heart extended beyond a mere corner. It was almost entirely hers, and in return, he wanted to bring her happiness. He wanted to see her smile, to hear her laugh. "It is I who am not the right one for this marriage. Ye deserve a mon who can give ye a future."

Claricia felt as if the air had been snatched from her lungs. There. It was said, and her heart was close to breaking. This marriage was to be nothing more than what he had intended from the first. She should not have expected anything more. She should have been satisfied with the security he was willing to give her. She should never have allowed herself to feel anything for him. She should never have allowed herself to hope, to dream.

A fortnight. That was all the future she would have with this man who was her husband, and she forced herself to smile up at Alexander, determined to make the most of every minute they would have together. If this was all she was to have, then every memory must be as sweet as the ones from the night before.

Chapter 15

"**B**y all that's holy, Rourke, do ye see what I do?" Alexander stood on a ridge overlooking Loch Awe. His head and torso were wrapped in furs against the brisk wind. A bow and a quiver of arrows were hooked over his shoulder. He pointed directly below them. "Look down there. Do ye see the woman and lad about to step out onto the ice?"

The two men were returning from a hunting foray into the hills. Four days had passed since the wedding. It was the second week of March. Very soon Alexander and Rourke would be heading south, and Alexander knew that it might be midsummer before he returned to Eilean Fidra, if he returned at all from the coming battle. Every morning, he had been into the hills to restock the larder, and that day, Rourke was accompanying him. Game was scarce. Only a red grouse that afternoon, but it was the best he could do.

"Who are they? Do ye know?" Alexander asked. To his astonished eye, the lad resembled Andrew or even himself as a boy, and the young woman bore an uncanny likeness to how he'd imagined a grown Caitrine might appear. But logic told him it could not be. One was dead. The other was lost among the ocean of refugees and *diobrachain*. Perhaps it was nothing more than a trick of the light. Soon the seasons would change. Already the days were lengthening, and as the snow and ice started to melt in the glens and ravines, it was not uncommon for strange shadows or sharp glimmers of sunlight to obscure reality.

" 'Tis my Viviane," replied Rourke. He knew that Lady Claricia had planned to visit the island that day, and it appeared that upon her departure, Viviane and Simon must have accompanied her on a portion of the distance across the frozen loch. They were now heading home. Claricia must have taken one of the paths along the shore to the spit of land north of the castle, where the crossing point was narrowest.

"And the lad? Who is he?" There was an abrupt edge to Alexander's question. A baffled expression marked his face. The similarity between the lad and his brother, the woman and his sister, was so striking, it wrenched at his gut. They were Kirkpatrick's, he was sure, and for a moment he wondered if his father had sired children with a woman other than his mother. No, that could not have been for although children of a mistress were not uncommon in the Highlands, Alexander did not doubt that his father had loved no other woman than his mother. He had been an uncommon man, a devoted husband, and would never have insulted his wife in such a manner. "Who is the boy?"

"Her son," said Rourke. He did not like lying to Alexander, but he had no choice, having promised Claricia that her secret was safe with him. Besides, he only had suspicions.

"The son of yer Viviane? The woman who rescued ye?" asked Alexander. Incredulity colored this query. "That is the woman who's been living on the Auld Believer's Isle all this time, and ye've been hiding her from me?"

A sort of wary uneasiness began to close in on Rourke. It was a familiar sensation, very similar to how he'd felt when it had seemed Viviane's past might threaten their future. He had used to fear that the secret she guarded might take her from him one day. Of late, Rourke's apprehension about her past had abated. Now, however, it returned with the realization that Alexander must have been looking at Viviane and seeing what Sorcha and the other women had seen when she entered the hall at Eilean Fidra. Alexander must have been suspecting what he himself had begun to suppose after learning from Claricia how it was that the woman she called Meg had come into her life. "I wasna hiding her from ye, Alexander," said Rourke, wishing that his Viviane's past were truly as blank as her memory.

But Alexander did not hear his kinsman. Having tossed aside the dead grouse, he was leaping over the gray rocks and down the steep trail toward the shore. "Stop!" he called out when the woman and boy began to make their way across the frozen loch. He had reached the bottom of the path and headed toward them. He cupped his hands to his mouth. "Wait!"

Viviane heard a man's voice. She paused and turned toward the shore. At first, she saw only Rourke standing on a ledge halfway up the rocky slope, and she waved up at him with a friendly smile upon her face. She did not see the man approaching her on level ground.

"Caitrine!" Alexander called out to her.

A chill worked its way up Viviane's spine. *Caitrine.* Someone was making the same mistake as the women in the castle. She did not like it any more now than she had then. She was Viviane, not Caitrine. The late-afternoon sun was in her eyes, and she could not see the man who had spoken to her, but she knew he was mistaken.

"It's me," Alexander called out joyously. He quickened his pace and began to run toward his sister. She had grown taller since that afternoon when she'd been taken from the misty forest clearing. Taller and fuller of figure, yet her hair was as black and curly as it had always been, and she was as beautiful as their grandmother had ever been. The physical resemblance to Lady Isobel was heart-stopping. Her stance was regal and proud as she returned his stare, the wind tugging at that long wild hair. She was dressed in a patchwork of furs, and her hands were bound in rags, no better than a beggar. It tore at Alexander to see his sister dressed like a common peasant. She was the daughter of a prominent laird, descended from the great king Canmore. A lump formed in his throat. What was wrong with him? None of that mattered as long as she was alive. *Alive. Caitrine was alive.* The years of wishing had not been in vain. Somewhere in the back of his mind a voice began a silent prayer of thanksgiving, and he held open his arms as he neared her.

Viviane screamed at the man's swift approach. It was a quick, shrill sound of fright. "Nay," she cried in denial, and took a step away from him, flailing her arms to maintain her balance on the icy surface of the loch. She glanced up to Rourke, hoping that he would hurry down and explain to this man how others had made the same mistake. She wanted Rourke to hurry to her side and keep this stranger away from her.

"Dinna ye recognize me?" Alexander asked, now only a few paces away from her. His pulse was racing. His heart was bursting with happiness. He wanted to sweep her into a brotherly embrace, to assure her that he had never stopped asking after her, never stopped hoping and praying that she might one day come back to them. He wanted to promise that he wouldn't fail her a second time, and that she would never be separated from her family again. But he saw her apprehension and spoke not a word. He did nothing except stop and wait for her to speak.

The man's urgent voice caused Viviane to look away from Rourke, who had begun to make his way down the slope. The man who had called her Caitrine was standing immediately before her. He had asked if she recognized him, and Viviane raised a hand to shield her eyes against the bright sun, thinking that even if she had once known this man, it was more than likely that she would have forgotten him along with everything and everyone else. Which was how she wanted it. She was content with Rourke and Simon. She did not want to search out her past, but she looked at him nonetheless, in part to humor him, in part to prove that he was mistaken. Then he would go away and leave her and Simon in peace.

Viviane's eyes widened at the sight of him, and

her breath caught, turning to a soundless shriek of terror in her throat. Her hand rose to her chest, her fingers clutching as if for air, and her mouth opened, but not a sound came forth. Aye, she did recognize him, and it was not a good thing. He was not a good thing, not a good man.

This was the man who had raped Claricia in the solar all those summers before. She would never forget that angular face, that black hair, those deep-set eyes.

"Dinna be frightened," Alexander said in a lower tenor, which was meant to soothe her. Still his voice rang with an unsettling urgency he could not control, and to his dismay, he saw that her panic seemed to be increasing rather than abating. In the hopes of calming his sister, he slid back a few steps from her before speaking again. "There is no reason to be frightened of me. I mean ye no harm. I am Alexander Kirkpatrick, laird of Eilean Fidra. And I have reason to believe I'm also—"

Simon's father! The unspeakable truth was imprinted upon Viviane's mind. *Sweet Saint Aidan. Believe what ye want, but I know ye're the mon who raped Lady Claricia, who put that bairn in her belly. And for God knows what distempered reason, the mon she's married.* The unspeakable thought made Viviane wonder if she had lost hold of her senses.

Of a sudden, a thousand images crowded her brain. For years, she had turned away from her past. For some reason, it had been easier to deal with Claricia's pain than with her own. Her past was a blank tapestry to be ignored, while Claricia's had been one of vivid horrors, which had to be avenged. Perhaps it was because Claricia had been the one to remember, not she. But now she could not prevent the sights and sounds of that dreadful afternoon from returning.

She had obeyed Claricia and hidden when the Highlanders stormed the castle walls. But when she heard Claricia's agonized screams, she had crawled out from the tiny space. A tall man with long black braids had been straddling Claricia on the floor, grunting and pounding his body into hers, and she had known what he was doing.

It had not mattered that he was a Highlander, as she was. It had been an evil thing he was doing, and when he had finished with her dear friend and mistress, the man with the midnight-black braids had wiped the sweat from his face, opened his eyes, and seen her crouched in the corner. How horrible it had been, for his expression had been jubilant when he'd stood over Claricia to readjust his leggings, and her stomach had lurched violently when he'd smiled and extended a hand to her.

"Quickly, come. It's time," he had said to her in Gaelic, and she had quivered with fear. She had screamed, "*No!*" He had started toward her and had taken hold of her arm as if to pull her from the solar. She had screamed again and again, and, kicking and fighting the man, she had managed to break free of his grasp. Claricia had dashed toward them, and in the next instant, an expression of utter surprise had washed over the man's face. She had held her breath as a small gurgling sound escaped his lips when he glanced downward at his chest and frowned.

Viviane remembered looking at the Highlander to see what had made him frown. There had been a knife in his chest, exactly where his heart should have been, and his twitching hands had moved upward as if to grab the knife, but it had been too late. A great red stain had burst across his tunic, and he had fallen to the rush-covered floor, his eyes wide with dismay and his lips moving as if to speak.

He had died.

So who was this? A demon? Nay, he had said he was the laird, *the man Claricia had married.* How could this be? There was a terrible buzzing in Viviane's ears, and she grabbed at her head to stop it.

"Meg?"

It was a woman's voice. Alexander and Viviane both turned toward the shore, and in the next second, Claricia appeared.

"What is wrong?" Claricia asked Meg, at first not seeing Alexander who was standing off to one side, and unaware of Rourke, who had reached the bottom of the hill and was a few paces behind her. She spoke in Gaelic. "I heard you scream. What has happened?"

Viviane's face contorted. She was angry, and stormy with confusion. "What have ye done?" she screamed at Claricia, feeling betrayed and threatened. Her frenzied words carried across the loch and into the hills, echoing and reverberating many times over, like the wail of a hundred *ùruis-gean,*creatures half-human, half-hobgoblin.

Alexander looked from his wife to his sister, then back to his wife "What are ye doing here?" he asked Claricia.

"Broad beans, white cabbages, beets and fennel," Claricia blurted out, sounding almost as irrational as Meg, for the sight of Alexander had momentarily confused her. "We were sowing the seeds. She has a small garden on the island. We were sowing the seeds."

"But why?"

"The moon is waning, and the planting must be done before the dark time comes."

Alexander had not meant, "why plant the seeds?" He still did not understand what was happening, and he started to ask why she had called his sister Meg, when the screeching started again.

Viviane shouted at Claricia, "Why have ye married the mon who raped ye? What madness is this? Did ye not kill him? What sorcery brings him back to life?"

Rourke had reached the edge of the loch, and, hearing his Viviane's hysterical speech, he momentarily leaned against a bare tree trunk, knowing in that second that Simon must be Andrew's child. *Why have ye married the mon who raped ye?* Viviane had demanded of Claricia, and Rourke shuddered at the whole of what that meant. *Did ye not kill him?*

The bits of truth had jagged, ugly edges, but they fit together. Rourke knew that Andrew had been killed while raiding one of de Clinton's strongholds in search of Caitrine. It had been six years before, which approximately fit Simon's age, and although Rourke did not like it, there could be no doubt that Andrew had raped Claricia, perhaps while his Viviane was watching. Andrew was Simon's father. And Claricia quite probably had been the one to murder Andrew, her rapist. Supporting himself against the tree, he stared at Alexander, wondering how much of this tale his kinsman had been told.

Christ's bones, the truth was an awful thing, and Rourke rubbed an arm across his eyes, trying for a moment to erase the next reality that derived from the first. If Andrew was Simon's father, that could have explained the similarity between Simon and Viviane. They were not mother and son. He already knew that. But what he had not imagined was that they were aunt and nephew, which was, of course, true, if his Viviane—despite what she believed—was indeed the missing Caitrine.

"This is not the same man," Claricia said to her friend.

"Impossible," Viviane hissed. She glanced in frantic desperation toward Alexander, then toward Simon, who was standing to her side with a bewildered look upon his young face. The similarity was unsettling. Father and son. The green eyes. The black hair. Even the nose and thin mouth were the same.

"They were brothers," Claricia said quietly, wishing that she did not have to say any of it aloud, wishing that Alexander might not hear the truth at that moment, not like this. But she needed to calm Meg. She had never seen her act that way, as if she were on the verge of some demented action. Claricia was afraid that Meg might injure herself.

"Ye brought him here." Viviane's expression contorted like that of a lunatic. "How could ye? Why?"

"I did not bring him," Claricia said calmly.

"Liar," she spat back.

Rourke intervened. "She doesna lie. The laird and I were returning from hunting when we spotted ye and the lad from above. Alexander Kirkpatrick was curious. Nothing more."

"Do ye betray me, too?" Viviane spun about to face Rourke. "The pair of ye bringing him here. Ye both betray me," she keened.

Alexander sensed the same rising madness that Claricia had perceived. He attempted to soothe the young woman. "They did not bring me. It is as my Irish kinsman Rourke O'Connor says. I was curious to meet ye. There was no other reason."

But Viviane did not seem to have heard either of the men. "Have ye not thought of the lad?" she demanded of Claricia. In the next heartbeat, a horrible prospect flashed across her mind. They were there to take Simon from her. The laird was the man who had raped Claricia, Simon was his natural-born child, and now that Claricia and the laird were married they wanted their son. That explained it. That was why they had married. That was why they were there.

"Come to me, Simon. Quickly." Viviane motioned him behind her, then she pulled out a dirk from beneath her patchwork of furs. "Ye canna have him, neither of ye, do ye hear me? Ye gave him to me. Ye asked me to keep him safe, to protect him with my verra life, and I did. He's mine now. Ye canna have him."

"What in God's name is she babbling about?" Alexander asked Claricia.

Rourke walked toward his Viviane and extended a hand to her. He took a breath and saw that his arm was trembling. "Give me the dirk. Hand it to me."

Viviane pointed the knife in Rourke's direction. She made several sharp jabs in the air. "Stay back. All of ye. Keep away from me and the lad."

Rourke stared at her in alarm as a terrible suspicion unfolded in his mind. He had always known his Viviane was different. So, too, did he know of the tainted MacWilliam blood. It flowed in his veins but did not manifest itself, and if his Viviane was Caitrine, it flowed in hers as well. It came from Murdoch MacWilliam, their great-great-grandfather, who had vowed to murder his every relative, his every enemy, anyone who defied or displeased him, anyone who stood in his way of holding sole title to the lands he'd stolen over a lifetime of greed. Murdoch MacWilliam was the reason the infant twins, Lady Isobel and Rourke's grandfather, Ingvar, had been separated at birth. Rourke touched the upper portion of the crucifix hanging about his neck. It was the only relic each twin had had of their mother, who had been murdered by her own father, the insane Murdoch MacWilliam.

Tainted blood. That was what people called it, and some whispered that it had flowed through Andrew's veins, making him wild and reckless, accounting for his lust for blood and the apparent pleasure he had derived from inflicting pain. It was said that that was why he had attempted to rescue his sister against all odds.

Could it be that his lovely, sensual Viviane was cursed with the tainted MacWilliam blood? Rourke wondered. Was that what made her such a passionate creature? Was it why she'd had the

courage to live alone with the child? And could
it be that he would lose her, even if she did not
find her past?

"Viviane." Rourke spoke in a voice that rose
barely above a whisper. "Ye must listen to me.
Dinna look at them. Dinna think of them or try
to understand anything. Ye must come to me, Viviane. I love ye with all my heart. *Le m'uile mo
chridhe.* Ye must come to me."

"Nay!" she cried out. Again, she made a threatening motion with the dirk.

The sun was setting and the night winds were
gathering, but that was not what caused the chill
to seep through Alexander's bones as he tried to
make sense of what was happening, of what he'd
heard. To begin, he did not doubt that this
woman was his sister Caitrine. It could have accounted for why a woman with no memory had
found her way to Loch Awe; somewhere deep
within her mind had survived the knowledge of
the Old Believer's Isle. That she did not recognize
him was not troubling. It did not surprise him
that his fragile sister had forgotten. Indeed, he
considered it a blessing that she had been able to
forget the young girl she once was, for with that
loss of memory she had no recollection of what
must have happened to that young girl when
she'd been taken from the mist-shrouded clearing. She had no recollection of their mother's being butchered in her sleep, of their father's being
executed. It did not trouble Alexander that her
mind had fixed the past in such a way that she
had not lost anyone and there was no pain. What
troubled Alexander was what she had said to

Claricia about the boy she was trying to hide behind her.

Ye canna have him. Ye gave him to me. Ye asked me to keep him safe, to protect him with my verra life, and I did. He's mine now.

Again, Alexander looked at Claricia to ask, "What is she talking about? Whose child is this?"

More than anything, Claricia wanted to tell Alexander the truth. But she was afraid of how Meg would react. "Simon is Meg's," she said in a clear, steady voice.

"I dinna believe it." Alexander turned away from his wife in anger, surprised at how it wounded his spirit to hear her lie to him.

"You must believe it," she said.

But Alexander did not acknowledge her admonition. "What do ye know of this, Rourke?"

"It is not for me to say," he replied, forever bound by his promise to Lady Claricia and equally determined not to hurt his Viviane in any way.

"So ye know something," Alexander retorted, not liking to consider that somehow these three people had been keeping secrets from him. He looked at them each in turn and was shocked by the uniform determination their faces revealed. These three people did, indeed, share a secret, and for a moment, it seemed to Alexander that he might be engulfed by a sensation of overwhelming betrayal. "I dinna understand any of this." The words were wrenched from him. They were an invocation for illumination.

Claricia could not bear to look at Alexander. She loved him and wanted nothing except good memories of the times they might share. She did not want to hurt or deceive him. But she was failing in every respect. She knew that afternoon would not be a good memory. He was being hurt and deceived, and, seeing the confusion and self-doubt that marked his countenance, Claricia blamed herself. It was as she had claimed. She was not right for him. There was too much of the past between them. She averted her gaze from his.

"Dinna turn away from me, *mo ròs geall.*" Alexander's softly spoken plea was almost swallowed by the wind.

Hot tears pooled in Claricia's eyes. The crisp wintry air filled her lungs, and she held the deep breath for several seconds. "Please, Meg. Please. For me. Just the truth. Just let me tell him the truth. Nothing more than words. Then we'll leave you in peace. You and Simon together."

"Don't go any nearer to her!" Alexander called out the warning to Claricia. He was thankful that she did not move.

"Ye would tell him?" Viviane cast a hostile glance at the man who had warned her friend to stay away from her. She took a step toward Claricia.

"I have no choice," she said, fighting the urge to step away from this alien, menacing Meg. "He is my husband, and there can be naught but the truth between us."

"Ye would put us all in danger, after ye made me swear never to tell a living soul? Ye know what will happen, don't ye?" She took another step closer to Claricia. "Yer uncle will find out that ye lied to him, that the bairn lives, and then he'll be coming after us."

Alexander heard every word of this, and the jumble of bizarre pieces started to fall into place, not like feathers coming to land, but like shards of broken pottery, hard and sharp, crashing to the ground. There had been a child, Claricia's, conceived out of rape; a child hidden from de Clinton, protected by his birth mother and sent away to survive under the care of this woman, who now loved him like her own. It was a tale so tangled, he almost did not believe it could be true. If Alexander understood what he'd heard, then his brother had raped an Englishwoman, who would one day be his wife; and his sister, unable to remember who she was, had raised her very own nephew.

This was the stuff of tragedies.

And of miracles.

Of a sudden, Alexander saw himself with Andrew and Caitrine as children. They were playing along the shore of that very loch. In a voice no louder than a whisper, he spoke to her. "Caitrine, do ye not recall? Snow angels, Caitrine? Remember how we would flop onto the snow, laughing, and taste the flakes when they landed on our mouths? Snow angels, Caitrine. Ye loved snow angels, and I taught ye how to make them. I wasna bad then. Ye loved me as a brother. Can ye not look at me and remember the good? Can ye not remember yer own brother?"

Everyone waited for her reply. It was silent on that gray patch of frozen ice, and the only sound was the wind bending the bare trees on the hillside above them. Rourke and Claricia watched as she stared at Alexander and shook her head, in neither denial nor affirmation, but in confusion.

The turbulent anger upon her features collapsed. She frowned like a lost child.

"Meg, listen to him," Claricia urged. "Believe him. He is not evil. He will not harm you." She took a tentative step toward Meg, but stopped when Meg lunged at her. There was a dull expression in Meg's eyes both odd and frightening, and the dirk remained clutched in one hand, raised in a self-defensive posture. But Claricia would not give up. She could not. "No one wishes anything bad for you or the boy. No one is going to be hurt."

Viviane continued to shake her head. She did not hear what Claricia was saying. Too many images, quicksilver specters that she did not understand, were flashing before her mind's eye. She saw two lads with a physical resemblance to her Simon, which was shocking. It made her head ache. The awful buzzing in her ears was louder, but not so loud that she did not hear the youthful laughter of the dark-haired boys. Another flash. An image of children moving their arms and legs in the snow. Someone was speaking, and with a jerk, she focused once again on Rourke and Claricia and the man with black braids.

"Mam, I want to go home." Simon spoke for the first time. His young voice quivered. He was frightened by his mother's behavior and the confusing things these adults were saying. "I'm cold, Mam."

"The lad is right. We should return to the island," said Rourke. "Lady Claricia and Alexander will return to the castle. There will be time enough on the morrow to make sense of this."

"Nay, never," Viviane said in a low voice,

enunciating each syllable slowly and surely. "Never."

"That is a sensible idea, Rourke. We will return to Eilean Fidra until the morning," Alexander agreed. He went to take his wife's arm.

But Alexander had moved too quickly. His sister misunderstood his intention. She screamed and lunged at him with the dirk. Alexander lost his footing on the ice and went down, and in the next instant, his sister was on top of him, the dirk raised high in readiness to plunge into him.

"No, Meg. Don't!" Claricia called. She saw a glint of sunlight reflect off the dirk as it swiftly moved downward. "Stop!"

Claricia and Rourke reached her at the exact moment when the dirk sank into Alexander's shoulder. Rourke tried to pull his Viviane off Alexander. Claricia bent to help her husband. And Viviane stabbed the man with the black braids again. This time, the knife entered lower, nearer to his heart.

"What have ye done!" roared Rourke. He yanked his Viviane to her feet: the bloodied dirk fell from her hand and skittered across the ice. "He is yer brother. Yer own flesh and blood," he yelled, ending on a rough groan of anguish. He gripped her shoulders, stared into her vacant green eyes, and shook her twice, as if to wake her from a dream.

Slowly, she turned her head to stare at Claricia, who was kneeling over the wounded man. She looked back to Rourke. He was furious. She did not want him to be angry at her. She did not want to disappoint her lover. She did not want to lose him. There were tears in her eyes. She blinked twice to clear them away, but they flowed freely down her cheeks. In a very small and bewildered voice, she whispered, "I am sorry, Rourke, but I dinna remember. I'm sorry. So sorry. This is not what I really wanted, no matter what I may have said to ye. Truly, I dinna want him dead. I didna mean to kill him."

The Irishman wrapped his great arms about her and held her to him, one hand cradling the back of her head where she nestled against his shoulder. "Dinna worry, my love. It will all work out. There is always a future." But he was not certain of the truth of his own words as he looked down and saw that Alexander's eyes were closed and that despite the frosty air his complexion had an uncommonly ashen cast.

"*Am beil e beo?*" Rourke asked. *Is he alive?*

"Just barely. We must get him to the Old Believer's Isle," said Claricia. "It is nearer than the castle. The wounds are serious, I think. There is no time to waste."

Rourke nodded. A circle of bright red blood was seeping across Alexander's chest, staining the fur of his outer garment, and Rourke was truly fearful.

Quickly, they made a sort of pallet from the woolen plaid Rourke wore beneath his furs, and, having rolled Alexander onto the fabric, Claricia was able to pull him across the ice with Simon's help. Rourke followed behind them, guiding his Viviane, who was preoccupied by her private thoughts. At the little beach, Rourke reluctantly broke his hold about her waist to sling Alexander across his shoulder, and with Simon in the lead, they proceeded through the woods to the clearing.

At the hut, it was Viviane who stepped forward to hold open the door. First, Rourke entered, next Simon and Claricia, then Viviane who watched Rourke set the wounded laird upon the bed in the sleeping alcove. His long legs hung over the end of the sleeping platform, and she gathered up a few extra furs to keep his extremities warm. The expression upon her face had lost its wild, confused quality. There was a calm about her, a sort of resolute control.

"Simon, light the fire and set a brazier close to the alcove for extra warmth," Viviane said to the lad in a voice that once again sounded like her own. There was no resemblance between this woman and the one who had wielded that dirk. At the sleeping alcove, she wedged herself between Rourke and Claricia. "Ye must let me tend to him," she said, thinking that perhaps if she gave him back his life, he would let her keep Simon. Mayhap he would recover and try to understand, try to forgive her. Rourke and Claricia did not budge, nor did they make room for her at the bedside. She went on, "I ken more of healing than either of ye. Dinna worry. I willna hurt him agin."

Rourke was the first to move aside. "Do ye remember now?" he asked, the relief he felt ringing in his voice. All trace of the frenzied woman on the loch had vanished. This was the Viviane he adored. The future might be theirs after all.

"Nay, I dinna remember." She saw how his hopeful expression collapsed, and quickly added, "But it doesna matter one way or the other if I remember. Ye know that I never wanted to go back and find the past. All I wanted was ye, Rourke O'Connor," she replied as she inspected the laird's wounds in a knowledgeable, proficient manner. At length, she glanced up.

"I am not sure what happened to me today. None of ye need forgive me, if ye canna find it in yer hearts. But hear me out if ye please. The truth as I know it is this: I love ye, Claricia, like a sister, and ye, Rourke, as my lover and companion, with all my heart. *Le m'uile mo chridhe.* And I suppose, if what everyone says is true, then I must have loved this mon once, too, as my brother. To each of ye, I'm someone else. Meg. Caitrine. Viviane. But I canna be three women. There is only one of me."

She slipped one of her hands into Rourke's, entwined her fingers with his, and smiled up at him. "I canna remember or make sense of it, but I do know one thing, Rourke. I know that I want to be yer Viviane, now and forever. I dinna want to stir up the past and go back. It is no more important to me now than it was before. I am not Caitrine or Meg. I'm Viviane." She looked from Rourke to Claricia, then down at Alexander. "If he survives, will the both of ye help him to understand? Will ye help him to forgive me and accept what canna be?"

"You need not ask, dearest friend," said Claricia. She could not yet call her Viviane, but would do so in time. For now, she put an arm about her shoulder to offer a sisterly embrace. Like the rest of the past, what had happened that afternoon would of necessity be put behind them. There could be no recriminations. It had to be that way if there was to be any hope for the future. "So much has happened. We've survived much worse than this, and—"

Viviane held up a hand to stop Claricia from saying anything more. "There will be time later to talk, for now we must tend to yer husband. I'll need some moss moistened with vervain oil for poultices, and I shall also prepare an infusion for the pain. Everything is on the shelf behind ye."

Rourke went to fetch the ingredients, and together, the women began to wash Alexander's wounds.

PART 3

THE HEART
AND THE ROSE

Chapter 16

"**A**re ye trying to poison me now?" Alexander gagged. His body jerked upward from the rush mattress, and the bitter liquid that was being spooned between his lips sprayed forth from his mouth.

This reaction did not disturb Claricia. It was an answer to her prayers to see him open his eyes and speak, despite the mess he was making and the unfortunate resistance to her ministering. The wounds were deep, his loss of blood had been extensive, and even now, as he tried to sit upright, she saw dark stains seeping through the dressings on his shoulder and chest.

"You must not move," she scolded in a soft voice as she held the spoon toward his lips once again. His mouth remained closed, and she coaxed, "It is valerian. For the pain. Come, you must try to have a little more. I am told it is good for you."

Alexander shook his head as best he could manage. "Nay, no more. The taste is putrid, and the smell is not much better. My pain isna so bad that I should have to suffer that noxious potion as well." There was a dull burning sensation in his shoulder, and Alexander closed his eyes as bits and pieces of what had happened on the loch returned to him. "How long have I been asleep?" he asked.

"A little more than a day."

"Where am I?"

"Viviane's hut on the Old Believer's Isle."

"Ye mean Caitrine?"

"I mean Viviane, Rourke's woman," she retorted in a quiet yet firm manner. She gave careful consideration to each word of response. "This is *Viviane's* home."

"But she goes by another name. I heard ye call her Meg on the loch."

"In another time and place I called her Meg. Who she was before that we shall never know."

"She doesna remember a thing?"

"Fragments, mayhap, but nothing of importance. Nothing to convince her she is your sister. You may have found her in body, but not in soul." Claricia paused. She could only imagine how difficult this was for him to hear. From everything that she had learned of the Kirkpatrick clan, she knew that Alexander had adored his younger sister. None of this was easy to say. Claricia had the uneasy feeling of being torn between her friend and her husband. But he had to be told. "And she does not want to remember, either. Can you understand that?"

Alexander closed his eyes again, and when he spoke his voice was slow and weary. "Nay, I canna understand. My memories of childhood are good and strong and vivid, and it seems impossible to me that my sister might forget any of that. But I can understand that I have no choice save to accept what canna be." He lay there for several moments. His eyes remained closed, and his breathing was labored. The little burst of energy that had enabled him to resist the valerian was almost depleted. But before he succumbed to sleep once again, Alexander had to know about the boy. "Tell me about the lad."

Claricia sat very still. In the long hours of the night, she had pondered this, knowing that if Alexander survived she would have to tell him about Simon. In hindsight, it seemed absurd that she had ever imagined the boy might stay on the island while she was mistress of Eilean Fidra, and that that would have been the end of it.

He opened his eyes for an instant and saw the uncertainty on Claricia's face. Using his last ounce of strength, Alexander reached out one hand to touch her forearm in gentle encouragement. He was only beginning to reckon with the myriad of reasons why he had married this Englishwoman and why it was that he cared so deeply about her happiness. She had, indeed, taken hold of his heart, and when he spoke his words were heavy with emotion. "No matter what ye tell me, ye will always be my wife. That will never change. Ye mustna worry."

Claricia's heart lurched. He had not said he loved her, but the tenderness in his voice told her there was much more behind his words than what he had said aloud. Quickly, she searched his face to see what his eyes might reveal, but they were shut, and her heart sank a bit. She was perhaps too eager, then she saw the trace of a smile turning up the corners of his mouth. Perhaps, he did not love her, but that did not mean she could not trust him. She was his for always, no matter what. It was a powerful sentiment—to feel a sense of belonging with another soul—and it gave her the courage to trust him enough to begin the tale.

"First, I was mistaken to imagine it might be possible to deny the truth. It was wrong to think I could keep the truth from you, or from anyone else, for that matter. What you must understand is that mine was not an act of deception. I believed it was the right thing for the boy. Simon has a home and a mother. Soon he will have a father, when Viviane weds Rourke, and perhaps, one day, there will be brothers and sisters. Childhood is such a brief thing, too soon shattered by reality. Can you fathom what a miracle it is that this one child has enjoyed something quite special on this island? It is nothing less than a blessing. He has not been wrenched from his mother's bosom at a tender age, or sent away to foster in a stranger's household. Think upon it. He has not seen the violence of war that you and I take for granted. Brutality is almost unknown to him. He has known naught but love and security, and I did not think it was right to upset that for the sake of truth. I did not wish to hurt him or Viviane in any way."

Alexander heard the tears choking her voice. He, too, felt a tremor of emotion. There was infinite wisdom in what she said, and he spoke in a hushed voice. "I dinna want to destroy any of this. To change his world. Or hurt anyone. But I must know who he is."

"I understand. I understand, and so you shall know," she said softly, looking down at his hand, where it rested upon her arm. "Simon was named after my father, and he is the reason I was able to survive all those years with my uncle. He was the reason I was able to hold my head high when I heard the other ladies whispering Beast's Bawd behind my back. When my mother and I first went to live in my uncle's household, I had a dream of finding a fair young lord who would be my husband and take me home to someplace in England, far away from the war in Scotland. But reality is a distant cry from dreams, and as time went by I abandoned that girlish fancy. Instead, I clung to the hope of one day being free of my uncle, of one day finding the child. My child, for he is—as I'm sure you have suspicioned—mine, not hers."

"And my brother's?" Alexander cut in with the harsh query, experiencing at once the contrary emotions of repugnance and joy. He was sickened with repugnance that his wife had borne a bastard conceived from rape, while he was elated with joy that there was, indeed, a Kirkpatrick heir. His emotions made no more sense than did this story, which he would not have believed if someone had told the whole of it to him less than a month before. "Simon is my brother's son?"

"Yes," Claricia whispered, praying that Alexander would not condemn her, as her uncle had done. "He was born nine months after your brother raped me, and at first, when my belly began to grow round, I believed it was my penance for having committed a mortal sin. I had taken a life. It made sense that I must replace it— an argument I found all the more convincing since I would be giving life to a child made from the flesh and blood of the man I had murdered."

Alexander opened his eyes and saw tears gathering at the ends of her lashes. Their eyes met, shimmering lilac melding with lush green. He saw her pain, but there was much more within her gaze than anguish and suffering as she held her head high in that familiar pose. As his eyes closed again, he was stunned by the depth of her bravery, her pride. It was common knowledge that a woman could not claim to have been raped if a child grew in her belly, for it was believed that that child was evidence of pleasure, and where there was pleasure, all legal and religious minds were in agreement, there was never rape.

Nausea cloyed at Alexander. The burning sensation in his chest worsened. It was his brother—not de Clinton—who had made her a whore. De Clinton had only taken advantage of the situation. And with this knowledge did Alexander begin to understand Claricia's reluctance to experience pleasure, and why it was she clung so resolutely to the notion of dignity. It sickened him to recall how he had mocked her. If only he had the physical strength to take her in his arms and give her the comfort she deserved. There was so much more that she merited, but which he could never give her.

As if to experience the totality of her pain and thereby take a portion of it from her, Alexander forced himself to delve deeper into the sordid story. "And when the bairn was born ye sent him away?"

"But not for the reasons you may think," Claricia hastened to explain. She did not want him to misinterpret any of it. "Before I saw the babe and held him in my arms, it is true that I perceived him as my punishment. But when he was born and I put him to my breast, smelled his sweet skin, and felt his tiny heartbeat, it was a mother's true love and devotion that seized my heart. He was innocent and helpless, dependent upon me, and I could not bear to think that anything evil might happen to him. He was my child, my dear, dead mother's grandchild, and I wanted to guarantee his survival by any means that I might. I knew my uncle would not let him live, so we claimed the babe had perished, and Viviane fled with him into the hills. I had saved her life. In turn, she would save my son's."

"Ye're a remarkable woman," Alexander mumbled, wishing that he had the strength to open his eyes and tell her what a blessing it was that he'd found her and made her his wife. There was so much he wished to say to her, and no time. Another woman might have gladly handed over the bairn to de Clinton or abandoned it to the elements, but not his gentle generous Claricia. He wanted to hold her and love her, to tell her the real reason he had married her. He moved his lips to speak, but his head was spinning, and irregular dots of light danced before the black landscape of his closed eyelids.

Claricia stared at her sleeping husband, and the love in her heart expanded until it seemed as if it might burst. Even after hearing the truth, he had nothing but kindness for her. The debt she owed this man was immense, and as she stroked his brow, she knew that even if the future they shared together extended over a lifetime, it would not be long enough.

For now she would watch over him and nurse

him back to health, and as she waited for the
hours to pass until he would awaken again, she
sang in Gaelic, "My love is sweeter than honey,
better than jewels, softer than wool."

Three more days elapsed. Alexander became
restless, tossing and thrashing about the under-
sized bed in the sleeping alcove. The women hov-
ered over him, sponging his brow and spooning
any number of decoctions and infusions between
his lips. Fever seized his body. It festered within
the wounds and inflamed his mind. He did not
open his eyes or speak except to rave about vengeance upon de Clinton, about Caitrine disappearing into the mist, and of Andrew's limp body
being tossed into an earthen moat.

Claricia could scarcely bear to hear any of it.
So, too, was Viviane profoundly influenced by
what she heard. With each hour a little more of
the past was returning to her, and although she
still did not remember Alexander Kirkpatrick or
anyone else, she had begun to remember details
of Loch Awe, somewhere in a time before she had
found her way there with Simon in her arms.

That morning, neither of the women was in the
hut, having gone across the ice to Eilean Fidra for
some supplies. Of course, Rourke could have
gone in their stead, but it had been his idea to
send Claricia on the errand. She had not left Alexander's side since he'd been injured, and it
worried Rourke that her health would suffer if
she did not get out of the hut for a few hours.
Hence, he and Viviane had made a list of items
that could only be found at the castle. Only after
Rourke had promised not to move from Alexan-

der's bedside in their absence had Claricia agreed to leave for the space of an afternoon. It had been several hours since they'd left with Simon, and they were soon due to return. Unfortunately, there had been no change in Alexander's condition.

"Sorry, auld friend, 'tis time again to check that wound," Rourke said as he peeled back the dressing upon Alexander's shoulder. The Irishman's jaw tensed at the appearance of the inflamed wound. There were glistening clots of blood along the forming scar. The skin itself was terribly bruised, which was a fairly commonplace sight for a warrior to behold, but it was the yellowish substance oozing from the line of raised flesh where the skin had been pushed back together that caused Rourke to be concerned. He spoke to the unconscious man.

"Dinna tell me ye're going to let this little peck pull ye low. Think about everything ye've been through, mon. Yer brave body is covered with scars much more dreadful than these, and every one of them was delivered from warriors far more fearsome than my Viviane. Ye wouldna let a woman be the one to deal ye a mortal blow, would ye?" he chided, then leaned closer to sniff at the shoulder wound. It was necessary to check for any odor that would indicate that putrefication had begun to set in. Rourke gave a sigh of relief. "Praise be, 'tis just an ugly thing to behold. Nothing worse. Now, let's be keeping it that way. Yer wife wouldna be pleased if she returned to discover I hadna been treating ye properly."

Carefully, Rourke sponged away the yellowish ooze. Once it had been cleansed, he drizzled vervain oil on the wound, as Viviane had instructed him, then reapplied another moss poultice to the shoulder before turning his attentions to the chest wound. As he worked, he continued to talk.

"When this is done, I'll be trying to feed ye, and while I know ye dinna fear passage into the netherworld, ye must be eating a little something. Ye mustna breathe yer last before fulfilling yer vow against de Clinton. Surely ye havena forgotten that, mon?" Having finished attending to the chest wound, Rourke pulled the fur over Alexander. He picked up a roughhewn bowl and crude wooden spoon. "Widen yer mouth and swallow. The women assure me this is good for ye. Helps with the pain and fever, they say. Can ye hear me, Alex? Open yer mouth and eat. It is not yer time. Ye must eat and rest and heal. 'Tis not yer time to be leaving this world. Not while de Clinton lives."

Alexander's mouth seemed to relax, and Rourke slowly spooned the warm liquid into his mouth. Behind them, the door to the hut quietly opened, but Rourke did not look up from his task or pause in his speech when Claricia slipped inside the room. She had hurried ahead of Viviane and Simon, partly because she was eager to return to Alexander, but also so that she might relieve Rourke of his bedside duties. Several of the warriors and *diobrachain* had decided to begin their southward journey to join the gathering army near the Torwood. They had already departed Eilean Fidra, and were bound for the trail that led to Crianlarich. If Rourke wished to travel with them, they had told Claricia, they would meet him in the pass below the peaks of Ben an Oir before the sun began its descent.

But Claricia did not announce her arrival, let alone her intent. She stood by the door, listening to the Irishman as he fed Alexander.

"I'm thinking of a verra clear memory. 'Tis of the first time we fought side by side, Alex, and I can see even now how ye swung yer lochaber ax with such power. I have a crystal clear vision of how ye leaped into the fray yelling yer Kirkpatrick battle cry like a demon. I marveled at yer courage, wondered at the risks ye were taking, and ye assured me that ye wouldna perish until ye'd had yer vengeance on de Clinton. It was determination and raw nerve that made ye such a dauntless warrior. Have ye none of that willpower left to get ye through this? *Danachd. Misneach. Boldness. Courage.* Where are they now? Listen to me, Alex," Rourke cajoled in a voice that pleaded to be heard. "There's still much to be done. De Clinton lives, and ye must still go after him."

Claricia covered her mouth to stifle a cry of despair. By Rourke's tone, it was evident that Alexander had not improved, and it was that fact, coupled with what Rourke was saying, that struck at Claricia's heart. Her mind sped back to the journey from Clar Innis, when Rourke had told her something of Alexander's past.

He will find the bastard, Rourke had said, referring to Andrew's murderer. *I've no doubt of that, and when he does, then Alex will at least have reclaimed his honor.*

But Claricia knew the truth. She was that murderer, and in sparing her life, Alexander had put her above his honor. It was a remarkable act, and now—as Rourke was suggesting—he might die before having his vengeance against de Clinton. If Claricia could have had her way, there would have been no revenge, only forgiveness and peace. But as she had come to know this Highland laird who had become her husband, she had come to understand that it was impossible to take away that desire for retribution from him. Indeed, it would have been wrong to expect him to deny the importance of clan and honor, which meant so much to him and to the generations of Kirkpatrick lairds who had gone before him.

Despite her English birth and the myths of savage Highlanders upon which she had been raised, Claricia had come to understand these people. They were not barbarians. They were decent men and women, who loved their families and honored their ancestry with a devotion that transcended any Englishman's, and it seemed to her that it would have been a grave injustice if her husband had not been able to achieve the retribution he desired.

No, she decided, she would not tell Rourke that the *diobrachain* were waiting for him in the pass. Instead, Claricia would join them herself. She would go south to find her uncle and kill him on her husband's behalf. It did not occur to her that this was warrior's work, and that she should not interfere. She could only think that she must not let her husband die while her uncle still lived. She had wondered how to repay her debt to Alexander Kirkpatrick, and now the method was clear to her.

She could not make Alexander better, but she could return to her uncle. She knew the kind of man her uncle was, and although he had refused to pay the ransom, he would have been more than willing to take her back for free. How easy it would be. She would claim to have escaped her Highland imprisonment, and once alone with her uncle, Claricia would repay her debt to Alexander Kirkpatrick. It was the ultimate loyalty she could envision a wife extending to her husband. She could exact venegance for his clan, and in settling her debt, Claricia would no longer doubt that she was the right match for a Highland laird.

Alexander's lids fluttered open, and he focused on the concerned little face hovering above him. It belonged to a lad with green eyes and ink-black hair.

"Uncle, ye awaken," the boy said. He smiled. "Good day. *Dhia dhuit. God today.*"

"Ye call me uncle," Alexander whispered, grateful that the child appeared to accept him.

"Aye, I am Simon, Viviane's son, and my mam says ye're my uncle."

"And how is that?" he asked warily. Surely they had not told the lad the whole tale. Claricia had seemed determined not to destroy the child's illusions.

"She says ye're her brother."

"Though she doesna remember me?" he cut in. Disappointment laced this query. There was something about the boy's tone that told Alexander his sister was no closer to remembering than she had been.

"Aye," Simon confirmed. "But she says that

shouldna matter between us, that I should get to know ye and yer clan."

Alexander nodded, experiencing a wave of something that he could only have called comfort. The disappointment he had earlier experienced had been tempered. Although his sister would not call herself Caitrine, she was willing to acknowledge their relationship, which, in turn, afforded the boy his rightful place in the clan. Alexander closed his eyes and pondered his brother's role in all of this, coming to the conclusion that it did not matter that Andrew had been left out of the equation. It would suffice that Simon believed his kinship with the Kirkpatrick clan derived through the woman he thought was his mother.

"Ye're feeling better?" the lad inquired.

"I believe so." Alexander stretched his arms overhead. His legs poked out from beneath the pile of animal pelts. "We are the only ones here. Where is everyone?"

"My mam is working in her garden, and Rourke is building a pen for the pigs. The ice is melting, and one of them drowned last night."

"And Claricia?" He looked about the small hut, eager to see her, to hold her and kiss her pretty lips, to spend time with her and tell her all the reasons he had married her. "My wife? Where is she?" "

"The *aingeal*?"

"Aye, the angel," Alexander agreed with a smile, then he noticed the apprehension on Simon's face as the lad tried to avoid his gaze. He sat upright to take a better look around the interior of the hut. "What is it, lad? What do ye keep from me?"

"I must fetch Rourke. He wanted to know as soon as ye awakened," replied the boy, and to Alexander's dismay, he dashed from the hut.

Something was not right. Alexander did not think Claricia would have left him on her own, not after their last talk together. Perhaps de Clinton had taken her. Minutes ticked by. Alexander tried to pretend the door would open and Claricia would enter. But he was no fool. The child had been transparent. Something had happened to Claricia, and she would not be coming through that door. Alexander gripped the wooden bed frame and swung his feet off the mattress and onto the floor. His head spun. He paused for a moment, then gripped the frame again as he tried to stand. But he was weak, and a pain shot through his shoulder and up his head to his skull, forcing him to close his eyes as he collapsed back against the pile of bedding.

"Ye are awake."

Alexander turned his head toward the door and opened his eyes. It was Rourke. "Aye," he said in a flat suspicious tone.

"And feeling stronger?" the Irishman asked. He went to a table, where a black kettle rested. "Viviane made a good thick soup of barley and leeks. Are ye hungry?"

"Where is she?" snapped Alexander. He was irritated and impatient. "Why are ye babbling about boiled vegetables when I ask about my wife?"

"It is not what ye think."

"Explain," he ordered in anger. *How could anyone know what he was thinking?*

"Seven days ago some of the *diobrachain* went

south to join the small people," said Rourke. The small people were camp followers—ghillies, nurses, cooks, drivers, and such—whose menial tasks were of vital importance to the day-to-day life of an army, and with such a large gathering of warriors and clansmen, the number of small people would be extensive as well. Within weeks, there would be thousands of Highlanders and Lowlanders massing near Stirling Castle, and the *diobrachain* hoped that among this swell of humanity they might find one or more of their long-lost kin. It was not unreasonable to imagine they might locate their fathers or brothers, their husbands or sons, but whether they would be welcomed back was far more unpredictable.

"And what has this to do with my wife?"

"Lady Claricia went with them."

"Why?" Alexander did not understand. Although they had not spoken of love, he had given her a future, which he knew was important to her. She would not have turned away from that. Besides, there was something between them of value, something more than passion. Alexander was certain of it. He stared at Rourke and waited for illumination.

"It was her intention to find de Clinton and kill him for the both of ye."

"*Air ghaol ni math!*" he exclaimed with an almost violent burst of breath. *For the love of God!* Amazement and disbelief stunned Alexander. For a moment, he could not say another word. A thousand thoughts crowded his mind. At first, he could only disparage Claricia for being so foolhardy, then he was touched by the fuller implication of what she was willing to risk for him, and finally, his emotions turned to anger at Rourke. Alexander raised his voice at his kinsman when he demanded to know, "How could ye let her go? Why didna ye stop her?"

"I had no knowledge of her intentions," Rourke yelled back in an equally angry voice. "She didna ask my permission. Had I known, I would, of course, have prevented yer wife from leaving. But Lady Claricia told only Viviane, who, naturally, agreed not to breathe a word to me. By the time I found out, it was too late. Two days had passed while I thought she was at the castle, but she was already many leagues gone by then."

Alexander made a sudden upward movement. The pain in his shoulder was excruciating, but he swung his legs out of bed once again. This time, he forced himself to stand. "I must go after her." A wife was a very precious thing, and he did not want to lose her.

"*Na caraich,*" Rourke admonished. *Dinna stir.* "Ye would go out and die on the trail?"

"We all die sooner or later. I canna lie here like a helpless bairn and let her face that monster on her own. If I can find the strength, I must try to find her, protect her, and bring her home before it is too late."

"Too late for what?"

"Ye're a warrior and may not understand, but I tell ye nonetheless: I must bring her home before it is too late to tell her that I love her."

"Och, but I do understand, Alex. I understand all too well. And if that is the reason, then ye must go."

Chapter 17

Rourke accompanied Alexander on the journey. It was a difficult trip. The snows in the mountains were melting, the burns were running high and fast, and Alexander had not recovered sufficient endurance to travel more than a few hours at a time. Their stops were frequent, their pace was slow, and although Alexander had initially refused Rourke's company, he was grateful that his kinsman had been by his side.

It was the last week of April when they arrived at King Robert's camp in the vast forest of the Torwood. There, lying almost midway between the most northerly and southerly points in Scotland, was the ground that many considered the gateway from the Lowlands to the Highlands. Already some eight thousand Scotsmen had answered their king's call for able-bodied fighting men. In addition, there were several thousand unarmed small people, who had made the trek from the farthest reaches of the country to that spot.

The Torwood was south of besieged Stirling Castle and some five miles north of the village of Falkirk. It was noisy and muddy. Dogs and pig-

lets ran free, barking and oinking and making a
general nuisance of themselves. Bonfires were
smoking day and night, not only for warmth and
cooking, but so that the three score of blacksmiths
attendant upon this swelling army might be
about their work of sizing horseshoes and honing
weapons.

"We look for a Highlander by the name of
Ewen. He is the *sennachie* of the Kirkpatrick
stronghold at Eilean Fidra. Do ye know the
mon?" Alexander inquired of the first group of
barefooted warriors he encountered. They were
gathered about one of the bonfires.

"Aye, we've met," someone replied. He
pointed in an easterly direction. "Yer Ewen of Eilean Fidra is camped with the rest of the western
Highlanders on the other side of the auld Roman
road."

The fighting men had been disposed into four
brigades. The clans from the western Highlands
would fight alongside warriors from the Western
Isles under the banner of the king himself. In that
encampment near the old Roman road, Alexander and Rourke found Sorcha's husband and a
handful of other Kirkpatrick clansmen engaged
in mock combat with the liegeman of Angus Mac-
Donald, from the Western Isles.

The Scottish king knew he would be outnumbered by the English in the coming battle, but he
was determined that his force would be superior.
His warriors, who would fight not by compulsion
of royal decree but in defense of home, family,
liberty, and country, would have the advantage
of patriotic purpose as well as that of greater skill.
The daily preoccupation throughout the Torwood

was devoted to discipline and training. The days were lengthening. Spring had come. The weather was turning milder, and across the meadows and rolling Lowland hills the patchwork of heather, grass, and bracken was brightened by blue and yellow wild flowers. There was more sunlight, and even in the waning hours of the day, the constant training continued. That afternoon it involved spears. The men assigned to King Robert's division were practicing moving together with their spears held at an angle, which formed a huge iron-bristling hedgehog of lethal points. This was called a schiltron and could pose a formidable obstacle, especially to mounted horsemen.

Alexander and Rourke stood to the side and watched for several minutes. At length, someone motioned to the king, who was conducting this training session. His majesty turned, and, seeing the two men, he stepped forward to greet them.

"Welcome to the Torwood, Alexander Kirkpatrick." The king greeted him in their native Gaelic. "We heard ye were injured. 'Tis an honor and a blessing that ye hurried along yer recovery in order to join us. And a most thankful welcome to yer Irish kinsman as well. Every able-bodied fighting mon is needed to defeat the *sassenach.*"

"I wouldna miss the chance to fight at yer side, my liege lord." Alexander made a low bow to the king. He glanced beyond his majesty to survey the men who formed the schiltron. Among them he recognized the young Highlander who was the father of Frances's babe. There, too, was the Colquhoun in whose company he and Claricia had traveled on the trip from Hepburn to Loch

Lomond. "I see many familiar faces, yer majesty."

"Aye. These men were among the first to arrive shortly after the great snow, and yer Ewen has been with me since ye left him in my service last November. He has been invaluable. Ye were right: he is particularly adept at certain clandestine tasks. Thank ye. In repayment I didna mind standing in for ye to train the others while ye idled in yer sick bed," the king replied, bantering with Alexander, who laughed and then promised to cease his idle ways. Robert Bruce was an amiable, good-natured man, respected for his devotion to independence and admired for the equality with which he treated all Scotsmen. "I shall withdraw now, Alexander Kirkpatrick, and leave ye to yer clansmen. Will ye and Rourke O'Connor join me for the evening meal at my tent this night? I would discuss the wee matter of yer negotiations with Sir Aymer de Clinton."

"Aye, yer majesty," Alexander replied humbly. "We'll be there."

The king strode away, followed close at his heels by two henchmen. Immediately, the schiltron broke rank and the men from Eilean Fidra rushed forward.

"What news have ye of our loved ones, *toìseach?*"

"Is all quiet north of Loch Lomond?"

"Are they prepared to defend Eilean Fidra?"

"I left Maxwel of Ballimeanoch and Lady Moira in charge of Eilean Fidra's defense, and a more able team I canna imagine. But it appears all fighting men are headed here. Yer families are safe. It is they who are worried, and who pray for yer safe return before the midsummer harvest," said Alexander. Some camp followers joined the group, and Alexander scanned the sea of faces for Claricia. But he did not see her among the women. There were more questions about wives and children left behind, and when he had answered them, Alexander posed some of his own. "What of the English king and his army? Where are they now?"

"King Edward and his forces are coming by sea. It is expected they will land at Berwick sometime in the next three or four weeks."

"And what of those *sassenach* who are already across the border?"

"Do ye mean Aymer de Clinton?"

"Aye," Alexander confirmed. His jaw stiffened.

"It is rumored that a full force of de Clinton's men-at-arms rode out of Hepburn a fortnight past, with the purpose of securing the inland road from Berwick to Edinburgh."

"What do ye intend?" Rourke asked Alexander later that night when they had returned from the king's tent, which had been nothing more than a patched length of sailcloth strung between two trees. The bonfires in the Torwood were burning low, the dogs and piglets slept, and the fighting men and small people were settling in for the night.

"Claricia isna here. I've located one of the *diobrachain*, who said she left the Torwood in search of de Clinton. She was bound for the Edinburgh-to-Berwick road. I must travel after her."

"Even after the king's warning?" Rourke wondered aloud. His majesty had advised Alexander to set aside the matter of vengeance against de

Clinton. Steady discipline at all ranks was crucial to victory in the coming battle.

"Aye. Even after the king's warning, I will go. I owe my fealty to Robert and to Scotland. My father died for the king, and I would gladly do so as well, but I willna surrender my wife to independence or to any mon's crown. I intend to go after her. *Alone.*" Alexander finished on such a firm note that Rourke clamped his mouth closed when he would have volunteered to go with him.

"*Soirbheas leat.*" Rourke bid his kinsman farewell as he had the last time Alexander had gone in pursuit of Lady Claricia. *Good luck to ye.*

There was much more at stake this time.

Several hours before dawn a tall friar left the king's camp in the Torwood. He reached Falkirk at sunrise, where a villager's wife gave him a piece of bread and allowed him to draw water from a well. The friar uttered his thanks to his benefactress in a low tone, mumbling a few additional words in Latin, for he did not want anyone to know he was a Highlander. Refreshed, he continued along the line of the old Roman road that led to Edinburgh. His feet were bare. His dusty black robe was short in the front, hanging to the middle of his calves, but in the back it dragged along the road. Beneath this he wore the tunic and belt of a warrior, with a dirk thrust in one side of the belt, a sword in the other. The generous cowl of the robe was pulled over his head to hide his face. His hands were crossed before him, dipping inside the wide sleeves, and he walked with a bent head.

Alexander did not want anyone to know what he intended or where he was going. He traveled on foot. It was twenty miles to Edinburgh from Falkirk. A horse would have been quicker, easier on his feet and health, and he hated to waste time, but a true friar would never have had a horse at his disposal. So Alexander walked.

At dusk, he spotted the ruins of Linlithgow. The old royal palace had been demolished after its liberation the year before. A few sheep were grazing for a bit of early spring grass along the ridge that had been the earthen mote. Here and there were piles of stone along the road and in the surrounding field, some of them were already coated with a thin layer of moss. An old man was sitting atop one of the great stones that had been part of the castle.

"Brother, good evening," said the old man when Alexander was near enough to hear him.

Alexander nodded a silent greeting.

"I wouldna continue onward, if I were ye. The *sassenach* devils are getting nearer by the day. Turn around and seek the protection of the Torwood, brother. King Robert and his good army will see ye safe."

As before, Alexander mumbled a few words in Latin and continued onward. The old man did not try to stop him. No doubt he thought the barefoot friar was quite mad.

On his second day, Alexander got a ride in a cart from someone else who was mad enough to be heading in the wrong direction. Despite the bumpy ride, Alexander was grateful to be off his feet, and he fell asleep, to awaken in the yard of a crossroads tavern somewhere south of Edinburgh.

He was on the right track. Alexander was certain of it. He could feel it. There was tension in the air. He saw it upon the faces of the women at this crossroads, and in their anxious eyes. He heard it in their taut voices. Eventually, the whole English army would pass by this tavern, and the road up ahead was being secured by de Clinton in order for that great army to pass. Alexander rode for another day in the cart, then had to resume traveling on foot when the owner of the cart reached his destination.

After several hours, Alexander found himself in a peaceful wooded area nestled between rolling hills. Of a sudden, the quiet was broken by the distant thunder of horses. Alexander hurried to the next bend in the roadway for a better view.

A long cloud of dust was approaching. Closer it came, and louder. The first of the riders appeared. They were English, and presented the singular sight of eagerness for battle. The sunlight was glinting off their helmets, chain mail was shimmering at their chests, and colorful pennons were snapping in the wind.

Alexander stood against a tree as the file of men-at-arms began to pass. He had no trouble recognizing the black-and-green banner of Sir Aymer de Clinton. Alexander clenched one fist beneath the black robe. He raised the other hand to touch the hilt of the sword secured in his belt. His head was bent, yet he stole an upward glance at the passing horsemen. Again, he clenched his fist. His gut lurched, and he forced himself to remain still. There she was, Claricia, his lady wife, his lovely rose, riding alongside one of de Clinton's knights.

There was no expression upon her face. She sat erect and proud, with her chin at that arrogant tilt. That familiar pose told Alexander everything that he needed to know. She was surviving, nothing else, and his whole being ached to reach out and comfort her.

I love ye, his heart cried out to hers, but she was not even looking in his direction. More than anything else at that moment, he wanted her to see him. *Look at me.* He wanted her to know that he was close at hand. He wanted her to know that he had come after her and that she would not be alone any longer. *I've come all this way because ye're my wife, and I dinna want to lose ye. I canna let any harm come to ye.*

Alexander stepped away from the tree as she was about to pass. He did not intend to speak to her. But perhaps she would notice the friar at the side of the road, and when she did, he would look up to meet her eyes. Alexander raised one hand as if to invoke a blessing upon the passing soldiers.

"Hey, you, there. Stand back." One of the knights rode straight toward the friar. He made a threatening motion, as if he intended to kick him or worse.

Quickly Alexander returned to his spot by the tree, and Claricia went past him. Her back was stiff. Her eyes were focused straight ahead. She had not noticed the black-cloaked friar standing beneath the budding tree, and his heart ached as he watched the column of soldiers disappear around the bend in the road.

After a while the echo of hooves died away, and Alexander began to follow. He might not have been fast, but he could follow their trail, and he would find them.

He caught up with them four days later. They had ridden in a giant semicircle and were bivouacked at a place called Soutra Hill. It was a strategic, well-selected point at which to await the arrival of the full English force under the command of the English king, Edward.

Easily, Alexander slipped into their camp. De Clinton was not there yet. The word was that he would arrive soon from Hepburn. But Alexander did not ask too many questions. He could not afford to do anything that might arouse suspicion or prompt the English knights to send him on his way. Instead, he assumed the entertaining persona of a friar overly fond of wine, dice, and bawdy talk, while he watched and waited.

Claricia was kept in a pavilion that had been readied for the arrival of de Clinton. It was a large tent of stripped canvas with two peaks on its roof, each flying a pennant, one for de Clinton and the other for England. Finally, Aymer de Clinton arrived, and at last, Alexander saw Claricia.

She stepped out of the tent, looking more Highland lass than English lady, wearing the purple kirtle Alexander's mother had stitched, her hair unbound and her feet bare. De Clinton took hold of her elbow. He escorted her down a path that Alexander knew led to a burn called Brothershiels, in which the knights liked to bathe.

Once again, Alexander followed.

Chapter 18

Claricia forced a smile to her lips as she tilted her head to one side and listened to her uncle. It seemed as if a million years had passed since she'd had to play the part of the obedient niece, and Claricia experienced a momentary fear that she might fail, and in failing, she might reveal her true motivations. Her smile quivered slightly, but she did not look away from him.

De Clinton grinned in return and gripped her forearm. He pulled her close to whisper in her ear as they walked by the sentry at the edge of the encampment. "What a surprising creature you are. I could scarce believe it when I received word that you had returned to me, niece. I came as quickly as I could, to see for myself."

"Surprising? But you are my family, sir, and have given me a home these past years. You are too modest a man to think I would not return to you after my ordeal this winter," Claricia said in a tone that dripped with flattery. "Indeed, Uncle, where else could I have gone and been treated with such generosity as you show me?"

This pretty little speech pleased de Clinton. His fingers upon her forearm stroked her. "Can I assume, then, that you wish to resume our previous arrangement?''

Claricia was sickened by the thought of letting him touch her as he had done in the past, and she fought the impulse to snatch her arm away from him. Instead, her free hand slipped inside the pocket of her kirtle to grab the knife she had kept there the past weeks in anticipation of what it was she intended to do that afternoon. She held her chin high and met his gaze. ''And what arrangement was that, Uncle?'' she asked in an ingenuous voice that held not a trace of challenge. She was stalling for time. They needed to get farther away from the camp. That was why she had asked him to take her to the stream.

De Clinton was perplexed, and he frowned. ''You are changed,'' he remarked, staring at the bright golden mass of unbound hair, which cascaded down her back. His niece wore no wimple, as was befitting a titled Englishwoman. It made no matter that she was a whore. She was a lady by rank and birth, and as such she had always worn a wimple. But why not now? And why that peculiar question, which implied she had not understood their previous arrangement? Her outward demeanor was as obsequious as it had ever been, but there was a suspicious high color in her cheeks, which he had never seen before. He knew she did not have any true affection for him. But that had never mattered, for she had always been obedient. It was not the lack of affection that bothered de Clinton. Rather it was a certain air of confidence that he detected in his niece. He had never seen that in her before, and it made him uneasy.

"Changed? I? Nay, Uncle," Claricia replied, forcing her tone to remain collected and sweet, forcing herself to continue smiling at him. Different? he had suggested. Claricia's stomach twisted into knots. It was a worrisome thing to speculate precisely what de Clinton meant by that comment.

"Do not be bashful, niece." De Clinton's gaze upon Claricia narrowed. A low lewd tone, which had not been there earlier, colored his voice. "My guess is that you were ridden well this winter, and that is what reveals itself in your *different* behavior." He paused on the path to turn so that they would be facing each other. His hold on her arm remained firm, and with his other hand he gripped her chin, forcing her face up to his descending lips.

It was a grotesque and revolting kiss, and without any conscious effort Claricia started to drift away. Her mind began the lullaby, *Sleep, my little darling, sleep. Dean cadal, seircean, dean cadal.*

One moment she felt his sloppy wet lips, then she didn't. Panic gripped Claricia. She must not let that happen. This time, she must be aware of everything, so that she would be able to do the deed at the best moment.

De Clinton was panting hard. He was grinding his belly against hers. "You are even more desirable. A better whore than ever," he mumbled, so caught up in his own lust that he was oblivious to her barely concealed disgust.

Hidden behind a nearby gorse bush, Alexander heard and saw every bit of this. His blood pounded with a furious anger, the muscles along his jaw and at his temple twitched, and it was all he could do not to spring out and throttle the revolting beast until he begged for mercy. But they were too near the camp. Even if Alexander had been able to overcome de Clinton, the scuffle might have attracted unwanted attention. It would have done them no good to rid themselves of the bastard if he and Claricia could not have escaped together. At the very least, he must guarantee Claricia's safety.

"Uncle, would we not be more comfortable at the stream?" she asked when his lips left hers to nibble at her ear. She swallowed the bile in her throat and injected a sultry quality into her voice. "There is a grassy bank there, I have heard, where you may lounge and watch while I am bathing."

"Ah, you are a clever girl," de Clinton murmured, His hold on her loosened, so that they might continue along the path. "I believe I like this difference."

Alexander followed at a discreet distance. Soon he heard the rush of water over rocks. They had reached the end of the path, and Alexander positioned himself between two large trees to watch and wait for the right moment to reveal himself. Sunlight was streaking through the treetops to illuminate the small clearing through which the stream flowed. It was a magical place. The water in the burn was silver, the fingers of light reaching through the trees and down to the ground sparkled with moisture. Perhaps true lovers had met there in better times. The pretty picture was, however, destroyed when Aymer de Clinton began to undress.

"What are you doing?" asked Claricia. She was

unable to keep the alarm from her voice.

"You wanted to bathe. It sounds a pleasurable pastime, and the water is most inviting. Instead of watching, I shall join you, and we shall take care of each other." He ended on a bawdy laugh.

Deep in the pocket of her kirtle, Claricia held tight to the dirk. She stared at him, uncertain how to respond. She did not know what to do.

"What maidenly modesty is this?" de Clinton asked when she did not move. "Do you flirt with me, niece? Tease me?"

"I—" Claricia was having a hard time thinking. This was not what she had imagined would happen.

"Perhaps your Highlander was rough with you and forced you," de Clinton said. "Did he tear the clothes from you, lovely Claricia? Is that what you want?" And without waiting for an answer, de Clinton pulled violently at one of the sleeves of the purple kirtle. It ripped at the shoulder.

Claricia gasped. She glanced down at where the sleeve had been torn away and her arm was revealed. Somewhere in the back of her mind she heard the lullaby. Not now! Nothing must cloud her ability to reason, and she cried out, "Stop!"

"Stop?" De Clinton's expression turned ugly. "Surely the Highlander taught you better than that. How dare you tell me to stop?" He had always liked obedient women, and Claricia was being bad. She must be punished. Roughly, he tore at the other sleeve, then he grabbed hold of the fabric at the neckline with one hand, but not to rip the bodice open. Instead, he swiftly yanked her to him, while the fingers of his other hand pulled and twisted through her hair.

Claricia cried out in pain. But she did not struggle. She dared not move, else her grip on the dirk in her pocket would have been lost.

"Put your arms about my neck," de Clinton ordered. His niece did not move, and he took hold of her arms to position them as he desired. Suddenly, he froze. "What is this?" he demanded. Having pulled her hand from the pocket, he'd seen the knife. He held her arm high, the dirk flashed in the sunlight, and he squeezed her wrist. "Drop it," he ordered, but she did not obey.

He was hurting her. Claricia wanted to loosen her grip on the dirk, but she thought of Alexander instead. She remembered his kindness, his tenderness, and the importance of honor to him. She thought of him, feverish, as he lay upon that bed in Viviane's hut, and she held the dirk in spite of the sharp pain, which was causing her eyes to water. They were at an impasse.

In his hiding place, Alexander waited. If he acted too soon he might jeopardize Claricia's safety. He was crouched to react. His hand gripped his sword hilt, but it was not yet time.

"If you do not drop that knife, I will call out to my men, and they will deal with you. I will hand you over to them, you treacherous little bitch," de Clinton snarled.

De Clinton's threat hit its mark. It terrified Claricia. But not into obedience. Instead, she lunged forward, raising her knee to his groin. De Clinton gasped and stumbled. Claricia lunged again, and this time, she nicked his arm with the knife, and he sprawled backward on the ground.

"You cut me," de Clinton exclaimed in a voice

made heavy with disbelief. He wiped at the bright red streak on his arm and then stared at his niece in shock. She stood over him with the knife poised to strike again. There was fire in her eyes. High color blazed upon her cheeks. If she attacked him, she would have advantage, and if he did not die right away, his wounds could have been severe enough to fester and kill him before Edward rode out of Berwick. The situation was not encouraging, and it took a few moments for de Clinton to regain some of his arrogance. "What? Murder me? I did not think you had it in you, niece."

"You were always a conceited fool."

"Perhaps. And you were always a weak and submissive whore. Are you truly changed, I wonder?" He was taunting her, trying to diminish the resolve he had seen so clearly upon her face. "Could you murder a helpless man?"

"Helpless! You are about as helpless as a serpent."

"How will you do it, then? Here?" He laid a hand upon his chest. "Come. Do it! Right through the heart."

Claricia hesitated. She had killed once before, with good reason, yet it had haunted her nonetheless. Now she had as much reason as she'd had the last time, but what, she wondered, had ever made her think she could take another human life, no matter how evil the man might be? Death was God's work. Not hers.

"You can't do it. Can you? You dare not. You're a coward, like your mother," de Clinton insulted.

"Do not speak of my mother." Claricia felt her

body sway as if she might lose her balance, and she tightened her grip about the dirk, until it seemed she had stopped the flow of blood to her fingers.

De Clinton sneered at her. "Do it, whore. Do it." And when Claricia did not move, he began to laugh.

"Perhaps the lady canna do the deed." A man spoke, and in the space of a heartbeat, de Clinton quieted. His laughter was swallowed by the gurgling stream, and the unseen speaker went on. "No crime attaches itself to the lady for her inability to act. In truth, she is too gentle a soul. I, on the other hand, am not." Alexander, still garbed in the friar's robe, walked into the clearing and stood beside Claricia to stare down at de Clinton. "There is nothing gentle about me, and there is nothing to stop me from killing ye."

"And who are you, good brother?" inquired de Clinton in an almost conversational tone. If he feared for his life, he did not reveal it.

The cloaked man tossed back the cowl from his head.

"Alexander!" Claricia, who had recognized his voice, cried out his name in joyous astonishment. He had recovered from his wounds and had come after her. He was there by her side, and for an instant, she almost wavered in her stance over de Clinton. She almost let the dirk fall from her grasp in an impulse to throw her arms about him. But she stayed the urge. There would, God willing, be time later for such a reunion.

"So this is the great laird of the Kirkpatricks," jeered de Clinton. "The mighty thief and kidnapper."

"He is no thief," Claricia protested. Despite her anxiety at their current situation, there was pride in her voice when she added, "He is my husband."

De Clinton sniggered. "How appropriate. The savage wed the whore."

"Nay. That isna the way of it. The laird wed his lady."

"Whatever you wish," quipped de Clinton on another irreverent sneer.

"*Mollachd ort*," Alexander hissed. He stared the Englishman in the eye. *Curse ye*. Swiftly, he drew his sword from beneath the folds of the black robe, and before de Clinton had time to react, Alexander placed one foot on his chest to hold him where he lay upon the ground. He placed the point of the sword at de Clinton's throat. "If ye believe in the Almighty, I suggest ye ask for his intercession now."

A flicker of fear lit the Englishman's eyes. In the next instant, it was gone. He swore a vile oath against the Highlander and God, and tried to free himself by rolling to one side with a sudden forceful movement.

Alexander invoked the Kirkpatrick battle cry. "*Dia is Buidaidh*." It was time. And with swift purpose, the last laird of the Kirkpatricks ran de Clinton through with the sword that had once belonged to his father and his grandfather before him.

Claricia's hands flew to her mouth to stifle a scream. Her body lurched forward, seized by the automatic response to help another human in need, but in the next second, her blood chilled. Instead, she stood with her eyes affixed to the horrible sight on the ground before her, and she began to cry, partly in relief, partly in sadness, and partly from fear and exhaustion.

The Beast breathed his last.

Alexander withdrew the bloody weapon from de Clinton, tossed it to the ground, and turned to his wife. He opened his arms to her.

Without hesitation, Claricia flung herself into his embrace. To feel his arms wrap about her was more than she could bear. How she had dreamed of this; but how she had always thought that it would never happen. Great wracking sobs burst forth from her, and although her body was shaking uncontrollably, she held tightly to him. It seemed impossible to believe that it was over. After so many years of pain and humiliation, her uncle was dead, and if Claricia had not held fast to Alexander, she was afraid she would have awakened only to find that it was nothing more than a dream, that her uncle lived and her husband had perished.

"Hush, my darling, it is over. It is done," Alexander crooned, tightening his hold about her trembling shoulders. "Ye are safe, *mo ròs geall*. There is nothing that will hurt ye ever agin. Not if I can help it."

At length, his words penetrated Claricia's consciousness and slowly she began to calm.

"Will ye be all right?" he asked when he tried to settle her some distance from de Clinton's lifeless body.

"Don't leave me!" She clung to him.

"Dinna fear. I'm not going anywhere, not without ye, but I must see to yer uncle."

She nodded in understanding and sat quietly a

few paces upstream. She averted her face from the dreadful scene.

Quickly, Alexander recovered his sword. He rinsed it off in the water, then hid de Clinton's body beneath a gorse bush, after which he used a leafy branch to brush at the sandy ground in order to remove all traces of what had happened by that pleasant burn. At length, he returned to Claricia, who had managed to compose herself.

"What are you doing here?" she asked when he held out his hand to help her rise. It was time to leave. They had to hurry away before de Clinton's men came looking for him. "I—I never expected to see you."

He smiled. It all seemed so simple now. "I came to protect my wife," was his soft reply. With one hand, Alexander cupped her chin and tilted her face, so that he might look into her eyes. "What were ye doing here, if I might ask the same of ye, my lady?"

Claricia returned his smile. Tears spiked the ends of her lashes, but there was a warm light reflecting from the depths of her eyes. Her voice was soft and steady in reply. "I intended to fulfill your vengeance against my uncle."

"Och, sweetling, there was never a truer wife for a Highland laird." Alexander's heart contracted with sheer delight, and the back of his hand, which had cupped her chin, gently stroked upward along the line of her jaw. "Despite yer earlier protestations, it appears we are perfectly matched."

Claricia's heart felt as if it had started to melt. She closed her eyes and sighed, feeling very safe and content, very pleased and satisfied. Then something caused a chill to shoot up her spine.

From the direction of the English encampment, voices called out to de Clinton. Some soldiers were coming along the path. The smile faded from Claricia's face, her eyes flew open wide, and she looked to Alexander.

"Answer them," he whispered.

"What?" She did not understand.

"Plead yer privacy. Send them away."

"Ah," she said, then took a deep breath and raised her voice. "Nay, sirs, you must not come closer. We are occupied." She ended by forcing herself to emit what she hoped sounded like a sultry flirtatious laugh.

It worked. Her laugh was met by a ribald remark, and the voices began to fade away. The men were leaving, and without a moment to spare, husband and wife joined hands and headed north to the Torwood.

At dawn on Sunday, June twenty-third, Scots pipers and drums roused King Robert's army to hear Mass. It was the Feast of St. John the Baptist, and many of the men made confession. When the service ended, trumpets blared, and the troops assembled for inspection.

The King of Scots rode before them on a sturdy brown pony. Robert wore full battle armor that morning, and a linen tunic embroidered with his coat of arms over a steel-link shirt. It was a warm summer day, and already insects were humming in the nearby meadow.

"Men of Scotland," the king began, "the moment of choosing is upon ye. If there be any mon among ye whose heart isna strong enough for what is to come, then let him now depart our company. I want no mon by my side who holds his own life dearer than freedom."

Battle cries and mortal oaths resounded up and down the lines. Every man stood firm for Robert, and when at last they fell quiet, the king spoke of the overwhelming odds they were about to face. He exhorted them to rely upon the strength of their bodies, their hearts, and their faith in God, and he ended by invoking the motto of William Wallace. "God armeth the patriot!"

The English army had marched out of Edinburgh the day before. It had been an awesome, glorious sight. In Edward's train alone there had been one hundred six four-horse wagons and one hundred ten eight-ox ones. One spy along the old Roman road estimated the English strength at nothing less than three thousand heavy calvary, five thousand light horsemen, and fifteen thousand infantrymen. Another claimed there were upward of forty thousand calvary and some fifty-two thousand archers. Whatever the actual size of the approaching enemy, its numbers were immense, and in response to this leviathan military advance, the Scottish army had moved from the Torwood to the thickly wooded New Park. The battle for Scotland was at hand.

"Come, my lady wife, it is time for ye to leave," Alexander said to Claricia. He helped her lift the sack upon which she had been sitting, and he guided her through the throng of soldiers and small people. They held hands as they walked. "Are ye frightened?"

"No," Claricia lied. Since their return from Soutra Hill, she had been assisting those who would tend to the wounded with their preparations. The sack slung over her shoulder was filled with neatly folded rags, which she had washed and dried in the sun. Claricia had never seen a battle, but those past weeks she had heard many stories, which paled the raid upon Goswick Keep those six years ago into insignificance, and she was absolutely, utterly terrified of what would happen that day.

Alexander knew Claricia was lying, and he smiled at his wife. He knew that there were many other things that this woman did for him, and for no other reason. He took in the sight of her pretty face, those plum-colored lips and lilac eyes, that soft golden hair, and he etched her image upon his mind. He spoke with a warrior's bravado. "This time tomorrow we will be together agin. Dinna worry. And dinna look upon the battle. I ken the sounds of the fight are unholy. The shrieks of the men and beasts will make flesh-bumps pop upon yer skin, but ye must promise me to wait in the safety of the valley until Rourke or I come back for ye. No matter what happens, ye mustna leave the others."

"I promise." *But I will not stay there if you need my help.*

The small people were being sent to a place of concealment under the cover of two hills called Gilles and Coxet. They would be safe in that valley during the battle, and afterward, they could make their escape to the north and west if the battle went ill for Scotland. Claricia made a silent vow that she would never leave without Alexander. She would find him dead or alive. But that was her secret.

"Ye will wear it always, will ye not?"

Claricia cocked her head to one side, puzzled by his words.

"The green heart. Ye wear it still?"

"Of course." She reached beneath her tunic collar to pull out the polished stone.

"That is good, for then I shall always be near yer heart, just as ye are in mine."

Tears pooled in Claricia's eyes. "There is nothing more precious you could have said to me."

"Nothing?" He wiped at the tears and gave her a wistful yet playful smile. His eyes were twinkling. "Nothing more precious? Are ye certain of that?"

Claricia's heart leaped into her throat, her breath caught, and she blushed. Was he teasing her? At that moment, of all times, did she dare to hope for more? she wondered as she stared into his dragon-green eyes.

"What of love, *mo ròs geall?*" Alexander asked in a soft whisper. "Would not words of love be more precious to yer heart?"

"Words of love?" she repeated, feeling as breathless as if she'd run up the tower stairs to his chamber at Eilean Fidra. A heavenly smile lit her face, for the warmth in his eyes reassured her, and she stood on the tips of her toes to kiss him gently upon the lips. "Words of love would be most precious, indeed."

"Och, how I've dreamed of this verra moment." Alexander moaned from deep in his chest. It was the reason he had come after her, and he cursed himself for waiting so long to speak of what was in his heart. He returned her tender kiss with one of his own, but it was longer and more ardent. "I love ye, *mo ròs geall*."

"And I love you, Alexander Kirkpatrick, my tender and kind husband, my bold and honorable Highland laird." Claricia took one of his hands and raised it to her lips in a lingering caress. A tear fell from her eye to trail down her cheek and stop at his finger. "I will wait as you wish."

"And I will return to ye, my dear wife. Dinna fear. I will come back to ye."

They were being separated by the crowd. Claricia's hand fell away from his, and she was swept away in the direction of the Gilles hill.

Throughout the day there were skirmishes, and when the light began to fade from the summer sky, the outnumbered Scots army had held its own against the mightiest army any English king had ever assembled.

The morning of the second day began much as the first. The Scots had spent the night in prayer, and the foot soldiers were still on their knees, receiving a blessing from the Abbot of Inchaffray, when King Edward rode along his lines.

"Look, the rebels are on their knees," Edward remarked with an air of satisfaction. "They yield! They beg for mercy."

"But, my lord king," Sir Ingram Umfraville was bold to reply, "I fear it is from God they ask for mercy, not from you."

"So be it," rejoined Edward, who immediately gave orders to sound the charge.

The fighting commenced with a charge against the Scots' right wing, commanded by the king's brother. It raged through the morning and into the afternoon, with neither side being able to gain advantage, and in the protected valley behind the hill, the small people were getting restless. Their chieftains and clansmen had thus far held out against the English, but the longer the fighting went on the more likely it was that the outcome would turn in England's favor.

Reinforcements, someone among the small people suggested.

The notion spread through the valley, and a plan was launched.

"Slay!" The cry surged up from the small people in a single voice. There were perhaps as many as fifteen thousand among them, and it was a cry that rose over the din of battle. "On them hastily! Slay! Slay!" they called out to their comrades already on the field.

The small people were drawn up in martial order. Some were mounted on baggage horses. Some were on foot. They carried sheets fixed to tent poles, and spears instead of banners; and, having snatched up shovels and pitchforks, pike handles and broomsticks to march from the valley, they displayed a long, extended front on the top of a rising ground at some distance in the rear of the Scots army and fully in sight of the whole English army. It was a formidable sight, and as was their intent, they descended the hill as if they were advancing to join the fray.

By that time, the English were weary, and disheartened by the obstinacy of their opponent, and upon seeing this formation of fresh soldiers as numerous as those against whom they'd already fought so long and to little purpose, they were greatly dismayed. Discipline began to fail, and the English began to give way along their line.

King Edward rode toward the safety of Stirling Castle, and from that moment onward, his army no longer held together. Confounded and panic-stricken, the vast English army separated and fled. Twenty-seven English barons were killed in the pandemonium. Many warriors were drowned in their attempt to cross the Forth, and the little ravine of the burn called Bannock was bridged by the carcasses of men and horses.

Such was the outcome of the Battle of Bannock Burn, as it was named by the Scots, for the stream that had protected the right flank and rear of their army. By the English it was called the Battle of Stirling or the Battle of Bannock-moor.

The hot summer day was drawing to an end when Alexander found Claricia in the valley. She was tending to a wounded lad from Kintyre, and, sensing someone standing over her, she glanced up. The warrior was caked in the gore of battle, but she recognized her husband in a heartbeat.

"You're alive," she exclaimed with humility and emotion. There were too many who had not survived the fray, and she had forced herself to stay busy, else she would have gone mad with worry. *I love you, Alexander Kirkpatrick,* her heart was singing, and in spite of the death that surrounded her, she was filled with joy and peace. "Praise be to God."

Alexander did not have to hear another word. He saw the affection in her eyes, heard the happiness in her voice, and, surrendering to exhaustion, sank to his knees beside her, but he did not have the strength to take her in his arms. His throat was parched. His voice cracked. "Havena I always proven to be a mon of my word?"

"Always," she whispered in reply. Claricia wanted to hold him, kiss him, embrace him, but her hands were full. All she could do was take in the sight of him, whole and alive, and blink away the tears.

The lad from Kintyre moaned, "Water."

"Ye must see to yer patient," Alexander muttered as he lay down on the ground, secure in the belief that everything was as it should be in his small corner of the world. He closed his eyes. For now, he would sleep. Tomorrow, there was a very rich future ahead of him with this woman.

Epilogue

~~~~~~~~~~ ◯◯ ~~~~~~~~~~

Through the summer of 1314 English prisoners were ransomed, and the spoils of the defeated army, which abounded in gold and silver, rich arms, costly apparel, and furnishings, were divided among the victors. It was only right and just that those who had been robbed of so much should have had a portion of their property restored to them. By mid-August, most of the chieftains and their clansmen had returned to their families.

At Eilean Fidra the welcome home was a jubilant one. Not only had every man survived, but the laird and his lady wife returned laden with the Kirkpatrick share of the spoils. There was much crying and embracing in the bailey. Someone broke open a cask of wine, the pipers and drums set up a merry tune, and everyone danced into the long bright hours of the Highland night.

Of a sudden, a triumphant cry burst forth from Rourke, who had been dancing a fling with Viviane.

"She has agreed!" the Irishman cried out. His voice echoed off the towers that rose at each corner of the bailey. The wives and warriors, the old

373

Maeris, Moira's *diobrachain*, and every other member of the household literally halted in the middle of whatever it was they were doing to stare at Rourke. He let out another hurrah, then kissed Viviane full and hard upon the lips, for all to see. "My lady has agreed to be my wife. Where is Brother Luthais? Bring forth the good friar. My lady and I shall be wed this verra night!"

Claricia embraced Viviane. "This is wonderful news. I am very happy for you, my dear friend." On a quiet whisper, she added, "And for Simon. And Rourke."

Viviane smiled at Claricia, but the glance she cast upon Alexander was somewhat hesitant. Her memory of the past was no better than when the laird had gone in pursuit of Claricia. *Perhaps ye will remember while I'm gone,* Alexander had said to her in parting. But that had not happened, and although she did not understand why, Viviane found herself in the peculiar position of wanting to please Alexander. How did he feel about her marrying Rourke? she wondered. Was this a good thing? Did he approve?

Alexander smiled broadly at Viviane. He wished to reassure her. It did not matter whether she remembered or not. He accepted that. What was important was that she was alive, he and Rourke had survived the past months, and the clan honor had been preserved. Rourke's announcement to marry his sister was good news, and Alexander clapped his kinsman on the back. "The lady makes an excellent choice. Ye are, indeed, a lucky mon this night."

Brother Luthais stepped forward. He directed the household to the chapel steps, and there, he joined Rourke O'Connor and Viviane of Loch Awe in holy wedlock. The crowd cheered. The rousing music of cymbals and drums filled the night air, and there was more dancing and drinking.

"*Slainnte leibh*," Alexander raised a wooden cup to toast the newlyweds. *Fare ye well.* "May ye enjoy long life, prosperity happiness and family."

Claricia stood at her husband's side on a bit of high ground that overlooked the merrymaking. Their arms were entwined about each other's waists, and they smiled at what they saw in the bailey before them. Rourke and Viviane and Simon had made a small circle with their hands, and they were going round and round, executing a gay little dance of their own design.

"The future is, indeed, going to be a wonderful thing," Claricia said in a quiet voice to Alexander. She took his hand and placed it against her stomach. "I am certain of it, for I can feel it here."

"Can ye mean what I think?" Alexander asked in a voice that crackled with emotion. He dared not breathe, dared not move his hand from her stomach or even look at her. He could not bear to see any hint of denial in her eyes, for the blossom of hope unfolding within his heart was a delicate thing.

"You were right." She tilted her head to look up at him. Her eyes were brimming with happiness. She wanted him to share the fullness of her elation. She wanted to see those green eyes sparkle with the same bliss she was feeling. Softly, she told him, "There was nothing wrong with me."

"Why did ye not speak sooner?" he asked,

turning her round in his embrace until they stood facing each other and he could glance down between them, where his hand touched her stomach.

"I was not certain until we returned and I was able to consult Sorcha. If my calculations are correct, we will be parents sometime around the New Year."

"The time of hope. There couldna be a more perfect time to welcome a babe into the world. 'After darkness comes light.' " Alexander recited the line from the Twelfth Night mummer's play he remembered from his youth at Hepburn. " 'After the dead of winter comes the sunny exuberant spring.' "

"I have heard that verse before."

"Do ye know how it ends?" Alexander moved his hands to pull her closer. Slowly, he bent his head to kiss the tip of her nose. Next he kissed one eyelid, then the other.

" 'After sorrow there is joy,' " Claricia whispered in the tiny space that separated their lips.

"Aye, joy, *mo ròs geall*. Always and forever. Yer future will be overflowing with joy. No more sorrow. That is my solemn promise," he murmured as his mouth claimed hers in a slow sensual kiss. He heard her soft moan as she parted her lips to his tongue, he felt her mold herself against him, her arms twining about his neck, and he knew that she wanted more than just that kiss. "I have missed the privacy of our tower chamber," he whispered between kisses.

Claricia giggled.

"Ye laugh at me!" Alexander raised his head and smiled, but he did not release her from his embrace. "Am I such a funny mon?"

"Nay, it is not you, but myself." Again, she laughed. It was a light merry sound. "I cannot help myself, for you make me feel giddy as a young girl being courted by an ardent young lover."

"And are your parents watching? What of the others? Do they frown? Or are they jealous?" With each question, he kissed her, squeezed her, nibbled at her.

Claricia could not stop herself from giggling once again.

"Must we escape their watchful eyes?" Alexander asked playfully, but before Claricia could reply, he had swept her into his arms. In a few great strides he reached the tower entrance and began to ascend the stairs to their chamber. "Aye, yer future holds naught but joy, *mo ròs geall*. There will be happiness and love and children for ye. And pleasure aplenty," he added on a husky little growl. "And this night, as I shall every night, I intend to give ye some of that pleasure."

Avon Romances—
the best in exceptional authors and unforgettable novels!

THE HEART AND THE ROSE   Nancy Richards-Akers
78001-1/ $4.99 US/ $6.99 Can

LAKOTA PRINCESS   Karen Kay
77996-X/ $4.99 US/ $6.99 Can

TAKEN BY STORM   Danelle Harmon
78003-8/ $4.99 US/ $6.99 Can

CONQUER THE NIGHT   Selina MacPherson
77252-3/ $4.99 US/ $6.99 Can

CAPTURED   Victoria Lynne
78044-5/ $4.99 US/ $6.99 Can

AWAKEN, MY LOVE   Robin Schone
78230-8/ $4.99 US/ $6.99 Can

TEMPT ME NOT   Eve Byron
77624-3/ $4.99 US/ $6.99 Can

MAGGIE AND THE GAMBLER   Ann Carberry
77880-7/ $4.99 US/ $6.99 Can

WILDFIRE   Donna Stephens
77579-4/ $4.99 US/ $6.99 Can

SPLENDID   Julia Quinn
78074-7/ $4.99 US/ $6.99 Can

Buy these books at your local bookstore or use this coupon for ordering:

Mail to: Avon Books, Dept BP, Box 767, Rte 2, Dresden, TN 38225   D
Please send me the book(s) I have checked above.
❑ My check or money order—no cash or CODs please—for $_____ is enclosed (please
add $1.50 to cover postage and handling for each book ordered—Canadian residents add 7%
GST).
❑ Charge my VISA/MC Acct#_____Exp Date_____
Minimum credit card order is two books or $7.50 (please add postage and handling
charge of $1.50 per book—Canadian residents add 7% GST). For faster service, call
1-800-762-0779. Residents of Tennessee, please call 1-800-633-1607. Prices and numbers are
subject to change without notice. Please allow six to eight weeks for delivery.

Name_____
Address_____
City_____State/Zip_____
Telephone No._____   ROM 0595